I0675339

LOVE, VICTIM OF WAR

Written by Rick Scott

Copyright ©2016 by Rick Scott

Published by Dressing your Book
www.dressingyourbook.com
Key Largo Florida

ISBN: 978-1-941912-25-6

All rights reserved. No part of this book may be reproduced or transmitted in any form without written permission from the author or publisher, except for reviewers who may quote brief excerpts in connection with a review.

This book is a work of fiction. Names, characters, businesses, organizations, places, events and incidents either are the product of the different authors' imaginations or are used fictitiously. Any resemblance to actual persons living or dead, events, or locales is entirely coincidental.

Table of Contents

Chapter One

Marc Metz stands in the middle of his cornfield, hearing some disturbances coming from the middle of the cornfield.

Marc readies his shovel high in the air as he slowly walks deeper in the field. The high corn stalks impair Marc's sight as Marc takes two more steps deeper into the field.

From the kitchen window Marc's wife Eva stands at the window watching Marc as he cautiously takes two more steps before he stops and take a deep breath as he readjusts his grip on the shovel.

Eva gives Marc a strange look as she wipes her hands dry and walks over to the back door and watches Marc as he moves from side to side hearing the grunting sounds as his vegetables are being eating. Eva unties and tosses her apron onto the counter as she walks outside and toward the field.

Not knowing that his wife was close by Marc slowly pulls back one of the corn stalks and reveals a small deer eating the corn.

Marc screams with fear scaring the young deer.

The deer leaps up to run away hitting and knocking Marc down. Eva with her eyes bulging sees the deer running toward her but dashes off to the side. Marc lies on the ground trying to catch his breath and rubbing his stomach. Seeing that her husband was all right Eva starts to laugh. "Did you see it, that beast tried to kill me." Marc said as he steadies himself using the shovel. Standing up Marc takes a deep breath as Eva continues laughing. "I could be dead right now and you're laughing?" Marc said as he falls down to his knees.

Eva walks up to Marc and places her arm around her husband.

"Honey that was a deer a very small deer." Eva said as she covers her mouth trying to stop laughing. "Believe me, that was a killer deer. Marc said defending himself. Eva smiles as Marc evaluate the damaged crops. "I could be dead by now and all you can do is laugh?" Marc said as he slowly picks himself up then wiping off the dust from the hoof print that the deer left on his stomach.

It's going to be hard to keep the animals out this year." Eva said ' she reaches down and pick up a half-eaten stalk of corn.

"They're hungry, so I can't blame them. Ever since the war had started the Allies had bomb all of their feeding and resting grounds as the war gets closer to here we will see more and more dazed animals around, well at least we will have enough meat for the summer and winter." Marc said as Eva gives him a sad look.

Could you really kill that baby deer?" Eva said as she helps Marc by patting the dust off of his shoulder. "In a war we all do what we have to do to survive." Marc said as he looks around at the damage crops. "We should have enough crops left to fill the army' contract, at least the German soldiers will eat well this fall."

Marc said as he. "How about the deer?" Eva said with a small grin. "My first duty is feeding our daughters, my second duty is feeding the German Armies, and there should be enough." Marc said with a small grin as he takes Eva by her hand and leads her toward the house. Eva grips Marc's hand tight. "It's time for the girls to come home from school; I need to finish with our supper." "What are we having, I can get you a killer deer if you like."

Marc said with a grin. "That killer deer wasn't big enough to feed a child much less a family of four." Eva said as she smiles and looks back over at Marc. Hand in hand Marc and Eva walk in the back door and into the kitchen where they hear the front door open.

That better not be the Allies coming into this house."

Marc laughs as he yells out. "Oh, Papa, you said that the Allies won't get this close to us because we are just a few miles away from Berlin." said sixteen-year-old Anna as her fourteen-year-old sister Hilda walks in after her. "There are a lot of boys from our school leaving for the Army every day; the war will be over by fall, that's what our teacher is telling us." Hilda said as she walks up to her parents and gives them a hug. "How was school today?" Eva said as she hugs Hilda.

"Every day, all of the teachers tell the same stories of how we prepare for victory as our boys go and fight for the Fatherland." Anna said as she follows the family into the kitchen where Eva pulls out the dinner plates and hand them to Anna to set the table. "Papa, you was in the first war wasn't you?" Hilda asks as she takes out the drinking glasses and places them onto the table.

Both Eva and Marc look at one and another. "I did a little fighting mostly the French, Why?" Marc said as he looks over toward his daughter who was placing the drinking glasses down.

Before the bell rung my teacher was going to tell us about this war hero from the first war. Herr Wienhert said it was a soldier named Sergeant Metz, Papa what was your rank when you were in that war?" Hilda asks as Marc fawn as Eva walks over and got an extra plate and glass and places it onto the table.

There are four of us why are you getting an extra plate?" Anna asks shaking her head. Hilda looks over toward her mother and smile.

"Remember, Papa needed some help on the farm today and he told Von that he could help after school today." Hilda said as she smiled and placed an extra glass closer to the extra plate.

I didn't say today, I said tomorrow." Marc said in a stern tone.

"Well I saw Von today and he was coming over after school." Hilda said with a smile. "I'm not paying him to eat, we only have a couple of hours left, and I need him in the morning, not now." Marc said shaking his head and looking out of the kitchen window where he sees the small frail looking boy walking down the road and toward the Metz's house. "Von needs us we're like his family now that his parents was killed in that bombing attack, he is all alone." Eva said as she places all of the silverware out on the table. "Where does he stay when he isn't here?" Marc asks as he watches the thin frail boy walk closer to the house. "I heard that he was staying at the school during the week." Anna said as Eva walks up to the window and stands next to Marc who also sees Von walking up.

"School will be over in a couple of weeks then what will he do?" Eva asks with a sad look on her face. "Maybe he will join the army like all of the boys in my class." Anna said as she helps herself to the roast that Eva ha place onto the table. "That boy won't last two days in battle." Marc said in a low tone. "Maybe that will make a man out of him."

Marc said as he looks over toward Hilda. "I need a strong man to help me in the fields, not some weak boy." Marc said angrily as Von walks up to the back porch steps. As Von walks up, Marc and Eva step aside. Marc opens up the door as the young weak boy gives them faint smiles as he enters the kitchen. Hilda returns the smiles and rushes past her parents and welcome Von in. Marc gives his youngest daughter a strange look as Anna reaches over and grabs the fork from Von's plate.

As Hilda and Von walk over to the kitchen table Eva smiles at the young couple as Marc closes his eyes and shakes his head.

Don't they make a cute couple?" Eva said smiling.

"I'm going out to the fields, I can't eat now." Marc said as Eva grabs him by his arm and pulls him over to the table.

Von sees the dinner table and notice that the family was ready to sit down for their meal. "I'm sorry I came too early, I'll wait by the barn unto you finish your meal." Von said as he tries to walk away only to be pull back by Hilda. "Von we set an extra plate for you, come and sit down with us and share our meal." Eva said in a soft motherly tone. Marc and Anna sat down and started eating as Von with tears forming in his eyes smiles and sat down between Marc and Hilda. "After dinner we can go out to the field and start working." Von suggested. Marc glances over to his young hire hand." I'm not sure of how much sun light that we have left, beside there is a storm heading this way. So it's going to get darker faster." For the rest of the meal no one said a word. Marc stared at Eva as Von stared at Hilda. Both Von and Hilda smiles at one and another Marc see this and throws down his napkin onto the table and walks outdoors. "We're wasting sunlight lets go." Marc orders. Von drops his napkins onto the table and follows his boss out of the door. "Where are you two going we haven't finished dinner?" Hilda said as she watches Von get up and leave.

We'll eat later." Marc shouted as he walks off of the porch.

Marc and Von sits on the ground pulling up the embedded carrots and place them into a bucket.

Marc looks over and sees Von having trouble pulling up the carrots. "Where have you been staying at?" Marc asks as he sees Von struggle. "I've been staying at the school for the last few months.' Von said as he finally pulls up the carrots.

"Your home was destroyed?" "Yes sir, they said that one of the Allies planes flew over dropping their bombs, one landed onto our house."

How about your family?" asks Marc. Von drops the carrots into the bucket and then took a deep breath. "I was told that they never knew it." With a sad look Von turns his head so he wouldn't show the tears that were rolling down his face. "My mom was in the kitchen, I'm not sure where my father was but I was told that they didn't know what had hit them." Marc also looks away.

"What are you going to do now?" Ask Marc as he moves the bucket closer to Von.

"Join the Army and shoot down every Allies plane that I see." Von grabs the next set of carrots and with anger Von has no problems pulling it out of the ground. Marc frowns as he stops and looks over to Von. "Do you think that the German Armies will take you, how old are you?" Still on his knees Von starts pulling up the next set of carrots. "I'm fifteen, but I have a friend who is already in the Army, he told me that he could get me in." Von pulls out the next set then places them into the bucket.

Then Von sat back. "You were in the first war wasn't you?" Marc loosens his grip on the carrots and sat back.

"I was a sergeant but the girls don't know about my war history and I want to keep it that way." A confused Von looks over to his boss.

"Why, because we lost that war? There is nothing to be ashamed about that, but we want lose this one, I'll make sure of that." Von said with confident.

~ 5 ~

Marc gives his young, weak and frail looking hired hand a deep look. "We lost from the lack of leadership, higher up in command; we fought battles like it was the last."

When the battles should had been drawn out and planned better. Find the enemy and kill him was good if you were a sniper. But for an outfit you needed to know where they were at all times if some troops were moving trying to sneak around you. Marc said as his eager hired hand listen to each word as the ex-war hero tells his story. "This time we have Adolf Hitler leading us in the war with the allies, this time we'll win the war." Von says as he defends his Fuhrer. Marc shakes his head in disbelieve as he reaches and pulled up the next batch of carrots.

"Where are you staying tonight?" Marc asks trying to change the subject. "I guess that I'll go back to the school," said Von as he started back working with his boss. "Yea but school will be out in a couple of weeks then what?" Ask Marc as he continues to work.

"I'm out now, the school let all of the boys out so we can go and joined the army, I was waiting until the fall after the harvest to join but all of the other boys are leaving this week and I still might go with them," said Von as he drops the newly pulled carrots into the bucket. "Stay here and help me on the farm that's the way that you can fight the war by feeding our soldiers, you can stay in the barn, there is an old army cot that I use in the first war, it's not very comfortable but it's better than the hard wooden school floor." Von smiles at the invitation. "Thank you Herr Metz, this way I'll never be late for work." Marc looks up and sees the clouds getting darker and darker. "Let's call it a day and I'll unfold the cot.

Marc and Von gather up all of the buckets and carries them to the barn. Where in the back corner of the barn is a small wooden floor Marc walks over and grabs the folded cot from the corner and started to unfold it as twenty plus years of dust fills the air. "I've been in this barn a dozen times but I never saw this area before." Von said looking around.

"I keep it dark back here so the pigs and cows won't venture back here; this is where I stayed after the war when Herr Lowenstein hired me." Hearing the words Lowenstein

Von gives Marc a strange look. "Herr Lowenstein is a Jewish name."

'Yea that's right Herr Lowenstein was a Jew, but he took me in and treated me like a son and taught me how to farm the land to feed my family, I owe Herr Lowenstein more than I could ever pay him." Marc said as he stares at Von. "So what happened, did you buy the land are did you take the land, being a Jew land."

Marc shakes his head in anger. "Someday I'll tell you the story about Herr Lowenstein. But for now let's get your cot ready, Go and get the lantern, you can use that for light." Von walks over and takes the lantern from a post as small rain drops hit the ground with the cows and small farm animals started coming into the barn to get out of the rain the barn started to smell. Von places his hand over his face trying to avoid the stench from the wet farm animals. "Believe it or not you'll get use to that smell, I did." Marc said as he smiles. There were two wooden crates standing one on top of the other. "Grab that top crate and use it as a bedside table, but leave the other crate alone," said Marc as he looks outside and seeing the rain letting up. "I'll go to the house and get some blankets and a pillow for you." Marc said as he shooed some pigs that were investigating the new area. Once inside of the house Marc wipes the wet rain off of him as he walks over to the hall closet and pulls out some blankets Eva walks up giving her husband a strange look. "Is the cows cold?" Eva said as she helps as the blankets fall down from the top shelf and onto Marc.

"Von will be staying with us." Marc says as he thanks his wife with a kiss. "In the Back of the barn, where papa made you a little home?" "That was my home for two years until I married the boss's daughter and moved into the big house." Marc laughs as he looks around. Eva smiles and walks into their bedroom and grabs a pillow from the foot case and places the pillow on top of the blanket. "That's how we met; Hilda and Von already know each other." With that though Marc's eyes widen. "I'll shoot him and send her away to be a Nun." Marc replied. Eva smiles and walks with Marc to the back door where Eva holds the door open. Marc gives his wife an evil but playfully smile. 'I still have my rifle and I know how to use it." As Marc enters the barn Von is making a make do fence keeping the animals from getting in his small compact area. "Yea, I was going to suggest that, here are some blankets and a pillow." Marc said as he drops his load onto the bed. Von smiles as he's starting to feel at home. "May I ask you Herr Metz, What's in the second crate?" Marc looks over at the crate then back toward Von.

"Just some old broken tools that Herr Lowenstein kept to someday fix and use them, we just never got around to repair them, so don't worry about them. What's in that crate can never be use anymore, it's dark now and the rooster will be loud at the sight of the first sun light, Come on in the house for breakfast." Marc said as he turns around and started walking toward the door.

"Herr Lowenstein" Von said as he shook his head. "It was your duty to proclaim this land yours" Marc stops at the door of the barn and turns around. "Herr Lowenstein was a great man he fought in the first war and almost lost his right arm defending the land that now would had hated him. But that's for another day, get some rest if it's clear in the morning that we'll be busy." Without another word Marc walks out of the barn and up to the house Von slowly follow his boss to the barn's door without Marc knowing about it. In the middle of the night Marc is lying in bed still awake from Vons words about claiming the farm from a Jew and the hatred for the Jews that Von has. Marc slowly slides out of the bed hoping to not to awake Eva. "Where are you going?" Ask Eva as she slowly wakes up. Marc reaches over and gives his wife a kiss on top of her head. "I'm thirsty, I'm going to the kitchen and get a glass of water, so go back to sleep." Marc walks into the kitchen and grabs a glass from the cupboard and looks out the kitchen window as he turns on the faucet. Marc notices that the lantern was still lit in the back of the barn. Marc place the glass into the sink and walks outside. Inside the barn Von stares at the crate that Marc told him of the old broken tools. "I bet that I can fix some of the tools that can save some money Herr Metz." Von walks over to the crate and pulls it over to his made up cot. As Von opens the crate he sat down on his cot as he sees the content of the crate. As Von pulls out a highly decorated world war one German uniform. Some dried up blood is on the front of the uniform. Von places the uniform onto his cot to look further into the crate. Where Von sees the army boots and then an ammo belt that had a pistol holster on it. Von opens the flap of the holster and pulls out an old Lugar pistol. Von holds the pistol in his hand and rolls it back and forth. "That's my uniform and my pistol, I ask you to not open that crate." "You was a war hero, just look at all of these metals, how did you get them?" said Von as he picks up the uniform displaying the metals. Still angry Marc gives in and walks over to the uniform and took it from Von. "I was like you, when the war started in 1914, I was too young to join. I was about fifteen are sixteen I don't really remember at that time when I enlisted, and like you I knew that I could win the war.

Chapter Two

Basic training was, here's a rifle aim then pull the trigger, Hit the target and move on before I knew it I was in France fighting, Every time that I aim my rifle and pull the trigger a Frenchman fell, I got to be known around as a crack shot.

"Machines guns was blasting cannons were erupting. Bullets was hitting all around me the shells from the cannons hitting close by they were trying to fix their position on me as I took out one Frenchmen at a time, I would take aim and fire, then I would pull back my bolt reloading and shoot again, I got them and they never touch me. I made Sergeant from that battle and I receive some of these metals. After the ceremony I pack away my metals and move to the next battle field this time I was making the decision, I place my men where I wanted them we was winning battles and moving through France. By 1917 the Americans join the English so my outfit was moved back to Germany to defend our homeland from them. The Americans brought in tanks along with 50 thousand fresh troops. By 1918 we were finished but before the war ended my outfit and me did some damage to the English and the Americans. About a month till the end of the war I was standing in front of my soldiers with high-ranking Officers and I receive more Metals and the rank of lieutenant. We never saw that the English was slowly moving in. After the ceremony they started shooting, I was never hit but the English wiped out just about all of the soldiers, I was capture along with three of four officers and I spent the rest of the war in a prison camp that both the English and the American ran." Marc says hoping to dissuade his young weak hired hand to stay on the farm and serve his country by feeding them. Von stared at the uniform and notices the old bloodstain that covers the front. "Whose blood is this, The English or the Americans?" Marc took a closer look at the uniform and shook his head. 'Neither.' Von gives Marc a strange look. "This blood belongs to me." Marc takes a deep breath as he continues to talk. "I had a Lieutenant insignia making me an officer, but I knew no secrets, no battle plans, nothing. But the British and the Americans though that I did so I was place in an officers P.O.W. camp away from what was left of my men. Separated from the rest of the other officers. In the morning the British would beat me for information that I didn't have, after their lunch the American would beat me for the same information.

But I knew nothing I was order to that base for the presenting of the metals and the rank; I knew nothing else. Only that it was the place that changed my life forever. I thought and wish that I had given up and just die. But I didn't die. It's been over twenty years ago now and our country's are at war with them again I still want revenge but now I have a wife and two daughters so I fight my war here in the fields making sure that our fighting men have enough to eat before they go into battle. It can be hard sometimes for soldiers to find food decent enough to eat." Von looks down after hearing Marc's story.

"Now is your chance to get revenge, go with me, join the army fight the allies." Von pleads. "Didn't you hear me, wasn't you listening I have a wife and daughters now." Marc said in anger. When the British and the Americans realize that I knew no importance information and that I wasn't going to die they would beat me more, it became a game to them who was going to kill me first."

Chapter Three

In a couple of months after my capture the war was over. I recover in a Red Cross hospital then they gave me back my uniform and sent me on my way. The town that I was from was now a ghost town the buildings all destroyed by the war the people was walking around shell shocked; I had no surviving family left. So I started walking. "But they gave you back your Lugar?" Von said holding up the old rusted pistol. Marc sat on the cot and leaned up against the wall.

"Everywhere I walk I would find a dead soldier some ours, some theirs. I would pick up their weapons just in case I see anyone in an American or British uniform. I must have walked for days, weeks I don't remember when I walked up this very street and saw Herr Lowenstein trying to rebuild his farm. His arms mangled from bullets. He was an old man struggling to pick up shell fragments that filled his land. I drop my gear and ask if he needed any help. Herr Lowenstein looked at me with tears rolling down his face, then he shook his head. (no) But he needed my help so without his permission I started helping him before long we had enough area clear to plant whatever." Marc said as he looks around the barn. "Herr Lowenstein fought for a country that now hates him."

Von tries to think of something to say. "Life has changed since Herr Lowenstein fought; some said it was the Jews that lost us the war." Marc outraged by Vons's comment place the uniform back into the crate.

"I told you not to mess with that crate, I'm your boss should I fire you for not listening or if we was in the army should I shoot you for disobeying my orders." "

Please Herr Metz my deepest apologies but why are you so grateful to a Jew?"

"After we got the farm up and running we started rebuilding the house. At the beginning of the war Herr Lowenstein sent his wife and daughter to Hungary to stay with some family and away from the war, five months after the war ended Herr Lowenstein and I hitched the horses together and rode out to get them. Frau Lowenstein a beautiful lady was glad to see us. She knew that the war ended but wasn't sure if her husband was dead or alive. There was no way to get in touch with someone in another country. Then I saw the prettiest girl that I have ever seen." Marc said reminiscing,

'How old was that girl?" Von asks with a smile on his face.

Marc just stared into the ceiling. "She was a couple of years younger than me."

"And what ever happen to her?" Asked Von.

"Her name is Eva, Eva Lowenstein Metz. The love of my life is a Jew, in some eyes, but in mine she is a gift from God." Von looks at Marc who rolls his eyes toward his hired help.

Frau Metz is Jewish and Anna and Hilda is part Jew, I'm not sure of Herr Hitler politics, if I was fighting I would fight the allies and not a group of people that has birth right to Germany." Marc said as he notices that all of the farm animals were asleep.

We only have a few hours before morning, you better get some sleep," said Marc as he stands up and walks toward the barn door. "Breakfast will be ready at daylight, come on in and share our meal with us." said Marc as he leaves the barn and back to the house, Von places the uniform and the pistol back into the crate and turns out the lantern. The morning starts out as the smell of eggs and bacon fills the air. Eva stands over the wood-burning stove cooking their meal as Hilda walks in. "Hilda will you go to the barn and milk the cow for breakfast."

Hilda walks over to the back door and looks out. Hilda smiles as she sees Von walking toward the house holding a pale in his hand.

Von looks up and sees Hilda standing at the door.

Hilda opens the door as Von walks in "Good morning Frau Metz." Then Von looks over toward Hilda. "Good morning Hilda." Von said with a smile. At that time Anna walks in and sees Von.

"You're here early aren't you?"Anna said as she walks over to the cabinet and pull out four plates.

"Von will be staying with us for a while." Eva said as

she places the plate of bacon onto the table. Hilda smiles as Anna frown.

'Where is he going to sleep, Shouldn't you be joining the army with the rest of the boys in our class." Anna said giving Von a dirty look. "Von is staying in the barn until the end of harvest, and then we'll go from there." Marc says as he walks into the kitchen. Von smiles as he places the pale of milk onto the counter. "I milked the cow for this morning breakfast."

Eva grabs the pale and places it closer to the sink. "Anna you'll need to grab another plate for Von. Eva took four glasses out of the cabinet and one coffee cup for Marc. Hilda slide out the chair next to her and smile. "Von this can be your seat."

Marc and Anna give Hilda a strange look as Von sat down. Von swallows his meal down without chewing for this was his first breakfast he has had since the allies bombing killed his family. "Slow it down; this isn't your last meal." Marc said as he grins.

"I haven't had this good of a meal since my mom died." Von said as he finishes his eggs and looks over toward Eva, his eyes begging for more. Eva gladly slides the plate of eggs in front of Von who slide off the last couple of eggs into his plate. No word is spoken as the family of four looks on trying to hold back the tears of this alone loner. Now he will be a part of a family his life regains conscious.

"Von, I need for you to go to town today and pick up some feed for the chickens." Marc said as he finishes his cup of coffee.

"May I use the truck?" Von asks not sure of the answer.

"Sure, I have an extra key for you." Marc said with a smile.

Von also smiles as he feels more a part of the Metz's family. "Maybe I can drop the girls off at school on my way to town."

Marc nodded as an Anna angry said. "I'm the same age as Von why can't I drive the truck. Marc waits as Eva refill Marc's cup. "Can you change gears without burning out the clutch."

"Can Von?" Anna replies. Marc just looks at her without giving an answer.

After breakfast the girls climb into the truck Hilda first so she could sit beside Von. Von and Marc walk to the front door as

Marc digs into his pocket and pulls out the extra keys to the truck.

On the way to school not a word is said as the moan and grinding sound as Von struggle with changing the gears of the truck. Anna shakes her head as she braces herself for each bump. And the bad smell of burnt transmission fluid.

Finally, the truck pulls up to the school Anna jumps out and quickly takes five steps away as she waits for Hilda who slowly exits the truck. "Come on we'll be late if we don't hurry." Anna yells as Hilda looks back and thanks Von for the ride.

Von watches the girls go into school as he drives away. Passing him on the roads is two German trucks driving past him. Von watches them as they pass. "They're going to the farm." Von said with a smile knowing that his hard work will benefits his country. Von continues his drive to town and picks up the feed that he was sent for. On the way back Von passed the two same trucks Von stops the truck and this time.

Von steps out of the truck and salutes the passing military truck carrying the product of his and Marc's hard labor. Back at the farm Marc sits in the kitchen trying to dry the sweat off. Marc hears the grinding of the truck's gear. Marc frowns as he looks away knowing it was his hired hand that was coming.

Marc reaches over and kisses Eva as he walks to the backdoor. "I need to go and help Von with the off load."

"CantVon handle the off load?" Eva said as she takes the two glasses of water to the sink.

"No, I need to help him," said Marc as he walks out the back door. With more grinding Von tries to back up into the barn. The grinding of the gars is unbearable as Marc walks up to the truck. "That's far enough." Marc says banging on the hood. Marc jumps in the back of the truck as Von stood on the ground grabbing the bags of feed that Marc hands him. Von stacks the large bags of feed high enough so the farm animals couldn't reach them.

"I saw the military trucks coming and going." Von said as he stacks another bag.

"Yea, they cleaned us out." Marc said with a smile.

"Two truckloads" Von added.

"Did you have any problems at the feed store?" Marc asks as he handed Von the last bag of feed.

"No sir, I told Herr Zimmerman that as soon as the army's quarter master pays you then you would pay him." Marc shook his head agreeing.

As the summer slowly changed into fall Von, while working on the farm, started growing into a man. His chest started bulging out with muscle his arms tight and large Von slowly became a man. A man that the German army would love to have.

The war in the west was getting closer and closer to the farm. There are more Nazi soldiers around town. A town where an abundance of Jews live free and in prosperity. In their unknown world tucked away in the small German town miles away from the precious Nazi army, now with the army in town Marc and Von takes their truckload of vegetable and meats to them.

Marc drives up to the building that houses the German command. Marc got out of the truck and stood at the door looking around the town where the people of the Jewish faith wore their Jewish armband, the town that was warm and friendly now is quite with the watchful eyes of the many armed Nazi guards. "What happen to this town?" Von asks .as he to notice the strange happening of the town.

"I'm not sure but I think that they has something to do with it." Marc answers as he watches the guards walk around. "I need to pay on my bill at the feed store, check around see just what's going on." Von nods and walks away as Marc walks toward the feed store. Once in the store Herr Zimmerman looks up noticing Marc. Marc walks to the back of the store and to the counter where Herr Zimmerman awaits.

"The war is getting closer." Whisper Herr Zimmerman.

"Why are the soldiers here?" Marc asks as he looks around at the soldiers who were checking out Zimmerman products.

"They said that they was here to fight the allies if they make it this far, but I think that they are here to check on the Jews that's here." Outside Von walks around looking at the Nazi who was staring at the Jewish people then he heard his name calling from a distance.

"Von, over here." Yelled the voice Von turn around and

see his old friend Wolfgang, who is now a sergeant. Wolfgang rushes over to Von and the two shakes hands." Von how are you? Still working on the farm?" Von looks at the patch. "'You'll made sergeant?" Von asks admiring Wolfgang rank.

"Yea, I had some good battles and they made me sergeant, you could be a sergeant if you was with me."

Von gives Wolfgang a long look. "Join the army." Wolfgang said placing both of his hands on Von's shoulder. "The Harvest is over, why not?"

Von says as he admired the sergeant patch. "Will we stay here in town, or will we be sent to war?" Von asks as he agrees to join. "Well first you'll go to basic training then they'll send you where you are needed, but I'm close to our Captain I bet that I can get you with us, Where ever we are," said Wolfgang with a smile. "Meet me here in the morning and we'll get everything started." Added Wolfgang.

"I need to talk to Herr Metz, but I'll see you in the morning," said Von as he shook Wolfgang's hand. Von walks away and toward the truck where Marc was also walking.

"What did you find out?" Marc asks as he started up the truck and drove off.

"The war is getting closer and the army is here to defend the town." Von said as he rolled down the window.

"Yea, that's what I heard too." Marc said as he changes the gears in the truck. Von waited until dinner to mention that it was time for him to move on to the army. As they were finishing their meal Von sat back in his chair. "All of the boys in my class joined the army a few months ago." With a nervous look Hilda took a deep breath knowing what Von was saying. "And some of those boys are dead now, I've heard from some of the people in town last week." Von looks over toward Hilda.

I saw Wolfgang Bauner today and now he is a sergeant and after Basic training he can get me in his unit."

"You don't need to fight in the war." Marc said as he finishes his glass of milk. "We already had this talk." Marc continues.

"But Herr Metz I was to stay on until the end of summer harvest, this is the end." Von said pleaded his case. "Now what?" Von added.

'Now we get started on some winter wheat and get prepared for the spring." Marc said in a stern voice. "I need to fight for my country and the time is now, beside Wolfgang's outfit is guarding our town I'll be sent here." Then Von looks over toward Hilda. "We still can see each other every day."

Hilda looks down at her empty plate with tears forming in her eyes. "I think that Von should join the army, I heard that we are losing on the Russian front." Anna said with a sarcastic grin.

"I will be stationed here in the town, Wolfgang said."

"You'll go where they tell you to go," said Marc. Eva grabs some plates off of the table and carries them to the sink.

"Von, you can stay here, you know that you are a part of the family now, one less soldier won't hurt the army." Von closes his eyes knowing that he will be leaving the family that he became to love.

"I told Wolfgang that I will be meeting him in the morning." Not another word is said after that. Hilda and Von glances at one another, as the rest were speechless.

By the next morning the five gather for breakfast. Silence filled the air as Eva, Hilda and Anna place breakfast onto the table. "I hope that you thought about the army last night." Hilda said as she places a plate in front of Von.

Von thought about it for a second. "Yes, and I still believe that I should go." said Von as he picks up his fork and roll it back and forth looking at it. "I owe it to my country." Von replied.

You can supply your country with food the way that you did for the summer." Marc added as he hoped that Von would change his mind.

"And what about us?" Hilda said as the rest of the family look up to her giving her a strange look.

'What I mean is us, we are now his family, so what about us." Von dropped his fork and also looks at Hilda. "I want to end the war before good people are hurt; we're fighting a war on our own land. No one is safe from the war, Wolfgang told me that he could get me in his outfit; they are here to protect our town. That is what I want to do protect our town and ---my family." Von said as he looks around to his claimed family.

Chapter Four

"Von I have rifles and pistols here in the house if we are attacked then you and I will arm ourselves and defend our land." Marc said.

"Von I need to talk to you, follow me." Hilda said as she walks toward the back door.

"Whatever you have to say you can say it here," yelled Marc.

"No papa, I need to talk to Von outside." Reluctantly Von follows. Hilda walks over to the far end of the porch with her arms folded. Hilda never looks up as Von approach her. "What about us?" Hilda said in a quite tone.

"I can protect you better as a trained soldier." Von said as he places his hands onto Hilda's shoulder. As tears run down her face as Hilda falls into Von's arms they both cried for a second Von stop and rubs his eyes dry then he wipes the tears from Hilda's face. "I'll be alright, I promise." Von, with all of his belongings, started out of the barn hoping to sneak to town before the family knew that he was leaving.

As Von walk past the truck, the truck started up. A stunned Von looked over into the truck and sees Marc behind the wheel.

Von looks at Marc as Marc waits for Von to climb inside of the truck. Reluctantly Von opens the truck door and steps in. "I thought that you would like a ride to town." Marc said trying to find the right words to say. Von sat back into his seat and look down the road.

"As a soldier I can make sure that our secret will be safe." Von said as he looks over toward Marc.

Marc stops the truck and looks over toward Von. "I will keep the secret from the soldier. Von, I've been in a war, I had seen the evil of war, dead men with bullets holes and in some soldier's multiple holes, but all it takes is one bullet. One bullet that ended the lives of young men. I looked at you not as a weak boy but more like my son, Eva treat you like you are her son. And the girls, you're like a brother to them." Von looks over at Marc who has a scared look on his face. "Von I want you to stay on the farm and be a part of our family." Marc pleaded. Von raises his head back keeping the tears from running down his face.

"The four of ya'll are my family. You fought for our country and now it's my tum, I will come back after the war and we can be a family again, but for now I need to do this for myself." Von says as Marc nods his head and drives off. In town the Nazi population doubles as Marc drives up to the center of town. "Why are there more soldiers here, what is going on?" Marc asks as he looks around as the troop trucks pulls up and soldier's climb out. Von is also shocked at the sight. "Are the allies closer than we thought?"

"I don't know but I don't like it." Marc replied, "Maybe you should send the women to Hungary." Von said as he sees all of the soldiers standing at attention. "I believe so." Marc said as he also looks around. "Then come with me."

"What?"

"Come with me and join, with your background you should be an officer and it would be an honor to serve under you. Marc thought about it for a second as he notices more and more trucks filled with soldiers of the German army.

"What are they doing here, did the allies advance this far into Germany." Marc thought out loud. "There is no signs of the allies close by." Marc continued.

"Come with me, we can serve the German army together, we can fight side by side, I want to learn from your experience." Von begged.

Marc pays attention to each of the soldiers and the Officers who was yelling out orders. "I can't join now, I need to get the women to Hungary, I'll be back in a week or so, then I'll join" said Marc confused by all of the troops that were collected in the town that he called home. At that time Wolfgang is heard yelling for Von. Both Von and Marc look over toward Wolfgang.

Wolfgang runs up and grabs Vons's hand shaking it. "This is Herr Metz; I mean Lieutenant Metz." Von said proudly.

Wolfgang eyes widen. "This is the Lieutenant Metz; "I've heard stories of your battle field heroics". Wolfgang said as he walks over, grabs and shakes Marc's hand. "I'm sure that the higher command will make you higher officer than a

Lieutenant." Wolfgang said surprise that he is meeting the hero that he had heard of. "They should make me an Officer for finding you." Wolfgang bragged.

All Marc could think about was his three girls Eva, Anna and Hilda, what will happen to them. Eva being Jewish, as the two girls being half Jewish, Marc didn't feel safe about his girls. "I need to get my Family to Hungary." Marc repeats, "Why?

"We're here to protect your family and all of the German families in the town." said Wolfgang

Marc looks over toward Wolfgang then over toward Von. "Von, you go ahead and join I'll be back in a week then I'll join." The smile on Wolfgang face disappears. "But what about me, I found the hero." Marc looks over to Wolfgang.

I will mention your name." Marc said in a stern tone.

But first I need to finish my business. Marc said as Von agrees. "Yes, should I help you?"

'No, go ahead and go with Wolfgang; I'll see you in a couple of weeks." Marc said as he jumps into the truck and cranks it up. Marc drives off leaving Von standing with Wolfgang. Marc speeds as he drives home passing trucks and then more trucks heading for the center of town. As Marc pulls up to the front of the house Marc jumps out and runs into the house. Eva meets Marc at the front door.

'What's going on, you look like you'll seen a ghost?" Eva said as Marc rushes in "Where are the girls?" Marc asks as he looks around. "Anna, Hilda, where are you." Marc screams as he walks down the hallway. "Marc, what is going on, you is scaring me." Eva said as she follows Marc around.

Marc turns around to Eva and places his arms on Eva's shoulder. "Remember when you was a little girl and Herr Lowenstein sent you and your mom to Hungary?" Eva thought for a second then she looks up at Marc with a scared look on her face.

"Is it the war?" "Yes, the war is near there are hundreds of soldiers in town, they must know something." Marc said as the girls come running in. "What's wrong papa?" Anna said still holding the drying towel. "Where's Von?" Hilda asks looking out of the front door. "I need for you girls to go and pack your bags, everything that you will need, if you don't need it then leave it here." Marc said as he pointing to their rooms.

"Where is Von?" Hilda repeats.

"Von joined the army, he will be going away for a while. And so are you girls, now go and pack." As the girls runs to their room Eva helps Marc with packing the expensive objects.

"If the war last too long then sell what you can. After the war is over I'll come back to bring you and the girls home." Marc said as he filled a pillowcase with some gold silverware and other gold objects.

"But Marc you are going to stay with us isn't you?" Eva asks with tears running down her face.

"No I'm coming back here and join up with Von." Marc replies as he fills the pillowcase and throws it onto the sofa. "Girls, let's go, we need to leave as soon as possible." Marc yells out as Eva grabs his arm.

"Marc you have already fought in a war let the younger men fight this time." said Eva hoping to change Marc's mind.

"You girls will be safe with your family in Hungary, I need to stay here and watch over Von, I'll be alright." Marc said as he held Eva tight in his arms.

"But Marc you had already fought let them fight now." Eva repeats herself. "We need to go to the bank before they close the door." Marc remembers.

Marc runs to the hallway. "Girls place your bags on the porch and I'll put them in the back of the truck when we get back. Come with me, besides I want you to see what is going on in town." Marc said as he tugs Eva out the door. Without saying a word Marc and Eva rush out the door and jump into the truck. "This is bad honey, the war is coming here and I don't want you and the girls in the middle of it." As they drove into town, Marc parks as close as he can due to the many military trucks blocking all of the buildings. "Go to the bank I want to find Von and talk to him." said Marc as he waves Eva away.

Chapter Five

Marc went to the center of town where he drops Von off. As Marc looks around he doesn't see Von but Marc does see Wolfgang. Marc runs up to Wolfgang. "Wolfgang, where's Von?" Wolfgang started laughing as he sees Marc approaching him. "Herr Metz or should I call up Lieutenant Metz, I told my Captain about you and he would like to talk to you." Wolfgang said as he tries to lead Marc toward the new headquarter. "Ok I'll talk to him, but first I need to talk to Von, where is he?" Wolfgang shakes his head as he continues to lead Marc away. "Von is already gone; they shipped him out to Berlin for basic training just after you left, now come on Germany needs great officers like you." As Marc is led away Eva walks toward the bank. None of her friends would look her way. The Jewish people kept their heads down. Eva sees Herr Popolish the town's baker. Eva is confused by the way that Herr Popolish just walks by not paying any attention to her, a friend and customer for many years. "Herr Popolish, are you alright, it's me Eva Metz." Eva then notices the arm band, "Why are you wearing that arm band?" Looking around Herr Popolish with his head still pointing toward the ground and whispers.

"Make sure that you tell the Nazi that your name is Metz not Lowenstein, the Nazi hates us and they want to kill us just for being Jewish. Don't worry about the armband just tell them that your name is Metz and they will leave you alone."

At that time two German soldiers walks up. "It's illegal to talk to this lady, is he bothering you fraulein, you know the penalty for talking to a beautiful lady is death." said one of the Nazi soldiers as the other soldier grabs Herr Popolish arms while the first Nazi started beating him.

"What are you doing this man didn't----" "He is not a man he is a Jew, Don't worry fraulein he will be dealt with." With each punch Herr Popolish screams out with pain. "Stop it, leave him alone." Eva begged, as she tries to pull the Nazi soldier away. As blood filled the Nazi's balled up fist Eva pulls her arm back and with an open hand slaps the soldier. The soldiers drop Herr Popolish and turn their attention toward Eva.

"What are you doing, I was defending you from this Jew." The surprised soldiers said as he wipes his mouth wiping away the blood from his lips. "You want to hurt this man because he is a Jew, well so am I. My name is Eva Lowenstein Metz. Both my father and mother were Jewish." "Eva, no they don't have to know," cried Herr Popolish. "Shut up." said the Nazi as he gives Herr Popolish a slap causing him to fall to the ground.

"So you are Jewish, where is your armband?" Ask the second soldier. Knowing the mistake that she had just made Eva stared to the ground. "Let's take her to the back of the store and see if she is a Jewish trash or a German fraulein, the fraulein will have a beautiful body.

The two soldiers grab Eva and started dragging her toward the store. "Marc, help me, Marc." Eva screams. As she is being dragged Eva kicks one of the Nazi soldiers. The soldier loses his grip on her then Eva knee the other Nazi between his legs and tries to run away. As one soldier grab is midsection the other grabs his leg. "You can't escape the law." Yells the soldier with the hurt leg as he pulls up his machine gun and takes aim. As the trigger is pull several rounds of bullets brought Eva to her death. Before this had happen Wolfgang takes Marc to see Captain Mullar. The Captain was happy to see the legend that he had head of all of his army life.

"Captain Mullar, this is Lieutenant Metz." The Captain with a smile on his face raise from his chair and walk over toward Marc with his outstretched hand ready to shake the hand of the legend of the first world war. The two men sat down as Wolfgang stood behind Marc. 'How long has it been since you was a member of the German army?" Marc thought about it for a second, 1918 when the war ended so did my career." Because of the loss of the First World War Captain Mullar smile became a frown but only for a second.

"But this is a new war and believe me we are winning this war. And now we have a war hero to train our future soldiers, Marc gave the Captain a strange look. "I would like to fight the allied; I have some old revenge to settle." Marc said as he looks back and sees Wolfgang standing to close to him.

Wolfgang backs up a few feet. "Revenge," laughs the Captain. "No, no, no we need you in Berlin training, and away from the bloody mess that war causes." Marc sat back into his set and thought. "My son, I mean my friend just join the army and I need to be with him." Marc said as he looks sternly into Captain's Mullar face. "Non-sense, stay in Berlin and with your war record then I'm sure that you'll start out as a Captain or maybe higher." At that time the shots are heard. "What is that?" Marc asks as he turns around. "I'm sure that it's nothing, some people that shouldn't be here has just left." Captain Mullar said with a small grin. "The allies?" Marc asks. 'No, I mean other people." "Eva is out there." Marc says as he jumps out of his chair and out the door. Captain Mullar looks over toward Wolfgang. "Eva, who is Eva?" Ask the Captain. "She must be his wife; Frau Metz shouldn't get to close to those people." With the Captain agreement Wolfgang salutes his Captain. "Heil Hitler." And leaves the room. Marc runs out side yelling." Eva, Eva." Marc yells as he pushes through all of the soldiers repeating his yells. Marc franticly looks around the town. A lady walks up with tears in her eyes places her hands on Marc's shoulder. "Herr Metz, I'm so sorry." Hearing this Marc pushes the lady aside and continues his search until he sees Herr Popolish kneeling down. Hiding the body of a woman as blood flows around him.

Marc runs toward Herr Popolish still screaming out his wife's name. Herr Popolish slowly stood up and turns toward Marc.

Marc sees a body lying on the ground. "Eva." Marc yells as he runs up to his wife. "Herr Metz she save my life, I should be laying there not her, I'm so sorry." At that time more and more towns' people gather around. "Where are the soldiers that did this?" Marc demanded, "I don't know they walked away," claims Herr Popolish crying.

Marc falls to the ground and held his wife's lifeless body, rocking her back and forth Marc screams with the pain that he feels "Why did I bring you, you could have stayed at home and finished packing why, why did I bring you?" As the towns people gather around blocking the Nazi. "What about the girls? What will I tell them? Marc said rubbing Eva's hair, 'Please don't die, please wake up and I'll take you home so that the girls can see you." Marc cries.

"We have to do something with the body," someone said.

'Leave us alone, everybody leave us alone." Marc said angry 'who did this?" Marc asks as he lifted Eva head onto his shoulder.

"It was the Nazi; they shot her just because she was defending me." said Herr Popolish as he reaches down and touch Eva's hand only to have Marc pull her hand away 'Herr Metz we need to do something with her body before the girls find out about it, think about the girls." said Frau Dutchmire

'I need to find those Nazi who did this; I need to take revenge I'll kill all of them if I have to." Marc said as he looks around at the many German troops that now fill the town.

"Go home and be with your daughters, we'll bury Frau Metz next to her parents. "Where did the soldiers go?" "Go home to your daughters, they don't know that their mother is dead, go home to them, they are going to need you more than ever now." said one of the Jewish women who knee down beside of Marc and place her hand on top of his. Marc continued looking up toward Herr Popolish.

'I'm not sure they all have on the same uniform." said Herr Popolish then Marc looks over at Herr Popolish armband.

"Let me borrow this." Marc said, as he tries to pull the armband off of Herr Popolish arm.

'No, no, I must wear this all of the time." Herr Popolish pleads. Marc is able to pull the armband off Herr Popolish Marc then looks down at his lifeless wife. "Where are those soldiers at?" Marc screams out.

"There are two over there." Points out an elderly lady. Marc rushes over to the two soldiers who were acting as though they just woke up from a mid-day nap.

"Hey Nazis, I've just became a Jew how do you wear this." Marc said as he slides the armband up and down his arm. The confuse soldiers looks at each other as Marc walks up to them. Even though they weren't the right soldiers they would due. Before they could draw up their weapon Marc hit the first soldier with a right hook snapping the soldiers head backward breaking his neck. As the soldiers was falling to the ground Marc grabs his machine gun and starts shooting at the second German soldier.

Hearing the gunfire Herr Popolish runs up.

"You must get out of here; the Nazi will come to see what had happened, said Herr Popolish as he pushes Marc away.

Marc looks down at the dead soldiers thinking of his next move. "Help me take the cloths off of this soldier." Said Marc as he knelt down and unbutton the soldiers' shirt. Herr Popolish gives Marc a strange look.

'Herr Metz you must leave now, I'll tell the Nazi that the Resistance killed these soldiers, please leave now," begged Herr Popolish.

"I believe that I can wear these cloths." Marc said.

"Here come the soldiers," said one of the spectators.

"Help me drag this man away." said Marc as he grabs the soldiers and started dragging him away. Giving up Herr Popolish helped Marc undress the soldier, taking his cloths with him to the truck Marc throws the uniform into the truck and drives off. "I've got a plan Marc said as he drove off." I'll get revenge for you, I promise." Not knowing what or how he was going to tell the girls. But he has only a few more miles before he reaches home. Marc doesn't even know how to explain it to himself. The country where he was born raised and fought for just killed his beloved wife. Who was also a native German. Marc pulls off to the side of the road and jumps out of the truck where he looks to the heavens and screams then Marc closes his eyes as tears rolls down his face Marc screams "Eva." Marc looks up and down the now vacant road. "Resistance, who are they?" Marc asks himself. 'Who's side are they on?" Marc thought out loud as he walks back to his truck and climbs in.

The time lost on the Resistance cost him miles as Marc pulls up to the house still not knowing how to tell the girls that their momma was dead. Marc grabs the Nazi uniform and took it into the barn and tosses it aside. Then Marc heads for the house where he saw the couch filled with the girls belonging.

Marc looks around at the picture on the wall of the four of them; Marc takes the picture off of the wall and stares at it as tears run down his face. "Papa, is that you?" Anna yells as she walks thought the hall and into the living room, "Where's Momma?" Hearing this Marc starts crying.

"Go get your sister." Marc tries to say.

"Papa, what's wrong, where is my mother?" Marc holds the picture close to him. "Go and get your sister." Knowing that something was wrong Anna cries as she went into Hilda's room. The two girls walk into the living room both in tears. Marc pushes some of their belonging off of the couch.

"Both of you sit down." "

Papa, where is our momma?" Anna asks again but this time in a stern voice.

"She's dead." Marc said as he grips the picture closer to him. Both girls cry harder.

"How?" Hilda asks as she falls into her sister's arms.

"There was an accident in town."

"I need to see her." Anna says as she stands up and walks toward the front door.

"Wait, there's more to it." Marc didn't want to tell the truth but now he felt that the girls had the right to know. As Anna reaches the front door she sees Herr Popolish riding up on his bicycle.

"Why is Herr Popolish here?" said Anna as Marc jumps up and headed outside.

"Stay in here." Marc said as he walks to the front yard.

"Herr Metz, we were able to take frau Metz away before the Nazi found her, some of the women change her dress and clean her up, so that you and your daughters can say your goodbyes, but we have to be fast before the Nazi finds out, oh by the way I have to have my armband back, without it I can be shot." Confused from what Herr Popolish had told him Marc reaches into his pocket and pull out the armband and hand it over to him.

"Girls load up the truck with your stuff then we are going to see your Momma." Marc said as he turns around and walks back into the house. "I'll help." said Herr Popolish as he follows Marc into the house. As the truck is loaded Marc places a cover over the bed disguising the girl's belongings. Marc as well as the girls walks around loading the truck frozen with the loss of Eva. As the last bag is placed onto the truck Marc walks into the barn and brings out several gallons of petrol and places the metal cans at the rear of the covered bed of the truck. Herr Popolish covers the cans of petrol.

"Wait I have a couple more gallons to bring out."

"Papa, are we still going to----" Ask Hilda before she is interrupted.

"We're going there for a while, and then we'll be back." said Marc as he glances over toward Herr Popolish.

"I'll meet you in town." said Herr Popolish as he stood up on his bicycle and started pedaling down the road.

At first inside of the truck was quiet as the three try to understand what had happened. "Papa, what happen? This morning Momma made our breakfast now you're telling us that she is de---." Anna couldn't finish her question. "There was as accident in town." Marc said as he wipes the tears from his face using the sleeves from his long sleeves shirt. "She will be buried-" Marc said, as he could no longer hold back his tears." She will be buried beside your grandparents."

Marc pulls into town and drives up the church. "I don't want to go in." Hilda said as she sees the Church.

Marc reaches over and places his arms around his daughter. "I know honey, I know." They sat inside of the truck as Herr Popolish rides up on his bike.

Herr Popolish walks up to the driver side window and knock on the glass. "We need to do this before the Nazi's find out about this." Anna looks over toward her father.

"Why the Nazis, what do they have to do with it?'

"Yea, Papa, The Nazi is on our side, they're here to protect us." Neither Marc nor Herr Popolish said a word. Then Marc opens his door. "Come on let's go in." Marc held the girls tight as they walk into the church. Everyone who was in attendance was wearing the armband. In the front of the Church is an open casket. Both of the girls tighten the hugs on their father as Marc led the girls down to the casket. Not sure of what to expect Mark was relieved that Eva was placed in a new dress and there was no sign of the shooting. Marc lost it as did the girls as they saw Eva lying there peaceful. As the Priest walks up Marc and his girls sat down. The funeral was quick; the town's people wanted the funeral to be finish before the Nazis found out linking Marc with the killing of their two soldiers.

Even though Marc wanted the funeral over due to the fact that he didn't want to say good-by as Marc wanted to get revenge. After the funeral Marc and the girls walks to the truck.

"Anna, can you drive to Hungary?" Anna looks at her father.

"But Papa, why are we going to Hungary, I'm not leaving Momma."

"No Papa, me neither, we should stay, this is our home and Von is here, he can help you protect us." Marc looks down.

"Yea, like I protected your momma." Marc said quietly to himself. "Von is gone, he joined the army this morning and they had already shipped him out." With a surprised look on their face the girls look at one and another.

"Well we want to stay here with you Papa." Hilda said as Anna shook her head agreeing. Marc just looks at the girls then he notices some Nazis walking around.

"Your momma wasn't in an accident, she was murder by the Nazi's, because she is Jewish that's making you girls half Jewish so you must leave, I'm staying behind to get revenge, But I want you girls to go and stay with family until this is all over then I'll come and get the two of you." Anna couldn't find the right words to say so she just wraps her arms around Marc and got behind the wheel. Hilda grabs her father and the two held on tight. "Go with your sister." Marc said as his voice trembling and tears rolls down his face. "There is enough petrol on the back of the truck so don't stop. When the petrol in the truck is gone add more in but make sure that you aren't seen," said Marc as he stood at the driver side door. "I love you two girls; I love you with all of my heart." The truck pulls away leaving Marc standing in the road crying as well as the girls inside of the truck.

Then Marc dries his eyes and walks over to Herr Popolish. "On my farm is enough vegetables and farm animals, tell our people to take what they want, I don't want the Nazi to get anything, leave them nothing." The two men shake hands then gave each other a hug. "Look at us a Protestant and a Jew hugging, both of us would be shot if the Nazi saw this." Laugh Herr Popolish. "My war isn't with the Jews; my war is with the Nazi." Marc said as he turns to walk back home.

Chapter Six

As Marc reaches his house Marc stared at the house that at one time was filled with love and life, now the house is vacant and dead. Marc shakes his head as he walks into the barn. Where he walks over to the wadded up Nazi uniform and stretches it to get the wrinkles out. Marc then looks over at the crate where he had kept his first war uniform and his metals Marc opens the crate up and pours out the content into a small pile and using the fuel from the lantern Marc pour the fuel over the uniform and metals and started a fire. "That war end, this war just begun." Marc told himself. Marc walks over to the Nazi uniform and tries it on. A little tight but this is the first of many uniforms that Marc would have. By now some of the towns' people gather around the farm and started helping themselves to the vegetables and there are sounds of pigs squealing Marc walks out of the barn wearing his new uniform. As the people seeing the Nazi uniform they become scared and drop all that they gather and starts to run.

"No wait; I'm not a soldier, take all that you can, leave nothing for the Nazi to get. Marc said as he places the ammo belt around him then checking his new Lugar out, making sure that it was fully loaded.

Herr Metz, what are you doing?" Ask Herr Popolish.

"The best way to kill the Nazi is to join them." Marc replied. "You cannot take on the whole Nazi army, just look around town there are too many of them." said Herr Popolish.

Let the Resistance help you." Added Popolish, Marc shook his head. "I work on my own." Marc said as he checks out the handle of the Luger. "I know some people in the Resistance they are going to defend our town, they are waiting for the Allies to join in." Herr Popolish said as he places his hand onto Marc's shoulder. "I need no help; if the Allies get in my way then they will become my target." Mark said as he smiles and walks away.

Miles away Marc slowly walks through the woods. From a distance Marc hears some soldiers. Marc kneels down to see where they were. Marc moves in closer to the sounds of the soldiers. Then Marc sees five Nazi soldiers taking a break from the war. Their rifle was stacks away from them Marc sat there to see if others were close by. The Nazi had a small fire burning and were cooking their meal Marc pays close attention to the amount of the ration that they were cooking.

That's enough for them." Marc said to himself as he moves in closer. Marc stood up with his pistol in his hand and walk toward the group of soldiers. "Hey, who you are, what are you doing here, we was sent here." said a soldier standing up and pointing.

"They sent me here as an extra man just in case there is some allied soldiers around."Allied soldiers" Laughs one of the Nazi; 'We're looking for the Resistance, why didn't you know that?" Asks the Nazi as the other Nazi stood up.

Ok I lied; I'm here to kill all of you." Marc said as he pulls up his pistol and took aim. For a second the Nazi soldiers started to laugh then they realize that Marc was telling the truth as they reach into their holster and try to pull out their pistol.

Marc fired five shot killing all of the Nazi soldiers. As the men lay dead Marc walks over to the fire and look at his meal,

Yep, perfect timing." said Marc as he helps himself. Then Marc look around making sure that no other Nazi soldiers heard the shooting. Marc ate what he could then poured out the rest. Then Marc rechecks the area around him making sure that he was still alone in the wood. Marc took one of the shovels and started digging a large hole. Then Marc grabs four of the five rifles and threw them into the hole. Then Marc took off the ammo belt from the dead soldiers and took the ammo that he would be needing and tossed the rest of the belts into the hole along with the pistol, four of the knifes and all of the hand grenades except what he put inside of his belt. With a good glance around making sure that none other Germans had heard the shooting. Marc then walks over to the dead Germans soldiers and undresses them. Pants, Shirts and Helmets. Marc gathers them all up and tosses them into the hole. Then Marc cover the hole up making sure that the ground didn't look disturbed. Marc looks over at the dead half dress soldiers.

"I ate your food, I took your weapon, I even took your clothes along with killing all of you, and yes sir I would say that

I had a good day in battle." Marc said as he smiles and turns around and walks away.

A few miles down the road darkness came quickly.

Marc decided to find the first good place where he could sleep. Deep in the woods Marc looks around. He sees a very small clearing where he could sleep for the night. Marc carefully check his surrounding making sure that he was alone then starts cutting thick bushes and planking them into the ground. Marc places them as close as he could. The bushes were enough to give him cover if German soldiers would be walking around. Marc places thicker bushes on top giving the look as one large bush and called it a night. The night was hard on Marc not only had he not slept this way since the first war but now it was quiet and his thoughts were on that morning when it started out meeting Von in the truck, Eva was still alive and the girls was asleep in their bed. Hours later Marc's world shifted. Eva was murdered by the men that was supposed to protect her, the girls was sent to another country trying to keep them safe, Von joined the same army that killed his wife, what was Marc to do if he was fighting Vons's outfit? What would Von do? As the sky became darker Marc drifted off to sleep but his dream was a nightmare as Marc dreamt of the day that he and Eva met, the wedding, the birth of Anna then Hilda, the days where a large smile never left Marc's face then the dream changed to the first war where Marc was captured. Beaten for being on the wrong side of the war. Marc was in REM sleep as he replayed his life as a man, soldier, husband and father. It took years to find happiness and only minutes to destroy it. Marc will fight for his wife and daughters and for the people that can't fight for themselves

The next morning a truck pulls up to the camp site of the five dead soldiers. The officer and the driver is the first to get out followed by five more soldiers that were in the back of the cover troop's truck. They stand around the dead soldiers, staring at their half-naked bodies. "Where are their cloths?" Asked one of the soldiers.

'Who did this?" Ask another.

"It was the Resistance." said the Officer as he looks around for some kind of sign. "This war has just changed for us, now we have some Resistance fighter dressed up like us. Beware of everyone just because they are wearing our uniform doesn't mean that they are a part of us." said the Officer as he sees some spent shells on the ground. "This is from a Luger. Call headquarter tell them of the imposters. " As the Officer notice five spent shell all in the same area. "This was done by one man." said the Officer as he picked up the shell and looks at it. "How can you tell?" Ask one of his men. "The spent shells are all together, in the same place, if there was more than one man then there would be shells all over in this area." But there all in one place leading me to believe that there was one shooter." "Then how about the clothes and the weapons?" Ask another soldier. "The shooter was alone but he is working with others." said the Officer, we must be careful now more than ever." The radioman walks over and looks at the half naked soldiers. "Who would do this?" 'The Officer looks over toward the radio man. "Did you inform headquarter?"

The soldier nods his head (yes). "The Resistance is close by let's find them before they can use those uniforms." All of the soldiers gather into the truck as the truck heads down the road.

As they travel down the road Marc who was half awake heard the approaching vehicle. Marc has no time to jump from his homemade bed as the truck quickly approaches. As the truck passes Marc leaps up and grabs one of his hand grenades and pulls the pin. As the soldier in the back of the truck screams out 'Wait, stop the truck." As they try to pull their weapons out. Mark threw the grenade into the back of the truck before the soldiers could get a shot off. Mark falls to the ground as the truck explodes. The truck rolls off of the road and into the ditch Mark with his pistol in hand runs up.

Marc looks at the bodies in the back of the truck. The bodies were mangled from the blast. Then Marc moves up to the cab of the truck. Both the Officer and the driver were dead from the shrapnel of the grenade. "I can't use any of this." Marc told himself. Marc moves on. With one less grenade Marc must now replace it; Marc now looks for his next victims.

Marc sees a tiger tank off to the side where the tank's men was outside reconnecting the tracks. Being in a Nazi's uniform,

Marc looks at the men around the tank who don't pay too close of attention to him. "Where is your outfit?" said one of the soldiers.

Marc looks at the soldiers and places his rifle on top of the body of the tank. "Some of them captured some dead and the other is in the ground somewhere." said Marc as he takes off his helmet and wipes the sweat off of his fore head.

"Need some water?" Ask another soldier.

"Yea, if you have any to spare." The German soldier that was cleaning the 50- caliber machine gun that sat on top of the tank yells to the soldier inside of the tank.

"Hey toss up one of the canteens." From the inside a canteen is tossed up to the gunner and the gunner toss it to Marc.

'Danke?" Said Marc as he takes a drink. Then Marc watches as the men work on the tank's track. "What happened here?" Marc asks as he took another swig of water.

"It doesn't take much to throw a track, we have tonight to fix it then we must meet up with the rest by noon tomorrow," said the soldier that was busy working on the track.

Marc climbs up onto the tank and is amazed at the sight of this large machine. "I was in the first war, the tanks that I saw was much smaller than this one." Marc said looking around.

"Yea, these tanks are much better than back then but I think that the tanks back then was more comfortable." said the soldier sticking his head out of the inside of the tank.

Marc still looking at the tank then he pounds the tank with the butt of his rifle. "I've never ridden on one before, I only seen them from a distance."

The soldiers from the inside of the tank wave Marc in. "Well then come on in and I'll show you around."

Marc smiles at the chance to climb in, as the soldier was glad to show Marc around the inside of a tank. The driver shows Marc how to drive the tank as well as load the large cannon. He is also shown the escape hatches one in the bottom of the tank and the other was in the front of the tank. Marc took it all in. An hour later as the driver finishes his crash course as the other soldier finishes with the track.

"Where are you going from here?" asks one of the soldiers. Marc looks up to the sky and shakes his head. "Well it's too late for me now I'll leave in the morning."

'Then you should stay here tonight, besides we have enough rations for another soldier. Marc spent that night eating with his enemy, they laugh, told stories and one by one the soldiers fell asleep.

In the sunshine through the trees that the tank hides under from the allies' airplanes they begin to awaken. As each one awoke they began to store their gear that they use to fix the tank. Marc who had another bad night slowly woke up. "Get up you lazy foot soldier, it's time for us to leave." Laughs one of the soldiers. "Would you like to ride with us? Maybe you can join another tank." said the driver as he turns on the diesel engine the only sight that Marc hadn't seen. Marc pays close attention to the driver.

"Move the tank forward." said a soldier; let's make sure that the tracks are ready. As the tank moves Marc is jerked backwards, but he holds on then the soldier gives a swipe with his hand to his neck.

The driver stops the tank. "I thought that you said that it was ready." Yelled the driver.

"It just needs a little of tightening that's all."

"Well I'm getting out, I am in here for hours, and I need to stretch my legs whenever I get a chance." The driver climbs out of the tank and jumps to the ground. "Oh yea, this feels better." Marc grabs his rifle and pulls back the bolt action. "What are you doing?" Ask the driver as he stretches.

"This is a war, no telling who could be around here." All of the men agree. Marc walks up and shakes each soldier's hand. "Thanks for the meal and a place to stay last night." Marc said as he walks away.

"Hey wait a minute. s aid one of the tank's men "You still want a ride?" Marc turns around holding his rifle toward them.

"No thanks, I'm a foot soldier, beside I heard of bullets ricocheting off of the tank and hitting the soldiers around, when you meet up with your unit where then?" Marc asks as he grips his rifle.

"Who knows somewhere that there are American Sherman Tanks I guess, replies the driver. Marc drops his rifle down to his side.

"Well keep your heads down and aim straight." Marc said as he walks into the woods. The tank cranks up and pulls away.

As Marc walks deeper into the woods. "I'm sorry Eva, but they are fighting the allies not us. Marc said as he had one hand on his last grenade. Marc could have easy pull the pin and toss the grenade into the hatch of the tank before they close it up and drove off. "As days turn into weeks and weeks turn into months Marc fights and kills all of the Nazi that he could.

Back in Berlin Von graduates from basic training with all smiles on his face Von looks for Herr Metz to greet him; Then Von realizes that the only friendly face that he saw was Wolfgang who was waiting for him. "I just knew that you would be at the top of your class." said Wolfgang as he slaps Von on his back.

"Have you seen Herr Metz?" Von asks as he continues to look around.

"No, not since you left for basic." Herr Metz said that he had business to tend to before he joined up, and that was a couple of months ago, Herr Metz cost me a higher rank." said Wolfgang sarcastically.

"Well Im sure that you'll get a higher rank in battle." Von said with a smile. "So when do we leave for our town?" Ask Von as he ready to defend his hometown. Wolfgang shakes his head.

"The town is gone the German civilians left as the Jews were sent to a Concentration camp." Vons's eyes widen "How about the Herr Metz's farm?"

"We don't need his farm anymore the people in the Concentration camps now grow our vegetables, Forget about the town, it's a black blotch on a map now."

' Then where are we going?" Von asks as he follows Wolfgang to an awaiting troop trucks

"As soon as we get the rest of the replacements then we are going toward the French border, where we are going to make a name for our self." Wolfgang said as he points the replacements to the back of the truck.

"What are we going to do there?" Von asks in a nervous

voice.

Wolfgang looks over at his friends and laughs. "Are you serious? We are going to fight the Frenchmen." Von gives Wolfgang a strange look. "I thought that we were going to protect the town." Von repeats.

'From what, I told you that the town is a ghost town now, we're needed elsewhere and that's where we are going. Come on you can ride up front with me." said Wolfgang as he closes the back of the truck up and walk toward the front of the truck. Von didn't say a word as he climbs up into the truck.

Miles down the road Von look over at his friend.

"What's it like?"

"What do you mean?"

"Killing another man?" Wolfgang thought for a moment,

"Well, you're going to kill him or he's going to kill you, try not to think about it, your first kill is the worst, then it gets better, Remember you're a soldier for the Third Reich. The best trained soldier in the world is fighting for the fatherland," Wolfgang boasted.

"When we get into battle stay close by me, I'll keep you safe and, do as I say and I'll keep you alive and I can make sure that you move up in rank faster than the others." Said Wolfgang as he drives on. Von smiles as he sits back in the truck's seat. Before long Wolfgang pulls the truck up to the makeshift headquarter. Wolfgang and Von exit the truck and opens the rear door; the new replacements try to recover from the bumpy road. They waddled to the open truck door. As the Captain walks up. The new replacements uniform wrinkle from the road. "What happened here, straighten up your uniforms? Yelled the Captain as he looks over toward Wolfgang "Did you pick up these men looking like this?" 'No sir, Head Captain it must had been the truck ride."

Then the Captain looks over toward Von. "This soldier looks fresh." The Captain then looks over to Wolfgang. "This man can go out with your unit tonight." Wolfgang smiles as he knocks his heels together. "The rest of the men can set back and wait to be heroes." Wolfgang threw up his right hand.

"Heil Hitler." As the Captain walks off Wolfgang reaches out his hand. Von shakes his hand. "This is a very important battle a lot of Frenchmen will die tomorrow and you will be there to celebrate our victory." Then Wolfgang looks over to the rest of the replacements. "The rest of you will go and get assigned to different units, I only want the best in my unit and now I got it." Laugh Wolfgang. "Come with me, we need to go to the quartermaster and get you all of your weapons." said Wolfgang as he patted Von on his back. Von closes his eyes as Wolfgang walks ahead of him.

"Come on, follow me." Wave Wolfgang. "We were supposed to protect the town." Von said to himself.

Darkness fills the air as Von tries to sleep for the upcoming battle. Von noticed that some of the soldiers that came out of basic with him were assigned to guard duties along with their trainer. Von tries to sleep but he was too nervous to sleep, Von looks over to Wolfgang who was snoring. "A veteran of many battles." Von said to himself. Before the sun came up a soldier walks up to wake Wolfgang up. "It's time Sergeant." Wolfgang jumps up refreshed from his sleep as he looks over to Von, who hadn't slept all night.

"Are you ready to make history?"

Von gives a scared nod. "Yes, I'm ready."

Wolfgang grabs his pistol belt and wraps it around him. Von copies Wolfgang's every move. "The French won't know what has hit them when the battle starts." Wolfgang laughs.

As the ten soldiers climb up into a troop truck Von sat beside Wolfgang. "Like I said before, stay with me and do what I do and at the end of the day we can celebrate together as victors." Von nods and looks away as the truck comes to a stop.

The truck gate is open and the men jumps out. Von grips his rifle tight as he looks around for the French soldiers.

"There are not here, the truck drops us off a few miles away so we can secretly move in on them." said Wolfgang as he rechecks his map with the Officer. Wolfgang pointing at the map then he moves his hand across the map. The Officer nodded his head and started walking. "Alright men let's move out." Whisper Wolfgang. Von watches his steps as he moves forward, deeper into the wood. Wolfgang leading the march throws up his hand. All of the soldiers stop and kneel down.

Wolfgang quietly lays his machine gun down and takes out his knife. Von shakes as he kneels, Wolfgang walks up to the Frenchman standing guard. Wolfgang slowly reaches around the half asleep guard's neck and with one quick swing the guard falls to the ground. Then Wolfgang motion for the rest of the men to follow. As Von walks up to the dead French soldier he sees the blood flowing from his neck. Wolfgang pointing to each soldier where he wanted him to be placed. Wolfgang then motions toward Von to come up to where he was. "This is where we'll be for the ambush." Wolfgang said as he pointed down to the camp where the French Soldiers were sleeping.

"This is the last good night sleep that they'll get." Von said as he looks over toward Wolfgang who is waving his hands telling his men to shoot as one French soldier walks out of his tent. Trying to shake his sleep off the French soldier grabs his rifle as the German soldier looks back toward Wolfgang who is still waving his hand. Then Wolfgang leans down to Von, "That guard I killed?" Von nods his head.

"This is his replacement, we won't shoot him either, I need to know where the rest of the French are, they may be in those tents o r this might be a decoy." The French soldier took another route to the dead man that he was replacing.

'Let him find the dead body, whispers Wolfgang. Von watches as the Frenchman walks close by but not too close to notice that the Germans had laid out an ambush.

Ok men, get ready." All of the soldiers aim their rifles toward the French soldier's camp. "Don't worry about the French man concentrate on the base." Said Wolfgang as he stares down at the camp. Then the Frenchman started screaming, alerting his comrade who are quickly waking up. The French soldier runs back to his camp passing the undercover German soldiers.

As the French soldiers jump out of their tents with their guns in hand Wolfgang yells. "Open fire." As the Ambush starts Von sees a French soldier hiding behind a tree and takes aim. Von took a deep breath as he slowly pulls the trigger.

Von's bullet hits the tree as the French soldier returns fire. Knowing that he missed his target Von leaves the spot and gets closer to the French soldier. Wolfgang never knew that Von had left. Von runs close to the tree where now the French soldier knew that he was shooting at him. Shielded by the tree The French soldier had the upper hand on Von who was out in the open. Von shot his bolt-action rifle and had to pull out the bolt to replace the spent shell. Von ran to the right leaving the French soldier to readjust his position leaving in the open for the German soldier to shot him. The French soldier fell to the ground dead. As Von realizes that he was away from his outfit and closer to the French base camp Von had a better shot at the French soldiers that was hidden from the battle. One by one Von took aim and fired. With each shot a French soldier dies. Wolfgang laughs when he sees that the battle was being won. Wolfgang looks to his left where Von was supposed to be. "Von." Yells Wolfgang as he looks around. "Have anyone seen Von." The Germans soldiers glance around for Von but they were more concerned with the fighting. Then one of the German soldiers pointed to the French base. "There he is." Wolfgang looks down at the base and sees Von taking out the hidden French soldier one by one. Seconds later the battle was over. There were no surviving French soldiers left. Wolfgang and the rest of the ambush team celebrate as Von stands by the tree staring at all of the dead French soldiers that he was responsible of killing. Wolfgang notices Von standing at the tree Wolfgang was proud as he walks up and places his arms around his old friend. Wolfgang sees all of the dead French soldiers that Von had killed. "This is the reason that I brought you with us, out there we couldn't touch these soldiers because they were well hidden, but it took a brave man like you to break lines and win this battle for us." By now the rest of the German soldiers gather around Wolfgang and Von.

"Shall we call him Herr Sniper?" Ask one of the soldiers. "Herr Sniper, I like that." Wolfgang agrees as all of the ambush team patted Von on the back and Von stared at the dead French soldiers.   Wolfgang walks over to the dead soldiers and started going through their belongings

"What are you doing?" Von asks as the rest of the team started going through the dead soldiers' pockets. "We're looking for maps and other military materials, who was the first man that you killed?" Von looks down at the Man by the tree. "This man."

Wolfgang who pulls out some papers from one of the French officers' pocket and tried to read them. "Then take something from him."

'What?" Ask Von as he looks down at his first confirmed kill. "I took his life, that's all I want." Von said as he watches the blood flow down the ground into a small puddle.

The German Officer walks up and looks around the French camp. "This is a victory for now but, this is a small victory for us and nothing else." Said the German Officer as he turns and walks back toward the truck. "You have to take something from your first kill, thats tradition." said another soldiers. Von reaches down and grabs his knife from the ammo belt. Wolfgang grabs all of the papers from the Officer and shoved them into his pocket. "We must leave now, just in case there are other French soldiers around that heard the shooting." said Wolfgang as he picks up his machine gun and follows the Captain. Von stood there watching the blood flow as he grips his newly acquired knife and looks at it.

"Let's move it private." Wolfgang yells as he hurried up the trail. In camp Vons's tells the story of how he attacked the French soldiers and killed seven of them. The must kills of that battle.

The next battle led into the following and with each battle Von proves that he was someone to be followed, stay close and learn from. Wolfgang took all credit for Vons recruited.

As bullets fly by, Von approaches the enemy with arrogance and determination to win another battle. Before long Von is decorated as a Corporal under Wolfgang.

The two became a team as one thought so did the other. More and more victories were won under the two as the soldiers under them thought that it was a privileged to serve with them.

Chapter Seven

The girls did what they were told; Anna drove the truck down the dirty and bumpy road. Hilda holds on as if her life depended on it. Anna fights to change the gears. The grinding sounds as Anna goes from one gear to the next. Her legs tired from the hard clutch. Luckily, the road was empty as Anna swerves back and forth "Let me drive." Hilda would yell as Anna has a hard time steering the large truck down a bumpy dirt road. "Keep quiet, I'm trying to drive." Anna yells back.

"This is spooky." Anna said as she looks around. "There should be supply trucks taking this road." Anna said as she looks around. Then the truck started spurting. "What's wrong?" Said a scared Hilda. "I'm not sure." said Anna who is gripping the steering wheel tighter. As Anna pumps the gas pedal the trucks slowly come to a stop. "Anna, I'm scared." Hilda said as tears rolls down her face. "Is it dead?" Hilda asks as she looks out of the window at the bare area. Then Anna looks over all of the in dash instruments "We're out of petrol."

Anna hopes that this is the only problem. Anna and Hilda get out of the truck and walk to the back of the truck. Hilda pulls the tarps over where Marc had placed the Petrol. "Papa placed this on last." said Anna as she grabs a small barrel and pours it into the tank. "Keep a lookout while I refill the tank." Anna said as she struggles to pour the first small barrel. "What am I looking for?" Hilda asks as she turns around. "I believe that the war is near are there would be more trucks on the roads." Anna said as she pours the last drop of petrol into the tank. As Anna pours another small barrel into the tank she places the empty barrel into the back of the truck. "That should be enough to get us to Uncle Sol and Aunt Bertha's house.

As the girl's drive through town they saw the devastation of war. Buildings that are barely standing from the bombardments of all of the armies that enter the quiet, slow town where people live their life the simple way. Now that town is a shell of ruined lives and the loss of generations of love. It is now defined by fear, fear to be the wrong religion, fear of being in the wrong place at the wrong time. The girls were speechless as they drove through the town.

"Keep your eyes open we have no friends out there." Anna said as she looks around. Finally, the girls drive up to their aunt and uncle's house. The war made a path from the town and through the farm of Sol and Bertha Lowenstein.

The farm destroyed from war. Their house is shelled but still livable. Anna and Hilda slowly steps out of the truck not knowing what to expect as they slowly walk toward the house. "Stay right there." said a voice from behind.

"Now slowly get back into the truck and go back to wherever you come from." said Uncle Sol as he held his rifle tight in his hand ready to pull the trigger. "May we turn around?" Anna said as she raises her hands up in the air. "Please sir we just want to see our family." Hilda said with fear.

Sol takes a closer look. "Who are you two girls?"

"Our father is Marc Metz and our----" Anna and Hilda said as he drops the barrel of his outdated rifle toward the ground. The girl's turns around and see an old thin man with his gray bread hanging from his chin down to his belly.

The girls were glad to see their mom's uncle as they run up to him and both place their arms around the old, feeble man. "It's ok Bertha, it's Eva's girls." The front door opens and an old overweight woman walks out. The girls then run up to the door and hug their aunt. "What are you two girls doing here?" Ask Bertha as she holds the girls tight in her arms.

"Papa sent us here." Anna said tightening her hold on her aunt. "The Nazi----" Hilda tries to say as she started crying. "The Nazi killed our momma." Said Anna as she to start to cry. "And your Papa?" Asks Uncle Sol. Anna looks over to Uncle Sol who was walking up to them. "Papa is taking revenge." said Anna as she wipes her face dry from the tears. "Come on into the house, Bertha just made a big pot of soup, I need to move the truck." Sol said as he walks toward the truck. "Are you girl's hungry?" Both girls' nods their head as aunt Bertha lead them into the house. The girls are shock by the way that the house was filled with bullet holes throughout the walls also shows the damage from the shells of the cannons burst. "What happened Uncle Sol?" Anna asks as Bertha pours the girls a bowl of soup and Sol walks in the back door. "They are calling it World War Two, We've had the Nazi here then the Americans, neither side cared that families was living in the town. Both side fought their battle and left, leaving what you see here." Sol said in anger. "Why the Nazi Uncle Sol?" Ask Hilda. "Because they are after us, the Jewish people." "But why?" said Anna who ate some of her soup.

"The Nazi, just don't like us." said Aunt Bertha trying to play the nightmare down. "They hate us, and for once their hate fills my heart, I've killed my share of German soldiers, and I will continue to kill German soldiers until they kill me." Said Uncle Sol in an angry tone.

"Oh Sol, you're scaring the girls." Bertha said as she motions toward Anna and Hilda with her head. "The Americans has left and the German soldiers are slowly coming back, well me and the boys will stop them from coming back." said Uncle Sol who was getting madder with each word. "Sol, that's enough, you're scaring the girls." Aunt Bertha said as Sol stops his speech and looks away. "Your father is fighting for the Germans or for the Resistance?" Sol asks as he watches the girls eat their soup. "What is the Resistance?" Hilda asks as she drinks some of the milk that Bertha had sat down beside her.

"It's a group of old men trying to regain their youth." Said Bertha as she sat back down giving Sol a stern look.

"Life took our youth, but the Nazi are taking our lives and that we can do something about." Sol said in a victorious tone Anna places her spoon down and looks over toward her great uncle. "How can I join the Resistance?" Sol looks over toward his great niece "Young girls shouldn't be in a war. "Sol said as Bertha places a bowl of soup in front of him. "

"The Nazi killed our mother." Bertha closes her eyes as tear rolls down her face with Sol looking toward the girls. "Your father was a Great War hero; let him handle your mother's revenge."

"My father wants revenge, well so do we." Anna said as she looks over toward Hilda. "We're not staying. We should have enough petrol left to get us back home, we'll help Papa fight the Nazis." Anna slides back her chair as did Hilda.

"Girls, no." Aunt Bertha yells, "Stay here, you two girls

has no idea of what war is like. Your father does, let him handle it." Sol said as he stood up.

"You said that Papa was a war hero, when?" Hilda asks as she looks over toward her uncle.

"Marc Metz was a hero in the first war, there is a lot of dead Frenchmen lying across the battle fields." Sol said with pride.

"Well how come we had never heard of this?" Ask Anna.

"Because the war ended and he met our beautiful Eva. That part of his life was over now he wanted a new life with Eva, then with you Anna and after you came Hilda. Your father was not a war hero anymore now he was a husband and father and that's what he wanted. Now Marc is a soldier again but this time he is fighting his own battle." Sol said as he slowly sat down. The girl's stunned of hearing the word hero also sat back down. "I know that you two girls would like to fight along with your father, but don't give him any distraction.

Stay here and keep your aunt company." Sol said in a softer tone.

At that time a knock on the door is heard. Sol jumps out of his chair and looks at his three girls "go and get into the cellar." Bertha and the girls quickly pick up their bowl of soup leaving Sol's bowl left. Sol stands at the door with his hands on the doorknob waiting for the girls to hide. As the girls disappear Sol opens the door. The man at the door is one of Sol's friends Lew Roseblum. "Are you alone?" Sol asks Lew as the two men shook hands. "Yes, but we got problems." Lew said as Sol opens the door up with Lew walking in. "It's alright, Lew is here." Sol said. Hidden in the fake cellar Bertha and the girls emerged from the tiny cellar built for one. "Good evening Frau Lowenstein and these ladies are?" "They're my niece's daughters." Sol said as Lew walks over to greet the girls. "Sol, we have a problem and it's going to take all of us." Lew said as he turns his attention to Sol. "What is it?" Ask Sol as he looked out of the window. Lew looks at Anna and Hilda. "Let's go out to the yard and talk." Lew requested. "No tell me now, they are family." said Sol.

The Germens are returning." Lew said as he looks over at

Anna. "Why are they coming back, I thought that the Americans ran them off?" Bertha asks in fear.

They know that the Americans are gone, now they are back to finish the job." Lew said hoping that Sol was right about trusting the girls. "What job?" Ask Hilda. The three adults look at the two young girls. "The job is to kill the rest of the Jews in town." Lew said in anger. 'Tell the men to meet me at our designated sight. "Uncle Sol I want to go." Anna said pleading. "No, stay here." said Sol as he grabs his coat and rifle. "If you won't let me go then I'll follow." Sol looks over at his niece. "We're not playing some games out there, we will be shooting at the Nazis and they will be shooting back.

I don't need to be worrying about your well-being." said Sol as he walks out the door. Bertha walks over to Anna and places her arms around her. "Anna let the men protect us.

Beside we need to be here for Uncle Sol when he returns." Anna hugs her aunt then she walks over to the window and watches Sol walking away. Later that night as Bertha and the girls lay in Bertha and Sol's bed the battle in town is heard.

Gunfire from both sides fills the air. Hilda places her hands over her ears as the fighting continues. "Aren't you scared?" Anna asks her aunt. Bertha holds Anna.

"Whenever I see Lew come over my heart slows down, when I hears the shooting begin my heart stops. Only when I see Sol walks through the door dose my heart starts beating. But we need for the men to fight. We are hated because we are Jewish; Make sure that you have your papers on you at all times. Make sure that your last name is Metz on the papers. That will cause the Nazi to leave you alone, never tell them that your mother was born into our Lowenstein family." Bertha warns.

"But why, I'm not ashamed that my mother comes from a Jewish family." Anna said.

"How long does the shooting last?" Hilda asks as she tightens her grip on her ears.

"Whenever the last soldiers from either side is dead." Bertha replies.

"Do you ever get used to hearing the shooting?" asks Anna.

"Let's just hope that you girls can fall asleep soon, but

keep one eye open for we may have to go to the cellar if our men lose." As the fighting ends both of the girls are asleep. In the middle of the night Anna woke up and notice that aunt Bertha was out of the bed.

Anna makes sure that Hilda was still sleeping as she eases out of the bed and walks into the kitchen where she saw both her Uncle Sol and aunt Bertha sitting at the table. Sol had his rifle sitting on the table and is quiet as he stares at the wall.

Bertha sits beside him with her hand lying softly on Sol's hand. Happy to see that her uncle had survived the battle. But Anna could tell that something was wrong. "Did, Lew suffer or did he die without pain?" Bertha asks as she patted Sol's hand. "If Lew knew it was only for a second, Lew was hit in his chest." Sol said in a weak voice.

"But you're fine?" Anna asks as she enters the room. Both Sol and Bertha looks over toward Anna. Sol reach out his arms as Anna walks over and held her great uncle.

"We won the battle but we lost three. That's too many for us."

"Then let me fight, you said that Papa was a war hero and I'm his daughter, I can help the Resistance." Sol looks at his niece.

"War is no place for a little girl." Bertha reminded.

"Take me with you the next time." Anna begged.

"It's time for you girls to go back to Germany, tomorrow there will be twice the number of soldiers here and we are down to just four men to fight them off, we won't win." Sol said to Anna. "Your last name is Metz, which will keep you two girls alive. But we are Lowenstein that puts us to death." said Sol as he reaches over and kisses Bertha on the top of her head.

"Sol I will join the Resistance, either way I'm dead at least if I die it will be with you." Bertha said as she places her head into Sol's chest.

"It's safer if you girls were not here, leave in the morning. Hopefully before the Nazi get here.

Anna walks over and hugs both of her relatives. "We'll leave in the morning."

As the sun comes up Anna and Hilda were climbing into the truck. Bertha was out of the house holding a plate.

~ 49 ~

"This is for your trip, it's not much but it's all we got." Said Bertha as she hands the plate to Hilda.

"We'll drive north maybe we can find the American and tell them that the Germans are back."

"They won't have time to get here." Sol said as he walks up to the truck to kiss the girls good-by. "If you girls get stopped then show them your papers and don't let them know that you was here at a Jewish home, Your German name will keep you safe from the Nazi." Sol said as he kisses each of the girls. With tears in their eyes the girls drove off. Anna looks in the side mirror and sees the two elderly couple arm in arm waving at them. "We got to help." said Anna as she sticks her arm out to wave back.

Down the road Anna and Hilda saw where the battle took place. All of the dead Resistance men were removed but the dead German soldiers were lying on the ground. Anna stops the truck and gets out. "Stay here." Anna says as she runs over to a dead German soldier trying not to look at his face or wound Anna grabs his rifle and ammo belt that had a pistol on it.

Anna runs back to the truck yelling. "Get out, "Hilda jumps out of the truck." Here pull back of the seat." Hilda pulls on the back of the seat leaving a gap between the seat and the petrol tank. Anna places the rifle and the ammo belt in the small opening. "Get back in." said Anna as she runs to the other side of the truck. As the girls are now in the truck, Anna drives off. "What do we need with that gun?" Hilda asks as she leans forwards trying not to place any weight on the rifle. "I'm not sure why I did that, but now we are protected." Anna said with a smile as though she just did something important.

A few miles down the road a German troop truck rolls their way. The troop truck slams on its breaks as the men inside all jump out of the rear, aiming their rifle toward to approaching truck. Both girls mouths drop as they see the German soldiers aiming at them as the Officer inside the cab of the truck gets out and waves the girls to stop. Anna stops the truck in front of the German Officer. Scared of the soldiers all of which are aiming their rifles at them Hilda starts to cry. 'What are we going to do?" The Officer walks up to the driver side of the window.

"Where are you two girls going?" Ask the Officer as he peeks inside of the truck.

"We're leaving this town; our family said that's it too dangerous for us now." said Anna as she drops her hands away from the steering wheel because she was shaking too much.

Let me see your papers." said the Officer as he looks over toward Hilda. Anna takes Hilda's papers and adding her Anna hands the German Officer both of their papers.

"Why is she crying?" Ask the Officer as he looks over the papers.

"My sister is scared, we are German girls but we've been shot at by the Americans and the Resistance and I think by the German, we don't know who to trust."

The Officer looks up at the girls as he reads their paper." Your last names are Metz, but tell me why you are two girls in Hungary?"

"We are visiting our family in Budapest." Anna lied. 'Budapest is too dangerous for two young girls, Germany is safer then Budapest, because we control all of the Fatherland. Safe from the allies and other undesirable people, let's just say that Germany belongs to us. And we will protect our land. We're pushing out the Allies when you two girls get back Germany will be free and you can live in harmony, Germany will not be a battle ground, England and the United States will be the future battle field, go home and live the rest of your lives.

"Under the watchful eyes of the Third Reich." Anna gives the German Officer a faint smile as the Officer gives her back their papers.

"Go home." warns the Officer. Both girls' watch as the Officer and his men enter their troop truck and drive off.

"Anna lets go home." Hilda begged. Anna watches the troop truck in her side mirror as it disappears.

"Not just yet." Anna said as she drives away. Anna quickly pulls to the side of the road and turns the truck around.

Where are we going?" Hilda said, as she held on tight to the seat. "We're following the soldiers." Anna said as she makes the sharp u-tum. "They are going to fight Uncle Sol and the rest of the Resistance fighter." Anna said showing no fear in her eyes. Anna follows the cloud of dust on the road from the troop truck. As the cloud of dust slowly disappears Anna slows down the truck. Anna then jumps out of the truck and looks straight ahead. "Stay in the truck" Anna yells at her sister. 'But Anna where are you going?" Hilda asks as Anna opens the door to the truck. "Raise up." Anna said as she pulls the back seat up and reach into to grab the rifle and ammo belt.

Give me the pistol and I'll go with you." Hilda volunteer. "No, stay in the truck." Anna yells as she slams the door close. Anna places the ammo belt around her head and shoulder and walks toward the battlefield of the night before. From the tree lines Anna hides behind a tree and watch as the Nazi walks around their dead soldiers. The Officer kneels down and checks on one of his dead soldier. Then the Officer grabs a fist full of dirt and throws the dirt into the wind.

The Officer stood up and took out his binocular and looks ahead. Then the Officer starts yelling to his men pointing to the trees near Sol's house. All of the German Soldiers runs toward their Officer as he pulls out his pistol and start shooting. From the tree line fire is return from Uncle Sol and his men. "Uncle Sol." Anna said as she eases closer to the German soldiers. Anna takes aim and fires her stolen rifle.

Hitting a German soldier, Anna is knocked down by the recoil of the blast. From the truck Hilda hears the battle and jumps out of the truck hoping that Anna could use her. With her hands shaking Anna pulls back the bolt reloading the rifle. Anna braces herself for the next shot. Taking aim Anna fires the rifle again this time she remains standing as another German soldier falls to the ground. With all of the excitement the German never knew that they were being attack from behind. Seeing the German soldier fall to the ground Hilda runs up to Anna who was about to take another shot. "Great shot."

Hilda said as she runs up scaring Anna causing her to miss the next shot. The bullet hit the ground in front of the Officer.

Seeing this, the German officer turns around and points to the tree line where Anna and Hilda were. A couple of soldier turns around and returns fire. Anna and Hilda runs back to the base of the tree line where they were more protected. Being surrounded the Germans lost firepower from the front to the rear giving the Resistance as well as Anna and Hilda less to fight. As the bullets pop the tree around her Anna kneels down to the ground exposing the pistol on the ammo belt, Hilda grabs the pistol out of the holster and aims it toward the German. "What are you doing?" Anna asks trying to grab the pistol out of Hilda's hand. "I want to help." Yells Hilda as she pulls the pistol back away from Anna's reach. "If you over shoot then you'll shoot toward Uncle Sol." Anna said as she tries again to grab the pistol out of her younger sisters' hand as more and more bullets hit the trees around them. "I've seen Papa shoot a pistol before; I know what I'm doing." said Hilda as she takes a good aim and slowly pulls the trigger hitting the Officer in his back. Anna couldn't believe her eyes. As now both girls joined the Resistance without being ask to. The girls communicated whom they were going to shoot at so no bullets would be wasted on just one soldier. Before long the battle was over. Hilda was ready to approach the dead German soldiers as Anna stops her.

'Wait till you see Uncle Sol and his men first." Anna said holding her sister back. After a few minutes Hilda stood up to get a closer look. Anna watches Hilda as well as the Dead Soldiers. "Where is Uncle Sol?" Hilda ask as she places her right hand over the top of her eyes trying to see better.

I'm not sure, come on let's go and see." Anna said as she carefully stood up and walks toward the dead Germans.

"If you see one of the Germans move then shoot him." Anna told her sister. As the girls walk closer to the dead German soldiers they saw the darkness of war. As the dead soldiers lay on the ground bleeding from their wounds, a puddle of blood gathered between two dead soldiers. Hilda quickly turns her head as she falls to her knees and started throwing up. Anna tried not to look down at the soldiers. Anna walks her way toward her sister. Anna walks up to Hilda and places her hand on top of Hilda's forehead trying to hold back her disgust.

I'm so sorry that you had to see this." Anna said as she tries to comfort her younger sister. Hilda looks over to a dead German soldier and wipes her mouth.

"I'll be ok now." Hilda said as she pushes Anna away. The once loud battleground now has a quite spooky calmness.

"Let's check on Uncle Sol." said Anna as she moves

quickly away from the dead soldiers. As the girls walks past the soldiers they would turn around making sure that none of the soldiers was acting like he was dead.

As they got to the tree line the girls saw three dead Resistance fighters. "Where's Uncle Sol?" Ask Hilda as she again turns her head from the sight of death. Then a weak cried is heard.

The girls follow the cry where they see Uncle Sol holding their Aunt Bertha in his arm. Aunt Bertha was lying on the ground shot in her chest dead from the battle.

Aunt Bertha." Yells Anna as she drops her rifle and runs over to her Aunt.

"Stay back." said Uncle Sol with tears running down his face and in a weak tone. "She's dead." Cried Uncle Sol. "My baby is dead." Two more Resistance fighters walk up both wounded from the battle. They use each other to brace themselves as they walk. As they reach Sol and the girls both of the soldiers falls to the ground. "I told her to stay home but she wouldn't do it, she had to come." Sol said rocking his wife in his arms. Sol looks around and sees his wounded soldiers. Then he looks over to the girls. "I thought that I told you two girls to go home." Neither of the girls took their eyes off of their Aunt Bertha.

"We saw the German soldiers come up and we thought that we could help." said Anna in a low tone.

"Go home" Uncle Sol said as he looks down at his wife and cries.

"Let us join you, Uncle Sol we killed some of these soldiers, we can help." Hilda said.

"We are no more, we have dead soldiers over there these wounded soldiers will never be able to fight any more. Your Aunt is dead and I will fight till the end, I will be dead in a few days, When the second batch of soldiers come, go home, Go back to Germany. You are German girls and you'll be safer in Germany then you would be here." Anna looks over at the two soldiers that walks over to them one of the soldiers dies and the other gives her a near death look.

"Go home." Yells Sol as he lays Bertha down showing his wound.

"Uncle Sol, you've been shot." Anna cries as she tries to help her great uncle. "Get away from me and go home where you will be safe. "said Uncle Sol as he gives the girls a stern look." We can go north and fine the American and tell them about the Germans." Hilda suggested. "Go home, find your father, you two girls no longer have family here, we're all dead.

Hearing this Anna slowly turns to her sister taking her by her arm Anna leads Hilda away. Passing the dead soldiers Hilda reaches down and takes a rifle from one of the soldiers.

'Grabs his ammo belt." Anna said as she started picking up ammo belts from the German soldiers. Uncle Sol watches the girls as they replenish their arsenal.

"Stay out of this war." Yells Uncle Sol. Not hearing their Uncle's order, the girls grab what they could, they never look back as they work their way to their awaiting truck. Tears roll down their face as they place all of the weapons in the back of the truck. Each girl takes a rifle with them as they climb into the truck and drive off.

"Should we turn around and go and get Uncle Sol and his men?" Hilda asks as she watches Anna changes gears without the grinding sound.

"No he is determined to fight without us, Uncle Sol worried about Aunt Bertha being there and we shouldn't let him worry about us." said Anna as she drives away.

"Where are we going?" Ask Hilda as she looks over to her sister.

"Home I guess, maybe papa will be there." Anna said as she realizes that she has said papa and not momma and papa. Anna took a deep breath as she stared down the road.

"Papa won't be there; he is going to be doing the same thing that we're going to be doing." Hilda again looks over to her older sister.

"What's that?"

"Every German soldier that we see will be dead when we leave." Hilda gives Anna a hard deep look as she agrees.

"That's what papa is doing."

For the next few days the girls drive around looking for their next target. The petrol cans that Marc had placed on the back of the trucks run low. The girls find German soldiers close by. As they promised themselves, a lot of soldiers die in the battles that the girls could fight.

Chapter Eight

Marc also raises the death toll of the German armies.

Marc now upgraded himself with a German made machine gun leaving his bolt-action one bullet at a time rifle behind. Marc walks into a camp where a few soldiers await their meal as the cook's finish preparing the troops mid-day meal.

Marc walks past a tent where he glances in and sees a radioman talking over the radio as his Officer stands over his shoulder.

As Marc walks up to the middle of the camp Marc counts the men that he must killed. "Come on; let us eat the mess that you cook." Yells one of the soldiers to the fat cook. "When it's done it will be done." barks at the cook.

As Marc quickly counts the soldiers, he never sees the local Resistance outfit taking their place in the woods.

Marc wonders how he can make his kills with little problems then the cook opens up the soup pot and yells. "Let's eat." All of the men gather up in a straight line leaving the radioman and the Officer still in the tent. Marc smiles as he sees the opportunity. In the woods the Resistance outfit led by a man name Otto points to his men who were to be taken out in the upcoming battle. As Marc walks up and stands in the back of the line as the last man. Otto points to himself, as Otto would be the one that shoots Marc. Marc looks over to the tent making sure that the radioman and the Officer are still in there as he pulls out his pistol and pokes the man in front of him. The soldier feels the poke, turns around and looks at Marc.

"Hey wait your turn there is enough food for all of us." laugh the dune soldier.

"Sorry, I've haven't ate in a couple of days." Marc replies as he pulls the pistol down to his side.

From the woods Otto sees the pistol and stop his men by waving his hand back and forth. "Let's see what this man is going to do." Otto whisper to his men. Marc raises the pistol slowly backs up and pulls the trigger. With the soldiers standing one in front of the other five soldiers fall to the ground. As the men fall Marc aims his pistol at the next five soldiers. The second bullet drops the last five and also killing the cook that stood in front of the soldiers filling their soup bowl. Marc then takes a step back and shoots the radioman and the Officer who was trying to pull out his pistol.

Now there are no German soldier alive Marc walks up to the pot of soup and helps himself to their meal. As Otto and his men emerge from their hiding place in the woods Marc quickly turns to them taking aim with his pistol.

Otto raises his hand. "I think that we are on the same side." Otto said as he approaches Marc with his hands still in the air.

'Who are you?" said Marc as he takes a sip of soup.

"We are a part of the Resistance group in this area. And you are?" Otto said as he stands in front of Marc. Marc spits out the soup and looks Otto and his men over.

"We're not on the same side." Marc laughs as he looks at the men with Otto.

"Well this battle is over and we won." Celebrated one of Otto's men.

"Let go home." said another.

"That's it, the battle is over and all you'll want to do is go home?" Marc said in an angry tone.

"No, we have things to do." Otto said as he looks over to his men. "But first you never told me your name or what you are doing here? Are you a German soldier or are you apart of the Resistance group?" Otto demanded.

"Neither, I fight for myself." Marc said as he reaches over and takes a loaf of bread.

"You men keep a look out for more soldiers; I need to gather up all of the papers." said Otto, as he never takes his eyes off of Marc.

"Come on Otto, the battle is over let's go home." Begged one of Otto's men.

"The Allies want these papers." Otto said as he walks over to the tent and gather up all of the papers that he could.

"The Allies, what do they have to do with anything?" Marc said angry.

They help us by telling us where the Nazis are." said Otto as he glances over the papers before he shoves them into his pocket. "Come on Otto there are no more soldiers around so let's get going." Said Wilhelm one of Otto's man. Marc walks up to him. "Let me ask you something, when you was a child did you ever play war?" Wilhelm gives Marc a strange look.

Well sure I did." Answer Wilhelm. "Did you ever win?" Marc said as he shook his head and walks away.

Marc walks up to the soup pot. "Take a good look at the size of this pot. There is more soup in here then these soldiers could eat, the soldiers don't waste food. Look at the size of this camp it's too big for these dead soldiers, there are more soldiers out there and if you're not careful they will be coming in, especially now, if they are close by they heard the shooting." Marc then looks over toward Otto. Forget the papers, if the allies want them I'm sure that they have spies in the German Government, You, you and you can be the look outs the rest of the men gather up all of the weapons and ammo." Marc said as he points at the Resistance fighter.

"We don't take orders from you, as far as we know you could be a Nazi soldier, you are wearing the uniform." said Alfred.

"I wear this to blend in with the soldiers, and you are right you don't have to take orders from me. But let me ask you something, how old is your rifle?"

Alfred takes a long look at his rifle.

"This was my father's rifle." Marc frowns as he takes the rifle away from Alfred.

"This is old, that is new." Marc said as he points at the rifle of the dead soldiers.

"He's right; take all of the soldier's guns." Otto said as he walks up. "

Who are you, what are you doing here?" Otto again said.

"Look, I can tell just by looking around that you're fly by night fighters and you will all be captured, if the soldiers don't shoot you they send you to Berlin where the SS will be waiting for you. You will tell the SS what they want to know and I do not want my name mentioned so I'm not telling any of you my name."

"But you know our father" said Albert. "Yea and I have no plans to get caught." Marc said as he smiles. "Well what makes you think that we are going to get caught?" said Franz as he did as he was told and walk around the dead soldiers picking up their weapons. "And don't forget the knives." said Marc as he took another bite of bread. Then Marc kicks the pot of soup over. Leaving the table that held the dozens loafs of bread. "Hey what are you doing, we could eat the soup." said Wilhelm.

As he disarms the dead soldiers. "The soup was awful take the bread, it's not that much better but it is edible." Marc said as he started walking away in the woods.

"Wait, where are you going?" Otto asks as he tries to stop Marc from leaving.

"It appears to me that you and your men have all of the answers, you don't need me and I like working alone, so good luck Resistance fighters, May the war end in your favor." said Marc as he started walking away holding up the bread.

Otto watches Marc walk away then he turns around and sees his men doing as Marc had suggested by retrieving the weapons and each take a loaf of bread and fill their pockets. Alfred walks up to Otto.

"He's right we don't need him, He's a loner, and they always die in the first few days of battle." said Alfred as he finishes the last bite of bread as Otto watches Marc walk deeper into the woods.

Otto then looks around the camp. "He's right, there will be more soldiers coming, this camp is too big just for these men and the soup pot held more soup then these men could eat.

At that time the radio started calling. Otto looks over to the tent. "Answer the call." said Otto to Wilhelm. As Wilhelm answers the call Otto takes another look into the wood. Otto Hearing Wilhelm talking on the radio walks over.

"It's a patrol they heard the shooting." Wilhelm said as he waits for his order from his leader.

"Tell them that I was zero in on a pistol that I just got." Otto said as he held up his new pistol and look at it.

"Yes sir, I will tell him, Heil Hitler." said Wilhelm as he signs off. "Whoever that was wanted you to not to waste bullets and be careful because of the Resistance is out there somewhere." Wilhelm laughs.

At that time a large troop truck drives up catching all of the

Resistance fighters by surprises. "Everybody into the woods." Otto yells out as the troop truck nears. All of the men run into the woods where they could be safe from the German soldiers. The troop truck stops as ten soldiers jump out from the back and they all run into the camp. All of the Resistance fighters choose their new rifles and machine guns over their old out dated rifles. Marc was right on that account and Otto knew it.

"Take it easy, they don't know that we are out here, and they are in the open." said Otto as he and his men lay low hiding from the Nazi. They see the soup pot lying on the ground. They see all of the dead soldiers and they see the radio tent ransacked, as all of the papers and maps was gone.

"Get on the radio and tell headquarters that the Resistance was here." orders an Officer.

"Get ready." Otto whisper as the soldiers run to the tent to make the call Otto stood up. "Fire." The entire Resistance fighter group started firing. Knocking out most of the German soldiers. But not all as some are able to take cover at the base of the tree line. Now it is every man for themselves. As the more experienced German soldier's skill in their weaponry shot straight into the woods hoping to hit one of the Resistance fighter. The resistance fighter being protected from the sprayed bullets returns fire. As another troop trucks pulls up and ten more men jump out.

"Let's get out of here." cried Wilhelm as he is tempted to run.

"Stay where you are." yells Otto as he takes aim and shoots two soldiers that were beside each other. With fifteen German soldiers now fighting them the Resistance fighter was now ready to take their chance and run through the woods. A couple of fighters jumps up and started running deep into the woods. But they didn't' get too far as the Nazi shot both of them. "Stay where you are." Yells Otto as he sees the two get shot down. "Stay where you are." Otto continues.

At that time on the German side two explosions occurred. Otto looks over to the Germans side where most of the Germans were killed. "Keep firing." Otto yells as he takes aim and fires, killing a German soldier.

As the Resistance fighters shoot one by one the German

soldiers are killed. Within a couple of seconds all of the remaining German soldiers are dead. Otto and his men take full credit for the victory of the battle.

As the rest of the Resistance fighter celebrates Marc walks up. "One victory doesn't make you winners." Marc said as he walks past the men and toward the dead Germans.

"You came back." said Otto as he follows Marc toward the German's camp. Marc walks up to a dead soldier and grabs his hand grenade and places them into his belt. Then Marc turns around and faces the Resistance fighters.

"Always replace what you use." Marc said as he takes the ammo belts off of the dead soldiers.

"All of us have new weapons what do we do with the rest?" Ask Franz.

'Take what you need, bury the rest, don't let the Germans use these weapons." Marc said as he takes out the clips that held the bullets for his machine gun.

"What now?" Otto asks as he does as Marc.

"Well good luck in your war." Marc said as he once again walks back into the woods.

"You should be our leader." Otto yells. Marc stops for a second then he started walking.

"I fight alone." Marc said as he continues to walk.

"Otto what are you doing? We don't need him." said Wilhelm as the rest of the fighters agree.

"We won this battle because of him, we need him." said Otto as he runs to Marc.

"Excuse me Herr---, if it wasn't for you then we all would be dead, we need you to lead us into battle." Otto said as he stops Marc and places his arm on his shoulder.

Marc stops and looks at Otto friendly jester. "I am a German citizen, I taught my family the German way of life. I am proud to call myself a German citizen, but for the war it's my duty to fight the people that will ruin the country that I love and these soldiers wear the same uniforms that I wore in the first war twenty years ago."

So you were in the First World War, that's a start. If I find out who you are what do I get?" Otto said with a little humor.

Marc looks over to his new friend. "You'll get a bullet

from my machine gun." Marc said without a smile. "Look, the less you and your so call fighters know about me is better for me. And you should feel the same way."

At that time the rest of Otto's men walk up. They walk up to Marc but they speak to Otto. "We did what you said and buried all of the weapons that we didn't need." Albert said as he readjusts his backpack that is filled will ammo and assorted weaponry. 'The extra ammo can save you in a fierce battle someday." Marc said as he turns toward Otto ready to shake Otto's hand.

Otto with reluctance shakes Mares hand. "We still need you." Otto said as he tightens his grip.

You boys got all the ammo that you need, you have new shinny weapons and with that I'll be on my way." Marc said with a smile.

"Will we be in your way." Ask Franz.

"This man wants to fight by himself then I say let him, a man that fights alone dies alone, we'll buried him in a few battles down the road." said Wilhelm as he and the rest of the Resistance fighters stats walking away, all but Otto.

"What will it take for you to join us? Your leadership and our fire power, well the Nazi won't know what hit them." said Otto as he slowly turns and follow behind his soldiers.

At that time a troop truck is heard coming to the defense of the fallen Germans soldiers. All of the Resistance fighters turn around and look at Marc who is running to a clearing to see the approaching tucks.

'Well, what should we do?" Otto yells toward Marc.

"I see three maybe four trucks, which are too many for us." Marc said as he looks through his newly found binocular.

"Then we'll go to the safe house." Otto yells to his men. The men agree and start running. "Will you go with us?" said Otto hoping for the best. "There's too many, you won't last in this battle, come with us." Marc nods his head and follows Otto through the woods. All of the trucks stop at the campsite.

As the troops from the four trucks jump out and ready themselves for their orders. Wolfgang steps out of the first truck as Von jumps out of the second truck the two men looks over the campsite. "Where are their weapons?" Von asks.

It must be the underground (Resistance.) "Wolfgang said as he shakes his head in disgust.

"The underground?" a confused Von asks.

The Underground or The Resistance whatever you want to call them." said Wolfgang in anger. "What about the Allies?" Mention Von. "The weapons are gone the allies has their own weapons." said Wolfgang as he pulls out his pistol.

"I want all of the soldiers to scour the woods for signs of the Underground." said Wolfgang as he started walking into the woods. Von waves for his men to follow. Halfway through the woods Wolfgang holds up his hand. "There is a town about three miles from here, Bring up the trucks." Wolfgang orders.

As the men gather back into the truck Marc and his men run to the first house that they came to. "Open up." Otto yells as the door is open and all of the men run in.

An old man waves them into the bedroom where there is a trap door in the bottom of the closet. As all of the men climb down into the hidden cellar Marc shakes his head, as he is the last one to enter the hidden trap door. As the men gather around the small tight cellar. "This isn't right; I have a bad felling about this." Marc protested. "They are the----" Otto tries to say but Marc shakes his head. "This isn't right, now you are putting these people lives at risk." Marc Yells.

"Be quiet, the Nazi might hear you." Whispers Otto.

These old people are going to protect us; we're supposed to be protecting them." said Marc in an angry tone.   At   that time a step on a loose wooden plank on the floor makes a squeaky sound. Otto throws up his hand to silence Marc. Then several footsteps are heard roaming the house. "It's the Nazi, they're here." Otto whispers. The cellar is quite as Marc tries to hear the conversation above him. But the small tight room is too deep to hear. As Von walks up to the old man who is standing in front of his wife. "Where are they?" Von asks as he places his hand on his pistol holster. "I don't know what you are talking about; we are the only ones here." said the old man as he reaches around his wife shielding her from what could happen. "I saw a group of men, they was running past our fields." said the wife as the old man quickly turns around toward her. "Gertrude, what are you saying?" Ask the old man. Wolfgang walks over to the window and looks out.

In what direction were they going?" Wolfgang asks in a soft tone.

"I'm not sure, they was running so fast I didn't really pay any attention to them." Wolfgang nods as his men re-enter the living room. "There is no sign of them." said one of the soldiers who were looking around the house.

"What men are you looking for?" Ask the old man.

"The Resistance, they murdered some of our men this morning. We must go into town." said Wolfgang as he nods to the elderly couple as he orders his men "Back to the truck."

As the last German soldiers leave the house the elderly couple hug and kiss each other as the man walks over to the loose wooden plank and steps on it. "The Nazis have left." said Otto as the rest of the Resistance fighters give each other a smile of relief. "We can stay here tonight; by morning the Nazi will have left the town." Otto said mainly to Marc.

This is wrong." Marc said as he sits down.

"Why because you didn't come up with this plan?" Ask Franz as he walks toward Marc only to be stop by Otto.

"If we were found the Nazi would not only kill us but they would shoot the couple upstairs, do they deserve that? Now the Nazi are going to the next town putting them at risk. This is a joke and all of you are jokers." Marc said in anger as he hits the wall behind him with his fist.

"Then lead us." Yells Otto as his men look at Otto in shock.

"We don't need him." said Albert.

"We fought in battles before and we won without this man." Franz said as he looks over toward Marc who was yawning due to lack of sleep.

"Let's just say that you don't need me and I don't need you." Marc said as he closes his eyes for a second, "Besides I want nothing to do with the Allies, They're letting you do their dirty work while they sit around with their finger stuck up their----"

"The Allies are doing more for our cause then you could ever do." barks Wilhelm.

"Did they issues you good working rifles or even give any of you a little training, how to stalk the enemies find their weakness and pounce on it, let me guess (NO). They tell you to go out and kill the Nazi and take the papers that you may are may not trust as legit papers and not a decoy papers, I've seen it done before, I've did it before years ago." Marc said as he remembers the past. "Don't trust the Allies. And I say that as my last military speech, now I speak for myself because like I said earlier I don't need you and you don't need me." Marc said as he slowly falls asleep.

Otto looks over toward his men. "We need him; he doesn't need us." Otto said as he looks around to each of his men.

What about the Allies?" asks Wilhelm.

"Let me handle this man and the Allies." said Otto as he looks at Marc.

We don't even know his name." warns Albert.

"But we do know what he can do; he can win battles and keep us alive." All of the men give Marc a deep look as he sleeps.

Chapter Nine

The next morning Marc wakes up, as the rest of the men were still asleep, all but Otto who wasn't in the cellar. Marc walks over to the wooden ladder and climbs up where he walks out of the bedroom. Marc could hear Otto and Herr Leer was sitting down at the dinner table talking. "The Americans will meet you there." said Herr Leer as Marc walks in. Herr Leer quickly stops talking as Marc walks in. "This is a German soldier?" Herr Leer said as he pulls his pistol that was laying on the table closer to him.

"I'm not sure his name but he is the reason that fifteen to twenty German soldiers are dead." Otto said as he stood up to greet Marc.

"I preferred that no one knew my name." Marc said as he sat down and looks over at the coffee pot that was on the stove. Herr Leer looks over to Otto who nods his head. Herr Leer walks over and pours Marc a cup.

"Why are you wearing a Nazi's uniform?" Ask Herr Leer as he places the cup of coffee in front of Marc.

'Danke." Marc says as he takes a drink of the coffee. "I use this uniform so I can get close to the soldiers."

"Yea before he kills them." Otto interrupted with a laugh.

"Well we need to get him some regular cloths, or the Americans want mistake him for a Nazi." said Herr Leer.

Marc looks over to both Otto and Herr Leer. "I won't work with the Americans or the English, I thought that I made that clear." Marc said as he took another sip of coffee.

"I would like to know your name." Herr Leer repeats.

"Why is my name so importance?" Ask Marc as he finishes his cup of coffee. "Well go have fun with the Americans, maybe we can see one and another down the road, just don't bring any Allies with you." Marc said as he places his coffee cup in the sink.

"We need you." Otto said as he walks over and places his cup next to Marc's cup. "Go with us, when we team up with the Americans we will be double maybe triple the fire power that we need to win this war.

"Otto feels that you are the leader of this outfit." said Herr Leer as he walks over and stands in between the two men as Marc gives it a good thought.

Then Marc shakes his head. "I'll fight the Nazis and I'll fight the Americans and I have my reasons." Marc said in an angry tone

"Well, if you decide that you would like to lead us in battle just let me know." Otto said as he places his hand on Marc's arm and smile. "I need to wake up my men we have to meet the Americans this afternoon. Otto walks over to the bedroom and yells down to the cellar. "Let's move it." He yells as Marc and Herr Leer sit back down at the table. Herr Leer walks back over and takes the coffee cup out of the sink and pours them another cup.

"What is your secret?" said Herr Leer as he places the filled coffee cup in front of Marc.

Marc smiles as he takes another sip of coffee. "Aren't you afraid that the Nazi will catch us with you and your wife? You're putting your wife in too much danger."

Herr Leer sits back in his chair holding his cup close to his mouth. "Gertrude is a tough old broad, if there is going to be a shootout then I want Gertrude on my side." Herr Leer laughs.

"I would like to rid this area of the Nazis and that what going to happen when Otto and his men join forces with Americans Why do you hate the Americans so bad?" Ask Herr Leer as he then realizes part of Marcs secret.

"Was you in the first war?" Marc drinks the final drop of coffee as he looks over to Herr Leer.

"Yes, I was captured and beaten close to death by both the Americans and the British. Both are targets to me along with the Nazi." Marc said as he places the cup onto the table.

"Well I can understand why the Allies but why the Nazi?"

"I have my reasons, if I tell people then the hate might leave me so I keep this to myself and keep the hate burning within."

As the men climb up the ladder they gather around the table where Herr Leer and Marc are sitting. "So what will it be, are you coming with us or are you going to sit here and let the Leer's protect you?" Franz asks sarcastically.

Marc looks down at his empty cup of coffee. Then he

slides back his chair hard enough to make Franz and Albert quickly step back. I'm going to have another cup of coffee and then I'll decide." said Marc as he looks at the men as he walks over to the stove for his extra cup of coffee.

"Well if you decide to join us then you can find us in town." Otto said giving up on Marc. "Let's get out of here." said Wilhelm as he gives Marc a stern look as he walks toward the back door.

Wait a minute." said Marc as he takes a sip of his coffee. "Leave you rifle and machine guns here." Marc said as he walks over to the back window and takes out his binocular and looks over the yard and the tree line. "Only take your pistol and keep it in your pocket, but put it where you can quickly get to it, go out past the trees maybe one hundred yards and look around."

'Why?" Wilhelm interrupted.

"The Nazi left this house in that direction they may be waiting out in those woods for you, or their camp might be close by." Marc continues.

"Then what?" Ask Otto. Marc takes another sip of coffee. "Then come back here and I'll tell you my decision." Said Marc as he sets back down at the table. Otto smiles as the rest of his men reluctantly do as they were told.

As the men leave Gertrude walks into the kitchen. "What would you men like for breakfast?" She asks as she places her apron around her and lights the stove.

"A victory, with a couple of eggs." Said Herr Leer as he smiles at Marc. Who gives Herr Leer a faint smile as he takes another sip of coffee?

"So what is your story, why are you with the Resistance fighters. Leer isn't a Jewish name, why are you helping them and not the German soldiers? Marc asks as he watches Gertrude crack open some eggs and places them into her frying pan.

"My son who went to college in Hamburg was arrested by the SS." said Herr Leer as he looks over toward his wife. Gertrude glances back for a second then she went back to cooking their breakfast.

"The SS thought that my son was a part of the Resistance fighters." said Herr Leer only to be interrupted by Gertrude.

"He had no part of the Resistance fighters or the Nazi army, He just went to college." "Once the SS arrest you, you don't have a prayer, oh we had heard that he was killed while the SS had him, but he suffered and we would like for the SS and all of the Germans soldiers to suffer also including that beast in Berlin, Herr Hitler." Marc listen as Gertrude places a plate of eggs in front of him. "If you join the Resistance then we can help you and you can help us." said Herr Leer as Gertrude places his plate in front of him.

"How?" Marc asks as he takes a bite.

"We have people all in the Nazis army, they are helping us."

"Are you sure, your son was picked up by the SS how are you sure that the people on the inside didn't turn him in?" Marc asks as he helps himself to the eggs.

"Peter was pick up by the SS before I- we join the Resistance now everything is going into place." Herr Leer said as he stands up and walks toward the kitchen window and looks out. "After we kill Herr Hitler and his men we will take over Germany and fight the Allies." proclaimed Herr Leer.

"That is why we work with the Allies, we're leaning all about them, their weakness, where they hide their ammo dump. All of this is being taken in and when we take over the war we will know all that we want to know about them and victory will be ours." Said Gertrude as she sits down beside her husband and laughs. Marc looks the couple over as one by one the fighter's returns to the house.

"Does this group of misfits know your plans?" Marc asks as he sits back in his chair.

"What these idiots, no that's why they are working with the Americans, we will get information from them Otto is the only fighter that we will use in our war with the Allies. As for the rest of his men, well, they are a bunch of losers that will be killed unless you step in and run the outfit." said Herr Leer.

"Otto can keep them safe." Marc said as he looks at the back door as the fighter's returns.

Otto has a fat man that is good with explosives, (Wilhelm.), a drunk who is good with finding what we need. (Franz.), and the rest of the outfit is someone to pull the trigger, it will be you and Otto that will win the war, first with the Nazis then with the Allies." said Herr Leer as he finishes his meal and watches as the men gather in the kitchens waiting on Otto to return.

"So you're still here, why?" Ask Wilhelm.

"I decided to work with you, only if Otto and I can run this Resistance group. All of the men shake their heads as Otto walks back into the house.

"Well what had you decided?" Ask Otto as he walks in looking straight at Marc.

"It will be me and you running this outfit, we'll be a team. Otto smiles as the men, not sure of their newest member, look the other way.

"Well what did you see out there?" Otto asks his men with a grin.

"There is nothing out there the Nazis didn't stick around." said Franz.

"That was a waste to go out and look for something that isn't out there." Added Albert.

"But you wasn't sure, the Nazi could had been out there and no one knew that was a great call by your leader." said Herr Leer.

"That's co-leader." Added Franz.

"Ok co-leader, what should we do next?" Ask Otto as he sits down next to Marc.

Marc looks around his new team of soldiers and smiles. "First, we will need to find a new hide out taking these nice people out of harm's way. Then we'll meet the Americans and find out what they want. Then we'll go from there." Marc said as he stands up. "Grab your weapons." Marc said as he looks down at Herr Leer. "Danke for the place to stay last night but now we must defend our self." Marc said as he grabs his machine gun and reaches out his hand for Herr Leer to shake.

Herr Leer smiles as he shakes his head. "We are fighting for the same cause young man you and your fighter will always be welcome here." Said Herr Leer as he took Marc's hand to shack. Herr Leer grips Marc's hand tight.

We are on the same page aren't we?" Ask Herr Leer.

Marc feels Herr Leer tighten his grip. "Our mission is

the same as yours but we will be taking one battle at a time."
Marc says as he pulls his hand away. As the men leave the
Leer's house Marc leads the men into the woods.

"So if we all are going to be on the same team how about
telling us your name." Franz ask.

"Yea, why hide your identity from us how can we trust you
if we know nothing about you?" Wilhelm asks as he follows
behind the group of Resistance fighters.

"First you must gain my trust and right now I don't trust
anyone but myself." All of the men shake their heads as Otto
remains quiet.

"I know should we call you General?" Ask Albert
sarcastically.

Marc smiles as they continue into the woods. "Keep your
eyes open for the Nazi they can be almost anywhere up in the
tree tops or they could dig holes and place dirt over them."

'That's true I had heard of soldiers hiding that way for an
ambush." Otto said as he looks over to each of his men nodding
his head agreeing with Marc.

"We need to find a home base, where we meet and store
all of the weapons and ammo from each battle that we win." said
Marc as he looks up to the top of the trees.

I know a place." said Albert as he walks in front of Marc.
"It's close by, I used to play in a cave that is hidden." Marc
looks over toward Otto who shrugs his shoulder.

Where is this cave?" Marc asks as he follows Albert
through the thick trees.

"It's right behind these trees," Albert proudly said.

"Stop." said Marc as the men stop and looks at him.
"Make sure that the Nazis haven't found this cave." Marc said as
he walks up and points his machine gun straight ahead of him as
he enters the cave. The cave was perfect for them; the fighters
would be hidden from the Nazis when they are under attack. With
enough room left for them to store their captured weapons and
ammo. Marc was pleased with the cave Albert was pleased that
he could help. Marc walks over and pats Albert on his back. "This
is a good find for us." Marc said as he smiles. "Now we must find
the Nazis and destroy them." said Otto as he walks into the cave
and smiles. 'We can store the ammo over here in the back of the

cave." Marc said as he walks to the back.

"Well General what do we do next?" Ask Wilhelm. Marc looks over at his men.

"Well first we must go on patrol, let's see what's around us, "You" Marc pointing toward Albert "Go with this guy." Marc pointing at Wilhelm.

"If you won't tell us your name at least learn ours." Said Franz.

"Ok then you go and look for something to eat, by the time that all of you get back I will know your name." Marc said as he looks over toward Otto. "You and I will also go out. Otto shakes his head agreeing. "Alright let's move out."

As the men do what they are told Marc and Otto walk down a trail. "So how did you get involve with this useless group?" Otto smiles as he looks up at the top of the trees looking for snipers. "Believe it or not, before you came along we were in some battles and we did win some." Marc looks over toward Otto. "How many men did you have?" Otto frowns as he thought about that question. "We started out with ten soldiers now we are down to what you see." said Otto as he forgets to look out and reaches down and picks up a rock and toss it into the woods. "What do you know about Herr Leer?" Otto smiles as he watches the rock hit a tree.

"Herr Leer is a gentle man once he and his wife were the town's school teachers; they're great people to be around. They had one son. Peter?" Marc said interrupting.

'Yea Peter, He was my friend, my best friend. He was going to join the German army as soon as he graduated from college. We both were, but there were some problems with the Resistance group and he was arrested and the SS tried to pin the valance on Peter." "Was the SS right?"

"No, Peter wasn't a part of any groups. He was at the wrong place at the wrong time; The SS tortured him until he died. From what I have heard Peter died a long painful death. That's when Herr Leer and I join the Resistance fighters, The Leer's knows a lot of people in Berlin and they would let me know about the information and my men and I would act on it. As for the men, they are fighters; they left their family's to fight for the cause. Now we don't know your story and we will never know but they are committed to what they are doing and we're not too sure about you." said Otto as he continues to walk.

Marc glances over to his new friend. "If you and your soldiers are as committed as I am then we can fight together. But we are here to kill the Nazis not to hold hands and sing around the campfire." At that time some laughter'is heard. Both Marc and Otto stop to hear the sound and locate where it was coming from. They ease through the woods until they walk close to the camp. Both men squat down next to a tree and look around. They have a clear view of the Nazis, ten of them. The trees give Marc and Otto cover from the Nazi who didn't know that they were there. "Should we go back and get the men." Ask Otto.

"No, we don't have time; this is a rest stop for them." Marc whispers. He pulls out one of his hand grenades and looks over to Otto who aims his machine gun at the group of Nazis. Then Otto gave Marc a nod as Marc pulled the pin of the hand grenade and tossed it toward the relaxing Nazi soldiers. One of the Nazis soldiers saw the grenade land close by but the soldiers had no time to react as the grenade explodes. Marc then grabs his machine gun and takes aim. As the dust settles they see that all of the soldiers are dead. Marc and Otto waited to see if there were any other soldiers close by. As seconds pass and there are no Nazi soldiers coming to the aid of their fallen fellow soldiers Marc and Otto ease up from the base of the tree and walk into the German's camp. Otto quickly checks the dead soldiers for papers as Marc gathers up all of the weapons and ammo. "Leave the papers alone help me with the weapons. Finding no important papers on the dead soldiers Otto grabs the ammo belts from them.

Otto took a hand grenade from one of the soldiers and hands it to Marc. "Here this will replace the one that you threw." Otto said as he hands the grenade over to Marc. Marc smiles as he takes the grenade and places it into his belt.

"Let's get out of here." Marc said as he gathers up the last ammo belt. From a distance another shot is heard tat, tat, tat then another tat, tat, tat. Marc and Otto look at each other at the same time both men run toward the sound of the shooting. The rest of the men met them as they see Franz rumbling through the dead German soldiers taking their ammo belts and weapons. Otto walks up and looks for any military papers that he could find on the dead soldiers.

"They must be the cooks, over there is a case of food that they were about to prepare." Franz said as he points.

Otto looks toward Wilhelm. "Take the food, the rest of you grab the weapons." Otto said as he reads the papers that he got off of the dead German Officer. Marc grabs one of the dead soldiers and started dragging him away.

"What are you doing?" Albert asks as he watches.

"I'm getting rid of the bodies, this is too close to our base camp and we don't need the Nazis walking around. Looking for us."

"So I was wrong by killing these soldiers? Ask Albert.

"No, you did what you were supposed to do. We just need to hide the bodies." Marc said as he drags soldiers into the thick woods. Otto grabs the another soldier as do the others, before long all of the Nazis were hidden.

"Before long they are going to start smelling." Franz said as he pulls the last body over with the rest.

"Right now we will keep a low profile, before the sun goes down we will have to bury these men, but right now let's keep our eyes open for the rest of the men." Marc said as the others agree. Now that they had extra ammo they placed into the cave and with the case of food now they had some food. Before long the cave began to fill up with boxes of ammo and cans of food. With each victories battle came extra ammo and food. Marc walks out of the cave, knowing that Otto was on guard duty Marc decided to relieve Otto giving him a chance to have some hot food and rest.

As Marc walks through the woods he sees Otto and Herr Leer standing in the opening of the woods talking. Marc shakes his head as he slowly approaches the two men without them knowing that he was there. "Tell that new guy to change his cloths he can't be around the Americans dress like a Nazi." said Herr Leer as he gives Otto a stem look.

"Alright, we'll get him some street cloths before we meet with the Americans." said Otto as he places his hand on Herr Leer's shoulder and walks away. Herr Leer watches Otto disappear into the woods and turns to walk back to his house.

Otto sees Marc and smiles. "Herr Leer is pleased with the cave and the battles that we have won." said Otto as he greets Marc.

"You came out here as a guard; I didn't know that you need a guard." Marc said as he shakes his head in disgust.

"Herr Leer is just as important as you or I or any of the men that are in that cave." Otto said as he defends his friendship to Marc.

"I'm beginning to not to trust Herr Leer." Marc said as he follows Otto.

"We need him and he needs us." Otto said as he walks toward the cave. "We need to get you some new cloths." Otto said as he enters to cave.

"I know I heard Herr Leer tell you that, you're the soldiers he's the bystander." Marc said as he enters the cave.

"Well, when do we meet with the Americans?" Ask Franz. As the other soldiers gather around.

"Not today, their base was hit but a Luftwaffe raid last night so we'll meet them sometime tomorrow. Herr Leer will let us know when he finds out about the new time." Otto said as he places his Machine gun onto a small crate that the Resistance fighter is using as a table.

"Go guard the cave." Marc said as he looks over to Wilhelm. Wilhelm grabs his gear and walks out without saying a ward. Marc follows Otto to the back of the cave where Alfred was stirring the soup. Otto grabs a tin plate and hands it to Alfred who pours the soup into the plate.

"I don't trust him." Marc said as he watches Otto sit down on the floor to eat his soup.

"If Herr Leer could fight then he would be our leader, you may not trust him but I do." Otto said as he takes another spoon full and stair straight ahead.

"Franz the General here needs some new cloths, go to town and see what you can come up with." Otto said trying not to pay any attention to Marc. Franz takes his pistol out to make sure that it is loaded. Then Franz places his machine gun against the wall and looks over toward Marc. "What are you 32 or 34?" Franz asks as he size Marc up.

"I'm 38." Marc answers "But I prefer these cloths that I have on." Marc said referring to his Nazi uniform. "This uniform gets me closer to my enemy, that's where I need to be."

Confused Franz looks over to Otto. "But you still need some street cloths, like for tomorrow when we meet up with the Americans." Otto said as he finishes his soup and stands up to walk to the back of the cave for second.

"I'll just stay here and guard the cave." Marc said as he shakes his head.

"Do as you wish, but we need you tomorrow to be with us when we meet with the Americans." Otto said as he starts losing patients with Marc.

Marc shakes his head. "I told you that I want nothing to do with the Allies and I mean it, we can win this war without them." Marc said as he stands his grounds on his beliefs.

Otto stares at Marc and shakes his head.

The next morning as the Resistance gets ready for their rendezvous with the Americans Marc still in his Nazi's uniform watches as the men gather up their gear. "So general are you still staying?"Ask Wilhelm as he rechecks his machine gun making sure that it was fully loaded.

I want nothing to do with the Allies; I thought that I made that clear." Marc said as he looks over toward Otto.

Then stay here, but we still need to get you some street cloths." said Otto as he walks by without looking toward Marc. As the Resistance carefully leaves the cave Marc gather his gear and walks out in the other direction. Marc walks the two miles to Herr Leer's house.

As Marc walks closer Herr Leer not knowing that it was Marc fired a shot hitting the ground next to Marc. Marc falls to the ground and takes aim. "Herr Leer is that you?" Marc yells as he aims toward his target. "Who are you?" A voice from the house yells out. "I was with Otto and his men." Marc yells back. Marc lays silent on the ground as a Herr Leer reloads his rifle and looks out toward Marc. "Why are you still wearing that uniform?" Yells Herr Leer. "So I can mix in with the Nazis." Replies Marc as he still aims his Machine gun.

If we are on the same side, then why are you still aiming at me?" said Herr Leer as he places his rifle down.

If you fire at me again then I'm going to shoot you." Marc yells back. Herr Leer starts to laughs and waves Marc in. Marc is slow to stand up. "Why did you shoot at me?" he said as he wipes the dust off of him.

"I wasn't sure that it was you, you look like a Nazi to me. "Marc gives Herr Leer a small smile as he approaches the house. "What can I do for you?" Ask Herr Leer as he walks to the back door and opens it for Marc. Marc walks in and without invitation Marc sits down at the table. "What can I do for you?" Repeats Herr Leer. "I need to know about the outfit that I just join."

Herr Leer walks over to the cabinet and takes out two coffee cups. Then he pours the coffee and hands Marc a cup.

"What would you like to know, Otto is the leader I- we trust him with our lives, but then again we know all about Otto. He was my son's friend for a long time, but we know nothing about you and well trust is a word that we don't just throw around." said Herr Leer as he stares at Marc.

"I've seen you from somewhere, was you in the first war?" Ask Herr Leer as he motions toward Marc to drink his coffee.

"Well the men calls me General." Marc said with a small grin. Herr Leer with no expression on his face stares at Marc. "Look Herr Leer, you mention trust, I dont know you or the other men and all it takes is one of those guys to get captured by the SS and all of our names will be given, my war with the Nazi will last beyond the war and I still have some bad feelings toward the Allies and you and Otto wants me to work with the Allies. I'm afraid that I need to work alone and fight my battles, not yours, not the Allies, if they get in the way, then may the better man win." Marc said with a little anger.

"In the first war were you captured?" Ask Herr Leer with a faint smile as he begins to understand. "What was your rank?" Herr Leer continues.

Marc sat back into his seat and stares at his coffee cup. "I was a foot soldier and I did what I was told." Marc said as he shakes his head. "I was captured and held by both the English and the Americans, I was beaten by the English until they were tired then the Americans took over, I went years trying to forget about the beating but now we are at war with the same Countries, I was ready to serve the Fatherland one more time until my world change, now I'm in it for myself." said Marc, as he becomes more and more agitated.

Herr Leer sits up in his chair and looks straight toward Marc. "We are fighting the same war, like what I already told you when we destroy the Nazi and that Herr Hitler then we'll fight the Allies."

"But you can't win both wars team up with the Nazis or with the Allies. But now you don't have enough men nor intelligence to fight them both." Marc said interrupting.

Herr Leer sits back into his chair and smiles 'Oh but we do, we're helping the Allies by then we'll know all about them for when we turn on them and fight them, but we need men like you and Otto. Men who have hate in their heart for both the Nazi and the Allies. All of the rest of the men is someone that's pulls the trigger and we need that also. But we have had this conversation before, why are you here?" said Herr Leer as he walks over and pick up the pot of coffee and pour himself and Marc another cup.

"I'm not sure why I'm here. I want to fight alone and I want to fight the people that I want to fight. Otto can handle his men, but to me the Nazis are just as much the enemy as the Allies" Marc said as he takes the cup of coffee and drink it. "Otto likes you; He feels that he and his men could learn from you. Otto told me how you and the fighters met; Dress like the soldiers that you kill is perfect for what we are doing." Laughs Herr Leer as he finishes his cup of coffee.

I can't promise that I won't beat the Allies back to their Country." Marc said as he stands up and starts to walk toward the back door. "We can win both battles the first with the Nazi then with the Allies." Marc turns and thought for a seconds. "I want be a trigger man for the Allies." said Marc as Herr Leer looks at him. "Let the Allies think that we are on their side at the end we will smash them like will did with the Nazis." said Herr Leer as he starred at Marc. "General." Said Herr Leer as he gives Marc a stem look.

Otto and the boys are going to need you and your expertise in warfare, I know that we need you more than you need us, but at the same time we can help each other, first with the Nazi and then with the Allies. We can win this war twice all from one battle. I'm asking you to stay with us." said Herr Leer as Marc walks out the door. As Marc walks back to the cave Otto and his men were already back from their meeting with the Americans. All of the men are surprised to see Marc as he enters the cave. "Well look who is back." said Alfred in a sarcastic tone.

   "Well general did you decide to stay with us?" Ask Wilhelm as Otto looks on. Marc looks over each of the men. "I won't deal with the Allies." Marc said as he looks over toward Otto. Otto looks down in disgust. "We work with the Allies, we help them and they help us." said Otto as he shakes his head. "Then they better be of more help to us then we are to them." Marc said giving in and officially joining the outfit. Otto smiles as the rest of the men, still not sure of Marc's motives, stand still as Otto gladly walks up to Marc and shakes his hand.

Chapter Ten

The girls find a battle wherever they go. If the sounds of shooting were heard the girls would follow the sounds leading them to each of their battles. As they sneak up on the Battle from a distance they would scope out the battlefield and see who was shooting at whom and from what side would they get the best shot on the Nazi. Their truck is filling up with weapons and ammo, as they have to unload their young girls belonging to make room for their grown up deadly toys.

As the Germans had the Americans surrounded Anna and Hilda surrounded the Germans, as the battle tightens its grips on the Americans the girls' moves in. Anna takes out five German soldiers from the behind as Hilda eases up to three unsuspecting German soldiers that manned a machine gun Hilda takes out a hand grenade and pulls the pin. The doomed German soldiers never knew what hit them as the grenade blast knocks out the deadliest weapon the German had.

As the battle shifted more and more German soldiers die from Anna, Hilda and the Americans. As ten minutes goes by the battle ends with dead German soldiers filling the ground.

Anna and Hilda move in to restock their supplies. An American Officer spots the two girls rummaging through the dead German soldiers belonging. "Hey get out of here." Yells the Officer shooting his machine gun up in the air not aware that it was the girls that saved their lives. Scared the girls rush to grab what they could and run off as some of the surviving American soldiers chase after the pretty German fraulein.

Get back here." Yells the Officer to his men. "Anna and Hilda run deeper into the woods and spread out knowing that the Americans were following them, they aim their weapons toward the middle of the woods but the men do as they are ordered and return back to the battle field.

Anna and Hilda look at one another "It was because of us that they are still alive and they want to hurt us." Hilda yells to Anna who was ready to shoot the first American soldiers that came into the clearing.

"They're not following us." Anna yells back. We won their

battle for them and they want to hurt us." Hilda repeats herself.

"They are Americans; remember what papa said for us to never trust the Americans." Anna said as Hilda nods. Knowing that they are no longer being followed the girls decides to move on. They place their newly capture weapons and ammo in the back of their truck. Leaving no room for much more.

"What should we do?" Hilda asks as she sees the truck filled with most of their belongings and the weapons and ammo.

"We must find a safe place to live in." Anna said as she looks around the back of the truck seeing what they could get rid of next.

"How much petrol do we have left?" Hilda asks as Anna moves around some of the empty petrol cans.

Anna looks at the can. "Not much more, we'll have to get these cans filled, whenever we can." The girls check the area for Americans that may be following. As the girls see no one Anna looks over toward her sister. "They didn't follow us, let's leave." As Anna cranks the truck up Hilda watches out the window for the Americans. Anna places the truck in gear and rolls off.

Down the road the girls pass the Americans who try to stop the "Go, go, go." Hilda says yelling. Anna grinds the gears as she goes into the next gear. Picking up speed they pass the American soldiers with no problem. The girls flinch as a couple of soldiers begin to fire at them as they past.

Now down the road the shooting stops as the girls feel safer. As the Americans run toward their trucks only to be stopped by their Officer. "What are you men doing?" ask the Officer as he walks up to the truck.

"Those are German girls; we have to stop them." Replied one of the soldiers.

"Get out of the truck." said the Officer as he waves toward them.

"But sir those girls were getting the Germans weapons."

"So" said the Officer as he starts to lose patience with his men. "Go and search the dead Germans for information." Orders the Officer.

As the men jump out of the truck to do what they were told one of the soldier looks over to his friend. "Did you see them they was beautiful, I would love to capture them." said the soldier as he looks down the dirt road.

"Yea, you just wanted to give them a good body search." Laughs his friend. Down the road the girls see a small empty farm where all of the buildings are bombed out. Anna pulls up to the first building.

The girls look out of the window making sure that there was no one hiding inside. "What do you think?" Ask Hilda.

I'm not sure this could be a good place to hide out." Anna said as she looks around at the deserted farm,

"Pull over there." said Hilda pointing out at a large building that's filled with holes and burnt out walls. Anna drives the truck over to that spot and both of the girl's step out of the truck and look around. Gripping their rifle tight in their hands the girls started walking around the farm. "I wonder who won the battle here." Hilda said as she carefully takes a step.

Smell that?" Anna said as she slowly turns making sure that no one was following them.

"What?" Ask Hilda as she looks from side to side.

"The smell of death, People have died here." Hilda cringes at the though.

"There is the house." Hilda said pointing. Both of the girls slowly started walking to the house.

"Go to the front of the house and I'll go to the back." Anna said as she and Hilda split up. They carefully move throughout the house and into the middle where they met in the once lived-in living room. Bullets holes and the smell of burnt wood from the walls and ceiling decorated the living room as well as the rest of the house. The first bedroom was missing the outside wall and most of the flooring. "We can't stay in this room." Anna said as the girl's looks around. Next was the second bedroom. The odor of death is more present in that room as both of the girls had to place their hand over their mouth from the stench.

"This room is out." Hilda said, as she couldn't take the smell any more as she turns around and walks out. Before Anna walks out she notices a US Army medic bag with a red cross in the comer of the room. Anna grips her mouth and walks over to the medic bag.

Anna tiptoes through the dried up bloodstain that fills the floor. Anna gags with each step. "Anna, where are you?" Yells

Hilda from the other room. "I found something." Anna yells back. Anna finally reaches the medics bag. Anna carefully opens the backpack up where she finds some personal items.

Anna reaches in and pulls out a hand full of items that belong to the soldiers that fought in the battle

Anna looks at the silver cigarette lighter and wallets along with dog tags. Anna drops the items back into the backpack and picked up a wallet and went through it. A tear comes to Anna's face when she opens the wallet up and sees a young lady holding a baby. Hilda walks back to the room and sticks her head in. Hilda mumbles as she covers her mouth from the stench. "Anna did you hear me?" Hilda asks again.

"What, what do you want?" Anna asks as she stares at the picture.

"This room is unbearable, why stay in here?"

This must have been an operating room." Anna said in a low voice.

"How can you tell?" Hilda asks as she waves the odor away from her mouth

"All of the dried blood and this pack have the personal effects of the soldiers." Anna said as she holds up the lighter and dog tags

"Who do they belong to?" Hilda asks as she looks around the room at the dried up blood.

Anna looks at the dog tags but Anna doesn't read English. "I don't know, it's not in German." Anna then reaches into the wallet and pulls out the paper dollars. On the dollars it reads United States of America. "It's American." Anna said as she is surprised by the odd looking American Monies.

"Burn it all." Hilda said as she gives Anna a mean look. "Why?"

'Because we are at war with the American that's why." Said Hilda as she watches her step back to the door.

"Right now we're not at war with the Americans." said Anna as she smiles.

"Anna we are German girls and our country is at war with the Americans and the English. That means that we are at war with them also." Hilda said as she reaches the hallway and briefly looking in. Anna places the money back into the wallet and drops the wallet back into the backpack.

"I'm not sure who we are fighting, The Americans didn't kill mama, and papa isn't fighting the Americans he's fighting the Nazi, like we are." Said Anna as she picks up the backpack and carry it out of the room and into the living room and place it on the floor.

"What are you going to do with that?" Ask Hilda as she places her Machine gun next to a window and looks outside.

"I want to go through looking for maps." Anna said as she opens the backpack open and digging through it.

"We need food, check and see if there is any food in it." Hilda said as she glances outside.

"We'll need to find some food." said Anna as she closes the backpack and grabs her pistol. "Leave the gun here; take only your pistol so we can carry whatever we find." Hilda takes her machine gun and places it behind of the backpack and slides it against the wall. "What sounds good tonight?" Anna asks.

"Mama's fried chicken." Hilda said remembering. Anna looks over toward her sister and places her arm around Hilda.

"Well if you can find the chicken then I'll fine the oil to fry it in." Anna said with a smile. The girls walk out of the ruined house. Anna checks making sure that the truck was well hidden. Then the girls started walking in the woods for whatever that they can find to eat.

"What do we do if we find some soldier eating?" Hilda asks as she looks over to Anna.

"Then we'll have our meal but we'll need to---

"Kill the soldiers" Hilda said interrupting.

"Hilda this is a war and we're on our own side, we have no friends just enemy and we'll do whatever we need to do to survive." Anna said as she looks over toward her sister. "What do we do if we see an animal?"

Ask Hilda. "We can't shoot it, we don't know who is around us and we can't bring any attention to us." said Anna as she checks the surrounding area.

"Well it looks like fruits again tonight." Hilda said with a frown.

"Unless we can find some soldiers that had already cooked their meal." Anna said.

The girls walk a mile or so when from a distance they hear a language that they weren't familiar with, the girls ease up to the camp site holding their pistols tight in their hands. As they follow the sounds. Checking, making sure that the soldiers were alone, the girl's gets closer to the campsite. From the thick woods Anna and Hilda are covered as the men laugh and talk. "Who are they?" Anna asks herself.

"Are they Americans?" Hilda asks as she pulls back a tree limb to get a better view.

"I don't think so; they are wearing different uniforms than the one I found in the backpack." said Anna as she strains her eyes she looks through the branches and over growth of the weeds.

The men were a scouting team sent from Moscow hoping to find a weakness behind the German line. The scout team had finished for the day and were now relaxing as their dinner was being prepared. Anna and her sister looks at one another knowing that this was going to be the first meal that they have had in weeks since they left their uncle Sol and aunt Bertha house.

Chapter Eleven

Hilda checks with her sister as Anna counts the men that they must kill. Then Anna looks around for guards. "There are no guards." Anna whispers to Hilda, Hilda points at the men that she will kill as Anna agrees as she will take out the rest.

Checking one more time making sure that all of the men were around the campfire and not walking up behind them, Anna nods to Hilda and the two girls aim their pistols. Both of the girl's fire at the same time hitting two of the soldiers. The other soldier's tried to grab for their rifles but fall to the ground dead shot by the girls. Still not sure Anna and Hilda are slow to move into the camp. "Stay here." Anna tells her sister as she slowly walks into the camp looking from side to side passing the dead soldiers as she walks up to the campfire where a soup pot is being heated. Anna glances into the pot as she walks past and toward the back of the camp where she looks as far into the woods as she could. Feeling that all of the scout team were dead Anna motion toward Hilda to come in to the camp. Hilda also moves slowly in. Hilda kicks the dead soldiers making sure that they were dead. "Well our supper is ready." said Anna as she dips a spoon into the stew and tastes it. Hilda laughs at the sour look on Anna's face.

"Well this isn't mama's cooking but it's better than the apples and nuts that we've been eating." Anna said as she dips the spoon back in for a second helping. "What about their rifle?" Hilda asks looking around the dead Russian bodies. Anna walks over and pick up one of the rifle. "We don't need them; destroy them so they can't be used again." Anna said as she tosses the outdated weapon on the ground. "You know something sis, a couple of months ago we would cringe at the sight of a dead body, now look at us." Anna said, as she feels no remorse for what she and her sister have done.

Instead of gathering up all of the weapons now the girls gather up all of the dead soldier's mess kits and fill them up with stew. The girls quickly gather up what they could get from the stew pot and pour the rest of the stew onto the ground. "Let's get back to the house." said Anna as she tips the pot over.

"Who are they?" Hilda asks. "I'm not sure but they're not cooks." Anna reply's as the smell of the stew covers her.

Back at the house the girls eat their fill of the stew. The taste is horrible but it is food. A change from the nuts, berries and fruits. "This is getting too easy." Hilda said as she stares at her spoon full f stew.

"What is?" Ask Anna as she takes another spoon full then giving a sour expression.

"War."

'War." Anna asks as she swallows. "All we do is find the men that we are at war with and kill them; we haven't been shot at that much." Hilda said as she takes a bite.

"That's called an ambush, I've heard papa tell Herr Kohn that was the way that he prefers to fight." Anna said as she places the spoon back into the mess kit and places the mess kit aside. "I just wonder who side that we are on." Anna said as she pushes the mess kit away from her. Hilda thinks for a second.

"We're on papa's side." Hilda answers. "I wonder where papa is, is he fighting with Von or is he fighting Von?" Hilda asks as she finishes her meal and places her mess kit aside.

"We need to find papa; we can help him now." Anna said as she looks over toward her machine gun.

"When do you want to leave?" Ask Hilda as she agrees.

"Well the men that we killed will be discovered and their army will be looking for us, we'll leave in the morning." said Anna as she glances over to her sister.

The next morning came with the breaking of twigs and silent talks. Anna slowly raises her head looking out the window.

As five Russian soldiers slowly walk to the house, Anna quickly drops her head from the window and reaches over to nudge her sister awakening her. Anna places her index finger over her mouth.

"What is it?" Hilda asks in a soft, scared voice. Anna eases up to the window as she grabs her machine gun. Hilda reaches for her machine gun as she peers out the window. Not paying any attention Hilda knocks over her machine gun. The barrel of the machine gun rolls across the wall hitting the floor. The Russians hearing the noise hit the ground and starts firing. Both of the girls fall to the floor as the bullets hit the house. The bullets go through the house and across the room.

"We have to get out of here." Hilda yells as she covers her face from the falling debris from the wall. Anna grabs her machine gun and shovels it out of the window and starts shooting. With the Russians being pin down and out in the opening Anna shoots down making sure- that they stay put.

From the back of the house Hilda hears the sounds of the men walking in. Without thinking Hilda grabs her machine gun and runs to the door of the room that they were staying in. Hilda sees three men hunched over trying to sneak through the house unseen. Hilda sees the men at the same time that they see her. As the Russians kneel down and aim Hilda takes the first shot.

The blast of her machine gun riddles the kitchen killing all three of the soldiers. Then Hilda runs past the dead Russian soldiers and looks out of the back kitchen window making sure that there were no more soldiers trying to sneak in.

Then Hilda joins her sister, Anna stoops down to reload as Hilda runs to the second window in that room. "Where did you go?" Ask Anna as she pops another clip into her machine gun.

"They were coming in from the back." Hilda said as she reaches through the window and starts shooting. Anna glances at the door and toward the kitchen where she saw the three dead Russian soldiers. Anna then looks over toward her sister who showing no fear, aims in the direction of the Russian soldiers. Before long all of the Russian soldiers were dead. Both girls stand at their position taking a deep breath as the battle ends.

Anna then notices the new bullets holes that are in the walls. "This is too close." Anna said as she places her finger through the hole. "What should we do now?" Hilda asks as she drops the clip from the machine gun and places a new full clip in.

We can't stay here, they'll send more men, and we need to leave." said Anna as she stands up and check the yard making sure that the Russians hadn't moved from their spot. Hilda runs out the back door and toward the barn where they had the truck. Anna follows as they reach the truck Hilda was about to open the trucks door until she stops and yells to her sister.

"Wait, I have a bad felling about this." said Hilda as she

stands on the running board and looks inside. As Anna looks on Hilda's eyes grew wider. "What is it?" Anna asks.

Hilda jumps off of the running board and stands a foot away. "If you open the door then the truck will explode." Anna does as her sister says and steps backwards. "We need to check to truck over." Hilda said as she looks under the truck for more explosives. "They got this truck rigged with hand grenades, if we remove one grenade then there are others, what should we do now?" Hilda asks as she looks up the front to the back of the truck.

"Well looks like we're walking." Anna says as she notices the flat tires on the rear of the truck.

"We're just going to leave the truck and walk?" Hilda asks in an annoyed tone.

"The tire is flat, there are hand grenades all over the truck. They meant for us to die one way or the other." Anna said defending her decision. Hilda shakes her head in disgust as she walks to the back of the truck and looks at the flat tire.

"How do you change a flat tire?" asks Hilda as she leans down and look at the hole in the tire. "The hole is as big as a knife's blade."

Anna jumps back as she sees her sister jumping in the back. "Be careful, there are explosives all over the truck." Hilda pays her older sister no attention as she digs through for the weapons that they have collected.

"If we are going to walk then we'll need to take the ammo and weapons with us." Hilda says as she hands Anna some of the weapons. Anna reaches up and takes the weapons from her sister as Hilda takes ammo belts and places them around her neck and shoulder then jumping down off of the truck as she and Anna walks out of the barn.

"I'm hoping that our enemy will try to take the truck." Anna said.

"Let them blow up." Hilda said interrupting. The girl walks through the front yard passing the dead Russian soldiers. As they turn around and look back into the barn where they are forced to leave their truck and their belongings behind. Now there is nothing left from their home the girls frown as they realize that a few months ago they had a home with loving parents now they are veterans of many battles in a war that they knew nothing about. The soldiers that were supposed to protect them murder their mother and they lost their father who went to avenge their mom's death. Now it's just the two of them. They're lost, hungry and scared all that they have now is each other and the weapons that they stole and now they are in a different country and surrounded by dead Russian soldiers "Who are they?" Hilda asks as they pass the soldiers.

"They're not Germans and they're not Americans, who else are we in war with?" Anna said as she doesn't recognize the uniforms. "I know that they aren't Americans." said Anna

How can you tell?" Ask Hilda as she looks down at the dead Russians. Anna pulls out a shirt from the backpack and shows it to Hilda. "This is American's shirt." Hilda looks over at the shirt.

"Why do you keep that?" Hilda asks as she continues walking.

"I'm not sure, but I kept the wallets also and some of the metal tags."

"Papa is at war with the Americans, which means that so are we." Hilda said in disgust.

"Well I'm keeping all of this stuff." Anna said as she places the shirt back into her backpack.

"So where are we going?" Hilda asks trying to change the subject.

"I guess we need to find papa." Anna said as she looks down the long road ahead of them. "Or Von."

Hilda says. "Just keep your eyes open this isn't our land, no telling who is out here." Anna said as she looks around her. And hoping to change the subject away from Von.

Chapter Twelve

Von sits in his camp wondering where are Marc and his adopted family. Was Marc able to get his family to Hungary? Was Hilda ok, why wasn't Marc back in town when he said that he was going to be. Did Marc stay and fight the Allies in Hungary or did he make it back at a later date and join the Nazi army then. Von sat and wondered. At that time Wolfgang walks up carrying his machine gun with him.

"Let's go, there are reports that there are some Resistance fighters in the next town." said Wolfgang as he motions to his men.

"I can't believe that we have our own people fighting against us," Von said as he reaches down for his machine gun.

"We are to capture those for the SS but if some of them die then that's better for the fatherland." Wolfgang said in disgust.

"I'll do as I'm told but I would like to kill one of those Resistance fighters with my bare hands." Von said as he grips his fist together.

"I'll make sure that you will." said Wolfgang. As they approach the town the soldiers spread out making a long line as they enter the town's square.

"How can we tell if they are part of the Resistance fighters?" Von asks as he sees the towns' people walking around.

"Look at their face, those who are guilty of treason against the fatherland will show it. Check out their eyes, their eyes will follow you even though they are looking straight ahead. You can see the guilty ones." said Wolfgang as he watches all of the town's peoples.

Von walks up to a young man. The young man gives Von a nervous look. "Traitor." Von yells out as he hits the young man with the butt of his machine gun knocking the man down Von pounce on him as other soldiers help Von restrain him. "Very good Corporal, we have our first traitor." Wolfgang says as he slaps the young man in his face.

"Corporal we will interrogate this prisoner; the rest find

all of the Resistance fighters." Wolfgang orders. As the soldiers continue their search for the fighters Wolfgang winks at Von who smiles.

"Please sir, I am innocent." Begged the young man as Von reaches down and picks the young man up.

"If you are innocent then you would be in the German army." said Wolfgang as he hit the young man again.

"Just tell us what you know and we won't hit you again." Von said as he sees the fear in the young man eyes and the enjoyment in Wolfgang eyes. As the young man tries to talk Wolfgang hits him more and more as all that the young man could do was to cry out in pain as Wolfgang laughs. For a moment Von felt sorry for the young man until Wolfgang looks over. "What's the matter with you? Don't you want to get in on this?" Wolfgang says, as his bare fist is covered with blood. A shot is heard. Wolfgang drops the young man onto the ground.

"Take over; I need to see what is going on." said Wolfgang as He follows in the direction of the shooting. Von grabs the young man by his collar. As the young man resisted by hitting Von in Vons's face as he tries to escape. Feeling the pain Von hits the young man over and over as the young man screams out "I'm sorry, I'm sorry." Wolfgang runs over to a group of soldiers "What happened?" Wolfgang asks as he runs up and sees an old man lying on the ground dead from the gun shot.

Wolfgang then looks up and sees a man sneak into a side door of a building. "Keep searching." Wolfgang orders as he runs toward the side door. Wolfgang pulls out his pistol as he slowly opens up the door. As the door is open a man holding a knife lunged out stabbing Wolfgang in his chest. Wolfgang falls to the ground dead from the knife wound.

Von walks up to the group of soldiers. Covered in blood Vons innocence died with the young man, now Von is a killing machine of the Third Reich. "Where is Wolfgang?" Von asks as he looks around the town.

"He went in that direction." said one of the soldiers pointing.

"This man is dead, search for more of the Resistance fighters." Von orders as he follows the direction of the soldier. Von walks to the side of the building where he sees Wolfgang laying on the ground holding his chest.

"Wolfgang." Von yells as he kneels beside of his friend. As the rest of the men gather around.

"It's the Sergeant." Yells one of the men "What should we do?" Von with tears running down his face looks up at his men.

"Find his attacker." Von yells as he looks around hoping to find Wolfgang's assassin. As his men disperse throughout the town Von stood up and yelled new orders to his men. "I want all of the town's people to come to the front of this building." Von said as he then reaches down and picks Wolfgang's lifeless body up and carries the body to the center of town where he waited for the towns people to stand before him. One by one the soldiers yell into all of the buildings and homes telling all of the people what they were ordered to do. With their guns pulled, the soldiers march all of the civilians in front of Von who had laid Wolfgang's body in the center of town...

Von walks up to the people, as they all look straight down to the ground. Von uses the barrel of his machine gun to lift the people's head up. "Someone here just killed one of Germany's greatest war heroes. And I would like to know who did it? Did you kill the hero?" Von said as he stops at an old man. The man shook his head and look down. Von took two more steps.

"Well then you must have killed our hero." Von said as he stops at an old lady. The lady looks up at Von then quickly shakes her head as she looks down. "Well the whole town is innocent; this war hero killed himself I suppose. Berlin wants us to send all of the Resistance fighters to them; looks like we'll send the whole town to Berlin." Von said as he continues to walk up the line of the people.

Then Von walks up to the man that he felt killed Wolfgang. "But Berlin said that we can shoot some and give them the others, who shall I shoot first?" said Von as he looks over the man. "Is that blood on your hands?" The man turns and runs as the soldiers fixed their sights on the man as he runs toward the building. "Shoot him in the leg." Von yells as the men fire. All of the bullets hitting the man's legs causing both legs to explode leaving the man crippled. Von walks up to the man as the man holds the bloody stub where his legs were. "You wouldn't survive the trip to Berlin." Von said as he pulls out his knife and raises the knife high in the air. With the men watching Von brings the knife down stabbing the man in his chest. The man screams out as Von digs into the man's chest. "All traitors must die." Von whispers into the dying man ears. Von then stood up and wipes the dirt and blood off of his uniform as he walks back to the center of town where the rest of the soldiers are holding the town's people.

I need at least five men." Von said as he walks up and down the line of citizens. Von stops at one teenage boy.

How old are you?" Von asks as the kid shakes.

"I'm fifteen." Answers the kid.

"Well then you should be preparing for the German army shouldn't you?" Von asks with a smile. Von points at the young man and walks down the line as his men walk up and grab the boy.

"No, he is too young for the Army." Begged an old man as Von walks up to him.

'This is the leader, take him." As the old man resists Von knocks him down to the ground and points. "Their leader." Von continues to walk the line pointing at the men that were standing there. The once innocent farm hand now is a murderous killer for the Third Reich. Von stands back and grins as his men do as they are told. As the soldiers force the men to kneel down with their hands on top of their heads Von orders two of his men to go and get the truck as the remaining soldiers guard the suspected Resistance fighters.

"I should make Sergeant for this." Von told himself as he looks around at his accomplishment. As the two trucks pull up Von motions for the prisoners to be placed in the first truck.

"But Corporal, it should be you in the first truck away from the prisoners." said one of the soldiers confused by Von's decision.

"I would like to see the rats of the sewers as they are taken to Berlin, when we get close to Berlin then my truck will lead the way." As the innocent people are ordered to climb into the back of the truck the town's people beg for their lives. But Von who is drunk with the power thinks that he has just waves the people away with a threat. "I can call the whole town as a safe haven for the Resistance and have Berlin flatten this town." Von said in anger.

"These are good loyal people." cried out an old lady as she grabs Von's arm.

Von jerks his arm away from the old lady as he knocks her to the ground. "Would you like to go with them, I can tell you that these men won't be sightseeing when they get to Berlin."

Von laughs as he walks to the truck and climbs on board looking back at the town's people one last time giving them a victory stare as he sits down and the driver drives away.

Where is Wolfgang's body?" Von asks as he looks straight ahead. "We placed him in the back of our truck." said the driver. "Should we take him to his home town?" continued the driver. "No he will be given a hero's funeral in Berlin; I know that the Fuhrer would like to attend." Von said as he shook his head agreeing with himself. Von looks forwards seeing the Resistance fighters all bowing their head as some cry. "Look at them." Von said pointing

They laughed at us before, now they cry like a baby." Von said as he stares at the prisoners as one prisoner looks out seeing Von. The prisoner shakes his head and mouths the words

"We are innocents." Then the man looks down.

I change my mind that man is the leader." Von said pointing. Within an hour the two trucks pull up to a guard post.

The German soldiers place their hands in the air stopping the truck. Von steps out of the second truck and walks up to the guards handing them his papers. "We have a truck filled with some Resistance fighters." Von said proudly. The guard nods his head and hands Von back his papers and motions the other guard to raise up the board. Von walks up to the first truck.

My truck will enter first." Von then walks back to the back of the first truck. "Berlin is five miles down the road; make sure that the prisoners don't jump out." Von said as he starts to walk "But we are innocent and the SS will let us go." said one of the prisoners. Von stops and slowly turns around.

I'm sure that you are guilty of something." Von said as he turns and walks back to his truck. From inside of the truck's cab the prisoners see Von motion to his driver to drive on in front of the first truck. Once inside of the Headquarters in Berlin

Von smiles as the trucks are surrounded by the German soldiers as a Major walks up to Von's truck. Von sets out and clicks his heels together. "Heil Hitler." said Von as he raises his right hand up into the air. The Major returns the salute.

I've brought you some of the Resistance fighters that you wanted." Von said proudly

"Where is Sergeant Burma?" Ask the Major as he looks around.

"Our Sergeant was a victim of these traitors." Von said as he and the Major watches as the suspected Resistance fighter are lead away by the SS soldiers. Von walks the Major to the back of the truck where Wolfgang was laying.

"We will give him a heroes funeral." The Major said as he shakes his head in disgust.

"The traitors that murder Sergeant Burma died by my hands." Von said bragging.

"You should have brought that man with you and we would deal with him." said the Major as he turns and walks away. Von follows the Major to the large building where he walks up the stone steps up to the building as the suspected Resistance fighter are lead to the side of the building and down to the basement. Von follows the Major to his office. "Have a seat." said the Major as he places his hat onto his coat rack.

"With the murder of Sergeant Burma you will take over for him." Trying to hold back a grin Von stood straight and again he clicks his heels together.

"Yea Voe."

" Let your men go back to the home base as you stay behind." Von again clicks his heels.

"How about Sergeant Burma?" Von asks. The Major who was leaning against his desk peers up and looking from the top of his glasses the Major stares at Von.

"I thought that I said that Sergeant Burma will be giving a hero funeral, your main concern is your next battle." said the Major as he looks up toward Von. Von quickly turns his attention toward the map.

Back at the town Otto and Marc and his men walks in.

An old lady runs up to Otto crying as the other town's people follow. "Otto the Nazi was here and they took our young men away as Resistance fighters."

"Where did they go?" Otto asks the old lady. "They took them to Berlin." answers an old man.

Otto looks over toward Marc "There are no Resistance fighters here, we must save them." "We can't just go to Berlin and break the men out." Marc said as he looks over the people that gather around. "Who is this man?" Ask one of the old men. "We call him General." Answer Albert. "Well general whose side are you on?" said another old man looking at Marc who is now wearing street cloths instead of his Nazi uniform. 'Berlin is filled with more soldiers then there are all over the battle fields." Marc said as he shakes his head. "Was they the Nazi or the SS?" Otto asks. "They were Nazi and a Corporal killed my son for no reason." said a crying old lady.

We will revenge his death." Otto said reassuring the old lady with a hug.

"For here on out all Corporals will be shot twice." Marc said to his men, as the lady stares at him.

"And what about the rest of our men?" asks an old man.

"Could Herr Leer help us out?" asks another man.

Marc gives Otto a strange look. "I'll ask him as soon that we make it home."

"But we will find out more on our own." Marc said trying to keep Herr Leer out. Back in Berlin the screams are heard from the basement.

"We're getting information."said the Major as he grins. Von jumps at the loud sound of torture. "With your new responsibility means a higher rank of course, you are now A Sergeant." Von again clicks his heels together.

"Thank you sir." Von said as he smiles knowing that he had deserved it.

"Have your men go and restock their supplies then they can go back to camp, I'll need you to stay and go over the map with me of the area, we need to keep the Allies away from Berlin."

'Yea Voe." Von turns around and walks to the door.

"Sergeant." said the Major calling Von his new rank. Von turns around and smiles. "Hurry back we have a lot of work to do." "Yea Voe." Von said as he clicks his heels together again. The screams are louder as Von walks down the hall and out of the door. He tells his men of his rank as they all celebrate with cheers and back slaps. As the men leave Von walks back toward the Building. With the screams getting louder Von walks to the side of the building where the SS took the Resistance fighters. Von was about to walk down the stairs when he glances over and sees Wolfgang's body lying on the ground next to a hole where two Concentration camp prisoner was digging Wolfgang's grave as a Private overseeing the prisoners. Von stood and watches as the men finish the hole and then placed Wolfgang body in. The private salutes the body as the prisoners lower the flag drape body into the ground. "What a great hero funeral." Von said to himself as he turns and walks to the front of the building and up the stone stairs and into the building. The two trucks are filled with materials that they will need, and they drive off. Before Von enters the building, he watches as the trucks pulls away. Then he smiles and walks in. The truck passes all of the checkpoints and is now back on the main road. The driver never saw Marc and Otto as they hide for the ambush. Marc sees the approaching truck and walks out to the middle of the road and places his hand up slowing down the truck. As the driver gets close enough he sees the machine gun that Marc is holding.

The driver nudges the soldiers beside of him who was asleep. "Resistance fighter." Yells the driver. The soldiers besides the driver tries to point his machine gun out of the window as Marc takes aim and fires. Both of the driver and his partner are killed with the first blast. As Otto and his men aim for the second truck. The battle lasts for only a few seconds. As the truck with their dead drivers rolls off and into a ditch.

Otto and his men check the cabs of the truck making sure that the men were dead. Marc looks in the back of the cover truck to see if there were any men still alive. As Marc is surprise to see the content of the truck. "Hey check this out." Marc said as he yells out to his men. With all of the German Soldiers dead the men walk around to Marc who uncovers the back of the truck. The men now with wide eyes smiles at the finding.

"We need all of this." said Franz as he reaches in and grabs a box marked rations

"Check and see what is in the second truck?" orders Otto. Wilhelm runs to the second truck and looks in this time Wilhelm sees the rest of the German soldiers. The soldiers are leaning over.

"We have soldiers back here." yells Wilhelm as he points his machine gun toward the dead soldiers.

"Are they dead or alive?" Otto yells back as Marc climbs in the back of the truck.

"I think that they are dead." A nervous Wilhelm said.

"Climb up into the truck and nudge them with the barrel of your gun and see if they move." Marc yells out as he picks through the boxes. Wilhelm climbs up and into the truck as Alfred walks back to give Wilhelm some support.

"What do you see?" ask Alfred.

"Dead, well I hope that they are dead soldiers." said Wilhelm as he plunged through all of the supply's that are thrown from side to side by the crash. Wilhelm checks each of the soldiers and is relieved to find out that they were dead. "We must hurry up; I know that the guards at the check points had to hear the shooting."

Marc said as he rushes his men. "Check out the trucks the one that cranks will be the one that we'll take." Otto said as he moves his men. "Alfred go down the road and see if there are any German soldiers driving out here." said Marc.

Alfred does as he was told and started running down the road. "Is this the group that took the town's people in?" Otto asks Marc. "I'm not sure, but it will do." Marc replied

"Hey Franz, go and check the German bodies, see if there is a Corporal." Marc said as Franz jumps off of the truck and checks the bodies. Marc and Otto stand outside of the back of the truck as the men go through their captured goods. Both Marc and Otto glance toward the first truck as Wilhelm cranks it up. "Ok men let's move all of the supplies in to the first truck."

Otto yells as he points toward the first truck. With Marc and Otto's help the second truck is empty into the first truck.

At about the time Franz runs around the bend on the road and start yelling. "Here comes a truck." he yells as he points down the road.

"Let's hurry up." Yells Otto.

"Franz take cover, don't let them see you." Marc yells. Franz dives into a ditch and places broken branches from the trees over himself.

"Let's move this truck down around that bend out of sight from the Germans." Otto says as he and Marc place the last piece of equipment into the first truck.

"Go to the other side of the bend." Marc says as he and Otto check and make sure that their machine gun was ready to be fired. Both men move to the opposite side of the road and kneel down. Wilhelm runs up carrying his machine gun and waits to be told what Marc or Otto wanted him to do.

"Stay with the truck." Otto yells.

"If the soldiers get through us then take them out." Marc yells.

Wilhelm nods his head and runs back to the truck. As the German truck approaches Marc and Otto glance over to each other. First the German troop truck passes Franz. Inside of the ditch Franz lay still hoping to be disguised as the truck passes. The driver sees the down truck in the ditch. The German soldiers exit their truck and look around as the Officer walks up to the truck and looks in. "They're dead." said the Officer to his men.

"Keep a look out for the Resistance fighter." Continued the Officer. One of the soldier's walks the road and sees Marc kneeling in the ditch. Before the soldiers could get a word out Marc started shooting. First one of the German soldiers falls to the ground then two more fall, some of the soldiers ran to the back of the truck for safety, shielded from the gun fire. Franz stands up and shoots the men who was trying to take cover. Before long the battle was over. As all of the German soldiers lay dead on the ground, Marc and his men didn't have a scratch on them.

"Pull this truck to the middle of the road." Marc said as Alfred jumps into the troop truck and drives it where Marc was pointing. "Is that truck able to crank?" Marc asks pointing at the truck that was still in the ditch. Otto who was the closest to that truck jumps in and tries to crank it up. Finally, the truck cranks. Marc smiles. "Move that truck beside of the other one." Marc said standing in the spot where he wanted Otto to park. Not sure of Marcs decision Otto drives the truck where Marc wanted it.

Now raise the hood on the trucks." Marc orders.

Still confused Otto and Alfred lift up the hoods and stood back. Marc takes aim at the engine and pulls the trigger. Otto and Alfred jump for safety as bullets from Marc's machine gun ricochet off of the motors of both trucks. Marc finishes shooting as the motors start smoking and the fluids spill to the ground. "What are you doing?" Otto screams.

"I'm making sure that the Germans are slowed down by this blockade, now they can't move this truck and when they do we should be back at our cave." Marc told his plan. All of the men smile for they knew that Marc plan would save them.

Wilhelm smiles as he looks over toward his General. "What do we do now?" Ask Wilhelm.

"Go and get the truck." Otto said laughing at the blockade of the two German trucks. Wilhelm backs the truck to the men and they all gather in the back.

Wilhelm joined the rest of the men in the rear of the truck as Otto climbs into the cab of the truck behind the steering wheel. Marc climbs into the passenger side of the truck. Otto smiles at Marc as he drives off. A few miles down the road Otto drives up to the town where the suspected Resistance fighters were taken away. "Stop here." Marc said as he points at the town. Otto pulls over to the center of the town as the town's people look out their windows.

"What are we doing here?" Otto asks.

"The only way that we can help this town is to arm it." Marc answers Otto smiles as he agrees.

Then Otto stuck out his hand. Marc looks at Otto's outstretched hand. Marc smiles as he shakes Otto's hand. As the towns people notice that it was Otto and his men they all gather at their truck. "Any word on our guys?" Ask an old man.

"I'm sorry; we couldn't get to them in time." said Marc

"But I'm sure that after they convince the SS of their innocence, then they will be released." Otto lied to give them hope. Marc walks back to the rear of the truck.

"Alfred hand these people some of the rifle and grenades and enough ammo to last them a while." Marc orders.

"But we can't take your weapons, you'll need them." said an old woman.

"We have enough, we can spare." Marc said as he walks

to the back of the truck to oversee the distribution of the weapons.

"What is his name?" ask an old man.

"We just know him as the General." Otto replies with a smile.

"Alright that should be enough weapons." Marc said as he walks back around.

"Do we need to give you some training?" Otto asks as he looks at the old man. The old man shakes his head.

"No we have fought before, but the weapons will be a blessing." Otto nods his head.

"We've slowed the Nazi down for a while, we'll try to get back here to help out in the battle." Marc said as he climbs into the cab of the truck.

"Don't worry about us General, We'll be fine." said the old man with a smile. Hearing the word General Marc returns the smile. As the truck pulls away, Marc looks in the side mirror making sure that they weren't being followed. After a couple of hours, the truck pulls up to the hideout. Otto jumps out of the truck and looks at his men as they were climbing out of the rear of the truck. "Wilhelm go and break some tree branches to cover the truck from the air, the rest let's start unloading the truck." The men quickly unload the truck all of the contents.

"Just place all of the boxes into the middle of the cave and we'll go through them later." Marc orders. After the truck was unloaded and the truck covered from sight from above the men gather around the stacks of boxes that are in the middle of the floor.

"Do you think that they are booby traps?' Franz asks as he kneels down and looks around a box.

"Why would there be booby traps if they were giving them to their own soldiers." Marc asks.

"The General is right; these are for their own men they're not intended for us or there would be booby trapped." Otto said as he picks up one of the boxes and drops it onto the floor of the cave. Some of the men cringe as the box is broken open and Marc and Otto squatted down to see what was in there.

"What is it?" Alfred asks with a scared look on his face.

"Well it's Christmas morning here in the cave." Otto said

as he holds up a German uniform and throws it over to Wilhelm.

"That will be good when we need to mix in with the Nazi." Marc said with a smile. "The next box must contain the pants." Marc said as he holds the box off of the floor then lets it drop. "We have pants." Marc proclaims with laughter.

Franz picks up a long and large box and was about to drop it to the floor. "How heavy is that box?" Otto asks as he can see the strained look on Franz's face.

"It's heavy, why?" asks Franz.

"Then I wouldn't drop it onto the ground if I was you." Otto said as he backs away. Franz slowly places the oversize box down as Marc uses his knife to crack the corner of the crate open, then Marc pulls the rest of the top of the box open.

The men were surprised with what they saw in the box.

"This is Christmas." said Alfred as he reaches in and pulls out a cot for them to sleep on.

"How many are there?" Ask Wilhelm.

"We need to check all of the crates." said Otto as he opens the next box. "We have more cots." It felt like Christmas Morning and the war weathered men were young boys again as they opened all of the boxes. With the last box open all of the items were laid out in the open for them to look at.

"What do we do with the wooden crates?" Ask Franz.

"Keep them we can take each board off and stack them together one after the other. That will stop a bullet if there is enough wood stacked together." Marc said as he holds the boards together show his men what he wanted. All of the men stood around looking at their Christmas morning presents courtesy of the German Army.

"How many cots do we have?" asks Otto as he tries to count.

"There are enough for all of us, maybe two or three extra." said Wilhelm with a grin.

Stack the rest up against the wall so they won't collect dust." Otto said as he continues looking at the rest of the loot that they have.

"Place all of the weapons and ammo with the rest that we have," Marc orders as he goes through the empty wooden crate for the best one. "Here, let's keep all of the ammo in this crate, this should keep the dust off of the ammo." Marc said as he finds the right crate.

"All we need now is pillows and blankets." Laughs Franz.

"How about someone to sing you asleep." said Alfred as he also laughs.

"There will be more battles for us we can look for the blankets and pillows then." Otto said as the rest of the men stop smiling as they realize that there will be more battle, more chances to be killed. Otto also reacts to the way it sounds.

"We are at war, and we have enemies out there. And we have more wins than loses." Marc said trying to build up his men's confidence.

"We need to get rid of the German truck." Otto said as he tries to change the subject.

"What should we do with it?" Ask Franz.

"I'll take it to Herr Leer and see if he can dispose of it." Otto said as he walks out toward the front of the cave. Marc watches Otto leaving. "You can trust him." Wilhelm told Marc. Marc looks over toward Wilhelm and the others.

"At least we know his name." Mumbles Alfred. "And it's going stay that way." Marc said as he takes the wooden crate to the back of the cave and places the bare ammo in as the rest of his men watch. Marc them walks back to his men who are still staring at him. Marc grabs his machine gun. "Well I'll take the first watch." Marc said as he walks past the men and up to the cave. As Marc walks out he sees Otto drive off in the truck, he watches the truck disappear then Marc turns around and sees his men standing at the front of the cave. "You have cots; you might as well get some rest." Marc said as he walks deeper into the woods. A few feet away Marc turns around toward the cave and sees that all of the men have left the entrance. Marc started walking toward Herr Leer's house.

From a distance Marc saw Otto hand Herr Leer the keys to the truck and the two men shook hands. Marc shook his head in disgust as Otto started walking away. Herr Leer jumps inside of the truck and drove off. Otto reaches Marc at the base of the woods. "Herr Leer is going to get rid of the truck for us." Otto said with a smile.

"For some reason I don't trust Herr Leer." Marc said as he

stood with Otto.

"Herr Leer has helped us more then you have." Otto said in anger. "Besides Herr Leer doesn't trust you because he and we don't know your name." Otto said in his defense.

"I'm the General." said Marc with a smile.

"Who is guarding the cave?" Otto said as he starting walking, leaving Marc behind.

"I'm guarding the cave." Marc said as he follows Otto.

"Then shouldn't you be outside of the cave protecting the men that will be following you into battle?" Otto said as he walks faster trying to lose Marc.

"I am watching after the men, and what I see I don't like." Marc said as he slows down letting Otto walk away.

Otto turns around "We can trust Herr Leer; We've been trusting him since we started fighting the Nazi. We just met you." said Otto as he turns back around and walk away.

"I don't need this, I fight better by myself." Marc said out loud to himself.

As Marc gets back to the cave He sees Otto standing guard where Marc was supposed to be. The two men stare at one another. Without saying a word Marc walks into the cave as Otto follows. Marc walks over to where the men had placed all of the cots. "We put your cot here, hope you don't mind." Wilhelm said as Marc walks up and sees all of his belonging lying on top of his cot.

"I have a feeling that the General won't be staying with us much longer." Otto said as he walks into the cave.

Marc turns around and looks over toward Otto then to his men. "I don't trust many people, I have my reasons, but I can trust ya'll, if ya'll can trust me as the General and not my real name, I have my reasons." Marc said as he looks over his cot.

"From the battles that we have had General is the best name for you, I trust you." said Franz.

"With what you did with the German trucks, I can trust you." Wilhelm said as he glances over toward Otto.

"But we fight with other people, they may not pull a trigger but they help us when we need it. We trust them and they need to trust us." Otto said as he looks over toward Marc. Marc nods his head and places his machine gun on his bed.

"So this is where I'm going to sleep, this will work for me." Marc said with a smile as he looks over to Otto. Otto nods his head.

"I need to be on guard duty." Otto said as he turns to walk out of the cave.

"No stay in here, I'm on guard duty." Marc said as he grabs his machine gun and walks past Otto.

Chapter Thirteen

Back in Berlin Von sits at a large table going over a map of the area as the Major walks in. Von looks up for a second and then back to the map as the Major drops Von's new Sergeant insignia in front of him Von stares at the insignia for a second before he picks them up and smiles. "This is a start." Von says to himself.

"A start for what?" asks the Major as he overhears.

"Before I joined the Army I worked for Herr Metz, He was in the first war. He made Sergeant and before the war ended Herr Metz was a Lieutenant."

"Lieutenant Marc Metz." said the Major as he remembers. "I was there when Sergeant Metz made Lieutenant." said The Major "We were proud of Sergeant Metz; he deserves the rank if not higher. But we never saw the Allies sneak up on us. It was a blood bath; they came in firing at all ends I was hit in the legs. When I woke up I was in the hospital then they sent me to a prison camp, I never knew what had happened to anyone else. And you said that you work with him. Where?" said the Major as he sat down beside of Von.

"I was his hired help; Herr Metz owns a farm he fed the German Army with his vegetables." Von said with pride.

"If you worked under Lieutenant Metz then you will be an asset to the German Army. He knew how to mold the people around him. I hope that you learned from him, if you did then you learned from the best." said the Major as he patted Von on his back. "So tell me Sergeant, where should we place our troops in the defense from the Allies?" Before Von could say a word a German soldiers came in.

"Excuse me sir, but there was some trouble about five miles from here." said the soldier as he looks over toward Von.

"Well what is it?" Ask the Major.

"Well sir it has to do with the Corporal's men."

"That's Sergeant." Von said interrupted.

"Yes sir Sergeant, your men were ambushed."

"What?" Von said with a frighten stare.

"Ambushed, how?" Ask the Major. "We suspect the

Resistance fighters." answers the soldier. Von thought for a second.

"We captured some Resistance fighters about fifteen miles away." Von says in shock.

"Well you didn't capture all of them." said the Major in anger. Von looks away stunned at what he heard.

"Any survivors." Ask Von in a low tone.

"No sir, they all were killed." said the soldier.

"We'll send some SS over there to find the rest of the Resistance fighters." said the Major as he looks down toward the map.

"I would like to go with them and finish the job." said Von as he stood up.

"Nonsense, stay here and work on the battle plans. I was told that you were a very smart man. Now that you were a student of Lieutenant Metz, I'm sure that you will be more than an asset for winning the war for our beloved Fatherland." Von sat back down still stunned from the news of his men. " Have Captain Beckler meet me in my office." Orders the Major.

"Yea, Vol." answers the soldier as he leaves the conference room. Von stares at the map but his mind is elsewhere, the map is nothing but a large blank paper.

"Begging the Majors pardon, I would like to find my soldiers murderers." Von said worried of the Major's reaction.

The Major whose is bent over his desk concentrating on the future battle plan glances up and stares at Von. "Let the SS do the dirty work stay here and together we can win the war." said the Major.

"I'm not Lieutenant Metz, he was a fighter. So am I." Von said as the Major slowly looks up and agrees.

"I was told that you were a great soldier and a smart one. We need soldiers like you in Berlin. I will assign you to Berlin where you will shine." laughs the Major as he points to the map. "Now tell me where do you think that the Allies will be landing." said the Major as he points at the map.

Von looks down at the map and glances over the map then Von points at the eastside of the coast. I would be re-enforcing the coast." Von said as the Major smiles. "I've already ordered the re-enforcement of that beach front, brilliant minds like ours will win the war for the Fatherland." said the Major as he does a victorious dance. "Maybe I'll go with you to Berlin." Added the Major.

"Sir, I am a soldier I prefer to fight at that beach front where I can tell my men where to fight. Let me fight." Von said as the Major gives him a sad look.

"I will place you in a combat outfit. You can leave in the morning." said the Major as he looks away from the map.

"May I go after the Resistance fighters?" Von asks.

"We have no such outfit." said the sad Major as he sat down in his chair. "Give me three of four men and I'll end the Resistance fighters. The Major looks at Von and nods.

"I want to see the end of the Resistance fighters, you can have your men, but you work under my command, keep me informed of your every move." With a smile Von agrees and salutes the Major.

"Unfortunately all that I can give you is the new recruits from the training base." said the Major in a low tone.

"That will be the way I prefer; I can train them in my way of fighting." Von said with enjoyment. Von saluted the Major and walks out. Von drives to the German military school where he was given a list of names of men to make up his unit. As the men walk out of the school they are met with Sergeants waiting for them.

Von reads out the names on his list as did the other Sergeants that were there. As the men gather around Von, he looks over his new fighters. "My name is Sergeant Breubaker in time I will learn all of your names but first we will go to our camp and I will tell you what you should know and what I expect from you. Now jump into the back of this truck." As the men jump in the back Von smiles at his accomplishment. Now he is a leader, he will show that he is as great of a soldier then Herr Metz was in the first war. Von gets into his truck and drives off.

In the cave Otto and Marc sleep in the cots that they had gotten from the Germans. "Should we wake them?" Ask Alfred.

"No let them sleep, they've blown up a bridge by themselves, they deserve to sleep in." said Wilhelm. As he took his machine gun out for guard duties. Herr Leer walks down to the cave and Wilhelm escorts him in. Herr Leer stops and looks around the cave.

"Do you have in- door plumbing?" Ask Herr Leer in a sarcastic tone. Alfred walks up holding a pot of coffee

"Would you like some coffee?" Alfred said as Herr Leer glances over and sees Marc and Otto asleep in their cots.

"There is a war going on, and this is a hotel suite, wake these men up." Orders Herr Leer in a loud tone.

Both Marc and Otto wake up. "What time is it?" Otto asks as he looks over toward Marc.

"It's time to meet with the Americans." said Herr Leer as he walks over to Marc and Otto.

"That bridge you wanted destroyed is complete, we are now on a vacation." Said Marc as he tries to wake up.

"What about the Americans?" Otto asks as he sits up on his cot.

"You will need to meet them at four o'clock this afternoon."

"I don't do Americans." Marc said in an angry tone.

"This time we will need you." said Herr Leer. Marc looks over toward Otto who nods his head.

"Ok I'll go." Marc said as the rest of the men smiles. Alfred hands the two men a cup then he pours the coffee in them.

"How is your English?" Otto asks Marc as he drinks some of the coffee.

"Well I can say let's beat him again in English." Marc said with a smile.

Marc and Otto sit in the bed of a truck looking up in the sky for the American paratroopers to jump out of their plane. "Where is their drop spot?" Marc asks Otto

" From here to the edge of the foothill." Otto said.

"Edge of the foothill that's five miles away." Marc said in disgust.

"There is a high wind that could blow the Americans all over Germany." Otto said as he heard the sound of trucks approaching. "Get down." Otto yells at his men. The truck is well covered in the woods. Three German troop trucks rolls past them. 'Follow the trucks." Otto yells to Franz who was driving. Franz slams the shifter in gear as the truck shoots dust and gravel into the air.

"Where is the troop's truck going?" Marc asks as he stands up and leans against the back of the cab of the truck. "They must know about the paratroopers. We need to take them out before they shoot the Americans as they float down." Marc them pounds on the cab of the truck "There is a clearing down there that's where they are going." then Marc looks at the rest of the men. "Start shooting into the troop's truck."

"No let's surprise them at the clearing." Otto said as he stood up beside Marc.

"Three trucks that are around thirty men all together, we have a better chance to knock out the last truck then the one in front of it." Marc yells as the wind is pounding his face.

"Alright let's take out the last truck." said Otto as he pulls his machine gun up and aims it into the rear of the troop truck.

"Let them have it." Marc yells as the men start shooting. The rear truck quickly fills with bullet hole as the German soldiers try to return fire but are unable as Marc, Otto and their men mow them down. As bullet holes enter the cab of the truck killing the driver and his passenger, the troop truck veers off to the side, all of the men look inside of the now burning truck as they drive by. "One truck down and two to go." Marc said laughing. But the second truck is aware of the shooting of the third truck and they have their men sticking their guns out of the canvas and starts firing on Marc and Otto's truck. Neither Otto nor Marc saw that Wilhelm was hit as they return the fire. Franz swings the truck back and forth keeping the German soldiers from having a good target. Marc and his men must hold on and shoot at the same time. Otto grabs a hand grenade from the bag and pulls the pin. As the troop truck slams on its brakes hoping the smaller, lighter truck would slam into the rear of the larger, heavier troop truck. Franz slams on the brakes, as the German soldier is pulled backward from the quick stop. Otto tries to hold onto the truck as he tosses the grenade into the rear of the troop truck.

"Back up, back up." Otto yells as the grenade lands inside. Franz shifted the trucks gears and barely gets away as the grenade blows up killing all of the soldiers that inside.

"Follow the first truck." Marc yells as the first trucks gets some distance. Franz shifted the gears again and drives past the second German troop truck. In the air the men see the American plane fly by dropping out the men as the first troop truck reaches the clearing. The men gather around and point their rifles up to the sky and start shooting toward the Americans paratroopers. The paratrooper's try to return fire but when they let go of their parachute lines they are off balance and fall faster toward the ground. The Americans were an open target until Marc and Otto arrive and start shooting at the German soldiers. As the German soldiers fall to the ground dead some of the American paratroopers also fall to the ground dead. As the last American soldiers touch down on the ground all of the German soldiers are dead. An American Captain walks up yelling at the Resistance fighters. 'Why do I have dead soldiers?" yells the Captain as Marc and Otto notice the death of Wilhelm and Alfred.

As the Captain walks closer to Marc still yelling Marc grabs the Captain and starts strangling him as all of the American soldiers point their rifles toward Marc. "Your loss is not my concern but the loss of my men is." Marc said in his broken English, as his men also point their rifles at the Americans.

"What are we doing, we're supposed to be on the same side." said an American Sergeant Ogino. As he pulls the two men apart. "We were supposed to meet the Resistance fighters not the Nazis." said the Captain as he looks over toward Marc.

"Well it was us that killed the Nazis for you." said Franz in his broken English still angry from the shooting.

"So what, every time that the Allies land they want us to give them a safe landing?" Marc said to Otto.

"Who is in charge?" asks the Captain.

"Not you." Answers Marc.

"I am a Captain in the United States Army."

"Good, then tell your men it is because of them we lost two good soldiers" said Marc.

"We are dealing with a bunch of vigilante, no one in charge and their only concern is picking up the dead German soldier's weapons." said the Captain as he watches the Resistance fighters striping the dead soldiers from their weapons and ammo.

"This is how we get our weapons." Otto said as he looks at the bodies of Wilhelm and Alfred.

"They look like vultures." said an American soldier as he watches the stripping of the dead Nazis soldiers.

"Well, I would like to think that you're in charge." said the Captain as he glances over toward Otto who was giving him a dirty look.

I deal with you and only you." said the Captain as he turns his direction toward Marc. At that time Sergeant Ogino walks over and stands in between Marc and the Captain.

Sergeant Ogino is a large man of Italian decent stands as he looks at Otto and the Captain. Seeing Sergeant Ogino brings back memories of the first war. The beating by both the Americans and the British. Marc places his pistol at the top of his holster ready to pull it out if he needed to. "Let's go over here and talk." said the Captain as he motions to Otto to follow him.

Where he goes, I'll go." Marc said as he makes a motion toward the Captain as Sergeant Ogino places his arm out stopping Marc. "When an arm breaks it makes a loud snapping sound. Marc said to Sergeant Ogino. Sergeant Ogino looks over toward the Captain who nods as he drops his arm.

Why do you hate us so much?" Ask Sergeant Ogino as Marc takes a couple of steps. Marc turns his head and looks at the Sergeant for a second as he continues to walks with Otto.

This man stays." said the Captain. "He is also the leader." said Otto as Marc walks up.

"What is your name?" asks the Captain.

"We call him General." Otto responds.

The Captain gives Marc a strange look. "Well general can you explain to me why we were ambushed?" Marc looks over at the dead German soldiers and the dead American soldiers.

"There is a rat among us; I would say that the rat is from your side." Marc said in disgust.

"I don't think that's it on our side." said the Captain in his defense. Both Otto and Marc look at one another but don't say a word.

"We were told that you have a mission that you will need us." said Otto in his broken English.

The Captain looks over toward Marc. "Do you trust this man?" said the Captain to Otto.

"With my life and you should to." Otto said as he glances

over to Marc. Marc stares at the American Captain

"Can we trust you that is my question." Marc said sarcastically.

"There is a train station near here; we believe that the Nazi are moving men and equipment by rail. Headquarters wants us to knock it out."

"Why can't you knock the train out by air?" Otto asks.

"The Nazis have anti-aircraft guns and we can't risk the loss."

"But you can risk us?" Marc says.

"You're not the only ones at risk, we're here with you. But the Nazis might look at us wearing our uniforms different then they would you in street clothing."

Marc looks over at Otto. "The Nazis will look at us in street clothing. No one will be allowed to get close to the trains unless they are in a Nazis uniform." said Otto as rubs his face.

"Well we are here to blow up the train and we need you to help." Answer the Captain.

"No, you need us to blow it up and you take all of the credit." Marc said as he looks over toward Otto. "We don't need the Allies; we can do this on our own."

"Good then you go and blow up the train and we'll go to Paris and have some fun." said the Captain as he stares at Marc.

"Shouldn't we clear Paris out from the Nazis first for you?" Marc snaps back.

"We'll do whatever we can." Otto said as he looks over to Marc and shakes his head.

As Marc and Otto stand their ground the American Captain walks away. Sergeant Ogino walks up and holds out his hand in friendship. "I'm Sergeant Vito Ogino."

Both Marc and Otto looks at the outstretched hand of Vito. Then with a smile Otto shook his hand. "I'm Otto Linz and this is the General."

"Well general how are you doing?" Vito then stuck out his hand toward Marc. Marc at first stares at the outstretched hand then he slowly took it.

"How old are you?" Vito gives Marc a strange look.

"I'm 28, why?" Marc thought about it for a second.

"You weren't in the first war were you?"

"No sir I was just a small kid back then, but my father fought in the first war" Vito said with a laugh then he realizes how that sounded "But my father fought in Italy." Vito smiles and turn to walk away. "I need to check on my men."

"Does he remind you of someone?" Otto asks as Marc watches Vito walk away.

"All Americans reminds me of the first war, I don't trust any of them and you shouldn't either." Marc sees some of his men being laughed at by the Americans.

"Look at these fighters, no wonder why we are here, to save their sorry butts." Laughs one of the Americans soldiers.

"Then go home we don't need you." said Franz in his broken English.

"If you want us to help you fight then you must learn our language." said of the American.

This is our land you must learn our language." yells Marc as he and Otto walks up. "Or did they teach you words just to sweet talk our fraulein." Marc continues as he reaches the Americans.

"We don't need words for that." Laughs a soldier as he grabs his crotch. As the other American soldiers laugh Marc drops his machine gun and grabs the American as the other Resistance fighters try to pull him off as the Americans laugh.

"Scatter." Yells the Captain. "Tell your man if he can't control himself then he needs to go back where he came from." said the Captain to Otto.

"He will be fine, we need him with us, trust me." Otto said in Marc's defense. "Tell your men to show us some respect." orders Otto.

The Captain looks over to Sergeant Ogino. "Keep your men in line."

"Yes sir, the enemy is out there not here." said Vito to his men but he was looking toward Marc. Marc and the American soldiers stare at one another as they both walk away. Otto leads the American Captain over to his truck and opens up a map of the train station. Marc walks up and looks over the map as the Captain looks at Marc. "You'll be told after we plan this battle out." said the Captain as he places his hand over the site.

"This man is also in charge." Otto says as he lifts the captain hands away from the map.

'He is a renegade." Said the Captain.

"He's a fierce fighter." Yells Otto.

"Then you deal with him, are we straight on the plan?" asks the Captain as he rolls up the map and places it inside of his pocket.

"Just teach your men respect." orders Marc as he walks away.

"He is right, there is an informer and I don't think that it's on our side." Otto said as he looks at his men who had distanced themselves from the Americans.

"Who else knows about this?" Marc asks. As the two men looks at one another.

"Herr Leer" Both men said at the same time.

"No, he had helped us thousands of times." Otto said hoping.

"Like I always said we can't trust anyone." Marc said.

"After this battle we'll find out." Otto said as he grabs his machine gun off the truck and walks over to his men.

The Resistance fighters lead the Americans to the train station undetected. As both the Resistance fighters and the Americans watch, the Germans fills the boxcars of the train.

Marc and Otto makes their plans. "We can take some of the hand grenades from the dead Nazis and toss them into the boxcars." Marc said in a whisper.

"Yea but it's going to take a lot of grenades." Otto said in agreement.

"Hey you Germans talk in English." said one of the Americans.

"What are you guys talking about?" Vito whisper.

"We're working on a plan to save your sorry lives." Marc said as he looks over to Vito. Otto slowly went over to each of his men and told them of the plans.

"Stay here and try to stay out of our way." Marc told the Americans.

"Keep your rifles here just take your hand grenades and pistols." Marc told his men in German. All of his men give Marc a strange look.

"That's the only way that we can do this." said Otto. The men do as they were told. Laying down their weapons and placing their hand grenades into their back of their pants, waited for their next order. Marc and Otto place their machine guns down and look over at their men, the men were ready, they nodded to each other.

"What are your plans?" Ask the Captain.

"That is something that you have to see." Marc said as he and his men slowly move in position. Leading his men Otto sneaks down to the train tracks and mixes in with some other German civilians that were loading the boxcars. All of the men had to make it look like they were helping as each of the Resistance fighters were getting in place. The Americans shielded by the boxcars from the Nazis move into place to knock out the anti-aircraft guns. One by one each of the fighters placed themselves at each of the car. Then Otto, who was the last fighter, nodded and the Resistance fighters reached into their pants and pull out their hand grenades, pull the pins and toss them into the cars. "Get out of here." yell the resistance fighters to the rest of the German civilians. As each of the boxcars explodes all of the workers run for their lives. As the civilians runs the Nazis try to regain order. Some of the Nazis fire their weapons into the air. The Resistance fighters pull out their Lugar's and shoot most of the Nazis that were guarding the train. As the blast from the grenades ignite the ammo and other explosive materials Marc tries to run back into the woods, he is stopped by three Nazi. The Nazi hold Marc as they try to figure out what was going on. Marc notices that he wasn't with the rest of the civilian. "Resistance fighter." Yells a Nazi Officer.

Marc looks up into the woods, as the Nazi starts punching Marc, he sees Vito motioning him to fall down. Marc, now bleeding, nods and falls down kneeling as Vito and his men open fire killing the three Nazi and the Nazi Officer.

Marc remains kneeling waiting for the next shot from the Americans to kill him. But the shot never comes as Marc looks up and sees Vito motions for him to come to them. Marc looks around and orders his men to go into the woods. When all are safe the Americans shoot all of the remaining German soldiers. As the Resistance fighters lay on the ground trying to catch their breath. The Americans walk out and toss their hand grenades into the remaining boxcars. Before long their mission is over. Vito and his men return to the woods where Marc and Otto were waiting. Vito walks up to Marc who was sitting and stuck out his hand. "Thank you, if we were in charge of this mission then we all would have died." Vito said waiting for Marc to shake his hand. Marc smiles and reaches out his hand. Otto walks up and places his arm around Vito as Vito shakes Otto's hand. Then all of the Americans stood in line to congratulate the Resistance fighters. As the Captain was last in line.

"We all will win this war." said the Captain as he shook Marc's hand.

"We fight on the same team." Marc said in his broken English with a smile.

"Can you guys go with us on our next mission?" asks one of the Americans.

"I wish that we could but we must find out who informed the Nazi of your landing." Otto said as he looks over to Marc.

"Good luck, we have a fuel depot to blow up. And I will investigate the same on our end." said the Captain.

"Here I got these for you." said one of the Americans handing Otto all of the dead German soldier's weapons and ammo. Otto smiles as he picks up a Lugar.

"Thanks, these will go into our stock pile."

The Americans part as the Resistance fighters gather up their newly acquire weapons. All of the men took what they could carry.

The next morning Von and his men were at the train station looking around. "This was done by the Resistance fighters. Von said as he notices that there were no weapons.

"How can you tell Herr Sergeant?" Ask one of Von's privates.

"Look at the dead soldiers, their weapons are missing, that's the sign of the Resistance fighters. Like pigs they stripe all of the weapons and ammo from our dead heroes." Von said sadly as he looks over all his dead comrades.

"Well they won't get mine." said another private.

"Then let this be a lesson to all of you, keep your eyes open at all times, for all that we know they could be watching us right now from those woods" Von pointed up to where Marc and the Americans were. One of the privates pulls out his binoculars and looks in the direction Von was pointing. "Go and check the men, see if there is any that are still alive." Von said as he to pulls out his binoculars and looks.

"Those pigs." Yells one of the privates.

"What is it?" Von asks as he looks over toward the privates.

"The Resistance fighters took this Heroes wallet and medals; I can see where they ripped them off of his shirt." said the private in disgust.

"This one as well." Yells out another.

"This must end now." Von yells out in anger. "All Resistance must be killed on the spot no questions asked." Von continues.

As the Americans march to their next destination they pull out the medals they took off of the dead German soldiers and hold them in of their hands as they smile at their find.

Von looks over to his private. "I know who will tell us what we need to know." Von said as he turns and walk away.

Marc and Otto drive up to the cave. "I need to speak with Herr Leer." Marc said as he steps out of the passenger side of the truck and walks back to the back of the truck and watches as the dead fighters are lifted out of the back.

"I'll go with you." said Otto as he stands beside of Marc.

"Stay here, Herr Leer is your friend, I need to handle this." Marc said as he shook his head and started walking.

"No Wilhelm and Alfred were my friends and I need to know." Otto said as he walks toward Marc who slows down for Otto.

"What should we do with Wilhelm and Alfred?" Franz asks as he stood over them.

"Bury them in the clearing but save room for the rats." Marc said as he and Otto continues their walk. Herr Leer and his wife were in the fields working on their crops. As Herr Leer looks up to wipe off his sweaty face he sees Marc and Otto approaching. Herr Leer gives a sour look as he motions toward his wife.

"They didn't go to the drop site." Frau Leer shook her head in disgust. "Should we shoot them our self?" Ask Frau

Leer.

"No, let's see what has happened." said Herr Leer as he leans his weight against his spade. "Wells boys how did it go?" Ask Herr Leer as he smiles.

"I'll get us all a fresh glass of lemonade." said Frau Leer as she walks away. Marc and Otto looks at one and another.

"It went as planned." Marc said as he and Otto walks up to Herr Leer.

"Good, Then the Americans landed and now they are off to defeat Hitler and his goons." said Herr Leer with a confused tone in his voice.

"We were set up; do you know anything about that?" Otto asks as he points his machine gun in Herr Leers direction.

Herr Leer looks at Otto with a confused look on his face. "But how, you said that the Americans landed and that the trains were destroyed."

"We didn't say anything about the train being the target." Marc said as he leans in closer to Herr Leer. "Instead of the train the Americans wanted to blow up a Petrol station nearby." Marc said as he smiles.

"You told the Nazi that we were going after the train but instead we went after the refueling station. Berlin is going to be angry with you won't they." Otto asks with a smile. "But why? I thought that you were on our side what happen?" Otto said as he sees Frau Leer walking out of the house carrying a tray of the drinks. "We trusted you." Otto continues.

"My son gave his life for people like you." said Herr Leer in an angry tone. "He wasn't a part of the Resistance fighters but he knew some that were, He protected them up to the time that the Nazis found him. Up till his death he protected his friends and where were they when Peter was murdered, I wish that you and the Nazis have one huge battle where you kill all of the Nazis and the Nazis kills all of the Resistance fighters. Just wipe each other out. We can handle the Allies." said Herr Leer as he stops his wife from walking toward them. "Go back into the house." Yells Herr Leer.

"She has nothing to do with this, my wife's only crime is having a son that was loyal to the wrong group of men, so if you are here to shoot me, at least let her go." said Herr Leer, as he stands upright. Marc and Otto looks at one another. Then they shake their heads and without saying a word both men turn around and walk away toward the tree line.

"What, you are going to let me go? Cowards, that's what you are Cowards." Yells Herr Leer as he watches the men leave. Then Otto turns around.

"You have help us in the past, for that we will let you live. And for the memories of Peter. But you double crossed the Nazis, they will kill you." Marc said as he turns around toward Herr Leer. Then the two men turn back around and continue their walk toward the woods. Herr Leers eyes grow wider knowing that he will have to deal with the unforgiving Nazis. Without saying a word Marc and Otto walk back to the cave where they see the graves of Wilhelm and Alfred. Marc frowns as the men finish packing down the dirt onto the graves.

We must recruit more men." Marc said as he watches the final shovel of dirt placed on the graves. Otto nods but he doesn't say a word.

"What about Herr Leer and his wife?" Franz asks as he wipes the sweat off of his forehead.

"We'll let the Nazis handle them." Otto said as he stares at the graves of his friends.

"But we can't trust anyone." Marc said out loud.

"If they say that they are on our side, give them the benefit of doubt but keep your eyes on them." Marc said as he walks up to the dirt pile and picks up a dirt wad and crumbles the wad with his hands and watches the smaller dirt drop from his hand and back onto the grave.

"We will go into the surroundings towns looking for more recruits." Otto said as he squatted down and pats the graves with his hand.

Von and his men look over the dead Germans soldiers.

"These men are heroes and they will be treated like heroes." Von said as he sees some of the dead soldiers lying on their stomach and curled up in a fetal position.

"I want all of the heroes to be placed on their back like they were resting." Von orders as he points at the soldiers. All of Von's soldiers give each other an odd look as they do as they were told and turn the dead German soldiers onto their backs.

At that time the field radio goes off as the men finish Von's order. Von walks over to the truck and grabs the radio and answers the call. As his men finish they walk over toward Von who was standing by the truck with his head down. The men gather around Von. Von slowly looks up to his men. "The Petrol station was attacked this morning. The report was out that it was attack by the Americans. This must be the same group that murdered our fallen heroes." Von said in a weak tone.

Those pigs." Yells one of Vons men.

"We must go to the refueling station." Von said as he climbs into the truck and sits with a defeated look on his face.

"But sir what about these heroes' what should we do with their bodies?" asks a soldier.

Leave them for the burial unit." said Von as he looks over at the dead soldiers who now look like they are resting.

"There will be more." Von said in a low tone.

At the cave Otto and his men prepare themselves for the recruitment that they must accomplish. Marc walks up and looks the men over. "Leave your rifles and machine guns here only take your pistol." Marc said as he looks around.

"Talk to the men that you know and trust." Otto said as he checks the clip in his pistol and places the pistol in the back of his pants.

"We want men that can do more than just pull a trigger; we need men that are good with explosives, Men that can be used as medics." Marc said as he looks over to Otto.

"And what about you? Why do you still have your machine gun?" Franz asks as he places his pistol in the back of his pants.

"I'm not going with you. You know the men in the towns and what they can do; I'll stay here and guard the cave." Marc says as he swung his machine gun around his shoulder. All of the men nods and walk out.

Otto was the last to walk out. "Are you going to pay the Leer's a visit?" Otto asks with a smile. Marc thought about it then he smiles.

"Why waste the ammo, Let the Nazis waste theirs." Marc said with a smile. "Beside if the Nazis do pay them a visit then he will show them where we live, we can't have that." Marc said as he picks up his binocular.

"Maybe I should keep a man here with you?" Otto said as he shook his head.

"No I can manage it."

"I was thinking of keeping myself here." Otto said as he reaches down onto his cot and picks up his machine gun. Marc thought about it for a second then he shook his head (no).

"We need the men; I can handle this." Otto agrees and places his machine gun back on the bed.

"Ok General, but if you see the Leers tell them that I said hi." Otto said with a smile. Marc smiles back as Otto leaves the cave.

The Captain's off at headquarters with the room closed. After a while Von is invited to come in and the room is again closed. Von is told about the double agents close to the town. Von is handed two photos. The photos are of the Leers. "Those traitors." Von is heard from the tight closed in room.

The Captain gives Von the address of the Leers. Von stares at the paper with the address for a few seconds then he crumples the paper in his hand as he stands up to walk out. The Captain salutes as Von leave the room but the angry Von doesn't pay any attention to the salute and walks out.

Embarrassed the Captain slowly lowers his hand, knowing that he wasn't going to get his salute.

Standing on guard duty Marc watches the Leer's house. Marc waits to see when the Nazis are going to pay the Leer a visit. "When the Nazi come I can get in position to take them out." Marc told himself. After a few hours Marc decides to go back to the cave for his dinner. Marc sat on his cot eating some beans from a can. Marc wasn't there to see Von and his men pull up in front of the Leer's house.

Herr Leer was sitting at the breakfast table where he could see in all directions. He was at the back door but he could look down the small hallway and see the front door.

The loud truck rolling into the front yard of the Leer's house. Herr Leer looks over to the pistol that he had placed on the table beside of him either for his protection or final moment of his life. Frau Leer walks in. She is scared as Von walks up and to their surprise Von knocks on the door instead of breaking the door down. The Leers looks at one another.

"I'll go and answer the door." said Frau Leer as she turns and walks to the door. "They mustn't know anything." Herr Leer thought. But just in case Herr Leer picks up his pistol and places it in his lap. Von walks into the kitchen and places his hat on the table next to Herr Leer. Von notices the pistol that Herr Leer was trying to hide. But Von doesn't say a ward.

"You must be Herr Leer." Von said standing next to Herr Leer.

"Yes, yes I am." Said Herr Leer, as he remains sitting without looking up. All of Vons's men gather around the table with their weapon pointing down but ready for them to be lifted up for shooting.

"The word in Berlin is that you helped the Resistance fighters escape from us, is that true?" Von asks as he slowly walks around the table and to Frau Leer who was standing at the door of the kitchen. Frau Leer is being held by one of Vons's men. Von stops and smiles at the Frau then he moves on around the table.

"We are loyal citizens of Germany and we will fight for the fatherland when called to." said Herr Leer in anger. Von pulls out his pistol and places it against Herr Leer's head. Then Von reaches down and takes the pistol that Herr Leer had in his lap.

"But who do you fight for?" Von said as he pulls the pistol close to him to get a better look. "Where do you hide the Resistance when they are here?" Von continues.

'This is an old house, we are old people, we are not a part of this war but if we were we are Germans first that is who we would help not the rats that calls themselves Resistance fighters." Without saying a ward Von takes the pistol that Herr Leer had and points it toward Frau Leer.

"Now you wouldn't be lying to me would you?" Von asks as Herr Leer looks over to his wife and sees the gun pointed in her direction. Tears rolls down his face as he looks down.

"My wife had nothing to do with this, please let her go." Begged Herr Leer.

"Show me what I want to see." Orders Von as he steps closer to Frau Leer.

"I'll show you." Cried Herr Leer as he drops his head and slobs. Herr Leer slowly stood up and walks toward the door where he leans over and kisses his wife. "Please let her go, she had nothing to do with this."

"Yes I did." said Frau Leer as her husband with wide eyes tries to stop her from saying more. "I want to be with you." said Frau Leer as she reaches out her hand and softly caresses Herr Leer's face.

"Show me now are she will be the first to die." Orders Von as he lost his patience with the couple.

"I will show you. Herr Leer led the way to the closet where he shows them the ladder where the Resistance fighters would climb down into the unknown basement. "This is it, this is where we would hide the Resistance fighters, But Berlin knew about it all of the time. Talk to Major Cult he is in the SS division. He knows, he knew everything." Cried Herr Leer.

Von looks down the hole then over to Herr Leer. "Show me." said Von as he pushes Herr Leer to the ladder. Herr Leer climbs down the ladder and then he backs away as Von follows. Behind Von is Frau Leer then the rest of Von's men follows. As the last man climbs down the ladder Von orders one of his men back upstairs. "Go outside and guard the truck from the Resistance Fighters.

"Yea, Vol." said the soldiers as he does as he was told.

"Tell me something, when we were here were the Resistance Fighters down here?" Von asks as he thumps the barrel of his pistol against Herr Leer's chest.

"Yes sir, they were down here." Said Herr Leer, as he looks down scared from of could happen to he and his wife. "Please, I beg you, please let my wife go." Herr Leer pleads,

"This is a nice space down here, some people would store their vegetables down here for the winter or some people would keep all of their keepsakes down here for the future. But not you, you wanted to help the people that want to bring down their very own country. " Von said as he walks to the end of the long basement

"Have the woman walk over to this end." Von said as he points to where he wanted Frau Leer to stand.

"Please no." Cried Herr Leer.

"You can stand next to her if you like."

Von said as he smiles. The soldier's lead the couple to the spot that Von had shown them. "You will die and this place will be burnt to the ground, "Von said as he walks away. "Shoot the Frau first, let her husband see his wife die." Von orders as his men get in position. Frau Leer reaches out her hand for Herr Leer to hold, he cries as he reaches his hand out and held on tight. All of the soldiers aim at Frau Leer and wait for the orders to fire.

"This is what we do to traitors." Von said as he lifts his hand high up in the air. Then he smiles as he drops his hand. The signal for his men to open fire on the elderly couple. Frau Leer is push back against the wall as the bullets enter her body. Frau Leer slowly slides down the wall and dies in the sitting position. Herr Leer kneels down and cries as he holds his decease wife. "She would still be alive if you were on our side." Von said as he motions for his men to pick Herr Leer up and place him against the wall. Herr Leer stood there looking down at the blood that was flowing down the uneven floor. "You killed your wife." Von said as he lifted his hand up in the air, then dropping his hand as his soldiers fired their weapons. Herr Leer grabs his stomach as he falls to the ground landing next to his wife. Before long Herr Leer's blood mixed with Frau Leer's blood as the stream of blood flows down to the center of the basement.

From the cave Marc hears the shooting, he jumps up and runs out of the cave and toward the Leer's house where he sees the German truck. Marc slowly moves toward the Leer's house. Marc notices the guard that Von had sent out. The guard was leaning against the hood of the truck looking at the house. Marc eases up and using his knife Marc stabs the German soldier then pulls the dead soldiers body away. Then Marc places himself where he could get a good shot for when the remaining soldiers walk out. All of the men climb up the ladder and walks toward the front door. "Burn this house." Von orders as the first two soldier walk outside. Marc takes aim and waits for more to walk out. As Von notice a picture on the wall. Von walks over and looks at the picture of Herr Leer his wife and son Peter. Von walks over to the wall and takes the picture off of the wall to get a better look.

"There is some petrol in the back of the truck." said one

of the soldiers. As the men leave the house Marc takes aim with his machine gun. The first soldier looks up and sees Marc leaning against the back of the truck. "Resistance fighter." yells the soldier pointing at Marc. Marc pulls the trigger and within a few second all of Von's soldiers was killed before they could defend themselves. Von reaches around and pulls his machine gun up as he slowly creeps up to the front door. Marc who thought that he had killed all of the German soldiers began to walk closer to the dead soldiers. Von never recognizes that it was his best friend and mentor that he was about to shoot. Von slams open the front door and starts shooting. Marc not knowing whom he was aiming at fires his last bullet. Marc is hit in his chest. Marc falls back to the ground as his lifeless arm falls over his face. Von is hit in the shoulder and falls to the ground. Placing his hand over his wound Von walks toward the truck where he first sees the soldier that he had sent out to guard the house. Then Von sees the Resistance fighter lying dead on the ground. Von never knew that it was Marc lying there. Von pulls himself inside of the truck and as pain fills his body Von is able to crank the truck up and drive off. Tears rolls down his face as Von tries to change gears in the truck.

Chapter Fourteen

Otto and the rest of his men walk back to the cave. They were able to convince three other men to join them. Lugwic a farmer who lost his land due to the war. Lugwic is a large overweight man who is good with explosives.

Karl a thief by trade. Karl is best when it comes to sneaking up on the enemy. Erich a man for all men. Erich believes that he and he alone can defeat the enemy all by himself.

Otto along with Franz must train these men to fight the fight that Marc had taught them. But for now they didn't know that Marc had died in battle. They enter the cave as the new men look around in awe. "I was suspecting a tent and sleeping bags." Said Erich as he walks over to the cot and places his bag on top of Marc's cot.

"That cot has been taken." Franz said pointing toward Marc's cot.

"I thought that we was the only fighters there is in this outfit." Erich said as he picks up his bag from Marc's cot.

"The General sleeps here." Otto said as he walks up to Erich.

"You can sleep over there by the supplies." Otto said as he points over to Erich new cot.

"Who is the General?" Ask Karl.

"The General is the one that is going to keep all of us alive." Franz said as he places his pistol on his cot.

"This is a great place to hide out." said Lugwic as he looks around. "The cave is hidden with the thick trees and brushes; there is room enough for our living quarters and ammo and food storage." Lugwic continues as he walks back to the Ammo storage. Otto and Franz looks at one another.

"Where is this General?" Said Karl.

"He's guarding our cave." Otto said as he still stares at Lugwic.

"Well if he is guarding this cave then where is he?" Laughs Lugwic.

"The General should be coming in here soon." answered

Franz as he looks over toward Otto.

Otto walks over to the ammo space and pulls out some of the captured German weapons and hands then out.

"Have you ever shot a machine gun before?" Otto asks Erich. "Nine. (No)" Erich said. Otto reaches in and pulls out a rifle and hands it to Erich. "But you have shot a rifle before haven't you?" Erich nods as he takes the rifle from Otto.

Erich looks the rifle over. "This is a German made rifle." Said a confuse Erich.

"That's right all of our weapons are captured German weapons." Otto said making sure that all of the new men could hear him.

"We were expecting American made weapons." Said Erich.

"Yea or may be English made." Karl added.

"We shot the Nazi with their own weapons, that is a double kill for us, first we use the German made weapons and the German made bullets to kill them. And that save the bullet that could have killed us. A double kill." Franz said as he displays his German made weapon. All of the new men agree and took the weapons that they were used to. As Otto handed out the weapons Franz hands them the ammo belt that they would be needing. It's getting late and Otto and Franz starts getting worry that Marc was not there. "Should we go and find him?" Franz asks.

"No the General knows his way here, I wonder if he decided that he has had enough and went out on his own." Otto said as he looks over to Marc's cot and sees the small bag that Marc had kept.

"Did he go and kill the Leer's?" Franz asks.

"I don't know but we need to find out." Otto answers.

"But we need to keep a watch on Lugwic I have a strange feeling about him." Otto says as he looks over toward Lugwic.

"Yea remember what the General said, we should trust no one." Franz added.

"How do you feel about Karl?" Otto asks as he watches Lugwic every move.

"Karl is a good guy; He once dated my sister a few years ago." Franz said as he looks over to Karl.

"Once dated, what happen?" Otto asked as he looks over toward Franz.

"Karl loves the ladies and the ladies love him." Said Franz as he smiles.

"Well keep him away from my sister." Otto said in a stem voice.

"I can't do that; your sister will run you over to get to that man." Franz said shaking his head.

"Karl will you come over here for a minute." Otto yells out.

"What are you doing there no women here?"

"We need a guard here so we can go and find the General." Otto said as he looks out into the woods.

Karl started walking toward Otto and Franz empty handed. "Karl grab your rifle." Franz said in a sarcastic tone.

"What do you want me to shoot, chip monks?" Laughs Karl.

"If the chip monks are wearing a German uniform." Otto said in a smart tone. Karl turns around and walks over to his cot and picks up his rifle and walks back to Otto and Franz.

"No chip monk will attack this make shift base." Karl said with a smile.

"We'll be right back, no one comes and no one goes." Otto said worried that they had picked the wrong man to join them. Otto and Franz leave the cave and they started walking in the middle of the woods.

"If the General didn't leave us then where did he go?" Franz asks.

"He didn't leave us are he would had taken his small bag with him." Otto said as he looks around the woods."

"If he was out here then he would see us and he would approach us." said Franz as he looks up in the trees wondering if Marc had climb up a tree.

The General must have gone up to the Leer's house; we need to check up there." Otto said as he started walking in the direction of the Leer's house. At the edge of the woods at the rear of the Leer's house Otto and Franz stop and look at the house using their binoculars.

"There is no sign of any movement." Franz said.

"Let's get closer to the house." Otto said as he puts his binocular back into his pouch. "Let's walk slowly," Otto said as he rechecks his machine gun and moves in. Franz looks from side to side.

"For some reason I don't like this" Franz said, as he is cautious with his every move.

"The back of the house looks ok." Otto says as he slowly walks toward the back door.

"Shouldn't the Leer's be out here or at least where they could see us?" Franz asks as he and Otto enters the back door.

"Hello." Otto quietly speaks out.

"There is no one here." Said Franz as he looks around.

'They knew that the Nazis would be looking for them, maybe they move away." Otto said as he looks into the Leer's bedroom. Otto sees all of the Leer's belongings neatly in their place.

"I think that they are still here." Franz said as he walks over and picks up Herr Leer" favorite smoking pipe.

"Check the basement, maybe they're hiding." Otto said as he moves slowly from room to room. Franz leaves Otto and goes over to the ladder as Otto moves on. Otto walks to the front window where he sees the dead German soldiers. "The General was here." Otto told himself. Then Franz climbs down the ladder.

It smells like death down here." Franz told himself. As Franz looks around he saw the Leers sitting against the wall with blood pouring from them to the center of the floor where there is a puddle of blood in the middle. Franz tries to scream but no words came out, then Franz started walking backward to the ladder. With two steps Franz was up the seven-foot ladder.

Otto was outside looking over the dead German soldiers. Then he sees Marc lying on the ground with his arm covering his face. "Oh no General." Otto said as he sees his dead friend. Franz runs out of the house. Franz sees Otto.

"Otto, the Leers are dead." Franz said as he looks at all of the dead German soldiers.

"So is our leader." Otto said as Franz walks up to him and sees Marc lying on the ground.

"Did the General kill all of these soldiers?" Franz asks as he stares at the dead soldiers.

"Yes, but he didn't kill their leader." Otto said as he points at all of the private patches on the arms of the dead German soldiers. "Their leader is still alive." Otto said as he walks over to Marc and places his hand over Marc's nose hoping to feel some air coming out of his nostrils.

"He's dead." Otto said as he tries to pick Marc up. Seeing Otto Franz grabs Marc by his feet. "Let's take him home." Otto said as he and Franz take Marc to the cave.

At the cave all of the men gather around as Otto and Franz lay Marc down on the ground. "Who is this?" Ask Karl.

"This is the General, now I'm not sure just how this is going to play itself out." Franz says with tears rolls down his face.

"Without the General we may not win this war." Otto said as he looks down at the lifeless body of his leader and friend.

"What should we do with him?" ask Erich.

"Bury him next to Alfred and Wilhelm." Otto says as he takes off Marc's ammo belt.

Chapter Fifteen

Von drives to the closest aid station for help. As he falls out of the truck the Germen medical team runs up and carries him to the hospital where they rush Von into surgery.

Days later Von awakens in a hospital bed. Von still in pain holds his shoulder as a doctor walks up and reads his chart. "You were lucky young man. The bullet that hit you was two millimeters to the right then you would have been shot in the heart, dead on impact."

"The man that shot me, where is he?" Von asks as he tries to get up but the pain forces him back on the bed.

"You have lost a lot of blood, you need to rest and let your body heal." warns the doctor. Von lies back in his bed and quickly falls asleep. As Von sleeps he can see the face of his attacker clearer.

Von jumps up in his bed sweet pouring down his face. "It was Herr Metz." Von said out loud.

The nurse attending the soldier in the next bed rushes over to calm Von down. The nurse grabs an injection and stuck it into Von's arm to calm him down. "You will be fine, you have lost a lot of blood and your brain is playing games with you." Said the attending nurse Von calms down and falls asleep again.

At the cave the Resistance fighters finish with Marc's grave. Otto stood quietly as the men placed the last shovel full of dirt on top of Marc's grave. Franz walks out holding Marc's headstone.

Franz hands the wooden headstone to Otto who walks over and places it at the top of Marc's grave. Otto smiles as he reads the headstone. (General.) Otto looks at the other headstone of Wilhelm and Alfred, which reads (Fighters that saved the world) "Now we are more protected than ever." Franz says as Otto agrees.

Weeks go by as Von is recovering from his wound.

As soon as Von is able to move around he is sent to see the Captain at headquarters. Von stands by the German flag staring at it. The thoughts that filled his mind is of the last battle that he was in, and for a split second he could see his mentor Herr Marc Metz but Von couldn't be sure of what he had seen. By now Herr Metz would either be a German soldier or a German Officer giving orders from some desk away from the battle. That's the best war logic is place officers away from the danger but close enough to call the shots. Or did Herr Metz stay with his family in Hungary not wanting to fight in another war. Was he dead or alive? Von stood at the flag wondering as a Corporal walks up to the daze Sergeant

"Excuse me sir." Said the Corporal. Von didn't react until the Corporal asks a second time. Von still in a daze turns around.

"Yes." Von said as he waits for his salute.

"Sir, the Captain will see you now." Said the corporal as Von shows him no reaction. Then the Corporal realizes what Von wanted?

The Corporal clicks his heels together and threw his hand up in the air. Von returns the salute as the Corporal repeats himself.

Von follows the Corporal into the Captain's office.

Captain Heinbaker waits for Von at his desk. With a smile on his face Captain Heinbaker held out his hand for Von to shake. "It is an honor to meet you." Said the Captain with a smile.

Von who shows no expression on his face, shook the Captain's hand. "The honor is all of mine." Von said as he shook hands with the Captain then sitting down before he was asked to sit.

"I was talking to Berlin this morning about you and we feel that a hero like you would be more use to us if you ran a
P.O.W. camp where the prisoners would be more willing to give us their secrets." Said the Captain as he follows Von's direction and sits down.

"I would prefer to hunt down the traitors that calls themselves Resistance fighters or the Underground." Von said disrespecting the rank of the Captain

"Well how about a Concentration camp." Said the Captain with less of a smile on his face.

"Sir I am still able to fight and I feel that I am needed on the front line or wherever those dogs are." Von said not giving in.

The smile has now turn into a serious look. "Sergeant, we

~ 135 ~

feel that your war days are over. You were wounded in your right shoulder, how can you fire your weapon from your right side?" Von closes his eyes for a second.

"Sir, it will be difficult for me to fight with my right side but I am a soldier of the Third Reich, I will do what my superior and Country tells me to do." Von said as he stands up and salutes his Captain. The Captain sat in his chair and rubbed his chin.

"No, Sergeant you are needed to do what you are doing, Find the dogs that calls themselves Resistance Fighter. Bring me all of the leaders of the Resistance that you and your men can find, I will personally watch you kill the beasts one by one." said the Captain as he stands up and stretches out his hand for Von to shake. With a smile on his face Von is more than happy to remain a German soldier.

"Sir may I have more men?" Von asks as he starts to leave the Office.

"Yes but this time you will need double of the men that you had. And make sure that you have at least two or three battle ready Sergeants with you." said the Captain as he sits back down and start writing the orders. "I'll make sure that you will remain in charge by making you a Lieutenant. You shouldn't have a problem with that." Said the Captain as he looks up from his desk with a smile. Von returns the smile as he again salutes the Captain. Von walks out of the building with his head held high as he walks to the nearby barracks where he enters the room as the soldiers inside pay him no attention, Von looks around waiting for the respect that he deserves but no one jumps out of their cot to welcome their new Officer.

"When an Officer enters the room you will jump to attention no matter what you are doing." Yells Von as he slams the door.

"Get lost." Yells one of the Sergeants sitting on his cot reading his newspaper. Von slowly walks over as the Sergeant looks up watching Von. Von grabs the paper and rips it up and throws it back at the Sergeant. "What is wrong with you, you can't order your same rank around." Said the angry Sergeant.

"For here on out refer to me as Lieutenant." Von said with pride and arrogance. At that time a bell is heard and all of Von's new men rush out of the barracks and stood at attention as the Captain stands at the flag pole waiting for Von to walk up and stand beside him. Von click his heels together and salutes the Captain and walks up and stands beside him with his head held high. Von faces his men as the Captain introduces him as a Lieutenant, their leader. Von again clicks his heels together and stands motionless as the Captain places his new Lieutenant insignia on him. Von stood facing them as his new men click their heels and salute their new Officer. Von carefully checks his surroundings making sure that there was no Americans or English or even the Resistance fighters were hiding ready to ambush as they did with Herr Metz when he was giving the rank of Lieutenant. "Our main mission is to interrupt the Resistance fighters and let the people of Germany know that we will fight those who fight against the Fatherland." Von said as he held his head high. As his men cheers. "The Resistance fighters are in their final days." Von said as he saluted his men and then saluted his Captain as he walks toward his men. "We fight tomorrow." Von said as he walks past them and toward his barracks.

Chapter Sixteen

Otto and his men sneak into position as the Nazi tank unit takes a break from the war. Franz eases up next to Otto.

'We never had to take on a tank before; they will kill us in the first second of the battle." Franz said as Otto looks around toward his men who were shaking with fear from the presence of the large heavily protected metal armor.

"What would the General do? Would he run with his tail between his legs or would he stand his position and fight?" Snapped Otto.

Franz gives Otto a scared look. "The General would stay and fight, But Otto the General is dead Are you going to lead us into this slaughter?"Otto looks over toward the tank as the hatch opens up. All of the Resistance fighter grab and ready their weapons. "Wait." Whispers Otto. "I want to see if others will follow him. "The driver will stay inside of the tank." said Otto as he aims his machine gun toward the German soldiers who were standing on top of the tank looking around making sure that things were safe for the rest of the men.

"Come on out." Yells to German soldier as he knocks on the side of the tank. A second German soldier climbs out. Sweat pours off of the soldier's shirt from the tight quarters inside of the tank. "Awe, fresh air." said the second soldier as he points his head toward the sky. "If we have enough time then I would like for us to at least wash our cloths." Said the second soldier as he climbs out of the tank as the third soldier's pops his head out and smell the clean air.

"Karl, get a grenade ready, if they keep the hatch open you will need to throw it in." said Otto as he focusses on Karl and the tank at the same time.

"You mean for me to throw the grenade from here?" Karl said as he pulls out one of his grenade.

"No stupid, after we shoot the soldiers you run up and climb the tank, then toss it in." said Lugwic as he nudged Karl.

The three German soldiers still not sure of their surroundings grip their weapons tight as they all look around the area as the fourth soldier (The driver) sticks his head out of the

~ 138 ~

top hatch on the tank. "Well how does it look? "ask the driver as he took a deep breath of clean air.

"Wait till the driver goes back down inside of the tank. "Karl are you ready?" Otto asks as he glances over to Karl. Karl nods as Otto readies his machine gun.

"Everything looks ok." said one of the soldiers as he continues looking around.

"We'll go deeper into the woods; I don't want to get shot out there." orders the driver as the soldier's looks at one another and smiles. The tank driver pulls his head back inside of the tank as the soldiers continue their search deeper into the woods close to where Otto and his men were laying low.

'Wait." Whispers Otto. Karl grips his grenade tight and places his finger into the pin ready to pull it.

Lugwic taps Karl on his back and shook his head. "Pull the pin when you are ready to toss the grenade down the hatch." Karl nods his head and pulls his finger way from the pin. As the German soldiers walk deeper into the woods they look up in the trees for snipers. Then one of the soldiers looks down and sees Otto lying on the ground at the German soldier's feet. Before the soldier could get a word out Otto pulls the trigger followed by the rest of his men.

"Go, go, go." Lugwic yells as Karl jumps up and runs toward the tank. Karl leaps onto the tank and jumps to the hatch. As a pair of hand reaches up from the inside of the tank to pull the hatch down Karl pulls the pin and throws the grenade inside of the tank then Karl pulls the hatch down. The blast from the grenade pops open the hatch as fire and smoke fills the air.

With the rest of the German soldiers dead the Resistance fighters rejoice. "Let's check out the tank." Otto said in a victorious tone. Each of the men walks up to the tank and touches the body of the destroyed tank. "This is victory." Said Lugwic. "It's a dead tank." Erich said as he watches the smoke bellow out from all of the tank's openings. "This is one tank that we will not have to worry about in the future." Otto said as he smiles at the burning tank. "What now, do we leave go back to the camp?" Said Franz as he had seen enough and pulls away from the tank. "No not yet." Otto said as he looks up to the machine gun that is mounted on top of the tank.

"Take the machine gun with us." Otto said as he points.

"That has to be mounted to the tank, we can't take it off." Said Karl as he looks over to the 50 caliber machine gun.

"It should just snap off of the stand." Otto yells as Karl reaches around the machine gun hoping to find the place where it would snap off.

"That machine gun is too heavy for us to take into battle each time." warns Lugwic.

"We will keep it at the outside of the cave for our protection. Karl runs his finger underneath the machine gun where he hears a click. "I've got it." Laughs Karl as he pulls the machine gun from its stand.

"But what about the ammo, must of the ammo is inside of the tank." Said Erich as he stands next to Otto.

"Take what's in the ammo box that should be enough until we can find another tank." Otto said as he motions Erich to climb up the tank.

"You mean that we are going to go after tanks now?" argued Lugwic.

"Maybe." Otto said with a smile.

"Look Otto this is being here at the right time, we want find to many tanks like this one where the crew is taking a breather, and the next tank will be shooting at us." Franz said as he turns his head up toward the tank and see both Erich and Karl watching their step as they walk together holding the 50 caliber and the ammo box.

"Each day we are getting wiser in warfare." Otto said as he pats Franz on his back. "But the next time that we go up against a tank we will inform the Allies of its whereabouts." Otto said knowing that this time they were lucky.

With the 50 calibers and the ammo in their hands Franz and Otto strips the dead German soldiers of their weapons and ammo belts and follow the rest of the men toward the cave, that was still miles away. Back at the cave Karl drops the 50 calibers onto his cot. And took a deep breath. "That was heavy. From now on we should stick with rifles and small machine guns" said Karl as he wipes the sweat from his forehead.

"Are you going to shoot that from here?" ask Lugwic as

he walks by.

"No stupid, we have to make a stand for it first."

"Well you better get on it, that's my cot and I'm not sleeping with it." Laughs Franz.

The next morning Von and his men drive up to the destroyed tank. Von steps out of the truck and looks around. "Last night the Luftwaffe spotted flames from the air but they couldn't get close enough to see where the flames were coming from."

Von said as he looks at the German markings on the burnt tank. "Here are some dead soldiers." Yells one of Vons men.

"I hope that the dead soldiers are Americans." Von said as he glances over to the edge of the woods.

"No sir, where are their weapons?" said the soldier as he looks around at the dead soldiers. Von slaps the side of the tank.

"The Resistance fighters are to blame for this." Von said as he shook his head in disgust. Then Von looks up where the 50 calibers were supposed to be. "They also took the machine gun." Von said in anger.

Otto and Karl work on a stand that would hold the 50 caliber machine gun. "This should do it." Otto said as he stood back and looks the newly made stand.

"Should we go out and test it?" Karl said as he tries to lift the stand up. Karl drops the stand back down as it was too heavy for him.

"No we cant waste the ammo, beside all of the German soldiers in the area would hear the noise and start looking for us." he said as he cleaned his hands from the grease and dirt.

Back at the tank Von gathers his men around. "This is the work of the Resistance fighters, before we were fighting them hand to hand now they are cocky enough to fight against a tank that makes them bolder and dumber, we must now locate all of the Resistance fighters and kill them before we lose more tanks." Von said encouraging his men to fight harder. At that time one of Von's men walks up holding a radio.

"Sir, it's headquarters, they want to talk to you." Von grabs the radio receiver and places it up to his ear.

"Yes sir it is one of our tanks, no sir the Allies had nothing to do with it. It was the Resistance fighters, well sir they took all of the weapons from the soldiers and they even took the 50 caliber from the top of the tank, no sir the Allies have their own 50 caliber they don't need ours." Von said as he stares at the stand that held the 50 caliber machine gun. "Yes sir we will find the dogs who are behind this and we will bring them to Berlin, Yes sir I will continue my search." Von listens for a few more minutes then Von raises his right arm high into the air.

"Hail Hitler." Von says as he hands the radio back to his soldier. "Headquarters wants the men responsible for these murders to be found and sent to Berlin, I want those who did this to be shot in the legs then be sent to Berlin. Check for tire tracks." Von said as he looks around the ground for tire tracks.

"Sir, tires tracks, why tire tracks?" Ask one of Von's men.

"Because a 50 caliber machine gun is too heavy to be carried by hand there must have been a truck involved." Von said as his men shook their head.

"This is why he is our leader." said one of Von's men. All of the soldiers including Von started looking for tires tracks in the soft dirt.

"Herr Lieutenant, there are no tracks." said one of Von's Sergeants.

"Then we will check out this land, who ever took the 50 caliber couldn't have taken it very far, I want everyone to spread out and move in this direction." Von said pointing as all of his men, with their weapons gripped tightly in their hands, move forward into the woods. Von stays back with his radio man "We'll wait here for the men to return, if they find the dogs that did this then we may call in an air strike from the Luftwaffe and flatten them." Von said as he leans back against his truck's fender.

Otto and Karl places the 50 caliber onto the stand as the rest of the men gather fallen trees from the woods. The men place the dead trees around the stand making it high enough to cover must of the 50 caliber but still giving them enough room to move the 50 caliber from side to side. "This will protect us very well." Otto said as he stood back and smiles at the captured prize. "Erich, go out and stand guard." said Otto as he and the rest of his men go back into the cave Erich walks the half mile and sits on a stump behind a thick bush. Half asleep Erich is awakened by the sounds of the German soldiers walking toward him. With his eyes wide from the sight of the fifteen to twenty men walking in his direction Erich slips away from the thick bush and heads back to the cave as the German soldiers continue to complain.

"We are supposed to find a 50 caliber machine gun; do you know how big a hole a bullet of that size could put in you?" complain one of the soldiers.

"I would rather be looking for the Allies. They are my enemy." said another.

Erich runs into the cave. "There are some German soldiers coming this way." Erich said as he tries to catch his breath.

"Did they see you?" Franz asks

"No." Answer Erich.

"Everyone go to your place." yells Otto as he stood up from his cot.

"Who is going to be on the 50?" ask Lugwic as he grabs his rifle and starts for the cave's entrance.

"I will, Franz feed me the bullets." Otto replied. All of the men reach their spots as Otto and Franz prepares the 50 calibers. None of the German soldiers knew what was ahead of them as they walk in clear view. "Fire." Otto shouted as his men open up on the unsuspecting soldiers. The German soldiers had no chance as all of Otto's men started firing. Otto even got a few kills with the 50 caliber. Within second the battle was over.

Back at the truck Von and his radioman hears the shooting.

Call it in." Von yells to his radioman. Von walks a few feet from the truck as the radioman turns and makes the call.

Von pulls out his map and points to the spot where he thought that he had heard the battle. The radioman gives the Luftwaffe the maps number and stood next to Von. "Maybe it was our men who did the shooting and the Resistance fighters were the ones being killed." said the radioman as he walks up to Von.

"I heard the 50 caliber, our men are dead and as soon as the Luftwaffe gets airborne then we will be rid of the Resistance fighters."

"But weren't we supposed to send all of the Resistance fighters to Berlin?" asks the radioman.

"Unfortunately there will be others." Von replied as the sound of two planes flies toward them. Otto and his men also hears the planes.

"Everyone back into the cave." Otto yells as he and Franz try to unlatch the 50 calibers from its stand. As the planes are overhead bombs exploded around them. As the bombs get near, Von and Franz unhook the 50 caliber from its stand and run into the cave as the area around them explodes. The cave has saved them.

After all of the bombs were dropped Von and his radioman looks down to the ground. "Everyone in the woods is dead now." Said the sad radioman as he turns and walk to the truck.

"They were great soldiers." Von said as he nods.

"Who, our soldiers or the Resistance fighters?" Said the radioman sarcastically. Von slowly turns and looks at his radioman.

"Step out here." Von said as he motions to his radioman. The radioman gets out of the truck and walks over to Von. "I need more men all of my men was killed by the Resistance fighters." Von said as he pulls out his Lugar and shoots the radioman. Von then without an expression walks over to the driver's side of the truck, gets in and drives off.

Otto and his men dig graves deep into the woods for the German soldiers or what was left of them. Most of the German soldier's weapons were damaged by the air attack.

Von drives to Headquarters with an empty truck. Von goes into the Captain's office where he tells the Captain that he needed twice the men that he had before. "The Resistance fighters are bolder now, they have more men and they laugh at us in every battle that they cause." Von yells at the Captain as though he was yelling at a private. The Captain sits in his chair and listens.

"I need to call Berlin." said the Captain as Von stops yelling. "Go to the cook house and have something to eat." orders the Captain as he reaches for the telephone. "I'll call Berlin." Von does, as he was ordered.

At the cookhouse Von sits at a table by himself, his food in front of him but he hasn't eaten a bite. Then Von stands up and walks out. Von enters the Captain's office where he finds the Captain sitting in his chair asleep. Von slams the door waking the Captain. "Well, what did Berlin say do I get the men that I need?" Von asks impatiently.

The Captain motions for Von to sit down as he yawns. "I talk to General Dietrich." said the sleepy Captain.

"And what did he say, Am I going to get more men?" Von said interrupting.

"General Dietrich turned you down, we need men on the front line." Without saying a word Von slaps his hat against his leg.

"Captain I need men, well trained men to rid Germany of the filth that are out there. Give me thirty to forty men and five days to train them my way and you and General Dietrich will see a stoppage of the Resistance fighter's movement" Von said as he stares down to the Captain in anger.

"Five days." Laughs the Captain.

"In five days those new men that you wanted should have had at least five or six Allies kills under their belt." laughs the Captain.

"Well how many men do I get?" Von asks with high hopes.

"None, Berlin would like for you to take over a P.O.W. camp, at a camp you will have your thirty to forty men under you but they won't be allowed to carry a rifle for you." Said the Captain as he continues to laughs.

Von slaps his leg again with his hat. "All I need is myself; I'll fight the Resistance fighters by myself." yells Von as he turns to leave the office of the Captain.

"Halt." yells the Captain. Von stops and slowly turns around facing the Captain. "You are getting your men, but this time Berlin will give you your orders."

Confused Von walks over to the chair and places his hat on the back of the chair. "How many men do I get?" Von asks as he taps the back of the chair.

"Around fifty." said the Captain as he fumbles through some of the papers that are stacked on his desk.

Fifty, I will rid Germany from the filth of the Resistance

fighters." Von says with a gleam in his eyes.

"Not so fast Lieutenant, you will be assigned to a front line battle outfit, you are to report to Captain Vonvanorder's infantry, and you will be fighting the Allies."

"Sir, I fight the Resistance fighter." Von says in shock.

"You will be fighting who ever your commanding Officer tells you to fight and you will be fighting the Allies." said the Captain in anger as he stands up and places both of his balled up fists on the table. Von stunned from the order sat down in the chair." And you will stand whenever a high ranking Officer stands up."

Von in a daze slowly stands up. "Yes sir."

"Leave the Resistance fighters to the SS they can handle them better." continues the Captain.

"Sir may I joined the SS." Von said as he gives the Captain a worried look.

"I made you the rank of Lieutenant; I can make you a Sergeant with the use of an ink pen." said the angry Captain.

"No sir, I will follow my orders as an Officer." Von said in a low tone.

"Good then report to Captain Vonvanorder, he will fill you in on your next mission."

Sir on my free time may I pursue the Resistance fighters." Von said as he glances over to the Captain.

"Ask you commanding Officer." said the Captain as he sat back down. Von walks out of the Captain's Office as thou he had last his last battle. "Lieutenant." said the Captain in a soft tone. "You've been wounded and Germany has lost a lot of good fighting soldiers due to the Resistance fighters now let the SS pursue them." Without saying a word Von slowly turns toward the door and walks out of the Office.

Captain Vonvanorder was walking down the hall behind Von. "Lieutenant, I'm Captain Vonvanorder, you have been assign to my outfit." said the Captain with his hand extended out for Von to shake. Still in a daze Von shook the Captains hand. "I heard that you were wounded, how is your arm?" Said the concerned Captain.

"My arm? Oh it is well I still can fight." Von said as he slowly comes out of his daze. "I will lead your troops into whatever battle the Fatherland has for us." Von said proudly.

Chapter Seventeen

Otto and his men are once again teaming up with the Americans. Both Otto and Vito shakes hands. "I'm glad to see you and your men alive and well." Otto said in his broken English.

Vito smiles as he grips Otto's arm. "We have had some casualties since we last met; I'm the high ranking here now." Vito said as he looks over at his war weary men. Otto also looks over Vito's men then he looks over at his men.

"We also lost some of our key men."

'The General?" said Vito as he looks around.

"Yes, we lost the General a few battles back, but he took around seven Nazi soldiers with him." Vito frowns with the thought of the death of the General.

"What is your mission?" Otto asks trying to change the subject.

"A Nazi Hospital."

"A hospital, we're going to kill the wounded?" Otto said surprised that the Allies would disobey the Geneva war act making all hospitals a safe haven for the wounded.

"No, not the hospital but the factories five miles away from the hospital that build weapons. That is our target." Vito said as he looks at both his men as well as Otto's men. "The Factories will be heavily guarded and I'm not sure that all of us can handle the job." said Vito as he shakes his head.

"What about your airplanes?" Franz asks as he walks up and overhears the conversation.

"The factories are too close to the hospital; we can't chance that."

"So the Nazis place the factories close to the hospital knowing that the Allies want bomb it." said Corporal Dunn, Vito's second in command.

'But the weapons that the factory builds will kill us and the Allies." Said Karl.

"The Germans knew what they were doing." Vito said as he counts Otto's men. "We may have enough to slow the factory down, but to destroy it, I doubt it."

"We can spread our men out, even surround it with enough of men and weapons we should win this battle."

Otto said hoping that Vito had a better plan. "The word is out that there are also some tanks there to be fitted for machine guns and cannons." Vito said as he reaches for the radio from his radioman.

"We will win this battle." Otto said with pride. Vito looks over toward Otto then he thinks for a second before he hands the radio back to his radioman.

"We make our plan as we go." said Vito as he and his men starts walking into the woods.

"Here." said one of the Americans private. "When we heard that we was going to be teaming up with you we started gathering up all of the dead Germans soldiers' ammo." said the private as he pulls out his backpack and hands Otto some ammo. As all of the rest of the Americans do the same with Otto's men. Now all of Vito and Otto's men are fully stocked with the ammo that they needed.

The two groups of soldier's walk side by side without saying a word. They were in German held territories and are outnumbered. To communicate Vito and Otto whisper between themselves. Vito pulls out his map as he and Otto points at the way that they should be going. "There should be a base that holds men just in case the factory is attacked." Vito whispers as he looks the map over."

This is where we are supposed to be." said Vito as he points to the map. Otto looks at Vito's point then he looks over the land ahead of them.

"That's just a couple of miles away." said Vito as he glances over toward his men then back at Otto.

"Sergeant Ogino, do you trust us?" Otto said with a strange look. "You and your men are the only ones in this Country that I do trust."

Otto looks to his men then back toward Vito. "Our camp is five miles from here; Give us four hours before you attack." Otto said as he motions toward his men to follow him.

"What are you going to do?" ask Vito as he looks through his binocular at the German camp.

"We are going to do what the General taught us." Otto said

as he and his men rush away. Confused Vito looks at his men. "Ok, let's find out more about this camp." Vito said as he continues looking through his binoculars.

A couple of hours went by. Vito readies his men for the attack "The replacements are here." said a private pointing down to the building.

"Great now we have twice the number of Germans to fight." Vito said as he pulls up his binoculars and looks through them.

"This doesn't look right." said Corporal Dunn looking through his binoculars.

Vito took a closer look. "Is that Otto and his men dressed like the Germans?" At that time Otto who was dressed like one of the German soldiers glances up knowing that Vito was looking at him. Otto smiles. "Hold your fire." Vito orders his men who pull their weapons back.

"What are they doing?" Dunn asks as he looks over toward Vito.

"I'm not sure." answers Vito.

"Hey whose side are they on?" ask one of the privates. "What do we do?" ask another private.

Vito thinks for a second. "We'll become Otto and his men's backups." Vito said as he motions to his men to move up. As the Americans advance up toward the building they see hidden guards in the woods. Vito motions to his men to drop their weapons and use their knife to take out the guards. Vito watches through his binoculars at both Otto, his men and the soldier that he has sent out to kill the guards. As the surrounding area is cleared of the German guards Vito and his men reported back. Then Vito pulls out his binoculars and looks around the building hoping to see Otto.

Otto dressed like an Officer walks out of the building and raise his binoculars to his eyes searching for some sign of Vito and his men. Both Vito and Otto focus in on each other. Vito gives Otto the thumbs up.

As Otto who was surrounded by unexpected German soldiers places his right hand by his side and gives Vito a thumb up.

"What is your next plan?" Vito said out loud. Otto pulls

off his hat and folds it up and places it in his back pocket.

"What is he doing?" ask Corporal Dunn.

"I'm not sure, maybe this is his way of telling the real Germans from them." Vito said as he sees a Higher-ranking Officers walk up to Otto.

"What they saying?" Ask Dunn as he and Vito watch through their binoculars.

"The Officer is yelling at Otto." Vito said as he pulls out his rifle and points it at the Officer. Otto quickly places his hat back on his head. "The Officer was yelling at Otto for being out of uniform." Vito said as he drops his rifle back to the tree that he was standing next to. As the Officer walks away Otto grabs one of his men and pointed to the woods where Vito and his men were waiting. "Keep your eyes on Otto's man, he's coming up here." Vito said as he watches Otto's man sneak his way from the building to the woods and up to Vito.

"We are about ready, keep your eyes on the main road for the reinforcement." said Franz in his broken English.

"What about those tanks down there?" Vito asks.

"They are ready for the drivers to come and pick them up."

Vito looks over to his men. "Alright who can operate a tank?" Vito ask hoping to find someone.

"I was in one at Ft. Benning. Yea so was I." Answer two of Vito's men.

"Great go with him when the fighting starts jump in one and pull it over to the main road." Vito said pointing to two of the five tanks. "I will talk to Otto, maybe your men could use two of us to help out inside of the tank." Vito nods and both of his men follow Otto's man down the hill and close to the tanks. Then Otto was found and told the plan.

Otto agrees by nodding his head. "The rest of us will split up. Half will focus on the building and the rest will focus on the Main road." Vito watches from the hill using his binoculars.

Scanning from side to side Vito can see the whole compound. "What are they doing?" Vito ask as he peers through the opening. As his men hid, Otto's man eases up to the German soldiers who were guarding the Tiger tanks. As the guard nears the Resistance Fighter, he would sneak up and with his knife in hand stab the guards then taking their place guarding the large massive German made Tiger tank. Otto stands at the opening at the building waiting for his men to finish their mission then report to him. One by one Otto's men walk out of the building giving Otto a slight nod as the completion of their task. As the last fighter walks up to Otto, Otto nods to his men who were guarding the tanks. Then Otto took off his hat notifying Vito that everything was in place.

Otto and his men slowly walk away from the building and wait. Around the building a group of German soldiers walk in formation around to the front of the building. "They must be the replacement guards." Vito hopes. Before the guards spread out they all looks around, as though they were about to get in position for a battle. "What is going on here?" Vito ask as he looks through his binocular.

"Maybe the real Otto and his men are coming out." says Vito's corporal.

"I'm not sure but keep your eyes open." Vito said as he glances over to his men that were with Otto's men guarding the Tiger tanks. As the German soldiers spread out the building explodes sending body parts through the air. Vito who ducks from the explosion, regains his posture and fixes his binoculars on the Tiger tanks where he sees Otto's men as well as his own men jump inside of the tank. The smoke from the tank billows out of the muffler stacks as the Tigers engines are turned over. "Find the right frequencies on the radio into the tanks." Vito said to his radioman.

"Babe Ruth to Lou Gehrig, Babe Ruth to Lou Gehrig." repeats the radioman hoping to find the right radio frequencies. As the Radioman turns the knobs each time he makes the call and no response. Inside of the Tiger tank the call is heard. "What is that?" Ask Lugwic.

"That is for us." answers private Mitch Bonner. "Go ahead Babe." said Private Bonner as he grabs the tank's radio.

"Ty Cobb is rounding third base and running for home, I repeat Ty Cobb is rounding third base and is running home." Lugwic gives Bonner a strange look.

"What does that mean?" Bonner grabs the steering wheel and turns the tank toward the main road and starts moving.

"The Germans are responding to the explosion and we need to cut them off." Bonner said as he orders Lugwic to place a shell into the cannon. Bonner pulls the tiger tank to the front of the main road and swings his barrel toward the approaching German trucks.

"Come on, don't let them in. "Vito said as he watches through his binocular. As the trucks drivers see the tank moving into place they slam on their brakes not knowing who was inside the tank.

"Are you in the clear?" Bonner asks as he places his hand on the pulling pin that fires the cannon.

"Yea, I'm in the clear." Lugwic said as he presses his self against the wall of the tank.

"Fire." Bonner yells as he pulls the pin. The tank jumps as the shell leaves the barrel. The first truck goes up in flames blocking the second and third truck from passing. "Reload." Bonner yells as Lugwic places another shell into the barrel.

"Ready." Lugwic yells back.

"Fire." Yells Bonner and he pulls the second pin. The second shell rips through the first truck that was burning and hits the second truck. "We're dead on." Bonner yells as Lugwic places another shell inside of the barrel. With the first two trucks burning the third truck pulls to the side making Bonner adjust his barrel giving the soldiers time to jump out of the truck and find safety in the woods. Bonner grabs the radio. "Babe Ruth, Babe Ruth, Cobb is running into the grand stand. Bonner said as he and Lugwic grabs the machine gun inside of the tank using the 50 Caliber. "Aim into the woods." Bonner yells both of the Tiger tank machine guns open up into the surrounding woods where the Nazi flee for cover. Some were killed but must take cover and were safe from the machine gun bullets. The first tank rolls over to the entrance of the burning building and starts shooting its machine gun inside. Otto and his men fight the remaining German soldiers that did not die in the explosion. On the ground, Otto never saw that the German soldiers were trying to surround him and his men. "Take a close aim, don't let Otto get surrounded.

Dropping the radio Vito and his radioman take close aim at the Germans. One by one the Germans drop dead. Hearing the shooting Otto quickly turns around and sees the dropping soldiers. Otto smiles as he continues to take aim and kill all of the Nazi soldiers that he could aim at. At the end of the battle Otto looks up into the woods and smiles at his friend that had saved his life. Vito motions to Otto to come up to the hill where they must fight off the Nazis that found refuge in the woods. 'Babe Ruth comes to the center of the ground and start shooting up into the woods." Vito said as the tank rolls backward and moves to the middle, aiming its cannon to the higher ground. "Fire at will." Vito said through the radio. "The Tank two use your machine gun and make sure that all of the Nazis are dead."

"Our call sign is Walter Johnson." said Private Smith.

"Ok Walter Johnson protect us from the ground force." Vito said in his radio. While the soldiers from the third truck move into position as they avoid the bullets and machine gun fire from Walter Johnson. The Nazis that are in the woods, find their safe spot and start shooting. Otto and his men search for the German soldiers that survived the attack. Vito and his men return fire into the woods. "Babe Ruth aim your cannon toward the woods and blast the Nazis." Vito yells into the radio. With the blast from both Babe Ruth and Walter Johnson the Nazis that fled into the woods had no chance as both blasts took out the hidden Nazis. Before long the building is safe and secure. Otto and his men rejoice from the victory. Vito scans around the building looking at all of the dead German soldiers. Vito smiles at his find. "Alright let's head to the building." said Vito to the men that were on the hill.

As the Americans joined the Resistance fighters the two armies shook hands at victories well fought. "What do we do with the Tigers?" Ask Dunn.

"The Tigers belong to the German Army so they can keep them." Otto said with a smile.

"If we let the German Army keep these tank then they will use them against us." Vito said with doubt.

Otto looks at his men. "If the General was here what would he do?" all of his men smiles.

"The General would sabotage the tanks." Karl laughs. Otto widens his smiles and looks over toward Vito.

"We will need some of your hand grenades. "Otto said as Vito still not sure of Otto's intention reaches into his grenade bag and pulls three of them out. Otto takes one to demonstrate. "We will pull the pin and place them under the back of the track when the Nazis roll away the grenade will explode, this should take out the rear end of the tank." Otto said with a smile.

"If they move just one tank then they will check the other tanks for the grenade, we may lose just one tank." Vito said as he shakes his head.

"Then we place objects into the barrels of the tanks. We'll make sure that the Nazis can't see the objects, when they fire their cannons the shell will hit the object and explode the whole tank."

Vito thinks about it for a second then he slowly smiled and shook his head. "That may work." Vito said with a smile.

Otto turns to his men. "Look for whatever would fit inside of the barrel that can side down the barrel and get stuck in the middle of the barrel." Otto said as his men start looking.

"Dunn, take three men and guard this base. The rest of us will help the Resistance fighters with their search." Vito said as he joined Otto.

The men find the parts from the burnt building that could be place in the barrel. "Make it tight in the middle of the barrel." Otto said as his man Franz walks out of the smoking building carrying a wooden box

"Here is some steel sludge; they should fit into the barrels without going all the way through." Franz said in his broken English.

"Try it out." Otto said with a smile. Franz places the round sludge into the top of the barrel.

The round sludge rolls down the barrel and stops in the middle. Otto looks down the barrel to see how far the sludge has gone. "Check on the inside." Otto said as one of his men climb inside of the tank and looks in the barrel.

"I don't see anything." yells Erich as he reaches inside of the barrel of the cannon.

"Place a shell in the front of the barrel." Vito said as he motions for his men to retrieve a shell. Vito eases the shell down the barrel. "How about now?" Vito ask.

"Everything looks good." yells Erich.

"Good, we must now do this to all of the Tigers." Otto said

as he reaches out his hands to Vito.

The two men shook hands with a smile. "When they fire these cannons the blast should carry into the main compartment of the tank. "I would love see the blast." Otto said, as he looks the Tiger over. As the rest of the Tigers were fitted with sludge filled barrels the two armies once again parted ways.

As the Americans parted. Otto and his men went back to their cave. All happy at their accomplishment and their renewed friendship with Vito and the American soldiers, they never knew that a few miles ahead of them was the German Army, camped out and waiting for the Allied forces to appear.

"Now we are Soldiers." laughs Erich.

"We may have won the that battle but not the war." said Karl as he passed an opening where he was spotted by a German guard.

"Hey." yells the guard. "Where have you been?" ask the guard as he walks up to the Resistance Fighter still wearing their German uniform. "Are your boy's hungry?" asks the guard. Not knowing what to do Otto and his men follow the guard to the camp. "I found some stragglers." said the guard as Karl and Erich looks to Otto for their next move. As the men get closer to the camp Otto throws up his machine gun and starts firing. "Find a safe spot." Otto yells to his men. Several German soldiers' fall to the ground dead as all of the Resistance fighters commence firing. Otto finds the time to get rid of his German shirt and toss it away. One by one the Resistance fighter's discard their German shirts. The battle was more than what they were expecting as one German soldier fell to the ground, another took his place. "Use your grenades, save your bullets." Otto yells out as more and more Germans soldiers enter the battle.

"We are outnumbered." Erich yells out as he starts to run.

"Stay where you are, they will kill you if you stand up to run." Otto yells to his men as they all wanted to run. As the Germans take cover and return fire toward the Resistance fighters they didn't notice that Anna and Hilda were sneaking up on them.

"You take that half and I'll take this half." Hilda said as she pulls up her machine gun.

The German soldiers were well hidden from the

Resistance fighters but they are out in the open with the two girls.

Anna aims her machine gun at the end of the line and made a sweeping motion as she pulls the trigger. As did Hilda.

With one blast from their machine guns all but a few Germans are killed. The rest of the Germans turn and start shooting at Anna and Hilda giving the Resistance fighters a better shot.

Within seconds twenty-five German soldiers lay dead.

Not sure of what was going on Otto and his men waited to see if the German soldiers were reloading or making plans to attack. Anna and Hilda saw the dead soldiers so they moved in and collected the soldiers weapons. Karl sees a movement on the German side. Karl takes aim and fires his rifle hitting wooden crates that hide the soldiers from the shooting.

Hilda falls to the ground as the bullet hits close to her.

"Hilda, are you ok?" Anna yells not knowing if her sister was hit or not. Anna took her machine gun and pulls it over a large stone and starts firing. All of the Resistance fighters flatten themselves to the ground as the bullets from Anna's machine gun rip above them. Hilda jumps up and joins her sister and starts firing her machine gun. As the Resistance fighters push themselves closer to the ground Hilda and Anna stops firing.

"Who were the Germans shooting at?" Ask Hilda.

Anna gives it a hard thought. "Who is out there?" Anna yells as she reloads.

Otto and Franz looks at one and another. "Who are you?" yells Otto as he grabs his machine gun.

"Why are the German soldiers shooting at you?" yells Anna.

"Because we are Resistance fighters." Otto said as he gives Franz a strange look.

"So are we." yells Hilda as she reloads her machine gun. Otto took a deep breath as he slowly stands up. Both Anna and Hilda aim their machine gun toward Otto and the rest of his men as they slowly stand up. Anna looks over to her sister.

"What should we do?" Anna asks.

'If they were German soldiers then why would these

German soldiers be shooting at them?" Hilda said as she slowly stood up. Anna follows but she still aims her machine gun in their direction.

Otto starts walking toward them with his hands held high but he is still holding his rifle. "Are you two girls a part of the Resistance fighters?" Otto asks as he walks closer to the girls.

"We are not a part of any group." Anna said as she lowers her weapon.

"Would you like to join us?" Otto asks impressed as he looks around and sees all of the dead German soldiers.

"No thanks." Anna said as she looks around at Otto's misfit like unit. Hilda walks over to the pile of weapons and starts picking them up.

"What do you think that you are doing?" Erich ask as he also was picking up the weapons.

"These are ours." Hilda said as she pays Erich little attention.

"Put those down." sells Erich as he slaps the weapons out of Hilda's hands. Both Hilda and Anna quickly raise their machine guns aiming them toward Erich. Stunned the rest of the Resistance fighters stood still not knowing what they were to do.

"Try that again and you're a dead man." Hilda said as she aims her machine gun toward Erich's face.

"We are on the same side." Otto yells as he stood in between Hilda and Erich.

"We killed these soldiers; these weapons belong to us." Anna said defending her sister.

"Your weapons are over there." Anna said pointing at the dead soldiers on the other side of the wall.

"Look fraulein, there are enough weapons for all of us." said Otto as he tries to calm the tension.

"Take what we need and leave the rest for them." Anna said as she stares at Otto.

Hilda reaches over and takes some of the ammo belts that Erich had picked up. "You can have those." Hilda said as she grabs the belt and pushes them toward Erich. Erich looks over toward Otto who smiles and looks the other way.

"Are you fraulein hungry?" Otto asks as he tries to make

peace.

"We don't need your food we have theirs." Anna said pointing at the pot on the fire.

"Well there better be enough for all of us." Karl said as Hilda walks up to him and takes the machine gun that he had just picked up.

"Our camp is two miles down the road." Otto said with a smile as he watches Karl almost falls down as Hilda takes the weapon from him.

"Then go to your camp, have all of the food that you can eat, just leave us alone." Hilda said as she stands in front of Franz who without a fight gives up his ammo belt that he got off of the dead German soldier.

"Where is your camp?" Otto asks Anna.

"Right here, in the morning our camp will be somewhere else." Anna said as she hands the ammo belts to Hilda.

"Like my sister said, this is our camp, Better move on." Hilda said sarcastically.

"Here is some good information for you, at night we shoot first then we see what is out there." Hilda added.

Otto smiles. "Thanks for the information; may we now take what we need?"

"What are you going to do with the bodies?" Franz asks. Anna and Hilda look around at all of the dead German soldiers.

"We'll bury them." Anna said as she motions for the men to leave. Otto smiles, as he is motion to leave.

The girls are now left alone Anna and Hilda look over to the bodies. "Maybe we should have let them help us with disposing of the bodies before they left."

"Yea, maybe."

Back at the cave Otto and his men were in their cots trying to sleep. Every time that Otto closes his eyes he sees Anna.

"In the morning we'll check on the girls." Otto said out loud.

"Why, they are bad news." Erich said.

"They save our butts." Karl added.

"We'll check on them in the morning." Otto repeats.

Chapter Eighteen

As the sun comes up Otto and his men arm themselves for the trip back to the girls. "We need to be careful, remember what they said, they'll shoot first." Franz said as he added an extra clip to his belt.

"That's why we are going at daylight." Otto said. "Those girls need us and we need them." Otto continues.

"Well, I don't need them." Erich said as he looks at his ammo belt wondering if he has enough clips in it.

As Otto and his men make their journey to the girl's camp, the girls awoke to the sound of a motorcades rolling toward them. Anna jumps up still covered in the dirt from where she and Hilda buried the German soldiers. "Hilda, wake up." Anna said as she nudges her sister. Hilda also wakes up with the noise of the three approaching trucks.

"What are they?" Hilda asks as she wipes her face of the dried dirt. Anna grabs her newly acquired binocular.

"They're Nazis." Anna said as Hilda quickly grabs her machine gun and gets ready for the battle. "Grab a couple of hand grenades." Anna said as she places her hand on Hilda's machine gun. Hilda places her machine gun down and grabs the two hand grenades as Anna had told her. The girls get in position as the trucks drive up to the camp. Hilda hands Anna one of the hand grenades and Anna pulls the pin. As the German Officer opens up the door on the passenger side of the truck and calls out for the men that the girls had just killed the night before. Anna tosses the grenade under the truck without the Officer seeing it. The lead truck explodes killing all of the soldiers inside the back of the truck. Anna yells to her sister to throw the grenade under the second truck. The second truck explodes leaving the third truck out of the girls throwing range. Both of the girls grab their machine gun and start shooting. Hearing the shooting Otto and his men starts running toward the camp. Several German soldiers fall out of the back of the third truck and take cover from the girls shooting at the burning first and second truck.

The Germans outnumber the girls in men and weaponry. One German soldier pulls out his rocket launcher and aims it toward the girls. With the truck on fire the German soldiers could see through the flames but the girls' view was hidden from the same flames. Otto and his men rush up from the other side where the German soldiers are poised. Before the soldier could shoot his rocket toward the girls Otto kneels down and takes aim. Otto hits the soldier in his back but the bullets impact causes the soldier to fire his rocket. On the other side where the girls were they could see the rocket going through the flames and over their head exploding in the woods behind them. The rest of the Resistance fighters also kneel down and finish killing the remaining German soldiers.

The Battle was over but the girls weren't aware of the killing of the Germans soldiers by Otto and his men. "Hold your fire." Otto yells as he stands up and holds his gun straight up in the air showing the girls that the battle was over. Both Anna and Hilda stop shooting for a second.

"Who are you?" Anna said as Hilda reloads her machine gun.

"I will tell you but you will still shoot me." Otto laughs as he approaches the girls by walking around the burning trucks. Still not sure Hilda hands Anna her loaded machine gun, Hilda takes Anna machine gun, reloads it and aims it at the approaching stranger. Otto walks through the two trucks and between the smoke and fire. Otto smiles as he holds his weapon in the air. "Last night you saved us and this morning we saved you, that makes us even don't you think?" Anna smiles as Hilda aims her machine gun at Otto.

Seeing this Otto stops and the smile left his face. "Fraulein, trust me we are on the same side." Otto said as he shows fear in his eyes.

"Hilda put your weapon down this man is on our side." Anna said as she reaches over and tries to pull the barrel down.

"Stay right where you are." Hilda yells out.

"Anna, we don't know this man, how do we know that he wasn't with the Germans in the third truck?" said Hilda as Anna glances over to Otto. "Where are the rest of your men?" Hilda asks as Anna removes her hand from Hilda's machine gun.

"They are behind me." Otto said as he motions for his

men to join him. All of Otto's men walk through the two trucks and through the smoke and flames and stood beside of their leader. "We killed the soldiers for you. Now we are even, Good luck in the future battles." Otto said as he slowly turns around and walks back through the burning trucks to leave. As his men follow the girl's looks at one another.

"Wait "Anna yells as she jumps up and runs toward the two burning trucks. Otto walks back through. "We learned to not to trust anyone." Anna said as she looks down at all of the dead German soldiers. "I was told by a great fighter once not to trust anyone." Otto said remembering Marc their General.

"We are what the Nazis called Resistance fighter or the Underground. Well whatever that they call us we are a threat to them." Otto said as Hilda joins them.

"You killed all of these soldiers, why?" Ask Hilda as she looks around at the dead soldiers.

"Because like it or not we are on the same side, the side where the Nazi die when they get in our way." Otto said as he motions for his men to follow him back to his camp.

Leaving Anna and Hilda behind Otto turns around. "Have you two fraulein had breakfast?"

"No." Anna said.

"We're not hungry." said Hilda.

"Well good luck." Otto said with a smile as he and his men walks back to the cave.

"We can trust them." Anna said as she watches the men walk farther away.

"Would papa?" Hilda asks. Anna thought for a second.

"No, probably not." Anna said as she reaches down and took what the ammo she needed. As Hilda watches the Resistance fighter's walks out of sight. "I would like to have some of those rockets that they had." Anna said as she picks up the empty rocket launcher.

"Well whatever we get we have to carry it." Hilda said as Anna has trouble picking up the heavy launcher. Anna agrees and drops the launcher. "We need to destroy it." Hilda said as she walks over and kicks to launcher under the burning truck. "What about the third truck?" Hilda asks as she looks down at the untouched truck.

Anna grabs a grenade and walks down to the third truck. "Bring me some of the Ammo that we don't need." Anna yells. Hilda gathers up what they needed and places it away from the burning truck. Then Hilda took the rest of the ammo and grenades down to the third truck where Anna had opened up the hood of the truck. "Place some loose bullets around the motor." Hilda climbs on the fender of the truck and places several clips around the motor as Anna drops a grenade into the fuel tank. "Ok place a grenade under the close hood." Anna said as Hilda closed the hood then places the grenade under it as she was told. "Jump off then pull the pin." Hilda watches her sister as she pulls the pin then runs. A few seconds later the grenade explodes. The girls fall to the ground as the truck's motor catches fire with the hood flying off. Then the clips started shooting off. As the oil and fuel that are in the motors lines ignites the fire follows the line to the fuel tank

Where the explosion separates the truck. "Well the Nazis won't be able to use that truck either." Anna said from the ground as she and Hilda watches the truck leap into the air and back to the ground burning out of control.

"You know Anna we could have used that truck to drive us, now we have to walk carrying all of the ammo." Hilda said as she and Anna looks at one another.

"Let's get out of here, there will be more soldiers." Anna said as she and Hilda grab their new ammo and walk away. Without knowing the girls walk in the same direction as Otto and his men.

As the girls reach the tree line the third troop truck exploded again this time the fire and smoke shoots high in the sky. Both of the girl's turn and watch from a safe position. "The Nazi will see the smoke." Hilda said as she and Anna continue their walk into the woods.

"This is creepy." Anna said as she looks into the tall trees. At that time an airplane is heard flying above the trees. "I wonder if the Nazis are checking out the smoke." Said Anna as she tries to look past the top of the trees. But the trees are too tall and spread out where she couldn't see the low flying plane. "They have to be the Luftwaffe checking out the smoke from the trucks." Anna said as she tries to look through the high thick trees.

"Well when, they see that the trucks belong to the Nazis they will send more Nazi soldiers to this area." Hilda said as she cups her hands together as she looks up into the thick trees.

"Let's get out of here the pilots will radio in their location." Anna said as she and Hilda started walking faster. As the girls walk deeper into the woods they hear the sound of the planes flying overhead. The girls hear the eerie sounds, and then they hear the explosion hitting the ground around them.

"Did they see us?" Hilda asks as she runs dodging the bombs.

"No the pilots know that this would be the best place for the Allies to hide." Anna said as she falls to the ground at the eerie sound of bombs dropping from the air. The bomb hit close by Anna. Hilda looks back and sees her sister lying on the ground.

"Anna!" Hilda yells as she tries to make it to her sister. Anna looks over to Hilda who was running toward her.

"Hilda, get down." Anna said as she motions her sister down. At that time the bombing stops.

"Let's go." Anna said as she notices that there were no more bombs dropping through the trees. As the girl's stand up their legs are wobbly from being scared by the dropping of the bombs. Then they hear some trucks pulling up at the base of the trees. "The Nazis are after us." Anna whispers. Anna looks ahead and sees a good spot that her and Hilda could hide from the Nazis and defend themselves. "Follow me." Anna whispers. Hilda is looking at the base of the tree line and sees the Nazis off-loading from their trucks and gather together making their plans. Hilda joins her sister at the spot. "They aren't sure that we are in here, or even if we are still alive after the bombing." Anna said as she grips her machine gun tight in her hands. The Nazi walks through the woods in a single line.

"Look for their bodies." ells an Officer. Anna seeing the number of soldiers that were walking toward them reaches into her ammo bag and pulls out more clips for her machine gun.

Seeing this Hilda does the same. "Wait till they are closer." Anna said in a low tone. As the Nazi get closer to the girls three more trucks are heard. Anna and Hilda look at one another. Anna then smiles a faint smile at her sister thinking that this was going to be their last fight. Then Anna stands up and with her machine gun she shoots the first batch of soldiers. Hilda joins in as the two girls shoot most of the soldiers. The soldier that still was alive was the one that found protection from the shooting. The Nazi soldiers' return fire toward the girls as more and more German soldiers run into the woods.

Anna and Hilda drop down as the German bullets fly over their heads "Stay down said a voice from the woods behind them.

Anna looks back and sees Otto and his men running in and start shooting. Hilda tries to run to the Resistance fighters as Otto motions her to stay down. All of the Resistance fighters move from tree to tree as they shoot. Anna jumps up and continues firing her machine gun as Hilda joins her.

"Stay here, I need to go over there for a better shot. "Anna says to Hilda. Hilda braces herself and starts firing, covering Anna Hilda spreads her machine gun bullets from side to side. Anna reaches her spot and starts shooting, killing five German soldiers.

"Everyone to the cave." Otto yells out as he continues firing. All of his men slowly move deeper into the woods.

"Come on follow us." Karl said to Hilda.

"I'm not leaving my sister." Hilda yells back.

"They will over run us if we stay here." Karl pleads. Anna reloads her machine gun and looks over toward Hilda who was motioning for her to follow the Resistance fighters. Knowing that the coast was clear Anna nods and started shooting as she runs deeper into the woods along with Hilda as the Nazis advances.

Now all of the Resistance fighters including Anna and Hilda are together. "Where are we going?" Hilda asks Franz.

"To our cave we will be safe there." Franz told her as he turns around making sure that they weren't being followed. Hilda and Franz pass Karl who was knelt down behind of a tree.

"What is he doing?" Hilda asks.

"Making sure that we aren't being follow." Franz said as he and Hilda runs past Karl. At the cave Otto placed his men where he wanted them.

"You two fraulein can stay in the cave." Otto said as he uncovers the 50 caliber and aim it toward the woods.

"I'm not going into the cave and sit while you and your men fight, we can fight just as well as anybody." Anna said in anger.

"Then stay out of the way, we are used to fighting as a team." yells Erich.

"Then team up with someone." Otto yells. Anna kneels next to Franz as Hilda kneels beside Karl. In the thick woods the sounds of approaching men are heard.

"They went this way." yells a German soldier.

"Get ready." Otto said in a low tone. Then some of the German soldiers come into clear view and Otto and his men open fire on them. As Anna shoots her machine gun she looks over toward Otto who was shooting the 50 caliber, Then Anna looks over toward her sister who was shooting her machine gun into the woods. Anna nods her head "This is where we are supposed to be." Anna told herself.

At that time Anna used her last clip. "I'm out of bullets." Anna said to Franz.

"Go into the cave and in the back is our ammo boxes, get what you need." Franz said as he continues to shoot.

Franz stood up and fired into the woods, giving Anna time to run into the cave. Once inside Anna sees the cots where the men sleep then Anna notice a blanket hanging from the ceiling in the back. Anna runs to the back and pulls back the blanket where she sees the stacks of boxes filled with whatever she needed. Bullets, hand grenades, pistols, rifles, knifes and clips for her machine gun. Anna grabs a handful of clips and places them into her ammo bag. Then Anna places some grenades into her bags along with ammo belts filled with the bullets for the rifles that some of the Resistance fighters were using.

As Anna turns to walk out she notices the German uniforms hanging on some rope that hangs from the ceiling. With an angry look Anna walks over and touches the uniform. "Who are they?" Anna said to herself.

"Does anyone have any extra ammo, I'm low?" Karl yells out, Anna having what Karl and the rest of the men needed lets go of the uniform and started running out.

"Cover me." Anna yells as she runs out of the cave. Anna ran up to each of the men and handed them what they needed.

"Let me have a grenade." said Erich as he took the clips from Anna. Anna pulls out a grenade and hands it over to him. Then Erich lifts up and started shooting as Anna moves to the next fighter. Anna went from one fighter to the next giving the men the ammo that they needed.

Anna runs over to Otto who was getting low of the 50 caliber bullets. "I didn't see any bullets for your 50 caliber.

"This is it, there are no more bullets for the 50 caliber." Otto yells out as he continues to shoot. Seconds later the battle was over as both side ceased shooting.

"Is it over?" Hilda asks.

"I'm not sure, I hope so." said Karl as he looks around.

"Karl, Erich go out and look around." Otto orders. Karl and Erich do as they are told. Hilda also follows the two men into the woods and look around.

"What are you doing here?" Karl asks as Hilda stands beside him as they look at all of the dead German soldiers.

"I'm just helping out." Hilda explains. Karl and Erich looks at one another and smile. Anna went back into the cave and looks around as the shooting ends. When Anna walks out she looks around to see that Otto was checking out the 50 caliber and the remaining bullets. Franz was looking at the dead German soldiers that were around the cave.

'Where is Hilda?" Anna asks as she looks around the small area.

"I believe that she went out with Karl and Erich." Otto said as he pulls the short line of bullets for the 50 caliber.

"Why did she go with them?" Anna said as she went straight into the woods looking for her sister.

"Hilda." Anna yells out.

"We're over here." Hilda said as she starts to walk toward her sister.

"Can you be a little more quiet out here, we're not sure if there is any more Germans around." Karl said in a low tone.

"I believe that there are more Germans out here than we know." Anna said as she leads her sister back to the cave.

"Are we staying?" Hilda asks.

"Long enough for us to take the ammo that we need." Anna said as she walks toward the cave where Otto was sitting on his cot with his face cupped in his hands.

"We had a good battle. " said Hilda as she and Anna walk in.

"We had a great battle" Otto said as he looks up with a smile. "You two fraulein did more for us then we could had asked for, please join us." Otto begged.

"Come with me." Anna said as she grabs Hilda's hand. Anna leads Hilda in to the back behind the blanket.

Look at all of the boxes of ammo." Hilda said as she walks past the Nazi uniforms and to the well-stocked wooden boxes of ammo and military equipment. "Look behind you." Anna said as she lifts up one of the German soldier's uniform sleeves.

"They are German soldiers?" Hilda says with her eyes wide open.

"I can explain." Otto said as he walks up to the blanket and looks in. Anna grabs a hand grenade from an open box.

"Stay where you are, or we all will die." Anna said as she raises the grenade up toward Otto and places her finger inside of the pulling ring.

"Wait, wait that will go off." Otto begged.

"We are here to kill Nazis and that's what I will do, even if we die with you." Anna said as she tightens her grip on the grenade.

"Please let me explain. We are not Nazis, please trust me." Otto said fearing for his life. "This is a trick taught to us by a Great War hero." Otto said referring to Marc.

"We wear these uniforms then we mix in with the Nazis and we take them down, we win more battles that way." Otto said as he walks over to the German uniform and looks at them.

"If we were a part of the German army then we wouldn't have killed all of the Nazi soldiers at the troop trucks." Otto continues as both Anna and Hilda look at one another.

"Can we trust him?" Hilda asks as Anna stares at Otto.

"I'm not sure." Anna said as she continues to stare at Otto.

"I like to think that you have saved us and we have saved you that makes us even, now if we work together then we can make a bigger different together." Otto said as the rest of the men enter the cave. Anna walks in the middle of the cave still holding the grenade.

"Why is she holding that grenade?" Ask a worried Karl.

"She thinks that we are working with the Nazis." said Otto as he follows Anna to the middle of the cave.

"We need some of those ammo belts." Anna said as she sees all of the men wearing several ammo belts around them.

"Anna I think that we should stay." Hilda said as she walks up behind Anna.

"We make a great team." said Otto as he places his arms around Anna who quickly moves her shoulder away keeping Otto's arm off.

"If we stay we will not cook your meals, wash your cloths, or have your babies." Anna said with anger.

"Well, we all take turns cooking, we all take care of our own cloths and I would be too afraid for you to have my baby, we are soldiers and so are you two frauleins." Otto said hoping to convince the two girls to join them.

"Well, I sleep with a knife in my hand." Anna said as she looks around at the men.

"I've seen what you two fraulein can do, believe me you will be safe." Karl said waving his outstretched hands.

"Come on Anna, we can trust them." Hilda said as she places her arm on Anna's shoulder.

"Ok, we'll join." The men cheer as Anna looks over to her sister. "We've been fighting by our self for a long time now." Anna said to her sister.

"We took a lot of chances; this time we'll have men to back us up." Hilda said with a smile." Anna looks at her sister.

"When we find Papa, we're going with him." Anna said as she looks over toward Otto. Hilda nods her head agreeing.

"Now, we must clean up our area, Karl you and Franz gather up the dead soldiers and bury them, the rest of us will go out to the trucks and gather up the dead soldiers from there."

"Maybe we should bring one truck here to the cave." said Anna as she looks through the woods making sure that there is room enough for the truck to be driven in.

"What do we need a truck for?" Otto asks giving Anna a

strange look.

"If we had a truck here we can cover it up with trees limbs and dead trees, it will be cover from the plans with the thick trees around us. And we can place all of the weapons and ammo from the soldiers, we need a truck, trust me." Anna said looking for a good area to keep the truck. Anna and Hilda grab their machine guns and started walking. Then they turn around waiting for the men to follow. Franz walks up to Otto.

'Who does that remind you of?" Otto smiles.

"The General." said both men at the same time.

"Well the General did save us in many battles." said Otto as he reaches for his machine gun.

"Yea but they are fraulein; do we take orders from fraulein?" Franz asks as he grabs his rifle and follows Otto. As they walk to the trucks they are careful to make sure that there was no German outfit already there. They crept around making sure that the coast was clear.

"Keep an eye on the main road for any German soldiers." Otto tells his men. Then Otto looks over the three German trucks. Each truck had a 50 caliber machine gun on them. Otto smiles at their fine. "This may just work out." Otto whisper to himself.

'Take the first truck, place all of the weapons and ammo in the back of the truck, take the 50 calibers form the other trucks and put them in the back of the first truck." Otto orders.

"What should we do with the other trucks? Erich ask.

"Drive them over to the burnt trucks and we'll destroy them." Anna said pointing across the way.

Erich looks over toward Otto. 'Are we going to take orders from a fraulein?"

"If we leave these trucks here the Nazis will be coming in here, if we take the trucks over there then they will be looking over there." Anna said and Otto agrees.

"And what about the dead soldiers?" Erich said as he looks around at all of the dead German bodies.

"Place them in the back of one of the trucks, Bodies will also burn." Anna said as she walks over to a dead soldier and grabs his ammo belt. Erich gives Otto a strange look.

"Do as she said." said Otto as he jumps on the second

truck and pull off the 50 caliber. Hilda climbs up on the third truck and also takes the 50 caliber. But the heavy machine gun is too much for the young girl and she has problems carrying the large oversized gun. "Leave it on the back of the truck and I'll grab it." Otto said with a smile knowing that at least the fraulein knows how to work.

"There are a lot of bullets for the 50 caliber back here." Hilda said as she pushes the crate of bullets to the back of the truck. With the first truck filled with the dead soldier's weapons and the two 50 calibers and the crates of bullets Otto smiles as he sees the first truck loaded down with useful material. As the second and third troop trucks were filled with the dead bodies of the Nazi soldiers.

Anna motions over toward the other side of the field. "We should take these bodies over there with the dead bodies from yesterday's battle. Hilda and I will gather up all of the left over weapons and ammo and place it in the back of the trucks and exploded the other trucks." Anna said as Otto looks over to the burnt out German trucks.

"Follow us." Anna said as Erich and Otto stood there stunned at the answer from Hilda. Otto got into the first trucks as Erich got inside of the third truck and the two men follow the fraulein over across the fields to the burnt out trucks. She motions Erich to pull up behind her as Hilda motion for Otto to back up his truck up close to the last truck. Then Anna and Hilda open up the fuel cap on the tank. As they look at one another then Anna looks over toward Otto who was waiting for them. Anna nods, Anna and Hilda pulls the pins of the grenade and drops them in and ran to the awaiting truck. With his outstretched hand Erich reaches down and pulls Anna onto the back of the truck than Erich reaches over and pulls Hilda up in the truck, all of this while Otto was driving down the road. With the girls now on board Otto shifts gears and picks up speed getting away from the trucks.

At the same time the two trucks explode. The petrol inside of the tank made a fire ball that reached up into the shy. Otto looks back in his rear view mirror and sees the fire ball. "Who are we working with?" Otto asks himself. Erich and the girls duck their head from the heat wave from the burning trucks. Otto quickly drives into the woods where he and his men have their cave.

"What are you doing, slow down?" Erich yells as he holds on for dear life.

At the cave Franz and Karl hears the approaching truck.

"Is that a truck?" Karl asks as he grabs his rifle from a nearby stump and leans against a tree and takes aim. As Franz grabs the 50 caliber and points it toward the road where the speeding truck was coming from.

"How many bullets do you have for the 50 caliber?" Karl asks as places a clip into his rifle and takes aim. Then the truck started blowing its horn and flashes its headlights. Confused Karl and Franz still took aim at the approaching truck and with their finger on the trigger.

Both men ready themselves to defend their cave. Before he pulls the trigger Karl notices Otto sticking his head out of the window.

"Hold you fire." Karl said as he and Franz stepped back pulling their weapons down. Otto drives up and jumps out of the cab of the truck.

"Well, what do you think?" Karl walks back to the rear of the truck and helps Anna and Hilda down from the truck.

"What do you mean, Otto you stole a German truck, don't you think that they will want it back?" Franz asks as he shakes his head.

"They will want it back but they will have a hard time getting it back." Hilda said as she walks up to the front of the truck. Erich stood in the bed of the truck.

"If they want it back it will take a lot of them to get it back, we have more machine guns than they do." Erich said as he looks around the bed of the truck. "We have more ammo than most ammo stations, there are pistols, hand grenades, two 50 caliber machine guns and all of the 50 calibers bullets we will need for the rest of the war." Erich said with pride.

Both Karl and Franz look at each other. "There will be a big battle ahead of us won't there?" Karl asks with a frown.

Without saying a word Otto nods. "This is why we are here, to fight the Nazis "Hilda said showing no fear in her voice.

"Are you sure that there will be a big battle, maybe the

Nazis think that the men finished us off and are returning back to their base." Karl said hoping that it could be true.

"And when they didn't show up their Officers thought that they were fighting in another battle." Franz said adding to Karl's thoughts.

Otto shook his head and walks over to the door and reaches in and pulls out a radio microphone. "There is a radio mounted inside of the truck. The German army knows that we won that battle and they will be coming here." Otto said in a low voice. "This time we will be ready for them." Anna said as she reaches up and pulls out an ammo belt from the open side panel in the bed of the truck. "We need to prepare for battle." Erich said as now he realizes that this could be his final days.

Otto looks over to Anna. Neither knew what to do.

What would the General do?" Ask Karl as both Anna and Hilda looks at one another.

"Who is this General?" Anna asks.

"The General led us in many battles and all of us came back." said Franz.

"Where is he at?" Hilda asks. Karl pointed over to the side of the cave.

"We buried him over there." Anna steps away from the group and looks over toward the area then she smiles.

I know what the General would do. First fill the cab of the truck up with dirt, add another 50 caliber to the top of the truck. Then place the other 50 caliber out in the woods, the bullets for the 50 caliber will be with the 50 caliber, if you run out of bullets then have a machine gun beside of you." Anna said as she walks around the truck. "Place heavy rocks around the sides of the bed of the truck so they can't shoot in the bed of the truck. Place all of the ammo that you have in the back of the cave inside the bed of the truck."

"Yea the truck will be home base." Otto added.

"They may try to surround us so we must protect the rear of the truck by having two are three of us scatter behind the truck. Just make sure that you have enough ammo around you they can't get to us from the rear we have to make sure of that. And make sure that all of us have enough hand grenades with us, are there any questions?" All of the men tried to catch up to what Anna was saying.

Karl raises his hand. "Why do we fill the cab of the truck up with dirt?" said Karl as Erich nods in agreement.

"They will be shooting at the 50 calibers if the 50 calibers are on the roof of the truck then they will be shooting inside of the cab, the dirt is there to stop the bullets." Otto said as he rubs his chin and smiles. "That is what the General would do." said Otto as he nods.

"We will need an evacuation plan." Hilda said as she looks around.

"Fraulein, if I may, Erich mount a 50 caliber onto of the roof and make sure that the bullets for them will be where we can get to them, then place the other 50 caliber over in the woods make sure that it is well hidden with enough bullets for it, Franz you and Karl go out and dig up the dirt for the cab but leave the microphone free so we can listen in to where they are at." Otto orders.

"Digs holes not trenches." said Anna as she points in three directions.

"Why holes?" Ask Franz.

"A trench will give them cover from us; a hole that is covered up with leaves can break their foot making them an easy target." Anna said as Otto nods his head.

"Anna, what should I do?" Hilda asks as she notices that all of the men had their orders.

"Go in the back of the cave and bring out all of the ammo and place it onto the back of the truck." Anna said as Hilda nods and started walking toward the cave.

"Anna you and I will look for our evacuation route." Otto said as he tugs on Anna's arm. Anna looks over to Otto and smile.

"It depends on how many soldiers the Nazis are sending here, but I like our chances." Anna said with a smile.

"We will need an evacuation route." Otto said with worry in his eyes. As Otto and Anna walk the path up to the Leer's house they pass the graves of their fallen. Otto stops at Marc's grave. "This is the General we owe him our lives." Said Otto as he and Anna looks at his grave.

"What was his real name?" Anna asks as she kneels

down and picks a flower out of the ground and lays it on top of his grave.

"We never knew, he wouldn't tell us so we call him General, He was a great man." Otto said with a tear in his eyes.

"That sounds like my Papa, he's a great man, and I wish that I knew where he was." Anna said as she also has a tear in her eye.

"Well we need to continue walking." said Otto as he started walking he looks over at Marc's graves. "Over there is Herr Leer's house, that's where I found the General dead. The Leer's were working with us but they were also working for the Nazis. We found out about it and the General confronted them, he didn't see the Nazis who were there for the same reason."

The Nazis killed the Leers and the General killed the Nazis, but before one of them died they killed the General, both sides lost that day." Otto said as he and Anna walked to the Leer's house. "Inside of the house is a hidden cellar that is where the Leer's hide us from the Nazis." Otto said as he pointed toward the house.

"If we go in there they can surround us." Anna said as she stared at the place where her father had died. "But they won't know that we are there, we should place some machine guns over there where we can get to them if we are being chase." Otto said pointing into the woods in front of the Leer's house. Anna agrees by nodding as she still stares at the ground where her father was killed. "What are you looking at?" Otto said with a grin. Anna shakes her head.

"I'm not sure but, I'm not sure." Anna said as she looks over to the edge of the woods where Otto wanted to stash some extra machine guns. "If the Nazis come from this road then the extra weapons will be lost to us." Anna said as she looks over to the edge of the woods and then back to the spot.

"They won't, it will take them more time to get here than it would be from the direction that we came from." Otto said hoping that Anna would agree.

Anna looks up at Otto and slowly nods her head. "Then we must place weapons and ammo in the woods."

Otto smiles as he points. "About three hundred yards past the trees is a town where they will protect us from the Nazis, if we can make it there then we'll be safe." Otto said with a smile. Anna we can beat the Nazis." Otto said with a smile.

Anna looks up at him and shakes her head. "No but we can slow them down." Anna said as she turns around and started walking back to the cave looking down at the spot as she walks. As Otto and Anna walk back to the cave Karl finished putting the last shovel full of dirt into the cab of the truck. "Where is Franz?" Otto asks as he and Anna walk up to the truck.

"Franz is placing leaves over the holes like you wanted, or what we call foot holes because if you step in them they you'll break a foot." Karl Laughs. "Did you leave room for the microphone?' Otto asks as he looks at the dirt fill cab. Karl reaches in and pulls the microphone out. "We left room around the radio so the dirt won't hurt the radio." Karl proudly said. Franz walks up covered with sweat and dirt.

They will have a hard time getting to us." said a smiling Franz.

"Where is Hilda?" Anna asks as she looks around.

"She is helping Erich with the 50 caliber, they went over there." Karl said pointing into the woods. At that time Hilda and Erich walks up.

"Well, all of the ammos from the cave is in the back of the truck and the third 50 caliber is stashed away in the woods." Hilda said with a smile.

"Ammo for the 50 caliber?" Ask Otto.

"There is a case, we have a case of 50 caliber bullets for each machine gun." said Erich as he motions into the bed of the truck.

"What now?" Karl asks as he finishes his assignment.

"We might as well have supper." said Otto as he looks at his pocket watch. "Erich stay by the cave's entrance make sure that you can listen in on the radio and keep an eye on the woods, make sure that we are left alone." Otto continues.

"We need to make plans for the battle." Anna said as she walks along side of Otto.

"Let's eat first." Otto said with a grin.

"Well what are we having?" Hilda asks as she looks over toward Franz.

"Whatever the Nazis left us." Replies Franz. Karl walks

over to the captured German portable stove and starts cooking.

"Karl was a chef in Berlin before the war." Otto said bragging on his friend.

"Yea but he ate all of the food by himself." Laughs Franz who sat down beside of Hilda.

"My customer's ate more than I did." Karl said with a smile defending himself.

"When do you think that they will hit us?" Karl asks in a serious tone.

"If they hit us then it will be sometime tomorrow afternoon. First they must wait to see what time that the soldiers should be returning. Then they will try to figure out where the soldiers were at on the last call in, then they will check the map to see what was around them, were they in Ally held territory. It may be a day or two, that's gives us plenty of time to prepare if they come at all." Otto said giving his men a little hope.

"We may have prepared for nothing." Anna added. Otto smiles as Karl brings in the hot dish.

"The best that the Nazis can provide." Karl said as he hands plates out to the rest of the Resistance fighters.

"I'll take Erich his meal." Karl said as he walks away from the group.

"I would still like to know about your plan." Anna said before she ate her meal.

Otto takes a bite of food and shows his enjoyment. "If the Nazis do attack then we will handle the guns and you two fraulein will go to the Leer's house and wait for us if we don't come then you can handle the Nazis with the weapons that we had left for you." Otto said knowing that there will be an argument.

"We can fight as good if not better than any of your men." Hilda said as she looks over toward Anna who drops her spoon inside of her prepared meal.

"If we are in the way then we will leave." Anna said in anger.

"That's not what I 'm saying, it's just we have fought together and we know what to do and when to do it." Otto said hoping to keep peace.

"And you don't think that we do?" Anna said getting

madder.

"I think that I'm going to relieve Erich." Franz said as he places his plate off to the side.

"I'll go with you." Hilda said hoping that Anna wouldn't be so defenses. As Hilda walks out of the cave she sees Franz and Erich talking. As Erich see Hilda he walks past her and into the cave.

"If we are in the way then we'll leave." said Hilda as she walks up to Franz.

"Otto didn't mean it the way that it sounds, trust me I've known Otto for a long time now. All of us have seen you fraulein fight and all of us know that when the battle starts we want to be on your side." Franz said as he tries to look through the dark woods. "If the Nazis hit us tomorrow then they will hit us from all sides, you and your sister can maintain the roads up at Herr Leer house." Franz says as he glances over toward Hilda.

"My sister and I have been fighting for a long time now and we have been on our own, neither one of us could tell you where we are right now or how far we are from home." Hilda said as she glances around into the dark woods.

"Why are you fighting?" Franz asks as Hilda looks up to him.

"I'm not sure anymore, revenge for our mother's murder, or we're just looking for our father." Hilda said as she looks at the truck making sure that the radio microphone is free from the dirt that they filled the cab of the truck with.

"Where is your home?" Hilda thinks for a second.

"Where ever Papa is." answer Hilda.

"Where is your home?" ask Hilda trying to change the subject.

"Right here and inside of the cave is my family and now I can say that my family grew.

"Oh come on now you don't have a wife or kids?" Hilda asks with a smile.

"Not anymore." Answer Franz. "What about you?"

"I had a boyfriend his name is Von but he's in the German Army, He's guarding our town from the Allies." Hilda said as she looks away. Anna walks up and sees the two of them talking. Anna smiles at the way that Hilda had opened up. With both hands placed around her coffee cup Anna takes another drink as she walks away.

"You need to get some rest; tomorrow might be a long day for you." Franz said as he notices that it was getting later. Hilda smiles and starts to walk away then she turns back and gives Franz a little kiss in his check as she walks into the cave.

In the morning Hilda awoke and saw that no one was in their cot "Where is everyone?" Hilda asks herself. "Anna" Hilda quickly calls out as she slowly gets out of her cot. Hilda then grabs her machine gun and walks outside. Where she sees all of the Resistance fighters standing beside the truck where the microphone was listening in. "What is going on?" Hilda said as she walks up relieved that they all were still there.

Karl places his finger up to his mouth. "We are listening in." Karl said as he turns his attention back to the radio.

"They're calling out trying to locate this truck." Anna said,

"The Nazis should be getting a search team up." Otto said as he glances over to Hilda. Then from above they hear the sounds of a plane flying by. "That's the search team." Otto said as he looks up.

Then the sounds of bombing are heard from the other side of the woods. "Do they know where we are?" Otto said as he looks up into the thick trees that cover them from the planes.

"If they don't know where we are at, then they will be bombing over here next." Anna yells as she grabs Hilda and moves toward the entrance of the cave.

"What are you talking about?" Erich said as he laughs. Then the sounds of bombing are heard close by as the sounds start getting closer.

"Everyone back in the cave." Otto yells as he pushes Karl, this blast is close to the truck.

All of the Resistance fighters enter the cave and look out. "Get away from the entrance." Anna yells as Franz and Erich start to run deeper into the cave as a bomb blast enters the cave. Anna looks over to her sister as they lay on the ground with the rest of the fighters. Safe from the bombing. Minutes later the attack was over.

"Is it over with?" Ask Erich.

"I think so." Otto said as he sits up from the floor of the cave. Otto walks over and looks out- side.

"How close was it?" Anna asks as she stands up and walks over to Otto.

The truck is safe but they know about where we are and they will be coming." Otto added.

"What should we do?" Franz asks as he walks up to Otto and Anna.

Otto looks over to his men as though he was looking at them for the last time. "We must get in place." Otto said as he looks over toward Anna.

"I don't want to fight but---'We'll go up to the back road and make sure that none of the Nazis can sneak up the road and attack from the rear." Anna said giving Otto a deep smile.

As the Resistance fighters gets in position Anna and Hilda walk up to the road and passed the house where their father was killed. "Something happened here but I just can't think of what." Anna said as she and Hilda reach the spot.

"I know; I feel it too." said Hilda as she looks around.

Otto and Karl jump up to the truck to man the 50 caliber as Franz runs out into the woods where the third 50 caliber was hidden. Erich grabs a bag of hand grenades and his machine gun and runs into the woods next to Franz as the Resistance fighters wait. Before long the sounds of troop trucks are heard from a distance. "They are checking out the burnt truck on the other side of the fields. Then the troop truck is heard moving toward them. "They want pull the trucks into the narrow road so they will let the men out." Otto yells. The sound of the trucks are getting louder. As the men dismount from the troop trucks the German soldier that stands at the top of each of the troop truck sprays the woods with their 50 caliber machine guns. As the bullets from the 50 caliber fly across the woods, some miss the trees and fly in all directions, hitting the truck where Otto and Karl were waiting. The bullets ricochet off of the truck and hit the nearby trees. "Get ready Otto yells to his men. Then a deadly quite is heard.

"What are they doing?" Karl asks as he points his 50 caliber from side to side. "The Soldiers are coming in." Otto said as he rechecks his 50 caliber. Otto and Karl wait as crunching of dead leaves is heard as the Nazi moves in.

"Wait till you see them." Otto whispers. From the nearby area Franz and Erich are the first to see the Nazis and they started firing, killing the first wave of German soldiers. Then from all directions the German soldiers started shooting. Otto and Karl join in. The air filled with the smell of the 50 caliber as each bullet was fired. Erich would pull the pin on the grenade and toss them at the approaching German soldiers. Anna and Hilda look at one another with fear in their eyes.

As the Germans get in position they make better shots now that they know where the Resistance fighters are located. A bullet bounces off of the truck where Otto and Karl are standing and shooting their 50 caliber. Bullets are busting through the glass of the windshield imbedded into the dirt that filled the cab saving Otto and Karl from being hit in the lower part of their bodies. The three 50 calibers were too much of a match for the German armies and their mostly bolt action rifles. As the blast from each of the three 50 caliber machine guns that Otto, Karl and Franz fired dozens of German soldiers fall to the ground dead.

Seeing this, a German Officer orders his men to go back to the trucks. None of the Resistance fighter notice the retreating soldiers, as they maintain their steady firing. "There is a road that will take us to the other side of the woods, take us there." orders the Officer to his driver. The troops fill the trucks and take the longer but safer route to the other side of the woods and toward the Leer's old house where Anna and Hilda hear the roaring trucks, run and take position for shooting the trucks.

"Here they come." Anna yells to her sister pushing her into thick hedges across from the Leer's house.

The trucks pull up in front where Anna and Hilda wait. The two fraulein waited as the Officer steps out of the truck and looks through his binoculars at a spot where he and his men could enter the back of the woods and sneak attack Otto and his men.

"We will go in through that section." yells the Officer and he points to his driver. Then the Officer orders his men out of the back of the truck.

"Get ready." Anna whispers to her sister. Hilda grabs a grenade and readies herself for the right time to pull the pin and toss into the group of German soldiers. All of the soldiers exit from the trucks and stand, waiting for their orders. Anna took a deep breath as she stood up and with her machine gun Anna shot and killed the Officer and his driver. Hilda pulls the pin and tosses the grenade at the feet of the Nazis. The blast killed most of the soldiers as Anna shot the rest. "We must move the truck." Anna yells as she hands Hilda and her machine gun and jumps into the cab of the truck as she had done before with her father's old truck Anna had trouble with the gears but she was able to move the truck out of sight in case Otto and his men had to run to the designated area. With the truck parked Anna ran back to the hedges where Hilda was waiting for her. The two frauleins waited as they heard the sounds of the fighting in the woods. With most of the German soldiers laying on the ground dead. Otto sticks up his hand. Karl was the first to stop shooting then Franz stops. "What is it?" Ask Karl.

"Listen." Replied Otto as the sounds of tanks roar their way. "Tanks." Otto yells as he and Karl jumps off of the truck.

"What about Franz and Erich?" Karl asks as Otto pulls him away.

"Go to the fraulein I'll get Franz and Erich." Otto said as he runs in Franz direction. Before Otto could move Franz and Erich run up to them.

"There are tanks heading this way." Franz yells as he runs past Otto. And toward the fraulein.

Seeing the men run out of the woods Anna and Hilda stand up and wave the men toward them. Halfway through the woods several German soldiers' run to the edge of the woods and kneeling down they take aim at Otto and his men. "Wait here." yells Anna as she runs over to the truck and drives it up. Hilda runs to the side of the road where Otto and his men could see her. As Anna climbs into the cage that held the 50 caliber Hilda motions for Otto and his men to run to the side and out of the German's aim. Anna pulls back the hammer of the 50 and took aim. "Get out of the way." Anna yells as the German doubles it numbers at the edge. Otto see Hilda motioning them to move in a different direction and yells for his men to do so as Anna pulls the trigger and with a left to right motion dust and dirt hits in front of the remaining German soldiers killing them. Otto and his men reach the truck as Anna finishes firing. As they reach the trucks four tanks roll out of the woods and with their cannon pointing toward the Resistance fighters.

"What are the chances that they are the tanks that we sabotaged?" Erich ask as they stare at the tanks. Inside of the tank the gunner loads the cannon and closes the hatch to the barrel and yells fire. First the barrel of the cannon on the tank lights up and explodes as the rest of the tank exploded. Then one by one all of the remaining tanks exploded. All of the Resistance fighters rejoice with their victory from the day when they work with Vito and his soldiers. Otto looks around him then gives the fraulein a confused look. Otto and his men look down and see the dead German soldiers. Then Otto looks back at the woods where he sees the dead German soldiers. Then Otto looks over toward Anna.

"Been busy." Otto said with a smile as Anna climbs out of the cage and sits at the driver side of the truck.

"Yea, you can say that we've been cleaning all morning." Anna said as the men laugh.

Then the sound of a plane is heard. Otto grabs Anna and pulls her out of the truck as the plane nears. The line of bullets hits the ground approaching the truck as Otto pulls Anna to safety. As the plane passes, the truck is destroyed with several bullets holes filling the truck, The German plane gains altitude and swings around for the second attack as two Americans P-32 fly up and chase the German plane away, as the Resistance fighter's cheer. Seconds later the German plane is hit as the plane's engine starts smoking then exploded in mid-air. "The Americans chased them away." Otto yells as he celebrates by waving his machine gun in the air and waving at the disappearing Americans planes. Then the Resistance fighters notice the bullet riddled truck.

"Looks like we are walking." Karl said as he stares at the now burning troop truck.

"There is a town a few miles down the road, they will

feed us and put us up for the night." Otto said as he looks around at the victory that they all had shared.

Chapter Nineteen

A few days later, in Berlin, Von is ordered to Captain Heinbaker's office. Von still is not fully recover from his wounds is order to investigate the battle. "We think that it was the Allies due to the magnitude of the slaughter of the forty men and the loss of four tanks, but Leer and his wife were working with us and with the Resistance fighters so we're not sure who was responsible for the murders of German top soldiers and the destruction of the great war machine of the Third Reich." said Captain Heinbaker as he points to a map that is laid out on the table next to his desk.

"I know this is the area where I was wounded on this side road." Von said as he steps closer to the map.

"That's right, right about here is where the Leer's lived they was working for us and at the same time they were helping the Resistance fighters." said the Captain as Von looks up at him. "We knew what the Leer's was doing, and it benefits us for them to be working with some man name Otto. We learn where most of the battles would be that the Ally were planning, The Leer's were very helpful to us, but now they are dead, I ask for prisoners. If you had brought them in, then we would have told you about them but they are dead and you took the blame." said the Captain as he starred strait into Von's eyes.

"I take full responsibility for the death of Herr Leer and his wife." Von said with sadness.

"Well this is the time for you to regain our trust in you, go out and investigate the battle and report back here, I want to know if the Allies are behind this or was it the treason act of the Resistance fighters. And I want this Otto and his men standing in front of my desk when you come back if this was the act of treason." said the Captain as Von stood up straight, clicked his heels together and raised his right hand in the air.

"Heil Hitler." Von said as he nods and leaves the Captain's Office.

Von gathers his men up and stretches out his map over the hood of his troop truck. Von points to the driver where he wanted to go and the driver nods as the men climb into the rear of the truck. Von and his men pull up to the entrance of the woods where he sees the burnt troop trucks." This is the work of the Allies." Von told himself. Then Von motions for the driver to drive across the field to the next set of woods.

The entrance to the woods is wider than the Tiger tanks. Von motions for his driver to follow the tank's track. The drive takes them deeper into the woods where dead German soldiers litter the surrounding area. As they drive, the driver hit a bump in the road. Von looks over toward his driver. "That was a stump." said the driver with fear in his eyes.

"It better had been." Von said in a treating tone. "Look at all of these dead heroes." Von said as he looks out of the window at the dead soldiers.

As the truck moves slowly down the trail that the tank tracks had made Von notices the troop truck that Otto and Karl used. "Stop up there at that truck." Von said pointing at the now flattened truck that was in the way of the four Tiger tanks.

The driver pulls up in front of the flattened truck. Von gets out of his truck as did his men. "Check the area." Von says as he walks up to the truck and see the remains of the two 50 calibers. Then Von glances over and sees the entrance of the cave. Von pulls out his pistol and enters the cave. Von shakes his head as he sees where the Resistance fighters lived. The cots, the small cooking area and as Von walks in the back, he saw where they stored their ammo, then Von notices the Nazi uniform hanging up. "Those cowards." Von said as he grabs a uniform and throws it onto the ground. Von walks back through the cave where he is met by some of his men. "I want every Resistance fighter found and brought to me, I will hang them myself." Von said as he kicks over a couple of cots and walks out of the cave. Von stands at the entrance of the cave and looks around where he sees the three graves. Von walks over to the graves and looks at the names. "These are the names of traitors." Von said. Then Von sees the headstone that reads General." Von pays closer attention to this grave.

"This must be the grave of their leader." Von said as he kicks the small headstone down. Von then notices the four destroyed tanks.

There was a report of two enemy planes flying by this

morning they must have knocked out our Tigers tanks." Von told one of his soldiers as he walks up to Von.

"Let's check out that house." Von said pointing up toward the Leer's house. All of the soldiers with rifles in hand follow Von to the Leer's house where Von sees the next troop truck. "Their planes were here." Von said pointing at the bullets holes that filled the truck. Then Von looks down where he shot the Resistance fighter who he thought was Herr Metz. Von stared at the spot where he shot the fighter.

"Excuse me sir." said one of Von's men. "There is a town about five miles down this road; we may find the soldiers down there." Von looks at the road then he looks over to his soldiers.

"They are not soldiers; they are the specks of dust under my boots." said Von arrogantly. "We will go to that town those who harbor these rats will pay with their lives." Von said of the town's people. The Resistance fighters knew that there was going to be a bigger battle ahead of them Otto posted guards at a ridge where the guard could see all roads that were around them. Otto knew that he and his men could never return back to the cave for the Germans now knew where they were hiding. Now the Resistance must live out in the open. The ridge is too narrow for all of the fighters to stay but down a small trail from the ridge is a flat area of land surrounded by thick trees where they won't be seen from above. The ground is cold in the morning where the fighters must now sleep as all of the cots are back at the cave, and the blankets that they use are from the nearby town where the towns people helped as much as they could. They fear of the Nazis finding out that they were supplying the Resistance fighters with food and aid will be their death sentences. The nights are cold as the fighter's try to stay warm but winter is coming and now all of their comforts were a few miles away in the cave.

One morning at daylight Erich is awoken by a small animal trying to get warm by climbing inside of his blanket that he had wrapped around him. Erich screams out as he jumps from his make shift sleeping bag. All of the fighters jump up and without thinking they grab their rifles and machine guns.

Thinking that the Nazis had found them and were in

their camp with the way that Erich had screamed. "What is it did you have a bad dream?" Anna asks, as she is relieved that there were no Nazis around. "Something bit me." said Erich as he waves his cover in the morning air. As Erich shook his blanket a small animal falls out and runs into the woods.

"What was that, a field mouse?" Karl laughs.

"I think that it was a chipmunk." laughs Otto as he places his machine gun against a tree then sits on top of his blanket.

"I am sick of living in the woods like this." yells Erich as he throws his blanket into the woods. "We live like animals out here." Erich continues. "I'm going back to the cave and get a good night sleep." Erich said as he walks toward the path next to Otto.

"We can't go back to the cave, by now the Nazis know about it, we're safer out here." Otto said as he stands up and stops Erich.

"We live like the animals and that is what they're calling us." Erich said as he tries to walk past Otto. "If you go back there the Nazis will find you and they will make you talk and all of us will be in front of firing squads." Otto said as he grabs Erich and holds him tight.

"Who was that American Sergeant that we liked, maybe he can help us get to the United States or even England." Karl suggested.

"We don't know where they are at. Besides I'm sure that they would like to go to the United States or England, why should they help us?" Otto yells out. "Besides we are fighters and that is what we will do, fight till the last Nazis soldiers is dead are the war ends, we can win this war. But we must stay strong and fight together that will win the war for us." Otto pleads with Erich and the rest of his men.

"It doesn't matter, it's morning we need to look for berries for breakfast." Hilda said as she uncovers herself and stands up to stretch.

"We need to check out the cave, maybe the Nazis over looked it." Karl said as Erich calms down "We'll go to the Leer's house first." Otto said trying to keep the peace. All of the fighters agree. "Karl go and relieve Franz from the ridge." Otto orders. Karl grabs his rifle and does as Otto said. "It's warmer on that ridge anyway." The Fighters walks past Franz who was overlooking the open fields from the ridge.

"I'm here to relieve you." Karl said as he takes over for Franz who was ready for the break and smiles as he shakes Erich's hand.

"Any action last night?" Otto asks as Franz stretch.

"Nine (no) it was quiet last night." Franz said as he grabs his rifle and starts down to the new camp.

"Well let's check out our old home." Anna said as she and the rest of the group head toward the Leer's house. The Resistance fighters watch their every step and they move closer to the house. Karl took the binoculars that Franz had given him and checks out the area in front of the fighters. Otto turns and looks up toward the ridge. Karl would give him the thumbs up, as there were no hidden Nazis waiting for them. The Resistance Fighters were cautious with every step they made. "Look up in the tree tops for snipers." Otto warns his fighters. What would have taken an hour for the men to reach the house took longer as the fighters knew that now the Nazis had seen their hideout. Hilda looks up at the house.

"They had been here." Hilda said as she stops walking.

"What do you mean?" Ask Karl as he to stop.

"Where is the truck we used to shoot the Nazis at the base of the tree line?" Hilda said looking around.

"And there were bodies of German soldiers around the truck." said Anna as she grips her machine gun tight.

"The Nazis was here, they removed the truck and the bodies." Otto said as he gives the old Leer's house a hard look. "Let's move to the house." Otto said as he slowly moves toward the house. As the Resistance Fighters approach the house with caution by bending over and making a fast run, as they watch all of the windows to see if there were Nazis hidden inside of the house.

As all of the fighters reach the house. Otto stood next to the front door. "We'll go in with caution." Otto said as he peers in the open front door. Seeing that the front room was clear Otto slowly enters the room as his men follow.

"I have a bad felling about this." Hilda said as she enters the room and looks around.

"The Nazis has been here." Karl said as he walks over

to the bedroom off of the living room and pears in.

"Check for bugs." Otto said as he slowly walks into the kitchen. Anna follows Otto into the kitchen.

"What are bugs?" Anna asks as she cautiously moves in the room.

"The Nazis might have placed microphones around the room in case if we came back here, they can listen to our conversation." Otto whispers as he walks to the back door and looks out toward the woods close to their cave. Anna walks up as they pull out their binoculars and look closer to the trees.

"When you were in the troop truck and shooting the Nazis with the 50 caliber how many men did you killed?" Otto asks as he scans the edge of the woods.

"Ten maybe twelve, why?"

'The dead soldiers are gone." Otto said.

"Then the Nazis have been all over the woods." Anna said as she also scans the trees.

"They know about the cave." Otto said as his men enters the kitchen. "How does it look out there?" Hilda asks as she walks up and takes Anna's binoculars. "Check for snipers." Otto said as he and Hilda looks up in the trees.

"There are no bugs in the house." Karl said as he walks over to the window and looks out.

"Be careful, Karl." Anna said as Karl steps away from the window and looks at her.

"If there were snipers out there they will be looking up here, you would be a target my friend." Otto said as he continues to look up in the treetops. As the treetops are clear Otto hands his binocular to Anna and looks around the kitchen.

"Maybe this house can be our new home?" Karl mentions as he looks around, we can go down to the cave and grabs our cots and some food." Karl suggested.

"We need to be very careful if we go down there, The Nazis know that we stayed there and if I was them, I would have a sniper if not a unit down there waiting for us." Otto said as he looks in the cabinets

Otto smiles as he finds a half used bag of corn meal. Otto pours the remaining meal out and onto the counter.

Using his finger Otto draws the area around them as the

rest of the group gathers around. "Hilda stay there at the window and watch the woods." Otto said as he points to where he had drawn the house. "Ok this is where we are; here is the field around us. This is the edge of the woods where our cave is." Otto said as he looks around to each of his men. "If we go in by this direction then we could be going into their trap. But if we go down this road leading us behind the cave and go in through there then we should be covered from the snipers or whatever they have for us." Otto said as Anna looks over the self-made map.

"We still need to be careful because we will be coming in behind them and all they have to do is turn around and see us." Anna said as Otto nods his head agreeing.

"Alright Karl you and Hilda go in and gather up what we need. Ammo, grenades and food." Otto said as he looks over to Karl making sure that he understands. Then looking over to Hilda who was at the back door looking out, she turns and looks over toward Otto and nods. "Anna you and I will watch out for the Nazis." Otto said as Anna also nods.

"What are our chances?" Karl asks as he gives Otto a concern look.

"If there is Nazis down there then I don't like our chances. But, if we are quiet enough then we can get the jump on them." Otto said as he stares at the corn meal map.

"If there is one Nazi then there will be others." Anna said as she also looks over the map.

"I wonder if Franz knows what we are doing, if we are wrong then he will be the remaining fighter." Hilda said as she turns around and looks over to the rest of the fighters.

"Well let's move out." Otto said as he wipes the counter clean.

Chapter Twenty

All of the fighters follow Otto out of the house, they check down the road making sure that the road was clear. Then they move down the road. The thick trees give a spooky scene as the fighters try to find the right spot to enter just behind the cave. "This maybe the spot." Otto said quietly as he looks up to the top of the trees for snipers. The ground made walking loud, with dried up leaves and small branches from the trees.

"Watch your step." Otto whispers. As the fighters move closer to the back of the cave Otto raises his hand stopping the fighters. "Follow the back of the cave." Otto said in a low tone.

"We should take off our shoes." Anna said as she reaches down and pulls off her.

"Why?" Karl asks as he watches her.

"The bottom of our shoes are rough and that is what is causing the loud noise." Anna said as Hilda also reaches down and pulls off her shoes. As all of the fighters follow Anna and Hilda by taking off their shoes and continue their mission to the front of the cave. They reach the front and notice a Nazi guard standing at the entrance of the cave. Otto motions for his men to kneel down as he looks around the surrounding where he sees two Nazi soldiers with a radio. The soldiers are tired and half asleep as was the guard at the cave.

Otto looks up for snipers that could be hiding in the tree tops.

Otto steps closer to the guard. As Otto pulls out his knife he approaches the guard by bringing up his knife and pulling the guard into the cave. The guard never made a sound as Otto pulls the knife across the guard's neck.

Otto gives the cave a slow look around as he motions for Karl and Hilda to come inside. The other two Nazi soldiers never saw Otto or knew that their fellow soldier was dead. Karl and Hilda move in quickly as Otto and Anna step inside of the cave and look out. "The Nazis were here." Otto whispers.

"How can you tell?" Anna asks as she quickly turns her head and looks. Karl and Hilda see all of the cots turned upside down and cut up.

"Hey Otto all of our supplies are gone.

"The Nazis must have taken them." Otto said

The Nazis that were over with the radio, they turn around and notice that the German guard from in front of the cave was gone. 'Hey Sigmore, where are you, are you taking a leak?" laughs the radioman. Otto and Anna pull the body into the cave out of the sight of the German soldiers. Otto looks back into the cave and sees Hilda and Karl throwing some empty boxes around as they look for anything that may be left.

"Let's get out of here." Karl said as he approaches Otto and Anna at the entrance of the cave.

"Stay out of sight." Otto said as he pulls Karl from the entrance as the radioman starts walking toward the cave.

"Let's go Sigmore, how much time does it take you?" At that time three more German soldiers come out of hiding and start walking toward the cave.

"We have to shoot them." said Otto as he slowly raises up his machine gun. "We'll start shooting, Hilda you and Karl start running to the Leer's house." Otto said as he looks out of the cave and sees the radioman walking closer to them.

"Get ready." Anna whisper.

At that time, Otto and Anna step out of the cave and start firing as Hilda and Karl do as they were told. More and more German soldiers popped up as they hear the shooting.

Anna swings around and shoots the unsuspecting soldiers as Karl and Hilda run. As they run toward the back of the woods and the old Leer's house, three more German soldiers pop up as they run. Hilda fires her machine gun killing the German soldiers. More and more German soldiers run toward the cave. Otto and Anna try to run as they shoot. "Spread out." Otto yells as he and Anna reach the edge of the woods. The battle took just a few minutes the Resistance fighters find a good spot outside of the edge of the woods and take aim as the Germans soldier's run up, are shot, and fall dead. "I'm not sure how many more there are, follow the edge to the place where we entered the woods, meet me at the Leer's house." Otto said as he motions his men to move. Hilda and Karl aim their rifle and machine gun toward the woods and follow their orders. Seeing that the coast was clear Otto motions for Anna to follow. Anna gives Otto a worried look.

"I don't want to leave you." Anna said.

"I'm right behind you." Otto said as Anna does as Otto said. Two more German soldiers run up as Otto aims his machine gun. Both fell. "There is more to come." Otto said to himself as he follows the path.

As all four Resistance fighters reach the road they quickly ease their way to Herr Leer's house. From the opposite side of the road, Otto yells, "Hilda you and Karl go back to camp. Anna and I will give you some time."

As Hilda and Karl run back to their camp, Otto and Anna walk to the other side of the road where they see three German soldiers running toward them, in the field. The German soldiers see Otto and Anna and they stop running. With nowhere to go the German soldiers raise their rifles toward them. Otto and Anna pull up their machine guns and pull the triggers. All of the soldiers fall to the ground dead. "Let's go." Otto said as he and Anna kneel down and look through their binoculars making sure that there were no more soldiers to fight. Otto starts to run back as Anna stays there still looking through her binoculars. "Anna lets go." Anna drops her binoculars and follows Otto.

As Karl and Hilda run up the side of the ridge Karl started waving his hands. "Don't shoot, don't shoot." Karl yells as Erich motion for them to run in.

"I wanted to shoot you for yelling." said Erich as he walks over to Karl and Hilda who run up the ridge and collapse.

"I was going to shoot you too." Hilda said as she stands up and looks out to the field.

"Where are Anna and Otto?" Hilda asks as she grabs Erich's binoculars and looks out.

"They should have been behind us." Hilda said as she hands Erich back his binoculars and starts to leave the ridge.

"Here they come." said Erich as he sees the couple running toward them.

"Get ready, there are German soldiers around." Hilda said as she walks up and takes aim toward the woods. As Otto and Anna reach the ridge all four lay on the ground to catch their breath.

"Where is the food?" Erich asks as all four start laughing.

"The Nazis have it, go and ask them for it." Otto said out of breath.

"Erich check the fields." Anna said as she turns over to her side where Hilda was laying. "I think that the cave is off limits for us." Anna said as she looks Hilda over making sure that she wasn't bleeding.

"We won this battle, but there will other battles." Otto said as he catches his breath.

"Yea, but this time we will have to fight on an empty stomach and sleep on the bumpy ground." said Erich as he looks down with sadness.

"We were there, the Nazis took everything, and we have no food or cots and no ammo." Karl said in a defeated voice.

"How much ammo do we have left?" Anna asks as she looks at the clips inside of her belt.

"Should we go back and get the ammo belts from the dead soldiers?" Hilda said as she looks inside of her belt.

"We can't risk it." Otto said as he looks over the ridge making sure that they haven't been followed.

"There was a radioman down there, when the Nazis call he won't answer it and they will be crawling all over this place." Anna said.

"We need to save all of the bullets that we can, we need to adopt the theory of one shot one kill, no more wasting bullets." Otto said as he looks at the others. "For those with machine guns we need to aim in one direction instead of spraying the area with bullets, how many grenades do we have?" Otto asks Hilda who usually carries the most.

"We went from a few to not many." Hilda said as Anna and the rest of the fighters give her a strange look."

"From now on we will only use the grenades when there are three or more soldiers." Otto said in a stern tone.

"If we use more grenades that will help us save bullets, won't it?" Hilda asks as she tries to defend herself.

"Three or more." Otto repeated himself.

"Who knows maybe in the next battle we can restock our

needs." Anna said hoping to get the pressure off of her sister. Otto looks over toward Anna who shrugged her shoulder and smiles.

"Well let's go back and rest, this was a rough morning for us." Otto said as Karl and Hilda walks past him.

"Hey is anyone going to relieve me." Erich asks as Otto and Anna starts walking.

"No stay here longer, we were in a battle, we need to rest." Otto said without turning around. Down the path Otto taps Anna on her shoulder. "Do you really believe that we are going to win the next battle?" Otto asks as Anna continues walking turns around.

"I had to, if I didn't then we will lose and I won't give up that quickly." Anna said as she continues walking.

"Then we will win." Otto said smiling.

As the four reach camp, Franz was standing beside a tree with his rifle aimed and ready. Franz smiles and drops the barrel when he saw who it was. "What happen out there, did we win?" Franz asks in a sarcastic tone.

"Yea, we won this one." Karl said as he walks over to where he was laying and sat down.

"Before we sleep we need to count our ammo, and I need a full count of the grenades." Otto said as he looks over to Hilda.

The radio back at the cave is sounding off. With all of the soldiers dead Von who was on the other end panics. "My men aren't answering me." Von told Captain Heinbaker who walks up to him.

"Are you sure that they aren't on their way back here?" ask the Captain.

"Nine (no) I told them to stay in case the Resistance fighters comes back, now I can't reach them, they must had been in a battle and lost." Von said as he looks up to his Captain. "I need more men." Von said as the Captain gives him a strange look.

"Do you think that it's the Resistance fighters?" said the Captain as he studies the map on his desk.

"I know this area, it's filled with the Resistance, let me end them now." Von pleads.

Captain Heinbaker looks over the map again. "Berlin has a report saying that the Allies will be attacking Frankfurt."

"When?"

"On the twenty-third, your men will be used as the second or third wave." said the Captain as Von looks over on the Captain's desk.

"This is the eighteenth I will go and destroy the Resistance fighter in one day then we'll be back, just give me one day." Von pleads. The Captain gives Von a long look. "Sir, I will personally guarantee that all of my soldiers that I will take out will return." Von said begging.

The Captain nods. "They will need to be back in two days." said the Captain as he reluctantly agrees.

Von slams his fist onto the table in joy. "We will bury each and every one of the Resistance fighters." Von proclaims.

"Nine (no) I want them here so we can take them to Berlin for hanging." Insisted the Captain.

"Sir the Resistance fighters killed the best soldiers that Germany has ever known. Give me the honor of killing them myself." Von said as he gives the Captain a sad look.

"Berlin wants the Resistance fighters standing in front of them and I will personally march them in myself, you Lieutenant can come along, but I want the Resistance fighters brought here, do you understand?" Yells the Captain.

Von stands back with a confused look on his face.

Then Von clicks his heels together and raises his right hand. "Yea, Vol." The Captain smiles and returns the salute.

Von turns and walks out. By mid-day Von gathers up all of the soldiers that he could find. Von stands on the hood of his troop truck to address the soldiers. "This is the most importance battles that you will ever fight." Von said as he looks around at all of the men. "In this battle we won't be fighting the Allies, we will be fighting the worst enemy there is, we will be fighting traitors of the Third Reich, our own people that spat in the face of our beloved Fuhrer. We will have the honor of destroying them with our boots." Von said as the rest of his soldier's cheer.

"It will be getting dark soon, let's make this their last night on earth." Von yells out as he pumps his fist into the air.

As all of the soldiers climb into the troop trucks Von looks up and sees Captain Heinbaker staring from his window. Von salutes his Captain and jumps into the cab of his truck.

"Sir, do you think that the Resistance fighters went back to their cave?" asks the driver Sergeant Hans Vandevolt.

"I planted some soldiers around the cave, if the pigs went back then they are dead by now."

Von said with grime in his eyes. "And if the Resistance fighters are still alive?"

"Then we will finish what I started a couple of months ago. The Resistance fighters are beaten, they know that all we have to do is show them that with force." Von said as he clenches his fist. Sergeant Vandevolt looks over toward Von and smiles. "Someday you can tell your kids and grandkids that you were a part of history, you were with me when I destroy the Resistance fighters." Von bragged with pride.

The troop trucks pull up in front of the entrance to the cave Von steps out and looks over the surrounding area.

"This is where we enter the woods to get to the cave where those animals hid. We will go by foot to the cave and join the men that I placed there." Von said, as he looks around the woods wondering where the men were that he had placed out in the woods. "They must be with the others, it's supper time, but they still shouldn't have left their post."

Von thought to himself. With an eerie feeling, the German soldiers with their weapons in hand, slowly walk up the path toward the cave. "There are our own soldiers out there we must be careful." Von looks over to the radioman.

"Try again I want to talk to the soldiers that are guarding the cave." Von said as he looks around the trees as he walks forward toward the cave. Von and his men move in with caution as they have their own men out there as well of the Resistance fighters. As the German soldiers reaches the place where Von placed the radioman a solider motions for Von to come over. Von is angry at the sight of the radioman and his guard dead. "Let's move on "Von whispers. On their way to the cave Von sees a couple more dead soldiers. "They were here." Von said as he looks inside of the cave.

"Why would they come back?" Ask Sergeant Vandevolt.

"To kill the heroes that I placed here, they have killed for the last time." Von said as he turns his head from the cave and toward Vandevolt. Von walks to the back entrance of the woods where he sees more dead soldiers. Von gives an angry look at what he has seen and sees scared looks on the others. Von looks up to the old Leer's house and points.

"That could be there new hide out, we will flatten that house." Von said as all of the soldiers gather around and aim their weapons toward the house. "These soldiers here will demolish the house as the rest of you go around this side of the woods and sneak up, when the pigs run out mow them down." Von said pointing out his plan. "Go and get in place when you are ready hold up your weapon and we will start firing." Von said as the men nod and do as they were told.

Von pulls out his binoculars and watches his soldiers get in place. As the soldiers gets in place Sergeant Vandevolt held his machine gun high in the air. "Fire." Von yells as he turns his sight on the house. As all of the Germans start shooting the house is hit several times. Before long the house starts breaking apart. Finally, the house falls to the ground. Von motions for his men to move in.

Chapter Twenty-One

Back at their new base Otto and his men over hears the shooting. Otto who was back from town, where he was able to bring back food for his men. Otto almost drops his two baskets. "They are here." Otto said as he places the baskets on the ground.

"Grab your weapons." Otto yells as Anna stands up and grabs her Machine gun.

"How close are they?" Karl asks as he grabs his rifle and checks on the remaining bullets.

"I don't know the Nazis could be in the woods or they could be at Herr Leer's house." Otto said as he and Anna walk up the path to the ridge Franz was guarding. Reaching the ridge Otto and Anna lean against the boulder that gives them protection from the fields.

"We aren't alone." said Franz as he looks over to Otto and Anna.

"What do you think that they are doing?" asks Anna.

"They are either spraying the woods with bullets hoping to hit us, or they are about to attack." Otto said as the rest of the Resistance fighter's joins them.

"If they come through those woods then aim carefully and save all of the bullets that you can." Otto said as he looks around to all of the fighters. Von and his men enter what is left of the Leer's house, seeing no bodies Von remembers the cellar in the bedroom closet. Von walks into the Leer's bedroom where all of the walls and part of the ceiling covers the closet.

"Clean this out, I want to get to the cellar." Von said pointing to the closet. Von's man wrap their rifles and machine guns around their shoulders and start cleaning up the mess. As the men clear out a pathway to the closet Von looks out through the bullet riddled walls. Von looks across the street at the field that leads to the woods. "They are out there." Von said as he points.

"Then should we stop and go out there?" asks Sergeant Vandevolt.

"No stay here, when you get to the closet then go down

the ladder and make sure that the pigs aren't hiding down there. Von starts walking out the bedroom door then he stops and looks over to one of his soldiers.

"That rifle has a scope on it let me borrow it." Von said to the soldier who pulls the rifle off and hands it to his leader. Von checks the ammo in the rifle and smiles. "I'll be back, if there is no one down in the cellar, then place hand grenades around the house and pull the pins, I want this house leveled." Von said as he walks out of the house.

Back at the ridge Von looks around through his binoculars and notices that there is no movement in the woods.

"We may have enough time for supper, Hilda stand guard. If you see the Nazis walking out of the woods, then start shooting we will join you." Hilda nods as the other fighters walk back down the trail to their camp.

"I'll bring you some food." Anna said, as she was the last to leave. Hilda smiles as she looks over the boulder and waits. Von slowly moves into the woods. As the sun quickly goes down Von hurries his steps through the fifty or so yards to the end of the trees and to the next batch of open fields. Anna leaves as Hilda stares out to the open fields.

Minutes later Anna brought some welcome food. Hilda turns around as Anna walks up carrying the food. "What is it?" Hilda asks as she places her rifle down against the boulder.

"Well, its chicken and potatoes and some bread." Anna said with a smile as she carefully gives the tray to her sister.

Von walks to the edge of the woods and looks through the scope of his rifle. First Von sees nothing, then Hilda raises up for a second to take the food from her sister. Von smiles as he sees the back of the Resistance fighter in his sight. Von slowly squeezes the trigger of his rifle. With wide eyes Hilda is hit in her back as the bullet goes through her and out of the front. Hilda slowly falls to the ground dropping her well-deserved meal. Anna covers her mouth with her hands as she sees her sister being shot. Anna drops down beside her sister and grabs Hilda. Anna cries out. "Hilda." as she holds Hilda in her arms.

Angry, Anna reaches up and pointing Hilda's sniper rifle. Von waited to see if there was going to be any more shooting from the ridge and felt comfortable enough to leave the safety of the woods and out in the open. Von runs to the ridge as Anna picks up Hilda's rifle and sees the approaching German soldier. Anna cries as she takes aim and fires. Von is hit in his chest and falls to the ground dead. Anna drops the rifle and holds Hilda. Hilda who was shaking from the gunshot looks at her sister. "Anna, promise me that you will look for Papa, I will also look for him." Hilda says in a weak voice as Hilda closes her eyes for the last time. Anna cries over her sister lifeless body.

From the camp Otto and his men hear the shooting and run up to the ridge where they see Anna holding Hilda. Stunned, Otto looks over the boulder and sees the presumably dead German soldier.

"There is only one soldier out there, we must prepare for others. "Otto said as he looks down at Hilda.

"Is she dead?" Karl asks as he runs up to Anna and tries to touches Hilda's hair. As Anna pulls her sister away from Karl.

"Leave me and my sister alone; we're out of the war." Anna said crying.

The German soldiers from the Leer's house start running to their Lieutenants aid.

"What should we do? "Ask Franz.

"We need to bury the body." Karl said as Otto pulls out his binoculars and looks into the woods. Otto gives Karl a mad look.

"A body, this is my sister, she saved all of your lives and all you can call her is a body." Anna said in anger. "I took care of her when she was young and I'll take care of her now." Anna said, as she holds Hilda tight in her arms.

At that time, all of the German soldiers reach the edge of the woods and see Von lying on the ground. Sergeant Vandevolt looks through his binoculars and sees Otto looking around.

"There are the Resistance fighters." Said the sergeant, pointing toward the ridge. In a mad dash all of the German soldiers run out of the woods shooting. As the ridge fills with smoke from the bullets hitting the boulder and the ground surrounding the ridge.

The Resistance fighters still manage to shoot toward the approaching Nazis. Several Nazis soldiers are hit and fall to the ground. "There are too many." Otto said. "They will overrun us, grab Hilda and we'll meet at the camp." Otto yells as he continues firing. Karl and Franz grab Hilda from the arms of Anna, as Anna resisted. "Anna let go they will help you." Otto yells in a firm tone. Anna lets her hold go as Karl and Franz grab Hilda and run down the path. Otto stayed at the boulder shooting at the fast advancing soldiers. Anna looks at her bloody hands and screams then with anger Anna grabs her machine gun and stands beside of Otto and takes aim.

"Anna, get out of here." Otto yells as Anna pays him no attention. Now with Anna shooting more German soldiers fall to the ground dead. The rest of the German soldiers retreat back into the woods. "They're gone for now, we must go to the camp and make plans." Otto said as he looks over toward Anna who is still holding her machine gun waiting for the next Nazi movement.

"Go ahead; I'm here for my sister." Anna cried.

"Their next movement maybe our last." Otto said as he places his hand on Anna's shoulder.

Anna turns and places her head on Otto's shoulder and cries. "I'm so sorry Anna." Otto said as he started crying

"What do I do now?" Anna asks out loud.

Otto holds Anna tight in his arms. "Stay alive, that's what Hilda wanted."

"I need to find Papa, I want to find him, he's all 've got left." Anna said as she pulls away from Otto. "I need to find Papa; he needs to know." Anna said as she pulls away from Otto's grip and walks down toward the camp sight. Otto looks over toward Anna then he looks into the woods. Otto pulls up his machine gun and starts shooting just for the death of his friend, for Hilda. Otto screams out in the pain that he and Anna were feeling. Then Otto follows Anna down the trail to the camp. When Otto reaches the camp all were standing around, except for Anna who is sitting on the ground holding her sister.

"I need to bury my sister." Anna said crying. "But where? Mama is buried at our home, I'm not sure where we are, how close is our home, is it too far from here, how about Papa, where is he at? Anna said in a weak voice. "Is he dead or is he alive, who's side is he fighting on? I need to find Papa he will tell me what to do, I want to go home and be his little girl again." Anna could barely say.

"We must go now." Otto said as he places his hand on Anna's shoulder. "The Nazis are planning their next move and there are more of them than us." Otto said as he motions for Karl and Erich to help Anna with Hilda. Both men take Hilda from Anna who puts up a small, weak fight. "Where are you taken her?" Anna yells out.

"We'll take her to town where she can be buried, years from now you can come back here and see her grave but for now we must move on." Otto said as he tried to comfort Anna. As the Germans attack they start shooting at the ridge. Otto looks over toward Anna. "Go to the town with the rest of the men." Otto said as he places both of his hands on Anna's shoulder.

"What about you?" Ask Franz.

"I'll stay here and give you time, GO!" Otto yells. Karl and Erich carry Hilda off as Franz helps Anna go down the path.

Anna stops and turns around. "Come on Otto go with us." Anna said in a cold tone.

"I'll meet you in town." Otto said with a faint smile.

"Come on Anna, Otto knows what he is doing." Franz says as he walks Anna away then turns back and looks at Otto who was watching them leave. Otto checks the clip inside of his machine gun. Otto replaces the clip giving him a full clip of ammo. As Otto waits he notices all of the fighter's weapons lying on the ground. "They left their weapons" Otto said to himself. Then Otto shook his head and walks over and grabs the weapons and tosses them deeper into the woods where the Nazis can't find them. "Let them think that I was alone." Otto said to himself. The Resistance fighters finally find the road.

"The town is about a mile away, they will help us." said Franz as he pulls a numb Anna onto the road. As the team runs down the road Otto prepared for the battle as the German soldiers enter the woods Otto lay low waiting till the German soldiers get close enough for Otto to jump up and shoot them. While the woods around him make the sounds of thousands of soldiers, Otto, in slow motion, rises up and aims his machine gun toward the group of soldiers. Otto fires a couple of blasts as he is hit in the arm.

Otto drops his machine gun and turns to run away as several bullets hit Otto's body. Before Otto could fall to the ground he was hit around fifty or sixty times his body fills with what looks like red dots as the German bullets go through his body. Otto slowly falls to the ground as all of the German bullets hitting him cause him to fall slowly. As Otto lay on the ground he died almost as soon as the battle started.

Chapter Twenty-Two

The Resistance fighters hear the shooting in the woods. Anna screams and tries to turn away from Franz and go back into the woods. Franz held his grip and pulls Anna toward town. "Otto is dead, he wanted us to get to town and that's what we're going to do." Karl yells.

All of the German soldiers move in and circle Otto who was lying on the ground. "Is he the only one or is there more?" asks a private of Sergeant Vondevolt.

"Check the woods for others, they will be armed and dangerous, keep that in mind." said Vondevolt as he looks down at Otto's blood filled body. "There must be around one hundred bullets holes in this man." said Vondevolt with a smile.

"Sir we found some weapons in the woods, but there is no sign of the Resistance fighters." said one of the German soldiers. Vondevolt looks back at Otto's body then back up to his men who were gathering around him.

"They are unarmed and scared, they will go into the town up that road." said Vondevolt as he stood and looked down the path where he sees some of Hilda's blood.

"Go get the troop trucks, bring them to the road we'll meet you there." Said Vondevolt as he follows the trail of blood. By the time that the troop trucks arrive the Resistance fighters reach the town. The town's people quickly took them in. Karl and Erich took Hilda's body to the store where the storeowner ensures that she will be put to rest and she will always be remembered.

Satisfied Anna agrees, then she looks down the road. "Where is Otto, he should had been here by now?" Anna said as she takes two steps toward the road. Franz and the cloths storeowner hold Anna back.

"Otto saved our lives today he was that way with the people that he loved." Anna started to cry as the storeowner holds her.

"We need to find a place where you can hide in case the Nazis comes here looking for you." said the General goods storeowner. Anna is hidden in the last store where they, the owners of the store, sell clothing. Franz was placed in the small hotel as Karl is taken to the first building where furniture is made as all of the products made with woods. Erich is placed in the restaurant. Karl is forced to fit in a crate that is standing up the height is big enough but there was barely enough room for him to fit in. "Take a deep breath and hold it for your life." said the wood builder. As Karl holds his breath the door of the crate is closed. With only tiny slits in the crate leaving Karl enough room to look out. The next slit is near the bottom around Karl's stomach. "Let him out." said the wood builder. "If the Nazis come this is where you can hide, they won't find you here." said the wood builder as he helps unlock the lock.

"Maybe they won't come." Karl said as he wipes the sweat off of his face from being inside of the wooden crate. All of the Resistance fighters went to meet Anna at the dress shop. Anna walks out wearing a new pretty dress. She comes out tying the belt of her new dress.

"Wow, Anna is that you?" Karl asks as he sees Anna in a dress. Anna smiles at Karl then she looks over to the storeowner's wife.

"How about my sister?" Anna asks not paying any attention to the men.

"Yes, I picked this dress out for her I hope that you like it." Anna follows the lady over to a dress table where the storeowner picks up a flowerily dress.

Anna picks up the dress and looks it over. Anna starts to cry as she sees the dress. "Hilda would love this." Anna said as Franz walks over and places his hands around her shoulders. Anna fell into Franz's arms.

"The Nazis are coming." yells one of the town's people. All of the Resistance fighters race to the store that was going to protect them. Karl runs in and the wood builder closes the crate and locks it up. Then the wood builder went on with his daily work. Vondevolt walks in and looks around the wood working store. The Store owner walks up and stands in front of the Nazi Sergeant "Yes sir, how may I help you?" ask the storeowner. Vondevolt looks around the shop.

"Is there anything that you would like?" The storeowner continues.

"I am looking for some Resistance fighters could they be here?" said the Sergeant as slowly walks around the shop looking around.

"Sir there haven't been anyone here in months, we stay alive by selling our goods to one and another," said the storeowner as he follows the Sergeant around the shop.

"What is back there?" Vondevolt asks pointing at the back of the shop.

"That is where the supplies come in, you know woods, hammers, nails all of the supplies that a wood builder needs." said the storeowner as he follows the Sergeant to the back of the store.

"What is in this crate?" Vondevolt ask as he places his hand on the lock.

"Those are maple planks, we use for locks to keep out the thieves." said the wood builder in a nervous tone. Vondevolt looks the crate over and slides his hand across the front of the crate.

"Careful, you may get a splinter." laughs the wood builder. Vondevolt brings his hand toward his face.

"I think that I have a splinter." said Vondevolt as he pulls out his knife and holds it up for the wood builder to see. From the inside of the crate Karl could see through the slit the face of the Sergeant.

Sergeant Vondevolt smiles as he shows the knife to the wood builder and the rest of the German soldiers. Then Vondevolt looks through the slit in the wood and plunges his knife straight into Karl's eyes.

Carl is stunned at the sight of the Sergeant staring at him. But the crate is too narrow for Karl to move as the Sergeant slides the knife into the bottom slit and into Karl's stomach.

The crate moves as the knife enters Karl's body as a whimpering sound is heard. The wood builder closes his eyes as he looks down. Blood fills the floor as the whimpering stops with Karl's death. Seeing all of the German soldiers the dress store owner runs to her back room where Anna was hiding. "You have to get out of here, now." said the storeowner.

"The Nazis will find you if you stay here." Anna follows the lady to the back door as the storeowner points to the woods. Anna runs toward the woods alone. She waits for the others to join her. Anna doesn't know what was happening. "Surround the building." orders Sergeant Vondevolt.

As the Nazis runs out Vondevolt looks at the blood on the floor. "I would tell you to clean this up, but I won't." Said Vondevolt as he grabs his pistol out and points it at the storeowner's head. "Come with me." said Vondevolt as he led the storeowner to the front of the store then outside where all of the town's people were waiting. Anna sees the Nazi soldiers circling. Anna moves deeper into the woods. Away from the German's sight. Vondevolt and the storeowner walk outside, all of the town's people are frightened. Vondevolt pushes the storeowner into the front porch rail. As the man bends over the rail Vondevolt laughs.

"This man is an enemy of the Third Reich and he will pay with his life, I will pardon those who are hiding any Resistance fighters in their stores, you will have five minutes to bring the Resistance fighter out. All of the stores are surrounded by my soldiers so don't be an idiot and try to let them escape. Bring them here and I won't destroy you and your shops." Vondevolt said as he looks down at his watch.

"You now have four minutes." All of the shop owners run inside their stores and retrieve their hidden Fighters.

"Please forgive me." says the storeowner to Franz. Franz smiles and places his hand on the shoulder of the storeowner.

"It will be alright, they are after us, not you." Franz said with a smile on his face. "Let's go outside." Franz said as he led the owner out of the door. One by one the Resistance fighters walk out and stand beside each other.

"Where's Anna?" Erich whispers.

"She got away." said the lady from the dress shop. All of the men smiles.

"How about Karl?" Ask Franz.

"Dead." whispered one of the storeowners. All of the Resistance fighters close their eyes and look down to the ground.

"Is this all of them?" Vondevolt ask.

"Yea vol." answered one of the store owners.

"Check the back see if any fighters try to get away." Vondevolt orders one of his men.

"I am a man of honor I will spare your buildings, all but this one." Vondevolt said as he points toward the wood shop building. "Bring these animals inside." said Vondevolt as the soldier he sent to the back of the shops returns and tells him that no one had escaped. Vondevolt follows his men inside of the building. The wood builder is forced at gunpoint to follow them. "Tie them up together and place them in the middle of the shop use that pole to anchor them down." Vondevolt orders. The German soldiers push the four men to the ground against the tall wooden pole and tied them up. Franz sat next to the shop owner. "Sorry for this." Franz said in a weak tone.

"No one talks." yells a German soldier as he hits Franz in the face with the butt of his rifle.

Chapter Twenty-Three

Where are they?" Anna ask herself as she waits in the woods trying to stay out of the sight of the German soldier who was still out there walking around. "This building will burn for at least five days." Laughs Vondevolt as his men carry in some petrol from their trucks. All of the men start screaming as the soldiers pour the petrol around them. Some of the men are splash with the petrol. "Don't worry about the splashing, it will burn off." Vondevolt laughs.

Anna hears the screaming of her friends then the building lights up with flames. Anna's eyes grow wide as she sees the flames and smoke form the building. Anna closes her eyes knowing that she could yell out but it would not help her friends. Anna slowly moves away from the sight of the German soldier. Stunned by the horrible killing of her friends Anna walks through the woods holding her stomach. Anna stumbles to a tree and leans against it as she starts to throw up.

For the first time in her life Anna was alone and scared.

Miles into the woods Anna finds a road that she walks down, still weakened by the death of everyone including her sister Hilda. How was she going to tell her father, if he was still alive, that she allowed his youngest daughter to die.

The thoughts returned of her mother and the last day of her life. The smiles, her loving way and gentle touch. Killed by her own people. Anna's mom might have been Jewish but she was still born in Germany and she should have been protected by the German Government. Anna could see Hilda as a child playing in the fields of their father's farm. Von at an early age always coming over and play with Hilda then trying to work with Marc who told him to get out of his way. Then Anna thought of Otto and the way that he always listened and made people that were around him feel good and wanted. "There are not too many people out there that can do that." Anna said to herself. Tears rolls down Anna's face as she thought of her love ones. Now here she is alone and walking down a dirt road. Wanted by the Nazis for her part in the Resistance fighters. For the first time in years Anna walks the road without her machine gun or a pistol in her military belt. Anna stops and checks out the pocket on her dress making sure that that she still had the pouch she found in that house where the Americans doctored each other. The American dog tag and the American dollar bills. First Anna pulls out her paper claiming that she was a German born citizen. "Good" Anna thought she would need to show the soldiers if she is stop. Anna looks up the long dirt road that she felt went nowhere and that was a place that she wanted to be at. Nowhere, No war, No hate and no killing." Is there such a place?" Anna thought. The smell of death fills the woods next to her. Anna moves to the center of the road away from the smell. From a distance Anna hears the sound of a truck approaching her. Anna thought of jumping into the woods protecting her from whoever is approaching.

Anna moves to the side of the road as the truck draws near.

"Too late to go into the woods." Anna said. The German troop truck pulls in front of Anna and stops as the German soldier's jump out of the back with their rifles, their Captain steps out and walks over to Anna. "Where are you going fraulein?" Asks the Captain, Anna looks at the soldiers and their weapons then she notices the pistol in the Captain's holster.

"My father's farm is over there; I went to see a friend now I'm going back home." Anna lied.

"Very good, may I see your papers?" asked the Captain who is smiling at the pretty fraulein. Anna reaches into her pocket and pulls out the papers that the German Captain asked for. Anna was pleased that she pulled out the papers and not the pouch that contained the Americans information. The Captain looks the papers over then he hands the papers back to Anna. "Thank you fraulein Metz could we give you a ride to your father's farm?" Anna gives the Captain a smile (of relief.) as the soldier's climb back into the troop truck. As the Captain turns to walk to the front of the truck he turns around. "Excuse me fraulein but what is your mother's maiden name?" Ask the smiling Captain.

Anna closes her eyes for now she was caught. Anna looks over toward the German Captain and in a soft voice "Lowenstein." Anna said as the smile on the Captain face turns into a frown.

"Then we will give you a ride but not to your father's farm but the concentration camp where you will be with your own people, who knows your mother may meet you there." Laughs the Captain. Anna close her eyes as the German soldiers jump back out of their troop truck this time the soldiers point their rifles toward Anna. A couple of soldiers help Anna climb in the truck and place her in the middle as they gather around her with their rifles aimed at her.

Anna gives in and places her cupped hands to her face and cries.

Chapter Twenty-Four

The road is bumpy Anna looks around and sees the German soldiers holding their rifle toward her with their fingers on the trigger. "I'm not a threat; you don't have to point your rifle at me." Anna said as she regains her composer.

"You are a Jew; we have to guard you." said one of the soldiers.

"But I'm unarmed and I'm afraid of rifles, please take your finger off of the triggers this is a bumpy road and it won't take much to bump your trigger shooting me." Anna said in a scared tone.

"Don't worry about us, you should be worried about the concentration camp that we are taking you to." mentions one of the guards. Anna closes her eyes and held her head down.

"But, I have a natural German name." Anna pleaded.

"I don't care we were told that you are a Jew and we have a place for you and your people, Good luck in there." Added another German soldier. As the truck stops at the gate of the concentration camp Anna could hear the conversation between the Captain and the guard at the gate.

"We found a Jewish fraulein and I would like to leave her here, who is in command?" asks the Captain. The guard motions for the gate to be lifted, as the truck enters.

"Kommandant Drabek is in charge."

"He will find us." said the Captain as he motions for his driver to drive in. As the truck stops at the Kommandant's office Anna is pulled out of the back of the truck and brought to the front of the truck, next to the Captain. Anna looks around at the prisoners of the camp. The prisoners work at their jobs slowly from being weak. Some of the prisoners glance up to see the new arrival but they look for only a second as an armed guard stands near them waiting to bully them for not working. Noticing that the Kommandant has not stepped out of his office The Captain motions for the driver to beep his horn.

As the driver presses the horn, the Kommandant walks out and salutes the Captain by clicking his heels together and raises his hand high in the air. "Heil Hitler." said the Kommandant as the Captain returns the salutes.

"I have a prisoner for you." said the Captain as the Kommandant walks down the steps and takes the paper from the Captain.

As the Kommandant reads the paper he becomes confuse. "But this is a German Fraulein; we only handle Jewish prisoners here at my camp."

"Her last name Metz, that is her father's name, but her mother's name is Lowenstein, that makes her half Jewish, she belongs here." orders the Captain.

"I never heard of this but we will take her." said Kommandant Drabek as he looks over to the papers then he looks over at Anna, the Kommandant smiles as he stares at his new prisoner. "I would like a report from you explaining the maiden Jewish name still makes her a Jewish prisoner. Your report will go with my report to Berlin."

The smiling Captain said, "Yes of course I will."

The Kommandant said as he reads the paper and glances over to Anna and smiles. "Come in my office and I'll have my secretary to type something up for you." said Kommandant Drabek as he looks at the pretty young fraulein. Anna looks away from the Kommandant. As The German Captain walks up the steps to the Kommandant's office Anna is forced to walk by the guards poking her with the barrel of their rifle. As they all enter the office of the Kommandant. Kommandant Drabek sits behind his desk and yells for his secretary to come into his office.

"Captain this is my secretary Frau Kellar, she will type up your report and give to you for your signature.

"That would be great." said the Captain as he follows Frau Kellar out to her desk leaving the Kommandant alone with Anna.

The Kommandant smiles as Anna looks away. "You are a Jewish fraulein and I'm a high ranking German officer, you will show me the respect that I earned and I deserve." said the Kommandant as he pours himself a glass of alcohol. "You are overdressed for this camp, here the prisoner's work in the fields and whatever I have for them. Those who do not do as I say will be put to death. Are you the type to disobey me?" Ask the Kommandant, he stares at Anna as he sips on his drink.

At that time a knock on the door is heard. "Enter" said the Kommandant as he hides his drink behind a stack of books. The Concentration camp foreman walks in wearing the same dull uniform with the arm patch of David carrying a Jewish worker uniform. "Ah, this is one of your own kind, this is a Jewish man who will drive you to work harder and if you don't then he will be the man who will inform me so I can submit punishment to the lazy animals that he watches over." Anna looks over to the camps foreman as Kommandant Drabek speaks.

"You would turn in one of your own people?" Anna asks as the camp Foreman glares at her. Kommandant Drabek walks over to Anna and swings his hand through the air slapping Anna in her face. Anna quietly cries out as she holds her face.

"I control this Concentration camp. But this man is my eyes and ears at the camp." said Kommandant Drabek as he walks back over to his desk and grabs his glass of whiskey and takes another drink. "Hand her the new dress that she will be wearing." said Drabek as he motions to his foreman.

The foreman tosses the dull white smelling dress to Anna. "It smells like death." Anna said as she turns her head.

"Are you sure that it is the dress and not you?" Ask the Kommandant as he takes another sip. "You may leave now." said the Kommandant to the camp foreman. The foreman turns to Anna and gives her a dirty look as he walks out of the door. "Put your new dress on." said the Kommandant as he sits in his chair sipping on his whiskey.

"Where, where is the dressing room?" Anna asks as she looks around.

"The dressing room is where you are standing." Replied the Kommandant.

Anna's eyes grew wider hearing this. Anna starts to untie her belt when the Captain walks in and sees what Anna is doing.

"You do know that touching a Jewish scum like her is illegal, you can be sent to jail or shot." said the Captain to the Kommandant.

I'm not going to touch this piece of trash." said the Kommandant as he slides his glass back behind the books.

"My daughter is about the same size that this Jew is and my daughter might like this dress, I'm making sure that this Jew is careful with the dress." lied the Kommandant.

"Well I got the letter that I need and I will be moving on, remember what I said it is illegal----"

"Don't worry I wouldn't touch this creature even if she begged me, I know the law." Laughs the Kommandant. Before the Captain walks out of the door he turns around and looks at Anna. The Captain shakes his head and walks out the door. "She wouldn't be worth it." said the Captain as he closes the door behind him. Not sure that the Kommandant would keep that threat in mind Anna looks over to him. "We'll continue." said the Kommandant as Anna closes her eyes and continues.

"Wait." said the Kommandant. " Change your cloths over here by the window." Anna walks over to the window and with her back facing the outside Anna takes off her dress and places the prison dress on. The prisoners outside look up and see Anna's bare back.

"What do you think that she is doing?" asks one of the women prisoners as she is raking the loose dirt in the vegetable gardening.

"Special treatment." said another prisoner. With the dull white dress on Anna stands at the window ashamed of what the Kommandant had seem.

"You may go out to the camp now the foreman will have a job ready just for you." Smiles the Kommandant as he finishes his glass of whiskey and stares at Anna as she quickly walks out with her head down. Anna walks up to the Foreman who was overseeing the two ladies with the rake in their hands.

"Here work with these fraulein." said the foreman as he tosses a rake to Anna. Anna misses catching the rake as the wood handle of the rake hits her in her face and head. Anna screams out as she grabs her face. "You're not working." said the foreman shaking his head as the two fraulein laugh. Anna picks up the rake and starts scraping the ground as the ladies were doing. The foreman continues shaking his head and walks away.

"What are we doing?" Anna asks as the ladies move away from her without saying a word. Anna stares at them as they continue to do what they were doing.

"Why are you out here, shouldn't you be in the kitchen are doing something easy?" whispers one of the frauleins.

"Why, they said that I belong here." Anna said as she rakes a dirt clog.

"We saw you in the window and we know what you were doing." said one of the fraulein who raise her rake high into the air with the teeth of the rake pointing at Anna. "He made me change from my dress to these work cloths."

Anna said as she stands up. "He never touched me, it's illegal." hearing this both of the women laugh, as the window in the Kommandant office is opened and the Kommandant stands yelling.

"Foreman these three women are having a good day, why is that?" The foreman runs over and pulls out his pencil and start writing.

"I'll take care of it sir, don't worry." yells the foreman as the Kommandant closes his window.

"This isn't good." said one of the frauleins as she pounds the ground harder. As both of the fraulein gives Anna a dirty look.

Darkness comes and the prisoners gather into their bare broken down shack where there are bunk beds and a small cooking area where the prisoners cook if they have any food.

Anna waited to see which bed was left empty so she could try to get a good night sleep. The first sleep that she has had since the death of her friends. "What is she waiting for the Kommandant to come in and invite her to his bedroom." said the fraulein from earlier. Anna sees an open bunk so she walks over and gets in. At that time the foreman walks in carrying a strap behind him and back in the darkness is the Kommandant. The Kommandant whispers something to the foreman.

The foreman nods his head and walks inside of the hut.

"You three fraulein come here." said the foreman pointing his strap to the two ladies and Anna. With a sad look on their faces the fraulein walk up to the foreman as Anna follows. "The three of you were having a good time out there, well you will pay for it now." said the foreman as he motions for the first fraulein to get into position. The first fraulein bends over and raises her dress up. Anna is frightened to see the foreman raise the strap back and swipes the fraulein. As the foreman smiles the fraulein screams out in pain. "Here the next one." said the foreman who gladly swings his strap again as the fraulein begs for him to stop. "It will be only two tonight." said the foreman as two men in the bunkhouse walks over and carry the fraulein back to her bunk. "Now it's your turn." said the foreman as he points his strap to the second fraulein. The second fraulein gets in the same position as the first.

Anna cries as she sees the strap swing high up in the air to the fraulein bottom. "The screams of the second fraulein were heard throughout all of the ten huts. Then came the second swipe as the screams are louder than the first. With the second fraulein who was holding onto the rail from the bunk is taken away by two more of the men and placed into her bunk.

"I'm so sorry." Anna cried, as the second fraulein is taken away "I didn't know the rules." Anna said as she continues to cry.

"There are no rules here, they make them up as they go." said Eva one of the prisoner in the bunkhouse.

"Quiet or you'll be up here next." yells the foreman pointing his strap toward Eva. Anna nods for the first time in the concentration camp a person had said something to her. Anna walks over and bends over. "You're not going to feel the strap tonight." said the foreman as the other two fraulein look over from their bunks. "No tonight you're going into the spa."

Hearing this both of the fraulein smile, then they start laughing. Anna looks back at them, and then she looks up to the foreman. "The spa." Anna asks not wanting to know about the spa.

"Come with me." said the foreman as he pulls Anna away. The foreman leads Anna as he pulls on her dress neckline to a small building in the middle of the camp. Anna looks the small building over as the foreman unlocks the door. "Get in." said the foreman as he throws Anna inside the cramped tiny room that was built out of bricks and steel siding.

There wasn't enough room for Anna to lie down or to stand up. Anna had to sit down on top of the brick floor. Anna gives the foremen a scared look as he closes the metal door.

"Stay in there a day or two." Laughs the foreman.

Anna sits on the cold brick floor. Anna leans back onto the metal siding where she closes her eyes. But the thoughts of her Father and her mother start her dreaming. Anna dreams of being home back on the farm where she and Hilda help their father with the farm. In sleep Anna smiles as she sees her mother walk out carrying a tray with ice cold water filled to the top of the glass. Anna and Hilda would laugh when they see their father pour the cold glass of water down him to cool himself off.

Von would show up and help out but the weak young man has problems with the potatoes and the carrots. They all would laugh as he tried to pull them out of the ground, then their neighbor down the street would come up and help with the harvesting. Otto would sit beside of Anna and laughs as Von pulls on the potatoes. Next Franz and Karl would walk up along with Erich. As her parents sat beside of each other and Otto sits beside of Anna they all laughs at Von, with sweat pouring down his face and Hilda trying to help him they both, with Hilda doing most of the pulling, bring the potatoes out of the ground. They all laugh until one by one each of the people stands up and walks away, disappearing into the sunlight.

Anna is left alone sitting on the ground, then the ground turns into bricks. As Anna awakens she noticed that she wasn't at home but in the metal box that they call the spa.

As the sun fills the sky the metal box heats up with no water to drink. Sweat covers Anna's face.

The heat inside of the box zaps the energy from her body. With the lack of water Anna can't yell out for help.

But who would come. The people that she trusted and depended on were dead. The fraulein in the hut didn't like her and she knew no one. The weak screams went nowhere. As night falls the bricks inside of the box cool down. Like she had to in the daytime Anna adjusted the way that she sat.

Anna's body became stiff from the lack of movement. At daylight Anna tried to stand up but the small ceiling and her now numb legs prevented her movement. Anna fell to the hot bricks. As hours went by Anna saw all of her family and friends waving to her from a distance. But they were too far for Anna to reach the more Anna tried to run to them the further they become. Right before the second day ended the box was opened and Anna was blinded by the sunlight, the foreman grabs her by her arm and dragged her to the Kommandant's office. As Anna and the foreman pass the two fraulein they laugh at the sight of Anna being dragged. Anna who still couldn't talk mouths the words "I'm sorry." Seeing this, the two fraulein stops laughing as the foreman drag Anna up the wooden stares and into the Kommandant office. Kommandant Drabek smiles at the sight of the foreman picking up the half lifeless body and places her into the chair. "You may leave now." said the Kommandant to the foreman. Then the Kommandant looks over to Anna who was barely able to lift one eye open. The Kommandant smiles as he pours a glass of water. Hoping that the water was for her Anna lifts up her weak head and watches, as the water is being poured out of the vase and into the glass.

"Would you like some?" Ask the Kommandant. Anna shook her head (yes) as she reaches for the glass that the Kommandant places in front of her at the edge of his desk.

As Anna reaches for the glass the Kommandant pushes the glass over and the glass of water falls to the floor breaking the glass. "If you want it then get on the floor and drink it like a dog." laughs the Kommandant. Anna falls to the ground and starts drinking the floor cover water not fearing the broken glass. "Here is some more water." laughs the Kommandant as he pours out the remaining vase of water onto her Anna lifted up her head, as the water is pour into her mouth.

With the water gone the Kommandant places the vase back onto his desk. Anna climbs up and sits in the chair as the Kommandant pulls out from a drawer the American pouch that was in her dress. "Would you like to tell me where you got this American pouch?" asks the Kommandant as he tosses it in- front of Anna.

"I got it when you went inside a building." Anna said in a weak voice.

"For some reason I don't believe you, would you like to try again." said the Kommandant as he reaches over and grabs the pouch from Anna as she reaches for it.

"I found it, I never knew who owned it, and the

~ 221 ~

Americans was gone." Anna said defending herself.

"Well it's not up to me to get you to answer my questions, that is for the SS and I shall make a call to them." threatened the Kommandant as he reaches for the phone.

"I never knew any Americans, I found that pouch." Anna pleaded.

"And there were some Americans dollars inside of the pouch wasn't there?" said the Kommandant as he reaches in and pulls out the American dollars. "You could be shot as a spy if the SS found these dollars on you, Lucky for you I collect American monies, you know for, after the war is over. Which side wins who cares, I will move to Hollywood and become an international star," said the Kommandant with a smile as he shows Anna his profile.

"I will place these dollars in my safe where the SS can't find them." the Kommandant said as he walks over to his safe and opens it. The Kommandant shows Anna a huge bundle of dollars that he has collected. "I was once a Kommandant at a P.O.W. camp before I came here, When I get to Hollywood how would you like to accompany me, I need a beautiful fraulein like you to go wherever I go with my arms around you." said the Kommandant as he shows Anna his second bundle of American dollars.

"You would be seen with a Jew?" Anna asks as she starts to get her voice back.

"Jew, remember your name is Metz, when we get to America your name will be Anna Drabek, how does that sound?" ask the Kommandant as he shows the two bundles of American dollars.

"If the SS come here who would say that to save myself I told them about the American dollars." Anna said with a smile.

"Ok fraulein Lowenstein, have it your way. At the end of the war I will be in Hollywood and you'll be dead, well life goes on with you or without you." said the Kommandant as he places the two large bundles of American dollars on his desk in front of Anna. "People in here die every day, that's why you have a bunk to sleep in, and your bunk can become available who knows." threatens the Kommandant.

"I'm a German girl just like the rest of the Jews out there in your camp. Why don't you pick one of the fraulein out there?" Anna said with a smirk on her face.

"Because they are dead and they don't even know it, in a couple of weeks you to will look like them, now I don't want that but I can't stop it if you choose that way." said the Kommandant as he looks over and sees Anna's dress hanging up. "I like that dress, try it on for me again." Anna looks over at the dress knowing what the Kommandant really wanted.

"I will try it on as many times that you like but remember it is against the law for you to touch a Jew that way." Anna said boldly.

"What me touch a Jew nonsense, your last name is Metz and I will say that I didn't know that you were Jewish" laughs the Kommandant.

What about that Captain that brought me here, he knows."

"What, that Captain, I'm a Major I could send him to fight the Russian on the Russian front with one phone call, trust me I have connections." bragged the Kommandant. "If you choose to die then you'll die, go back to your hut." orders the Kommandant as he pulls the bundle of American dollars off the table. Before Anna leaves she looks back and sees the new hiding place for the dollars.

Chapter Twenty-Four

Anna walks back to the hut where all of the Jews were getting ready to eat the small amount of food that they could find. Anna saw the food but she knew that she wasn't welcome to join them. Anna walks to the back of the hut and sits on her bunk. Eva reaches into the pot and takes a little of the so call stew out and place the mostly colored water onto a plate then she looks at the two fraulein that were earlier laughing as Anna was being dragged. The two fraulein nods their heads as Eva takes the plate to the back where Anna was laying down. "Here this isn't much but it's for you." Eva said as Anna sat up.

"No I can't there isn't that much food and that is for you to eat." Anna declines.

"No we will make it enough." said one of the fraulein. Anna smiles as she dips her spoon in the plate trying to get some of the stew in her spoon.

"Well, what did the Kommandant want?" Eva asks as

Anna looks up to her. "He wanted sex, but I told him no."

All of the people inside of the bunkhouse smiles. "We kind of knew that you said no or you wouldn't be back here." Eva said with a smile. The Kommandant picks up the phone to call the SS then he looks over at the dress and places the phone back down as he stares at the dress. "She will be mine." brags the Kommandant. As the days past Anna becomes weaker and weaker, her once pretty body is now turning into a skeleton like the others. Kommandant Drabek looks out of the window at the frail looking young fraulein then Drabek turns his head and looks at Anna's dress. "What a pity she will be dead in a couple of weeks." The Kommandant said sadly. Anna and Eva were working near the fence Anna who was digging a small ditch for the planting of vegetables looks over to the ten-foot fence. "With some help I bet that we could get over the fence and run to freedom." Anna said as she stares at the fence.

"There is no way, that fence is an electric fence if you

touch it then you will be executed, I've seen it happen to our people would tried to escape by climbing the fence but they are executed that quick." Eva said snapping her fingers. Anna frowns as her plan A is squashed and there is no plan B yet.

As time goes by Anna is getting weaker and weaker from the lack of food and the sun up till darkness work. As Anna is brought to the Kommandant's Office, she is sent out as fast as she was sent in, with nightly whipping from the foreman's strap. By the first of spring, rumors got out of the advancing Allied forces nearing Berlin. At night battles of the Germans and the Allies could be heard from a distance. "The Allies are near." yells one of the men inside of the bunkhouse.

"Soon the war will be over." Proclaims Eva.

Three weeks later the prisoners are awoken by the sound of tanks rolling around. "What is that?' Anna asks as she wakes up.

"They are Tigers tanks, every now and then the German soldiers brings them over here just in case the Allies start bombing the area where they normally keep them." answered another man. Weak and near death, Anna falls back into her bunk and waits until it is time for her and the others to get ready for the same routine of slowly dying out in the camp's fields. More and more prisoners have died in the past few weeks.

At that time the door is slammed open and a man walks in the room.

I am Lieutenant Ogino of the United State Army; we are here to set you free." Lieutenant Vito Ogino said as he looks around in disgust by the sight of the skeleton prisoners.

From the back of the bunkhouse Anna waves her hand and laughs. Vito walks to the back and sees the frail, weak fraulein prisoner. As Anna tries to stand up, her legs wobbly from the lack of food. Vito reaches down and picks her up and carries her in his arms as tears rolls down his face. With a weak voice the entire group of prisoner's cheers the Americans, as they are now free.

"I can walk; there are more people in here that need your help." Anna said as Vito held on tight. "They will be attended to." Vito said as he walks outside of the bunkhouse carrying Anna. Once outside Anna see all of the German guards standing in the middle of the compound with their hands clenched together on top of their heads.

We are free." Anna said in her broken English.

"That's right, you and your people are free, you speak English?" Vito ask as Anna hugs Vito's neck.

"Please let me down I can walk." Anna said as Vito helps her down.

At that time the foreman runs up to Vito thanking him for saving his life. The foreman kneels down and kisses Vito's hands. Vito quickly moves his hand. "Thank you American for saving my life." said the foreman in German.

"I don't know what you said I have no interpreter here, wait until you get to our base." Vito said as he stands back from the hand-kissing prisoner.

"He is no prisoner; he is one of them." Anna said as she points over to the German guards.

"You can speak English?" Vito ask surprisingly

"Yes, I speak a little English, and this man beat us and he has killed some of us." Anna said in anger.

"But he is wearing the same outfit that you're wearing." said the confused Vito.

Anna looks up to Vito. "If he is one of us then why is he fat and not skinny like we are?" Anna said as Vito motions for his Sergeant to come over to him. The foreman sees the armed Sergeant walking toward him. As the foreman panics he runs to the entrance of the Concentration camp.

"Hey stop him." Vito yells pointing at the foreman as the foreman see a large Sherman tank blocking the entrance. The foreman runs to the elective fence and jumps on it.

"Let him go that fence has electricity in it he will die the moment he touches it." Anna said as she watches the foreman jump on the fence and with sparks shooting out the foreman is dead within seconds.

"I decided to take him in and to hold him accountable for his action." Vito said as Anna has a smirk on her face.

"All of us wish this day would happen." Anna said in her broken English as Vito shakes his head.

At that time Vito's radioman runs up "Excuse me Lieutenant, but headquarters radioed that an interpreter is on his way."

Vito looks down at Anna "Tell headquarter not to worry, I already have one." Vito smiles as Anna smiles back at Vito.

At that time, two guards bring out the Kommandant.

"This is the Major in charge of this camp, he was hiding under his desk." said the private as he pushes the barrel of his rifle into the Kommandant's back.

"I surrender my camp to you." said the Kommandant in German as he cries.

"What did he say?" Vito ask as he looks down at Anna who was getting her strength back.

"He said that he is surrendering to you."

"Is this man in charge of the camp?" Vito ask as Anna smiles and nods her head.

"He was in charge until you and the Americans soldiers came." Anna said in a cheerful tone.

Vito grabs the whimpering Major and drags him over to one of the three tanks. "Bring the cannon barrel down." The soldiers inside of the tank smiles as he reaches down and pulls the lever that drops the barrel down. The barrel is lowered to chest high as Vito places the Kommandant in front of the tank's cannon barrel. "If he moves, blow him away." Vito said as the man inside of the tank gives his Lieutenant the thumbs up. Vito walks away leaving Anna behind. Anna smiles as she follows Vito.

For a second the Kommandant moves then he places himself back in front of the barrel of the tank as the man inside of the tank smiles and waves. Vito noticed that Anna wasn't beside of him. Vito looks back and sees Anna walking toward him. Vito stops so Anna can catch up to him as the two walk together. From the kitchen the smell of breakfast filled the camp. As they hadn't had a good meal in weeks all of the American soldiers look over toward the kitchen.

"Well at least you'll eat good here." Vito said as he like the other Americans soldiers turns his head toward the kitchen.

"That's not for us, that food belongs to the German soldiers as does that pig that is frying on that fence. Anna said as she looks over to the foreman that still was attached to the fence. Vito starts to the kitchen then he stops as he sees all of the cooks standing out in the middle of the compound with the other German soldiers.

"Send the cooks back into the kitchen." Vito yells as Anna frowns as she wonders who was going to eat the meal.

As Vito and Anna walk up the stairs Vito turns back around. "Bring me that Major."

"He is going to eat?" Anna asks in an anger tone.

"No, he is going to serve." Vito said with a smile Vito walks in followed by Anna.

"So this is the kitchen?" Anna said as she looks around. The cooks are rushed in by the Americans guards. "Tell then to finish making breakfast." Anna told them in German what Vito said. The cooks nod and bow as they walk into the back, as the Americans guards follow.

Vito looks over to one of his Sergeants. "Bring all of the residents in here, this is their meal."

The Sergeant gives Vito a sad look. "But what about us---sir."

"We will eat what is left." Vito said as he walked Anna over and sat her down where the Kommandant usually sits. The Kommandant is brought in at gunpoint and to Vito. Vito who had sat down beside of Anna turns to her. "Tell the Major that he will be serving this morning. Anna smiles and tells him what Vito said in German.

The Kommandant gives Vito a surprise look. "I am a Major, Lieutenant." said the Kommandant as he stood up tall.

"Yea and I have an M16 so move it." said the private that brought the Kommandant in the room.

"Sir are we going to eat?" asks the private.

"After the residents have eaten then we'll eat the leftovers." Vito said as he watches the entire camps residents file in and sit down. Most of them have problems walking and sitting but with the help of some of the American soldiers and some of the German soldiers all of the residents are brought in and seated. "Hey Major bring us some coffee." Vito said as he pounds the table and Anna laughs. The radioman walks up with his radio.

"Sir, Headquarters wants to know if there is going to be any evacuation from this camp." Vito looks around the dining hall.

"Yea tell Headquarters around five maybe six troop trucks will do it. We can use our troop trucks if we have to; we are going to be here for a while." Vito said not noticing that he places his arm around Anna as he turns to check on the count.

Anna moves closer to Vito. Vito stands up and motions to the residents. "Come on now, let's eat up." Vito said as he looks down making sure that Anna was eating. The tank at the front gate moves, Vito stands up and starts walking toward the door of the mess hall. Anna gets up to follow.

"No, no you stay here and eat." Vito said as he watches Anna sit back down.

"You may need an Interpreter." Anna said in her broken English.

"If the tanks are moving then the troop trucks are here to take resident away from here." Otto said as he motions to one of the guards who was in there guarding the Kommandant and some of his men that are serving the residents. The armed guard gives his Lieutenant the thumbs up as Vito walks out. Vito walks back in and tell the residents to remain eating, as the troops trucks will be taking the German soldiers first. The Kommandant places his tray of cooked eggs onto the table and starts for the front door. "All but you Major we need for you to keep serving your guests." Vito said as he drinks some of the Kommandant's coffee. Holding his cup of coffee Vito walks over to the door and looks out as all of the German soldiers are piling into the trucks.

"About fourteen more soldiers and the camp will be clear of German soldiers." Vito yells out so all could hear. But none of the residents could speak English so Anna rises up and tells them in their German language, they all started to cheer. Vito readies himself to sit down at the bench as he sees the Kommandant dishing out the eggs that the cooks had prepared. "All but the Kommandant that is." Vito smiles as Anna repeats it in German. The Kommandant finishes with the tray of eggs and walks over to Vito and places the tray onto the table. "This is beneath me, like you I am an Officer and I will not serve any more food for you." Drabek said in his broken English, with help of Anna.

"Well you can do what I tell you to do or this private will

take you out back and shoot you." Vito said with the help of Anna.

"I would rather die than to be treated like this." demanded the Kommandant.

"Ok" Vito said as he looks over to the private.

"Take him out back and shoot him." Vito said as the private pushes the Kommandant with the barrel of his rifle.

Both the private and the Kommandant walk to the kitchen. Seconds later the Kommandant runs out with a tray full of toast. As the residents finish their meal, it was time for the American soldiers to finish the rest of the breakfast that the cook had prepared for the Kommandant and the rest of the German soldiers.

"When do I get to eat?" asks the Kommandant.

"When you get to our P.O.W. camp." Vito said as he holds out his empty cup for the Kommandant to refill. The Kommandant reluctantly refills the cup.

As the last German soldiers are loaded in the troop trucks. After the soldiers ae removed the freed prisoners are loaded into separate trucks to be moved. Vito and Anna stands in the compound of the concentration camp. Anna couldn't believe the short time that she has stayed here and the many lives that were lost as the Nazis kidnapped them out of their homes and placed in different concentration camps though out several countries Most were worse than the one that Anna was forced to live in... Some were extermination camps where the occupants never left on their own two feet. Anna and Vito walk the camp side by side they were alone beside of the several Americans guards that stayed behind, but to each other they were alone. Anna and Vito walk over to the spa. Anna stops and looks at it for a second. Vito walks up and opens the door and looks in. "Who was this made for?" Vito ask degusted by the sight. "It was made for us, you can't breathe in it, and you can't move around, it is so hot inside that you sweat all of the time. There is no food, no water and no bathroom. And when the person goes in there the smells from the person before, the guards never wash it out, vomit, human waste it's all left in there. Anna said as she folds her arms around her stomach.

Vito places his arms around Anna's shoulder and gives her a little kiss on top of her head Anna falls in Vito's arms as she stares at the small brick and metal torture chamber that was called the spa. "Give me your pistol." Anna said as she holds out her hands.

"Well Anna I'm not sure of this heavy---." Vito said as he pulls the pistol out of his holster. Anna grabs the pistol from Vito and aims and shoots the spa. Each bullet Anna accurately places in to the spa. Vito didn't know what to say as Anna hands him back his pistol back.

"You've done this before." Vito said as he places his pistol back inside of his holster. Anna smiles as she continues walking, the American soldiers that were guarding the front gate run in.

That's okay fellows, we were target practicing." Vito said as he looks at the bullet holes all line up in order and side by side.

"Tell me about your life here." Vito asks, not sure if he should.

"I was here around five months, on my first day here I was humiliated by the Kommandant, I had two fraulein whipped with a strap, that was the first time that I was placed in the spa for two days, I was threatened by the Kommandant with the SS—"

"What brought this on?" Vito said interrupting.

"It's a long story," Anna said as she walks to the bunkhouse where she and Vito first met. Sadness claims Anna's face as she looks in the bunkhouse.

"We don't have to go in." Vito said as he tries to walk past the bunkhouse and toward the center of the compound

"I woke up this morning as a Jewish prisoner, four hours later I am free, I not sure why I can't realize that I'm free. No one will ever treat me like an animal again."

"Yea, you got that right." Anna looks up toward the Kommandant's office.

"And the beast is gone." Vito added.

"Wait here." Anna said with a smile.

"What, where are you going? You can't go in there we haven't secured that area yet." Vito said as Anna smiles back at him as she runs up the wooden steps and into the Kommandant's office. Vito stands outside looking around at the place that they called the spa and the shack that was calledthe bunkhouse. Vito shakes his head as the shock of what human beings can do to another human. Anna walks out of the Kommandant's office wearing the dress that she worn when she was brought in to the camp. Vito stood there mesmerized by the sight of a beautiful young woman. He couldn't believe his eyes as he stared at Anna who was swinging her dress from side to side. "Where did you get that dress?" Vito asks as his eyes are frozen on the beautiful lady.

Anna smiles as she sees the bulging eyes of Vito. "Do you like?" Anna asks with a smile.

"Very much Vito replies. At that time three Military Police's jeeps rolls through the gate. The men salute Vito and give Anna a strange look.

"Is this a prisoner of yours, sir." laughs one of the MP.

"Get that smirk off of your face Sergeant, this is a lady." Anna wasn't sure what the MP meant for her English wasn't that good; But Anna did know that whatever the MP said Vito was defending her.

"We are here to guard this camp, we didn't mean any harm." said another MP as he walks up and punches the first MP in the arm.

Chapter Twenty-Six

"This is a prisoner that was condemned to this camp; you will treat her with respect." All of the MP's who had gathered around Vito and Anna came to attention and saluted Vito as he gives all of them a dirty look as he leads Anna to his jeep.

Vito helps Anna climb into his jeep then Vito walks around to the other side and steps in as Anna stares at the camp for the last time. As Vito drives away Anna stares at the camp all the way down the road until the camp disappears from her sight. Not a word was spoken as they ride into the next town and to the American's base. As Vito drives into the base he sees the men cheering Vito drives his jeep up to a private. "Private what is the celebration?" Vito ask with a smile.

"It's Hitler sir." said the private laughing. "Did we capture him or what?" Ask Vito as he starts to laugh.

"We don't have to Hitler is dead he committed suicide today. Vito and Anna join in the laughter, as Anna understood what the American soldiers said.

"Hitler is dead." Anna said as she reaches over and kisses Vito. Vito grabs Anna in his arms and held on tight.

"Hitler is dead this war will be over soon." Vito said as he returns to kiss.

"The war is over." Anna said as she sits back in the seat."

"Now I can go home-----." Vito stops and looks at Anna. Anna also stops laughing as she looks back at Vito.

"Where is your home?" Anna asks in a sad tone. "Brooklyn, Brooklyn, New York. Anna tries to smile as she nods her head.

"I guess that I will also be going home." Anna said as she sits and stares at Vito.

"Where is your home?" Vito ask as Anna looks around at the bomb out town where the Americans proclaim it at their Army base.

"I'm not sure where we are, this is not a town anymore it's skeleton of lost lives." Anna said as she climbs out of the jeep and looks over toward Vito as a Major walks over to Vito.

"Lieutenant Ogino, You're just the man that I'm looking for." said the Major as he walks up and slaps Vito on his back. Vito watches Anna walks away as the Major continues to talk. "Adolf Hitler is dead, the Russians confirm it, and they have the bodies of Hitler and his mistress Eva Braun." said the Major. Anna turns and with tears in her eyes Anna waves toward Vito. "Lieutenant, are you paying any attention to me?" Ask the Major as Vito turns his attention from Anna to the Major.

"Yes sir, I'm sorry sir." There are German soldiers around that need to know that the war is over most of them already know but they still want to fight, even though the war is over if they want to fight then kill 'em. But if they give up tell them to drop their weapons and start marching over here, got it?" asks the Major as he pats Vito on his back and walks off.

Vito stands up in his jeep hoping to see Anna, but she has disappeared into the crowds. Vito then looks back at the Major. "The war will be over in a few days now; I'll be sent home as a civilian. What could that lifer do to me as a civilian, nothing." Vito told himself. Then he cranks up his jeep and drove down the street where he saw Anna last. Vito then closes his eyes and makes a U-turn and drives back to the base and gathers up his men. "We need to go and look for German soldiers that don't know that the war is over." Vito said in an angry tone. "Look Lieutenant, I came to this war to kill Hitler, now that he's dead then the war is over as far as I'm concern." Laughs one of Vito's men as he drinks some alcohol. Vito reaches over and slaps the bottle of alcohol out of his soldier's hand. "The war isn't over yet, there is a lot for us to do before we go home and this is one of them." Vito said in anger.

"Now get your gear, in an hour we're moving out." Vito said as he drives off leaving the soldiers behind. Vito makes one more attempt at looking for Anna, this time he sees Anna with her head looking to the ground walking down the street. Vito drives up and jumps out of his jeep. "Anna." Vito yells as Anna turns around. Vito runs up to her and the two embraces.

Vito wipes the tears from Anna's face. "Stay here Anna, please stay here, in a couple of days I'll be back and we can figure on how we are going to get you to the United States."

Vito said in desperation as Anna shakes her head.

"No this is my home I must stay here and find my Papa, United States is your home, and this is mine." Anna said as she pulls away from Vito and without looking back Anna walks away. Vito close his eyes as he watches Anna leave. Vito slowly turns and walks back to his jeep and drives back to the base to get his men.

Soon Anna walks by herself, as the town is many miles behind her. Not knowing where she was Anna walks in the direction that she feels that will lead her back to her Father's farm.

Anna passed the road that lead down to the concentration camp. Anna takes one quick glace over to the road as she walks past, then miles down the road Anna sees the spot where she was picked up by the Nazis and taken to the concentration camp.

A mile or two further down the road was the small town where the town's people saved her life Anna walks up to the back of the burnt down building where she cried knowing that all of her closest friends was murdered by the Nazis.

The town was empty now as the buildings were built side by side and with the burning of the wood builder's building the roaring flames went from building to building. Before long all of the building were set ablaze. Now there were only burnt out shells of the buildings that once were the heart of the area.

Anna walks past the buildings and looks around. Across the street is a small grave site. Anna took a deep breath as she walks over and sees the grave is Hilda's. Anna closes her eyes as she sees her little sister's name on the marker.

Otto is buried there also." said the familiar voice. Anna turns to see the lady who owns the dress shop that gave Anna her dress.

"What happen here?" Anna asks as she walks up to the lady and gives her a tight hug.

"The flames were too big and when it started to spread the whole town went up, the men tried to stop it but it was too late." said the woman as she stared at the place where her shop was.

"And the Nazis?" Anna ask as she places her hands on

the lady's shoulders

"They left right after you did, they didn't see what they caused, I was told that two days later they were ambushed by the British, with no survivors." said the lady in a slight daze.

"How did Otto get here?" Anna asks as she looks over to the side and sees Otto's head stone.

"When the men gave up on stopping the fire they went down and found Otto's body and brought him or what was left of him here and we buried him, next to your sister, I hope that it is alright." asked the lady as she glances over toward Anna.

"Hilda would have wanted that." Anna said as she patted the woman on her back.

"What are you going to do now, are you going to keep on fighting?" ask the lady as she bends over and tosses a pebble away from Otto's grave.

"I'm going home; the war will be over soon since Hitler is dead." Hearing the news of Hitler's death, the lady smiles and turns and walks away without saying a word.

Anna sat down in-between of Hilda and Otto; she sat there for what seems like hours. "Well family" Anna said referring to both Hilda and Otto. "I must go and find Papa. Anna said as she kissed her hand and place it on Hilda's gravestone then she kisses her hand again and placed it on Otto's head stone.

Anna stood up and gave the graves one last look as she continued on her trip. As Anna walked she was surprised by the lack of sound there was. No gunfire, no bombing no one was in pain. But the war was still very alive as Anna walks down the road. Anna could see the throwaway ammo belts that the German soldiers were wearing when they either surrendered or just gave up. Anna reaches down and wraps an ammo belt with a holster around her for the last minutes so that she was prepare to fight if she was called to do so. As Anna walks she realizes that she was wearing a beautiful dress with an ammo belt wrap around. Anna stops and pulls out the Luger pistol and several clips and places them into the pocket of her dress as she drops the ammo belt to the ground. For the first time in a few years Anna feels both safe and pretty.

Chapter Twenty-Seven

Not all German soldiers knew about the death of Hitler as in the background the war is still heard, "Why can't the fly boys drop Pamphlets telling the Germans that Hitler is dead?" said the complaining American soldiers. Vito keeps his eyes on the road as the driver complains. "I would hate to be killed on the last days of the war." The driver continues. "I don't like it either." said Vito as he glances over toward his driver.

"The war is over as far as I'm concerned, we should be packing up to go home, and look at this, we're out here in the open trying to tell the enemy that the war is over." Vito complains for the first time.

"Yea we're out here in the opens"

"A sniper's dream shot." added the driver. Vito and his drivers ride up to a group of German soldiers who knew about the death of Hitler. The German soldiers walk toward them with their hands held high as if they were surrendering. "Pull over at the other side of them." Vito said pointing. The troop truck pulls behind Vito's jeep. As Vito and his driver exit their jeep so did the men in the troop truck. Vito pulls out his revolver hoping that he doesn't have to use it, as his men gather around the surrendering soldiers. Vito sees the German Officer and walks over to him.

"Do you speak English? Vito ask the German Officer. With a sad look on his face the German Officer nods his head. "Yes, I speak a little English."

Vito smiles. "You and your men are aware of the death of Adolf Hitler?" Vito ask as the rest of his men search all of the German soldiers.

"Yes, we know, the war will be over soon, there is no reason to continue the war for us." said the German Officer as he watches the Americans soldiers with their search. "I assured my men that we will be treated well." said the Officer as he turns his attention toward Vito.

Vito motions the Officer to raise his arms up so he also could be search. "Sir, the war is over we are not your enemy any more but we have to make sure that the German Armies are dis-armed for our safety. Without any other choice the German Officers agrees, as he was being searched.

"They are clean." said one of the American soldiers.

"Ok then load them up in the troop truck and head back to the base." said Vito as his men motion to the German soldiers to move. "Sir I would like for you to sit up here in the jeep with us." Vito said as he points over to the jeep. The Officer nods and starts walking toward the jeep. The driver of the jeep pulls back his seat as the Officer climbs into the back of the jeep as Vito sits in the passenger seat. "Who is going to guard him?" Ask the driver. "'No one, we can trust him, and he can trust us, isn't that right?" Vito said as he turns back and looks at the Officer.

"The war is over and Germany has lost, we will surrender with dignity." said the Officer with his head held high.

In his broken English. "And that is what you will get, but I need to know, are there any more soldiers out there that will still fight, we need to bring them in." Vito said as he watches the troop truck turns around and drive back to the base.

There are some in the next town, but they are heavily armed and they will fight to the end." said the German Officer.

"But sir this is the end." Vito said, as he looks straight at the German Officer.

"Not to them, if they are alive then the war will not end." said the Officer with a stern look. Vito looks over to his driver.

"Well we have to go and get them." Vito said as the driver shakes his head.

"Let the fly boys know where they are at and they can blast them from the air." said the driver as he looks over to Vito.

"Well give them a chance to surrender; if they chose to fight then I'll call in the planes." Vito told his driver then Vito turns to the German Officer. "Show us where they are." Vito said as the driver quickly turns to Vito.

"Just the three of us, we'll be dead before we get to the town they must have snipers at the edge of town." said the driver in a panic tone.

"We at least have to give them a chance." Vito said as he motions for his driver to drive on.

"If I tell you where the rest of my men are I will be betraying them." said the Officer, as he has to hold on as the jeep drives off.

"No sir, you'll be saving them for the war is over. Let them live and go back to their families." Vito said as he looks back at the German Officer. As the jeep gets closer to the town the German Officer tells Vito and his driver to stop. As the driver stops the jeep Vito turns and looks at the Officer.

"There are land mines all over this road, we will need to be careful. Vito looks over to his driver who was giving Vito a scared look.

"You drive and the German Officer and I will walk in front checking for the mines." Vito said as he looks at the German Officer. The German Officer gives Vito a strange look.

"Sir you are with us if the jeep hits a mine then you will blow up with us." Vito said as he steps out of the jeep.

The German Officer takes a deep breath as he climbs out of the back of the jeep. Vito pulls out his knife and sits on his knees. "Give him your knife." Vito order his driver. The driver reluctantly pulls out his knife and hands it to the Officer. The Officer looks over the knife then he looks at Vito's driver who reaches down and pulls out his M 16 rifle and smiles. The German Officer smiles back as he kneels down with Vito and plunged the knife into the ground Vito and the Officer plunged their knifes in all direction where the jeep will drive on. A loud metal sound is heard.

"Here is one." said the nervous German Officer. "Ok mark it where my driver will see it.

With Vito and the Officer moving ahead ten feet Vito stands up and motion for his driver to move on. "Turn your wheels left there is a mine there." Vito said as he watches the wheels of the jeep turn and miss the planted bomb. With most of the mines planted in a zigzag pattern the German Officer stands off to the side making sure that the back wheels will past the mines.

"This is the end of the mine field." said the German Officer as he glances over to a hidden sigh.

"How can you tell?" Ask Vito with a little relieve.

"Because he probably planted these mines." Replied the driver.

"Well you still have a few more that you have to miss

before you get up here so drive carefully." Vito said as he motions for the driver to move over to the side.

As the jeep passes the German Officer cleans off the dirt on the knife and hands it back to the driver and walks to the back of the jeep and climbs in as Vito also cleans off his knife and steps into the jeep. "The soldiers will be past the trees." said the Officer pointing straight ahead. Vito pulls out his binoculars and looks into the trees.

"I don't see any snipers up there. The driver places the gear shifter into gear and starts to drive off as the Officer stands up in the back of the jeep. Vito looks up at him as the driver stops.

"The war is over lay down your weapons and come with us." yells the Officer in his German language. Both Vito and his driver were surprised when three Nazi soldiers drop their rifles out of the trees and climb down.

"I thought that you said that the tree was clear?" said the nervous driver.

"I didn't see them." Vito said in shock.

"Well they saw us." said the driver as the German Officer smiles.

"They were trained well." said the Officer with a wide smile on his face. As the German soldiers walk to the jeep with their hands lifted over their heads they were gunned down by the soldiers hidden in the town. Both Vito and his driver grab their weapons and starts shooting toward the town.

"They're not going to surrender." said the German Officer as a stray bullet hits the Officer and knocks him off of the jeep.

"Let's get out of here." yells the driver.

"Alright turn around. Vito said as he looks back and see the German Officer wasn't with them. "Wait I need to check on the Officer." Vito yells to his driver as he steps out of the jeep.

"Turn the jeep around while I check on him." Vito said as he runs over to the German Officer. The driver pulls away as he turns the jeep and continues firing at the town. As bullets hit the ground around Vito and the Officer, Vito kneels down and lifts the Officer's head.

"I didn't want to die by my own men." said the German Officer as he dies.

"I'm so sorry that I brought you up here." Vito said as he laid the German Officers head back down. As the driver turns around and drives toward Vito a German sniper zeroes in on Vito. The sniper fires his rifle hitting Vito in the back. Vito falls to his knees, seeing this the driver pulls up beside of Vito and jumps out of the jeep. Vito who is now bent over tries to lift himself up into the jeep as the driver tries to help, while bullets continue hitting the jeep.

"Sir are you ok?" asks the driver as he lifts Vito into the seat then runs over to the driver side and gets in and drives off.

Passing the mine field, the driver guns the motor and misses all of the mines that were planted. "Call for an air strike." Vito said as the driver grabs the radio and calls it in. Vito reaches around his side and feels the wet blood from his back. Vito pulls his hand back and see his bloody hand. "Anna, where are you?" Vito quickly said as he looks at his bloody hand. From the sight of his own blood and the pain Vito passes out.

Anna continues her walk that led her up to the old cave that she and her sister, along with the rest of the Resistance fighters, called home. Anna looks the cave over and smiles. Then she walks out and sees the graves of the dead Resistance fighters. Not knowing that her father was buried there Anna walks over and kneels down and pats the small handmade headstone.

"I wish that I knew who you are so that I could tell your families, but there is no last name and on the General there is no name. Anna said as she pats the headstones of all of the men all but the General. Anna kisses her hand and places it onto of the General's headstone. Staring at the General's headstone Anna stands up and continues her walk back home. It was getting dark as Anna searches for a good place to sleep.

In the woods Anna sees three trees in a triangle form, Anna walks over to the trees and places leaves down to make herself a bed. Now with the sun down and Anna almost asleep she has thoughts of her father working out in the fields as her mama bringing him something cold to drink. Marc drinks the cold water down and smiles as he gives the glass back to Eva as the two laugh, hug and finish with a kiss. Anna sees Hilda walking up to her parents and the three embrace. Anna could see them and as she starts walking toward them they all vanish.

Anna is alone until Otto walks up and stands beside of her. Anna turns and smiles as she sees Otto "I love you." Otto said as he too vanishes. Anna turns from side to side hoping to see her love once again. But no one is there as Vito walks up.

"They're all gone now, it's us." Vito said as he tries to place his arms around Anna but as Anna stands still Vito disappears. Anna awakes as her body jerks. Now it is daylight Anna must continue her march home. Anna stands up and wipes the dirt off of her dress and looks around her making sure that the war was not around her. Anna then walks up to the dirt road and continues her walk. Miles and miles down the road Anna could feel the hunger. From the side of the road Anna ate the berries that she found. Before long Anna was at the back of a one-time farm where the grounds were filled with carrots. Anna pulls up the carrots and smiles as she ate real food for the first time in a while. Anna took all that she could carry then she continued walking down the road. Anna comes up to a bombed out house. Anna stood and stared at the house. Anna drops the half eaten carrot as she realized that she was standing in front of her old house. "I'm home." Anna told herself in a soft tone. Anna runs up to the house and starts crying at the sight of the bombed out shell that was once her family's home.

With bullet holes that filled the walls, the kitchen destroyed by bombs and bullets. Anna looks out of the place where there once was a widow and sees the barn barely standing from a fire that burnt most of it down. Anna walks to her old bedroom and saw some of her old work cloths thrown in the floor. Anna took off her dress and put her work clothes on. "I'll get this farm going again." Anna told herself.

"When Papa gets back he'll be proud of me."

Anna said as she walks out to the burnt out barn to see if there is any equipment that she could use. Anna saw a rake and a shovel. "Well this is a start." Anna said as she walks over and picks them up. Anna walks out to the field and with the rake Anna started raking the ground as she hears a truck driving down the road. Anna reaches inside of the pocket but she feels no pistol, it was still in the pocket of her dress that was hanging inside of her bullet-riddled closet. Anna grips her rake tightly in her hands and watches as the American troop truck passes by. Anna was relieved that the truck didn't stop.

Anna started back raking up the ground.

For days Anna works on the grounds trying to get it ready for the planting. Every time that Anna would rake up the ground she has to bend over and pick out the bullets that hit the ground during the many battles that were fought on her land.

Anna would throw the spent bullets into a pile after a while Anna's pile becomes larger and larger. Anna would look up hoping to see her father walk up but he never came.

Chapter Twenty-Seven

The driver got Vito back to the base where the driver starts yelling for a medic. As the doctors and nurses run toward the jeep, Vito due to the lack of blood collapses. "The Lieutenant was shot in his back." yells the driver, as Vito is taken away. "Get him to the OR." Yells the doctor in charge. As the Major walks up and sees Vito being carried off.

"What happened?" asks the Major.

"He followed orders and look what happen to him." said the driver as he walks to the make-shift hospital.

After the operation Vito is placed in a hospital bed to recover from his wound. After a while Vito is able to sit up and stares into space. Vito thinks of the time that he spent with Anna.

Vito wonders where she is, what she is doing, if she was ok. The Major walks up and taps Vito on his bare foot that was sticking out from the bed. "How are you doing son?" Ask the Major as he walks up. "I'm doing fine; the nurses said that I will be leaving here in a couple of days." Vito said as he looks up to the Major. "I don't know if you heard but the German did surrender and the war is over." said the Major as Vito looks up at him. "When did this happen?' Vito ask.

"A few days ago, you've been out for a few days now."

"Anna." Vito said to himself.

"Who is Anna, your girl back home?" said the Major with a grin on his face.

"If she is then you'll get to see her when you get release from the hospital, you're going home son, with more medals to impress all of the women's in New York. I heard about the German Officer and what you tied to do, you are a war hero and I'm glad to have you under me when I get to Benning." Vito looks up to the Major.

"Benning, sir." With a smile on his face the Major walks over and stands in front of Vito's face.

"Now I know that Fort Benning is in Georgia and you're from New York but have you ever heard of the Georgia Peaches, that's what they call their beautiful women, I would like to take you there if you decide to stay in the Army."

I'm not sure of what I'm going to do now that the war is over." Vito said, in shock.

"Well as soon that you are well enough then I'll be back to get your answer." said the Major as he smiles and walks away.

"Uh, sir what about the German civilians that helped us in the war you know the Resistance fighters?" The Major stops and turns around.

"Some of them will be going to the States but they have to know that we were fighting for them to have a better way of life why." said the Major as he stops and turns around.

"How do we get them to the States?" Vito ask as he sits up in his bed.

"Well they have already left; they were in the first wave of soldiers that went home. You'll be one of the last whenever you're able to leave.

"All of my men have left already?" Vito ask as he has trouble sitting up.

"They was in the first wave to leave, they didn't want to leave without you but they did, your men love you and I know that I can use you in Benning. Think about it and let me know." said the Major as he walks away.

"I need to find Anna." Vito said. Vito tries to stand up but the lack of blood cause Vito to fall back on his bed as the nurses run over to help him up. The next morning Vito tries again to stands up. Vito is weak but he was getting stronger.

"You need to stay in bed." said one of the nurses.

"Where are you from?" Vito ask the nurse as she helps Vito back into his bed.

"Cincinnati, Ohio." said the nurse as she covers Vito up with the blanket.

"Do you have a husband in Cincey?" The nurse stops for a second then she continues to stuff the blanket under Vito.

"I did, but he was sent to fight the Japanese and he died in a battle that we were supposed to win no one was supposed to have been hurt." said the nurse as she gives a cold stair.

"I'm sorry, I didn't know." said Vito as he places his hand on the nurse's shoulder. The nurse moves her shoulder knocking Vito's hand off. "When are you going home?" Vito asks as the nurse looks over to him.

"I'll be on the last wave home, and I not going to replace my husband." said the nurse as she finishes and walks away.

"I need to find my love." Vito said as he lies back in his bed and thinks about Anna. Each day Vito is getting stronger and stronger on the third day Vito stands up and takes five steps, still weak Vito takes five more steps. "Anna, I'm going to find you and take you home with me." Vito said making Anna his inspiration to get better. Vito would walk the floor of the hospital for strength. Before long Vito was strong enough to walk outside. Vito sees a jeep and walks over to it and climbs in.

"Well here I am stealing a jeep, but Anna is worth it." Vito told himself. Vito drives around the surrounding towns looking for Anna. The towns now filled with former German soldiers still angry with the Allied Army for their losses give Vito an unwelcoming stare when he enters their town.

"Excuse me fraulein, but do you know a fraulein name Anna Metz?" Vito asks everyone that he had seen. Most women shake their heads and walk away with their husbands, who were still wearing their German uniform, who would grab their wife's arm and lead them away from the outsider American soldier.

"I come in peace." Vito said as he stood in the middle of the street.

"Go home American, there is no one for you here, besides you are out-numbered here." said one of the former German soldier.

"I'm unarmed I have no hatred toward Germany, I just want to find my friend, that's all."

"Go home so we can rebuild our homes and town."
Said an angry Frau. Three former German soldiers started walking toward Vito; they were carrying broken bricks from one of the bombed out building. Vito sees them approaching and quickly walks toward his jeep and drives off as broken bricks are thrown at him and his jeep. Vito drives out of the town and down another road where he passed several bombed out homes.

Vito shakes his head at the destruction of war. "I can understand why they hate me." Vito said to himself.

Vito passed the farm that was owned by the Metzs'.

Vito slows down and looks at the farm or what there was of it. Then Vito moves on passing the bombed out house where Anna was sitting on the floor and eating raw carrots.

Anna heard the jeep drive by but she didn't move. Anna sat there eating her so call meal. As the jeep was further down the road Anna stood up and look out of the window and saw the jeep drive away. "I wish that was Vito." Anna said as she sat back down and finished her carrots then lying down.

With tears in his eyes Vito drives back to the base where his Major was waiting. "Stealing a jeep is a federal offence." laughs the Major.

"I'm sorry, but I had to see someone before I left." Vito said as he steps out of the jeep and walks over toward the Major.

"A fraulein maybe?" said the Major as he laughs harder.

"Yes sir, I want to take her to Brooklyn." Vito said as he walks past his Major.

"That is also a federal offence, beside we're not welcome here and when we get back home and all of the wounded soldiers get home then even German civilians won't be welcome, even if they were German born in the States. But if both of us were in Benning then I may be able to pulls some strings for you and your fraulein." said the Major as Vito walks past him.

"My family lives in Brooklyn, I've been away from them for a long time and my parents are getting older every day that I'm here, I need to stay with them, my parents and my kid sister is all that I got, I need to go home." Vito said as he walks back to the hospital.

Then you're going home today get packed." said the disappointed Major.

Vito slowly packs his duffel bag with his belongings and walks over to the newly built airfield where he checks in with a Sergeant, they take Vito's duffel bag and hand it to a private that loaded it onto a cart to be sent out to the transport plane.

Vito sat down and waited for the plane to be fueled and loaded.

"Excuse me sir but the plane is ready for the Officers to board first." said the Sergeant that checked Vito in.

"You know I was a Sergeant when I first got over here.

Working with the Resistance fighters made me an Officer now I'm going home and they are here to suffer from the German soldiers that will be taking over when we leave." Vito said as he stands up and walks toward the plane with the Sergeant following him.

"Yea, I heard that some of the Resistance fighters have already disappeared." said the Sergeant as Vito quickly turns around and looks at him. Vito closes his eyes as he thinks of Anna and the danger that she is in. Vito climbs the stairs leading into the plane as the Sergeant salutes. Vito returns the salute and enters the plane.

"But that is what the Resistance fighters get for fighting their own side." said the Sergeant as he walks away.

Vito stands at the door of the plane and looks out at the Sergeant. Vito walks inside of the plane as he sees the enlisted men running toward the plane. The flight home was long and boring. Vito stares out of the window thinking about Anna.

Anna makes little progress on the farm. Days turn into weeks and with no sight of her father Anna realize that her father may be dead. Anna who was sitting on the floor eating some of the vegetable that she was able to grown rolls over and facing the floor cries for her father.

Back in Brooklyn Vito got his old job back as a truck driver. Vito would drive to all of the shops around Brooklyn and deliver their goods. All of his friends saw the change in Vito as he was no longer the women craze man who had a joke and a line to pick up all of the women in town. Vito would deliver his good to the stores and restaurant. Where before the war Vito always got a good deal on the products that he delivered as a good meal at the restaurant, as the cooks would prepare his meal as he unloaded their goods. When he was finished a waitress would meet him at the back door and flirt with him as he once did with them as he ate. Now Vito sat in quietness as he eats.

Finally, the waitress would give up and walk away leaving Vito alone.

Each day Anna works the fields hoping to bring the crops that one-day would also bring her father

At the end of the day Anna would look around a see what

kind of progress she has made. The field was ready to be planted but it was still far away from where Marc would have had it. Knowing this Anna drops her rake and falls to her knees.

"Papa would have this farm up and going by now." Anna cried. Anna looks over toward the house that was still a bombed out shell of a house. "Where is Vito?" Anna asks herself. "Germany is no longer my home; I need to get to the United States and to Brooklyn." Anna said as she drops her pack and walks over to her house and gathers up her dress the only belonging that she had. Walking away from the house Anna stops and takes one last look at the place where she and her sister grew up and where her parents made a home.

Now there is no one left and Anna knew that it was time to leave and start a life in America. But getting there won't be easy. "I need American money." Anna said as she remembers the two large stacks of dollars that the concentration camp Kommandant hid as she was walking out of his office.

That's my money." Anna said with a smile.

Chapter Twenty-Eight

Anna hoped that she could find the Concentration camp before it was too late as the Allies were leaving Germany as soon as they could. With her pistol in her hand and her dress in the other Anna walks the dirt roads. Being in the back of the German's troop truck Anna didn't see the surrounding area the first time that she made the trip to the camp. The second trip Anna couldn't take her eyes off of the young handsome American soldier. Now she is on her own hoping to find the place where she and other victims called home.

With luck on her side Anna saw the high gun tower that guarded the camp from the outside. Anna's eyes grew wider as she saw the tall tower, Anna ran up the dirt road to the first set of fences. But the smile left her face when she saw the American's soldiers walking around the camp. Anna walks toward the gate and drops her dress into the woods as she places her pistol into her pocket. Noticing the budge in her pocket from the pistol Anna place the pistol on her hidden dress and walks toward the front gate where she is stopped by an armed guard. "Wait a minute young lady, you can't go in there." said the guard with one hand in an outreach position and the other hand resting on his sling rifle.

"I use to live here." Anna said in her broken English.

"I'm sorry, but I still can't let you in." said the guard, as he stands in-between of Anna and the gate.

"Please, I need to go in there; I need some closure from this death camp." Anna said as a fake tear appears in her eyes. The sentimental soldier gave in to the fake tears and let Anna inside of the camp.

"Stay away from the prison barracks, we have people in there taking pictures, maybe you can answer some questions for us since you're a survivor from here.

"Just give me some time by myself and I will answer all of the questions you have." Anna said as she looks over to the spa.

The guard notices Anna staring at the small brick building. Did you ever stay in there?" ask the concerned guard.

Anna nods her head (yes) as the guard shakes his head in misbelieve. "Well at least you had some holes to get some fresh air." said the guard referring to the bullets hole that Anna shot the last time that she was there with Vito.

Anna looks up at the guard but doesn't say a word. The guard steps aside as Anna walks in. Anna walks directly to the Kommandant's office and toward the back of the room.

As Anna walks past the window she looks out making sure that she will be alone. The guard at the gate walks over to the barracks where the rest of the soldiers were taking pictures.

Anna could see that the guard talking to the men inside then pointing toward the Kommandant's office. As the three men walk over toward the Kommandant's office Anna knew that she had to work quickly. Anna walks over to the floor and quickly pulls up the small wooden slat from the floor and grabs the two bundles of American cash and walks over to the back window and throws it over the large electric fence. As Anna closes the window, the American soldier's walk into the room. Anna is sitting in the chair behind of the Kommandant's desk. "May we talk to you?" Said the Officer taking out his camera and starts taking Anna's picture. Anna covers her face and runs out.

"I'm sorry but I must be leaving now." Anna said as she runs past the three men. Anna runs out of the front gate and toward her dress and pistol. Anna looks at her pistol then she places the pistol in the back of her pants. She checks to make sure that she wasn't followed as she runs through the woods to the back fence near the Kommandant's office. Checking around her Anna looks from side to side making sure that she was still alone. Anna takes the two bundles of cash and places them in the front of her pants. Then place the bottom of her shirt over them hiding them from being seen. With a smile on her face Anna makes the long trip back to the American Army base hoping to find Vito before he leaves. It was getting dark as Anna reaches the Army base. Anna ducks behind some building and changes her cloths from the work cloths back to her dress.

Anna places the two bundles of American monies into the one of the pocket in the front of the dress; the Anna places her pistol and the clips in the other. "I must find Vito." Anna told herself as she tosses the work cloths away and started walking toward an American Officer who was looking over some papers. Anna walks up to him as the American Officer doesn't pay her any attention as he checks his papers then yells to his men. "Corne get that operation table loaded on the plane, don't worry about the tents, they can stay if we have to leave them." yells the Officer as he checks then rechecks his papers.

"Excuse me sir, but do you know a Lieutenant Vito Ogino?" Anna asks in her broken English.

"Yea, I do." said the Officer as he still concentrated on his papers and the way that his men were loading the plane. Anna moves around trying to get up with the Officer.

"Do you know where he is?" Anna asks as she finally stood next to the Officer.

"Yea, he's back home." said the Officer as he finally turns and looks at Anna "May I help you." asks the Officer as he looks at the beautiful woman standing next to him.

"That's ok." Anna said with a sad look on her face as she walks away.

"Are you sure I know Vito he's a good friend of mine, we share things." yells the Officer as Anna walks away.

"I'm going to Brooklyn." Anna said as she nods her head. Anna leans up against a tree as she watches the plane get loaded. Anna watches as the American soldier's load everything from an Officer's jeep to linens from the hospital. "Where is that plane going?" Anna asks herself. Anna walks up to the fence that separates the plane from the German people. Staring at the plane a soldiers see Anna and he thinks that she was staring at him. The small over weight soldier walks over toward Anna who was looking through him and at the plane. With his shirt off, from the heat of the day, the proud soldier tries to impress his new on-looker with his muscles. Flexing them as he pretends to wipe off the sweat and dirt from his arms. "May help you." said the Private as he smiles at Anna.

"Where is this plane going?" Anna asks as she points toward the plane.

"The United States, why?" said the private as he stops at the fence as Anna walks up.

"Where in the United States?" Anna asks as she still

~ 252 ~

doesn't notice the chubby little soldiers.

"I don't know; I think that this plane is going to New York City." said the private as he tries to flex his chest.

"I need to go to New York City." Anna said as she now notices the chubby private bouncing his flabby chest.

"I need to go to New York City myself, want to fly with me I can show you my cockpit." said the private as he gives Anna the eye.

"You get me on that plane and I will give you this." Anna said as she reaches into her pocket for one of the bundle of cash. The private's eyes grew as he sees Anna reach down and into her dress. Then his eyes grew wider as he sees the bundle of cash. As the private reaches for the cash Anna pulls it back to her. "Get me on this plane and you can have this."

"Hey where did you get this, oh I know your made it the old fashion way." said the private as he reaches down and tugs on Anna's dress. Worried that the Private was going to touch the pistol Anna backs away.

"Tell you what I'll take that cash and----" Before the private could say another word the Officer saw him and started yelling.

"Private, if you don't want to be left behind then I suggest that you get a move on and get this plane loaded."

Anna waves the bundle of cash at the Private as he walks off. The Private wasn't sure of what to do as his Officer was yelling at him and Anna waving the wad of cash in front of him. With a sad look on his face the Private decided to follow his Officer's order to get back to work. Anna drops her hand with the cash down to her waist as she hoped that the soldier would take the money and help her get to America.

Anna watches as all of the soldiers would go into the adjoining building and bring out what was needed to the place onto the plane. As all of the soldiers were away Anna climbs over the small fence and ran toward the open plane. Anna places the bundle of cash at the side door of the large cargo filled plane.

Anna quickly hides when she heard the American soldiers walking to the plane. "How many more trips do we have until we are finish with this plane?" ask one of the loaders to the chubby soldier.

"This should be it." said the chubby soldier as he looks and see the cash. With his eyes wide at the sight of the cash the chubby little soldier drops his end of the Operation table that they were carrying.

"What is wrong with you?" asked the chubby private helper.

"My hand slipped, hey grab that wheel before it rolls under the plane's engine." said the cubby private as he reaches down and picks up the bundle of cash that Anna had left him. The chubby Private looks inside of the cargo bin of the plane and sees Anna trying to hide in-between two Operation table. "You know if I was going to stay back here then I would lay on the back of the jeep that is in the front, the back of the jeep has a cushioned back seat." said the chubby soldier loud enough so that Anna could hear him.

As the second soldier walks up with the small wheel in his hand. He looks over inside of the plane to see whom his friend was talking to. "You're really losing it man, who are you talking to?" said the soldier as he tosses the wheel into the back of the plane.

"I'm talking to you, if I was going to fly home back here then I would sit or lie on the back of the jeep."

The second soldier looks over to the chubby soldiers. "Yea, but at 40 thousand feet in the air, it would be freezing back here, you wouldn't have a chance, and you'll be frozen to death." said the second soldier as he punches the chubby soldier.

"Then I would get some bed sheets from the crates labeled hospital linen." Yells the chubby soldier as he was ready to close the din door as two M.P. walks up.

"Hey wait a minute, we have to check out this compartment for stowaways." said one of the M.P.

"What stowaways, we have been right here loading this plane for hours now and we haven't seen any stowaways." said the chubby soldier.

"Yea beside this is our last plane for tonight now we get to eat." said the second soldier.

"After we finish looking this plane over." demanded the

M.P.

"Come on Sergeant we have been busting our butts since early this morning, we're tired and hungry and we have to stay here with you until we can button this bin up, now I heard that the Red Cross has sent over some hamburgers from the States and it's first come first serve." said the chubby soldier as he tries to close the cargo bin on the plane.

"Yea, delicious hamburgers." added the second soldier. The two M.P. looks at one another then they look back at the loaders.

"Fresh beef hamburgers from the States?" ask one of the M.P.'s as both of them looks at the loaders.

"Yea, beef from the mid-west, Oregon or someplace like that." said the chubby soldier.

"Let's go." said one of the M.P.'s as the chubby soldier turns off the lights and closes the bin door and the four men walk away. From the cockpit Anna hears the pilots going through their pre-flight checklist. With just a narrow door separating Anna and the pilots she is careful with her movements. In the dark Anna moves over to the bin door and searches for the light switch, rubbing her fingers across the wall Anna feels the switch and turns on the cargo light as the plane starts moving. Anna braces herself as the plane moves across the bumpy dirt tarmac to the better grade of dirt runway. As the cargo moves with each of the bumps Anna tries to make it back to the jeep where she climbs in the back. Anna didn't know what to expect on her first flight.

Anna feels all of the bumps on the runway, and feels the pulling of the G-force as the planes lifts off.

Anna holds on tight as the plane gain altitude then leveling off. Anna looks over toward the cargo light. "If the pilots come back here then they can see me." Anna told herself as she stares at the light switch. As the plane hits some turbulence Anna is knocked from the padded seat of the jeep and unto the jeep's floor. As Anna gives out a little scream as she lands in the jeep's floor. Anna places her hands over her mouth hoping that the pilots didn't hear her. With their headsets on the pilots didn't hear Anna scream. Anna lays in the jeep's floor for the next twenty minutes or so.

In high attitude the air in the un-pressurized cargo area becomes thin and cold. Anna stayed in the floor as long as she could until she could see her breath as she breathes.

Anna saw the operating tables and some of the hospital beds that were loaded. Anna slowly stood up and walks over to the beds hoping that she could find some blankets or sheets.

But the beds were bare so Anna had to search in the boxes around the tables and beds. Anna carefully pulls down a box that was stack too high causing it to fall down. This time the pilots hears the noise as the co-pilots pulls his headset and starts toward the back to see what happen. As the co-pilot walks to the door that separates the cockpit from the cargo area he pulls out his pistol. "What are you doing?" Ask the pilots as he laughs.

"If there is a stowaway back there then I'm going to shoot him." said the co-pilot as he tries to show no fear but the pilot knew better.

"Just don't shoot yourself, you're going to be taking over for me so I can get some sleep." said the pilot as he watches the co-pilot walk through the door and into the cargo area.

Anna hears the cockpit door slowly open. As the co-pilot walks back and sees the wooden crate and all of its contents scattered around the floor of the plane then the co-pilot slowly looks around to see if there was a stowaway.

The co-pilot gives out a little relieved sigh as he turns around and walks back to the cockpit. Anna watches, as the door is closed before she pulls herself from the many mattresses that the soldiers stacked up. Anna took a deep breath as she felt safe enough to walk back to the jeep. "Well what did you see?" ask the pilot as his co-pilot places his pistol back into his holster and sat back down.

"A crate fell over, those loaders had no clue on how to load a plane." said the co-pilot as he places his headset back on. Anna gave up her search for a blanket, as she starts back for the jeep. Then Anna notices the personal duffel bags of the pilots. Anna reaches in and pulls out an U.S. Army Officer's jacket. Anna smiles as she found something to keep her warm. Anna went back to the jeep and huddle up in the padded back seat of the jeep.

Still cold Anna rolls herself into a ball trying to keep the heat in. The long bumpy flight was more than Anna had expected. Anna shook her head as she realized what she was doing.

"What am I doing? I know nothing about the United States, My Country was in war with their Country, I know little English and I know nothing about New York, I need a map."

From the inside of the cockpit Anna could hear the pilots talking into their headsets asking permission to land.

Anna not knowing what to expect braced herself by holding onto the back of the driver's seat. As she feels the plane descending. Scared of the landing Anna breaths deeper than usual, at the sight of her breath Anna becomes more alarmed as she is knocked backwards, as the plane touches down. Holding on tight Anna is jerked from the back seat but Anna holds on tight and doesn't fall back. As the Pilots give each other a hand shake, Anna close her eyes and gives a little "Thank You."

Anna must now hide from the men who will be unloading the plane's cargo. But Anna wasn't sure how she was going to escape the plane. As the plane comes to a stop Anna once again must find a good hiding place just in case the pilots come out to gather up their belongings. Anna stuffs the Jacket back into the duffle bag and runs back to the mattresses where she hides as the pilots do come out and gather up their belongings.

What happened to your duffle bag?' ask the co-pilot as the pilot grabs his bag and starts looking around it.

"Did you see any one back here when you came back?" asks the angry pilots to his co-pilot.

"No, it must have fallen over when we touched down." answers the co-pilot with a small grin. "Have, you gone through my stuff looking for the medal that you said that you should have gotten instead of me."

"I didn't go through your duffle bag." Claims the co-pilot as he holds back the smile.

"Well then what happen?" ask the pilot as he checks his belonging.

"It was a tough landing and your duffle bag rolled over." answers the co-pilot, with the only excuse that he had.

Well, when I get to my barracks I'm going through my bag

and they're better be nothing missing." said the pilot as he walks back into the cock-pit and out of the door. Anna tries to follow but the cargo hatch is open. Anna runs back to the mattresses and hides as three men walk in and look around. "Start with these operating tables and I'll have everything broke lose when ya'll get back." said the man who was carrying the clipboard. The other two men nod and grab the first table and as the man in charge places his clip board onto the next table and starts untying the rope that held the tables together.

With the third man still in the plane Anna knew that she would be found. Anna closes her eyes trying to think of something she could do to get rid of the third man. Then from the outside a crash is heard. The third man grabs his clipboard and runs out. "Are you that stupid that you can't handle a table?" yells to the third man as he exits the plane. Anna slowly moves to the hatch and looks out. Seeing the third man place his clipboard onto the table and grab one end of the table and lift it as the other two men grab the other end. As other planes land, Anna sees the soldiers exit their planes and toward their awaiting family. "I need to mix in with their family." Anna told herself as she took one last look to see the men walk into a large building carrying the table. Anna jumps out of the plane and runs straight toward the crowds. Anna runs from one plane to another trying to get closer to the crowds and avoiding the men who were unloading the planes. As Anna reaches the returning troops, the returning soldiers thought that she was there to greet her returning hero.

With her beauty some of the returning soldiers grab her and kiss her. But Anna was there for one man and one man only, finding him will be Anna's hardest mission.

First Anna must find Brooklyn. "How hard will that be?" Anna asks herself. "Will Vito remember me?" Was another question? Anna reaches the family and friends section at the airport. Now Anna must find her way to Brooklyn.

Chapter Twenty-Nine

While her English wasn't that good and Anna didn't want the people to know that she was a German girl. Anna had to get to Brooklyn but Anna needed help by the same people that her homeland country was at war with. Anna walks up to a lady who was standing behind the crowd waiting to see her love one.

Anna places her hands over her mouth. "Excuse me Fra-" Anna stops herself before she blew her cover. "Excuse me miss, how can I get to Brooklyn?" Anna asks in a sick voice hoping that she could get by with a bad cold voice.

The lady glances over at Anna with tears rolling down her face the lady points to the right. Anna gives the lady a smile.

"Thank you, I hope that you can see your husband." Anna said as she starts in the direction that the lady sent her.

"He's dead, but he was with this group of men." said the crying woman as Anna stops and walks back to her and gives the crying lady a hug. "I'm so sorry." Anna said in her broken ascent.

The lady looks up to Anna. Her eyes widen by Anna's German ascent. Without saying a word, the lady returns Anna's hug. "Brooklyn is in that direction you can't miss It." said the lady as she turns her attention to the home coming of the troops. Before Anna left the airport's field Anna turns around and takes one last look at the returning soldiers and the families that gather around them with their love.

Tears rolls down Anna's face as she sees all of the men being greeted by their loved ones. Anna smiles as she walks away.

On the outside of the airport Anna see the thousands of taxicabs waiting for their next fare. Anna walks in-between the rows of cabs hoping to see Vito as one of the drives.

"Hey miss, where you want to go?" ask one of the cab drivers as Anna walks past him. Anna smiles as she walks by. Anna knew what they were because they had cab drivers in Berlin where her father Marc would take the family for a day trip to the city. Anna kept on walking to save the large stack of American monies that she had. As she glances from cab to cab Anna never saw Vito so at the end of taxi row Anna continues walking toward Brooklyn.

Anna reaches into her pocket making sure that the money was still there. Anna is surprised when she found the pistol.

For a second Anna had thought of throwing the pistol away. This is America, where she should be safe. But the pistol gave her comfort. For several years Anna carried a pistol or a rifle or machine gun it will be hard for her to just give them up even thou she was in a different country where the people weren't at war with each other. Anna reaches with her other hand and pulls out the stack of cash then she places the pistol into her pocket and the cash on top of the pistol.

Anna's journey to Brooklyn was long and tiring as she reaches the large sign reading Brooklyn Anna smiles "This is home." Anna said with a smile. As the sun goes down Anna looks for a place to stay. During the war Anna slept wherever she and Hilda found. Anna had slept on the coldest grounds and in the summer Anna sleeps on the dirt where bugs would crawl on her all night long. So sleeping in New York can't be that bad. As the sun quickly disappears Anna found refuge behind a building where there was an overhang at the back door where Anna could sleep and if it rains the overhang would keep her dry. "Tomorrow, I'll look for Vito and a better place to sleep." Anna said as she reaches up and unscrews the light bulb at the back porch with a discarded old newspaper Anna saw sticking out of the trashcan. Anna left the back porch light dim so it would give out little light. The hard but large back porch was Anna's first night in her new Country, a little excited but more scared of what she had heard of the Americans mostly from her father Marc, about the cruelty of the Americans that captured him in the first World war. Anna looks at her first home made bed the porch was made from bricks. Anna remembers the nights that she had spent in the spa. The cold brick floor in the winters and the hot bricks of the summer, but this time Anna was free, it was her decision where she slept as she chose the back porch of a small bakery in Brooklyn. Anna walks over to the trash can for more newspapers Anna goes through the trashcan hoping to find some cardboard to place on top of the bricks. Anna pulls up a bag of day old bread and pastries.

Anna stared at the bag; she hasn't eaten since the last time she was in Germany over a day and a half ago. And these bags were in the trashcan still the smell coming from the bags was good and Anna was hungry. Anna reaches in and pulls out a hard stale apple turn-over Anna gave the pastry a good smell. The turn-over still had the freshness smell so Anna took a small bite. Anna closes her eyes as she enjoyed the treat.

Anna continues searching into the trashcan for what she needed with one hand as Anna's other hand held the apple treat. After thirty minutes Anna's bed was completed using old newspapers and large cotton bags that held the flour for the treats that she was eating. Anna found enough bags to roll three of them up and place it into one bag giving her a pillow. Anna hasn't had a pillow since before the war now the homemade pillow was a comfort that she needed and used.

Before Anna lay down she looks for something to cut some of the large flour bags. As darkness cover the ground Anna uses the shining moon to look around for something sharp.

Next door to the bakery was a furniture shop where Anna found a discarded hack saw. The blade from the saw was worn down with no cuts left in it. Anna smiles as she took the hack saw and walks back to her homemade bed where she cuts the sides of the flour bags and spread the bags out giving her the blanket that she needed. Anna was now set for the night.

Lying on her back Anna enjoyed to pastry. Soon Anna slowly falls asleep dropping the pastry onto the ground.

As several old newspapers for a mattress and rolled up flour bags as a pillow and stretched out flower bags as a blanket. Anna had the first good night sleep in months or maybe years.

The next morning Anna is awoken by the sounds of the baker inside his kitchen baking his goods for the day. Anna jumps up and gathers up her bed and runs off of the porch and over to the side of the building hoping that the baker wouldn't come out and discover her. Anna looks over to the porch and sees that she had left the old newspapers that she had used for her mattress. Anna slowly moves to the porch only to be stop by the opening of the back door. Anna pulls back to the edge of the building as the baker walks out carrying more trash.

The baker drops his trash onto the porch and reaches down and picks up the flatten newspapers. "Vagrants." said the Baker as he looks around. The baker grabs the newspapers up in anger and walks over and places the paper back into his trashcan. Felling that she needed to leave Anna made sure that she still had the pillow and blanket and the bag of pastry and walks away.

A couple of buildings away Anna saw an old crate standing next to a building. Anna stores her new bed covering into the crate and she reaches into the bag for her breakfast of stale old pastries as she continues her search for Vito Ogino.

Anna looks at everyone that she saw. As they were looking at her. Anna's dress now wrinkled from the trip from Germany and the night where she had worn her dress as she slept.

The stale pastry wasn't filling, Anna wanted some breakfast. But Anna was afraid that she would have to order in her broken English, as she wouldn't know how the people in the tiny restaurant would act being that her language is more German than American. But Anna was hungry and she had no other choice but to go in. Still checking out all of the people around her Anna walks straight toward the restaurant.

Still no sight of Vito as she walks in. Anna sat down at a table where she tried to read the menu, but the menu being in English was Anna's next problem as Anna barley spoke English she knew none of the words that were printed in English.

A waitress walks up carrying a pot of coffee. As the waitress walks up to Anna she places the pot of coffee down on the table and wipes away some dirt that was on Anna's dress. "Look like you had a bad night." said the waitress as she cleans off Anna's dress around the shoulder

"What can I get you?" Ask the waitress as another waitress walks up to the man at the next table and ask him his order. The man told the waitress his order of Eggs, bacon and toast. Anna pays close attention to what the man orders and she orders the same as the man hoping that she could order something good to eat. "What kind of jelly would you like?" Ask the waitress as she started to leave Anna's table. Anna's eyes grew wide as she wasn't sure what the waitress had asked her. "I'll bring you a little of all that we have." said the waitress as she turns and walk toward the kitchen.

Anna slowly drank some of her coffee as she scans the room hoping to see Vito. Anna smiles as she sees all of the people laughing and talking among themselves. Anna felt safe there but she knew that the war in Germany ended just five months ago and she was scared if they found out that she was German born. How would they re-act if they had lost a love one by the hands of the German Armies? Then Anna saw two men staring at her Anna quickly looks away hoping not to bring any attention to her as both waitress brought the man his food as well as Anna's food. Anna tried to look over to see what the man and herself had ordered, the waitress places Anna's plate in front of her. Anna smiles as she saw her order and try to remember the American words so she could order it again.

Anna ate fast because of hunger. The two men couldn't take their eyes off of her. Anna watches their every move.

Anna waited for the man in front of her finish his meal.

When the man gets up and walk up to the register to pay Anna follows him. The man pulls out a five-dollar bill. Anna saw the bill and reaches into her pocket and without bringing the stack of bills out Anna looks over the bills and finds a five and pulls it out. Anna smiles as she waits her turn to pay. Anna glances over to the men at the table on the other side of the building.

They were still watching her. The men slowly talk to themselves as Anna looks on. Then it was Anna's turn to pay.

Anna notices that the man walks back over and place some coins on the table as tip. Anna smiles as the lady behind of the register took her money and tried to make small talk with her. "How was your breakfast?" Ask the lady.

Anna smiles and nods "It was good." Anna said in her broken English.

The lady behind of the register took Anna's money then she gives Anna a strange look, Anna knew that she has spoken too much. Anna grabs the change and quickly walks back to the table where she also places some coins on the table as a tip.

Anna starts for the door as she turns and glances over

to the men at the table; they both stood up and place their tip onto the table as they stared at Anna. Anna quickly walks out hoping to mix in with the people that were walking in the sidewalks. Feeling safe Anna started looking around for Vito. Anna never knew that Vito was in the restaurant dropping off the restaurant's order. Vito was out in the kitchen having his breakfast as he did every morning. Anna saw the two men walk out of the restaurant and look around for her. Anna started walking faster as one of the men notices her and pointed toward his buddy. Both men follow Anna as she walks down the street. Anna walks down an alley hoping to lose them on the next street. Anna walks faster as the men had followed her down the alley. "Where are you going?" Ask one of the men. As the men starts to run, Anna gives up and stands they're waiting for them as they run toward her.

"Are you alone?" Ask one of the men with a smile. "No, I'm not alone, I brought this with me." Anna said in her broken English as she pulls out her pistol and waves it at them. The two men seeing the pistol tries to stop running but their momentum causes one of the men to fall straight on his face on the wet and mucky road as the other man falls into some trashcans filled with the waste from the butcher's shop.

Anna smiles as she walks up to the men waving her pistol.

"I know how to use this." Anna laughs as she waves her pistol and continues her search for Vito. Vito finishes his breakfast and jokes with the ladies at the restaurant before he walks out to his truck and drive off. Anna sees the truck pulling away but she doesn't think too much of it.

As Vito drives he still thinks of Anna but knowing that she was still in Germany Vito starts to let go of her memory.

Still full from breakfast Anna spends the lunchtime searching the streets of Brooklyn for Vito. But everywhere she goes Vito wasn't there, or he had just left seconds before she walks up.

As days goes by Anna starts felling homesick. Even though she had no home, Germany is all she knew. With the once large stack of American bills now there is less than half of that stack and there was still no Vito.

"I need to go back to Germany." Anna told herself as she

looks down the street and sees a woman's boutique.

Anna not sure of how much money to spend leaving her enough for a ship's ticket back home decided to buy her a new dress. Anna walks in as Vito drives by in his truck. Anna walks in and looks around at the many new dresses that were on display. Anna has a sad smile as she looks around the shop. "These are beautiful." Anna said in her broken English as a sales lady was walking up to her.

"Are you German?" ask the sales lady with a concerned look on her face. Anna quickly turns around as she sees the lady with tears running down her face. Anna nods without saying a word.

"My husband was killed by the Nazis; we don't serve Nazis here." yells the sales lady.

"But, I'm not Nazis." Anna pleaded with the sales lady. "I fought the Nazis." Anna continued in shock at being discovered.

"My husband died in Germany fighting you Germans." said the lady as she walks closer toward Anna.

"I fought the Nazis." Anna repeated herself.

"I love Americans." Anna said as she turns around and quickly walks out of the store.

"Get out of here you Nazi." Screams the sales lady as she walks up to the door.

Anna walks backwards out into the street and doesn't see the approaching vehicle. As the driver slams on his breaks Anna turns to see the truck as it stops inches from Anna who fainted into the street. The driver jumps out of his truck and runs to the lady. Vito yells at the lady for standing in the middle of the street. "Are you nuts; I've could had killed you." Vito yells as he then notices who it was that he was bending down and holding in his arms. Hearing Vito's voice Anna comes to realize she has found him. Both Vito and Anna look at one another then they both smile and it ends with a kiss.

Vito and Anna sit on their front porch swing. Hand in hands they share a smile as Anna looks over to Vito Jr age five and little Hildy Age three. As their kids play on the porch Vito reaches over a give Anna a kiss on her cheek. "I love hearing the story on how we met, tell me again." Vito said with a smile. Anna returns the smiles.

"Well, I was a little girl on my father's farm." Anna said as time goes by and now a middle aged Anna sits on the porch swing with a middle age Vito as Anna is telling the story to a grown up Vito Jr. and a grown-up Hildy. Time goes on as an old Anna sits on the porch swing alone. Anna stares into the skies. Anna looks around but she sees no one. Tears rolls down Anna's face as the front door opens and an elderly Vito walks out carrying two glasses of water.

He reaches one of the glasses down as Anna takes it. Vito then sits down on the swing beside of his beloved Anna and reaches over and kisses her. "Anna tell me the story of how we met, I love hearing it." As Anna starts to talk two cars pull up. Vito Jr. and his family get out, as well as Hildy and her family. The whole family gathers around Anna as she tells the story on how she and Vito met. "I was a little girl on my father's farm ....

www.ingramcontent.com/pod-product-compliance
Lightning Source LLC
Chambersburg PA
CBHW020650030726
47498CB00002B/450